MEC
Publishing

Hi Mike

Hopefully this will
entertain you a little during
the lockdown.
Hope you enjoy it.

Janice.

RESTORING VINCENT

By JC Cole.

Published by MEC Publishing.

Publication Info

Published by MEC Publishing.

For details of our offices, customer services and for information about how to apply for permission to reuse the copyright material in this book please see our website at www.mecpublishing.co.uk

ISBN - 978-0-9955438-0-5

Dedication

This book is dedicated to my family who have supported me in completing one of my longest standing dreams. To my children, Sophie and Matt; my sister's, Sue Lawrence and Elaine Smith and my mum, Ann. Also to my cousin, Sarah, and my nieces and nephews (Kerry, Dan, Nicola, Jack and Amy) who all had to read and re-read the various drafts. I would also like to thank Tina Bell from Christie's for help with the technical details of the art world.

Prologue

Auvers-sur-Oise; France July 27th 1890

The fresh trickle of red viscous liquid looked vibrant against his pale skin as he lifted his smock to examine the wound. He was surprised there was not more blood after such an injury. The bright crimson smear reminded him of the tempera paint he'd used as a child, but this would dry quickly in the sun leaving just an ugly brown stain.

It was Sunday but he couldn't rest. The afternoon was unbearably hot and working outdoors after church had been difficult. Now his tools had been abandoned and dust clung to his battered shoes as he stumbled along the backstreets of Auvers-sur-Oise; the French town he'd known for only a few months but which had felt more like home than any he'd stayed in over the past few years. He could have settled here permanently if things had been different. That would never happen now. Not after this.

He clutched his abdomen and pain seared through his body until numbness crept into his extremities and he could no longer feel his fingers and toes. As blood started to seep through the fabric of the oversized blue calico shirt, his vision clouded.

Breaking the Fifth Commandment was one of the greatest sins a man could commit against God. Thou shalt not kill, not even yourself. The devout artist believed that. He'd spent his life trying to capture the essence of creation as death continually tempted him. In his 37 years he'd craved both; both had eluded him and it had slowly driven him mad.

His paintings were devoid of finer detail now and endless landscapes of wheat fields and unfamiliar buildings would be his last testament. His reward for employing his gift from God had been loneliness and poverty. Now despair flowed from his brushes to unbleached canvas, coloured by the pigmented oils he worked into its fibres. He'd been living off his brother for years even though he could barely support his own wife and their new child. Now they'd all been plunged into financial uncertainty as he tried to sell works that no one wanted to buy. His hope that they'd join him here in this rural retreat, allowing him to feel part of a family once again, had been crushed. His art was all he had left and it reflected the emptiness of his existence. It was his joy and his tormentor.

The heat warmed the fresh blood that enveloped his sticky fingers as he held them over the wound. He began to feel lightheaded from shock and his senses began to muddle, but he knew what needed to be done and time was running out. God wouldn't abandon him now after torturing him for so long and would know the truth of today's events even if man would never find out.

He had to get away from this exposed road and into the fields. It was a main route into the town centre and he'd be seen if he stayed on it much longer. The farmers would be inside their barns in this intense glare, allowing him some refuge, but even one innocuous glance could throw his hastily formed story into disarray. He had to tell his account of events to someone.

The shadows he cast on the white plastered walls of the cottages pushed him even further away from his path. He needed to rest and conserve his strength until it was cooler. It was essential that he made it back to the Auberge but his energy was fading.

He stopped to rest in the shade of the dung heaps that lined the farmyard borders of this provincial town. The wild summer flowers grew freely wherever their seeds had landed, taking everything they needed from the ground in which they survived. He envied their freedom to become exactly what God had intended, blooming into their glorious and colourful destiny so effortlessly. Why had *his* life been so difficult?

His last injury had been almost eighteen months ago. Then it had been a flesh wound, not a serious attempt at suicide. They'd called it a lunatic's bid for attention and had locked him away. The macabre act of self-mutilation was carried out in a fit of pique as he battled his overwhelming impulse to kill Paul Gauguin, his best friend and mentor, after a bitter argument. Such a murder would have rocked France had he not been able to force back his warring demons and control his rage. God had been with him that day, preventing a crime against Heaven that would have made the Devil triumphant. Instead his anger turned inward and he inflicted the grievous wound on himself. Every day, as he looked in the mirror, he was reminded of his desperate battle with his psyche. A bandaged head and a severed earlobe immortalised in an oil-on-canvas self-portrait for eternity.

He must have passed out as he lay in the grass. When he awoke the quality of the light had changed dramatically. It was darker and more chilling. The shadows of the mound under which he'd sheltered were longer and the flowers no longer glinted with sunshine. The foliage beneath him was spattered with dried blood that made the leaves look rotten - not that it mattered. No one would check this location once he'd told his tale. Rain would soon erase all signs of his brief and final presence. He moved slowly out of the fading sunlight into the cover of the evening shadows, wrapping his caked cracked hands in the tails of his shirt to cover his injury. The chestnut trees he'd gazed at so many times with a critical, appraising eye gave him protection from the windows of the farmhouses that lined the dusty roads. The white pensions, the subjects of so much of his recent work, were turning a pale washed-out grey as the sun set behind him.

As consciousness returned he cleared his head and recalled his plan. God had not taken him yet and he still had one final chance to make sure the truth of this day never surfaced. His tale would die with him. Why should he care what others thought? God would know the truth and that was all that mattered. At last he had shown mercy and presented him with a way out of his living nightmare. The moral dilemma that had haunted him for years had been taken out of his hands and now he'd be welcomed into Heaven. He would no longer be a burden on his family and they wouldn't miss him!

He made his way back towards the town hall to the Auberge Ravoux, where he'd rented a room. How little time he'd spent here but how much he'd accomplished. In the twelve weeks since his arrival in Auvers his work rate had been prolific. He'd produced a new painting every day, as if compelled to commit as much of his talent to canvas as he could in this final short burst.

Arthur Ravoux was sitting outside in the street with his family eating dinner, as was their custom. It was dusk and the church bells were peeling out their doleful matins. They barely noticed the artist as he bid them good evening and went straight to his room. He was hunched over and moaning slightly - but his behaviour was rarely normal. None of the family realised he wasn't carrying any of his materials or the canvas he'd left with after lunch.

As they ate their stew, the cries from the first floor room grew louder. Adeline Ravoux, the owner's 12-year-old daughter, looked up the window and then at her father.

'What's wrong with him this evening, Papa?' she asked.

'Maybe he's having one of his turns?' shrugged the innkeeper. 'I'll go and check on him.'

Arthur went upstairs to investigate and found the artist lying on his bed with his knees drawn up to his chest. His hands were covered in blood from the freshly reopened wound.

'I fear I may have done something stupid.' His voice was weak and strained. 'But do not look for any other cause. I appear to have shot myself.'

Ravoux stared for a moment at the expanding stain before recovering his wits. He called Adeline from the hallway, blocking her view into the room. Some things were not for the eyes of 12-year-old girls.

'Go and get the doctor, immediately,' he commanded.

Within 15 minutes she was back with Dr Mazery. He examined the wound but as a gynaecologist didn't have the skill to do more.

'There's relatively little blood loss in here and the entry hole is small, but the angle is strange assuming he was shooting at his heart. You say he claims to have done this to himself?'

Ravoux nodded and the doctor continued, confused at the seemingly conflicting evidence.

'He's missed by several inches and the bullet feels lodged in his abdomen. I don't understand how at such close range it didn't exit his body. But if he says he shot himself then I guess it must be so.'

'Maybe Dr Gachet will attend,' Ravoux said. 'He knows this man better than us. He may understand what he's done. Adeline, go and get him, and tell him it's urgent.'

Adeline returned within half an hour to tell her father that the homeopath was not at home but Gachet arrived an hour later after hearing the news by chance. Gossip was spreading fast throughout the town. Neither doctor was a surgeon capable of performing an abdominal operation all they could do was wait.

'The bullet is deep within his stomach,' Gachet explained to Ravoux. 'There is no way to remove it, or to repair the internal damage with our training. He's in God's hands now. Have you called his brother?'

'Our other guest, Anton Hirschig, has agreed to go to Paris in the morning and fetch him. No doubt he will return with him immediately.'

Doctor Gachet stayed for several hours, cleaning the wound as best he could with his homeopathic remedies. His patient was asleep before he left and had said no more about the events that led to his current injured state.

At dawn, Adeline was sent up to the bedroom with some bread and milk to see if the artist could eat. His wounds had been dressed and he was more presentable than the previous evening. As she entered the room she found him sitting up in his bed, in seemingly good spirits and smoking his pipe.

'Good morning, monsieur,' she whispered.

'Adeline, where's your father?' His smile faded as he leaned forward urgently in his bed causing his wound to bleed again.

'He's downstairs preparing breakfast for the other guests. Are you okay, Monsieur? He will be up shortly.'

'It's not your father I need to speak to. Close the door child. I don't want him to hear. There is something very important I must ask of you. There is no one else I can trust and this is a matter of life and death!' He tried to stand but his injuries pinned him to the bed as he stretched out his hand, beckoning her to come nearer.

Adeline closed the door slowly, considering the mental state of the man in front of her. She knew the rumours of his time recovering in an institution, but she'd spent a whole day alone with him as his model just six weeks ago and she was not afraid of him.

'I must ask you to deliver a letter whose existence or contents can never be revealed to anyone, especially not to your father, for his own sake. Can you do that for me Adeline?'

'I think so, monsieur. Is it dangerous?'

'Not for you, but others may ask questions that cannot be answered. In fact, they must not be answered. Adeline, you are a child of good heart but this is vitally important. This is my decision and mine alone. I ask you not to judge or wonder what is in the letter, but simply to deliver it. Will you do this for me?'

Adeline thought for a moment about this man she had known for only a few months; who had painted the portrait she didn't like but couldn't stop looking at. He always appeared more at ease with her and her two-year-old sister, Germaine, than with any of the adults in the house and he seemed to trust no one, not even his brother. How sad he looked. He'd been shot and was dying and had no family or friends around him. Hopefully his brother would arrive at some point today but who else would be here for him in his final hours if not her? Whatever it was he wanted her to deliver, she could tell from his expression that it was essential she comply with his wish. His manner was too urgent, too insistent for one so seriously injured. Why was he worried about delivering a letter when his life hung in the balance? His whole body leaned towards her, willing her to help him, as though he would not accept his fate and give up this suffering until she agreed.

'I will deliver it,' she said as she took the sealed envelope from him.

The artist's brother, Theo, arrived from Paris later that morning.

'What have you done?' he whispered as he entered the bedroom.

'This is nothing – I feel good! I will be back to work by the morning.'

And at that moment he truly felt fine. Maybe he'd been dreaming? Maybe God had decided he wasn't ready to greet him yet!

But just after midnight on July 29th 1890, Vincent Van Gogh died in his brother's arms - a penniless failure wracked with demons and now apparently abandoned by God.

Chapter 1

London – Sunday 21st September 2014

Tia Hall could tell by his body language that today wasn't going according to the meticulous schedule her father had drafted. She'd never actually heard him swear before but his cool façade was definitely cracking. He hated not being in control, especially on his own turf. They were stuck in traffic on Camden High Street, just north of London's West End, on their way to her new Halls of Residence and he was clearly pissed off. He'd been planning her move to university since before she was born but he hadn't considered that she'd chose one in the heart of Central London.

Outside in the street Camden's hectic bustle reflected the changing youth culture of the last sixty years, since teenagers first began to rebel against their parents and experiment on themselves. Now remnants of a multitude of bygone fashions lingered amongst the body-piercing studios and tattoo artists. Tourists mingled with a few uniquely dressed goths and punks with green hair. The constant stream of visitors ignored the crowded pavements and spilled into the roads weaving randomly between crawling cars; watching each other instead of the traffic.

Stephen Hall was becoming increasingly agitated by their lack of progress. The chaos surrounding them had already put his entire plan for the day off track. He was the Assistant Commissioner for Operations in the Metropolitan Police and wasn't used to waiting for others to get out of his way. He wondered how many laws were currently being broken as he sat and watched and did nothing. As horns blasted around them he could feel sweat pooling around his shirt collar and his usually calm exterior was starting to crack.

'What the hell is wrong with these people!' he shouted to himself, alarming his wife, Frances, who was sitting beside him. 'Why are they walking in the roads? Do they have a collective death wish?'

Tia slouched in the back of the car staring out of the window and contemplating her new life of long-awaited independence. She knew better than to answer his rhetorical questions. It would only make him worse. She felt a twinge of disappointment that the eclectic boutiques had been replaced by chain stores and coffee shops. The Avant-garde shops that remained were now largely confined to the converted stables up by the Lock, where authentic memorabilia blended alongside cheap Chinese imports. Instead Boots, Sainsbury's and Starbucks occupied the premium sites around Camden Town Underground Station, much as they did outside every other station in London.

In contrast, the infamous pubs had hardly changed. It was only 11am but already two drunks were fighting in the doorway of one illegally open bar as their equally drunk girlfriends tried to pull them apart. Tia wondered if this was a very late end to last night for them or an early new start. Whatever it was, she knew that it was just reinforcing her father's view that his daughter was not ready to face the world without him. He probably had police surveillance of her halls planned from the moment he drove home.

She picked at the poorly applied nail varnish she'd used for the first time that morning. It was a feeble and smudged first experiment to feel more grown up. It had failed. Tia tried not to stand out from her peers, just as few of these shops were now truly original. She was mixed race, and at 5'11", very tall; but otherwise she appeared to be a typical teen, filled with insecurities about almost everything in her life. She'd never had a boyfriend, had only ever been on holiday with her parents and had never been drunk. Her curly dark hair was pulled back into a ponytail. Her jeans and t-shirts came from Top Shop and her face was normally scrubbed clean and devoid of makeup before today.

Tia kept her one unique feature secret, even from her few friends. For fifteen years studying to be accepted onto the desired university course had come second to mastering a martial art called Wing Chun. Even getting straight A-star grades at GCSE and A level didn't match the enthusiasm of her father's dedication to her relentless training in the little known form of self-defence.

As they pulled into the car park of Ifor Evans Halls Tia's nervousness returned. She wasn't sure she would even be able to find her way back to the tube station in the morning, never mind look after herself on her first night away from her parents ever. She instantly dismissed the thought as she knew her dad would insist on walking the route with her before he left to drive the 16 miles back home to Orpington, in Kent.

Her father's brand new Volvo 400 was full of her possessions, some of which she'd never seen before and didn't realize she owned. The first aid kit her mother had prepared was almost as big as her suitcase, containing all the supplies necessary for a girl dedicated to fighting for sport. As her family helped transport kitchen equipment, stationary and sports kit from the car to her new home, the luminous green Perspex box with the huge white cross drew stares from the other arriving residents who assumed all they would need over the next few months was a large supply of Resolve for their hangovers.

'Looks like the paramedic's arrived!' sniggered an unwashed lanky male who was currently scouring the car park for new talent. His numerous piercings and self-inflicted tattoos suggested it wouldn't be long before he'd need the contents of her mobile pharmacy – particularly the antiseptic wipes. 'I know where my next stash is coming from!' he laughed to his friend, but his bravado quickly dissolved as Tia's 6'3" Jamaican dad lifted his head from inside the boot of the car. With an imperceptible nod the boys retreated and disappeared back into the building.

Tia felt her face flush, knowing her fellow students who were currently unpacking their normal-looking luggage wouldn't be able to tell. Her darkened skin pigment had hidden her shyness well over the years, making her frequent blushes almost impossible to detect. She'd grown up with the occasional rude remark about her black, police-chief father and white, tax lawyer mother, but nothing that would have registered enough to make her conscious of how she looked. She'd never even really been sure what the ignorant few had objected to most about her family. Was it their unpopular professions; the colour of her father's skin; or the fact that there was a difference in the colour of his wife? She was just thankful that her own generation were more enlightened than her parents' generation seemed to have been.

'Have you got the security kit I gave you?' her father called from the front door of the building. 'Take that up first so we can mark everything as we unpack it.'

'Yes, dad!' Tia replied, picking up the combination-locked briefcase that looked like it should belong to a city banker, and the contents of which would have foiled even the most competent thief. Only a policeman would think that a mobile security camera hidden in a coffee jar, a baton disguised as an umbrella and a rape alarm were really necessary as items of self defence for a first year student - especially one whose martial arts proficiency technically classified her as a lethal weapon. Only a senior officer would have access to such equipment, some of which had been custom made by the boys back at the Yard. Tia already planned to hide the case under her bed before her new college friends labelled her psychotic.

'So!' Frances whistled, bringing in a tray of tea as they squashed the last of Tia's belongings into the now-cramped en suite bedroom. 'What's the plan for the first few days?'

'Registration is tomorrow morning then I guess I'll spend most of the day in the computer science building. Fresher's Fayre starts on Tuesday so I'll see what the fight club situation is then.' Tia could feel her father suppressing a reprimanding comment and smiled at him. He hated it when she called it that, but he managed to stop himself reacting to her teasing!

'Just make sure you get a partner who knows what they're doing,' was all he said.

Tia had been studying the graceful but unpopular discipline of Wing Chun since she was 4 years old. Her father had been an avid Bruce Lee fan and loved the speed and fluidity of the sport. Having grown up in Brixton during the 1980s and witnessing first hand the escalation in violent crimes, he'd insisted that Tia learn to protect herself from the threats he saw for real every day in his job. To Stephen Hall, Wing Chun was a philosophy for a safe and peaceful life, not a lesson in violence.

'Do they have a martial arts club here then?' Her mother smiled sarcastically, knowing that her husband would never have agreed to Tia's choice of college if they didn't. Tia's promise to maintain her training regime had been top of the list of requirements he'd laid down before he would concede that a Central London university was a viable alternative to a safe campus with security guards, set in the middle of nowhere; and it was a very long list.

Tia dispatched her parents just after 5pm, promising to visit next Sunday for dinner. Their agreement to her living in halls had been non-negotiable when she accepted a place on the computer science degree program at University College London – one of the top universities in the country, but only 16 miles away from home. Tia knew, however, that her father's access to traffic cameras, facial recognition software and various security networks meant he could find her pretty much any time - day or night - if he really wanted to.

Registration day passed without incident, as she suspected it would. Her timetable was fuller than she'd expected and the daily hours of maths had not been anticipated, but she would cope. Studying was one of Tia's strengths and she felt comfortable immersed in her books and laptop, which removed the need to make small talk with people she barely knew. She was happy to sit behind a screen hacking her way through weak security programs looking for glitches she could share with her dad. He encouraged her borderline illegal activity, not least because she'd made him look good on more than one occasion at work after highlighting potential loopholes in various business and police systems. She was already a proficient programmer in several languages and had spent many school holidays at her father's office, learning from some of the Met's finest security specialists. It was one of the coolest things about her dad - his office was New Scotland Yard! Looking around the seminar room at the pallid faces of her fellow students she guessed many of them had led similarly sheltered lives.

Fresher's Fayre began on day two and, in contrast, was not what Tia had expected. Too many American high school movies had created an anticipation of organized booths with cupcakes and smiling faces welcoming her to social events and friendship possibilities. She couldn't wait to broaden the social horizons that had eluded her throughout her school years due to her father's vetting processes. Alcohol and boys had both been forbidden despite being the top two conversation topics amongst her school friends. She was desperate for a social life now she had a glimpse of freedom but acting on that need was going to be tougher than she thought. Throughout the length of the Victorian stone cloisters the alphabetical arrangement of ancient trestle table 'stands' placed opposing college societies within firing range of each other. A full-scale argument was already taking place between the communist society and the neighbouring Conservative's association. Every conceivable club was competing for the attention of the fresh intake of potential members who would secure their on-going funding and existence.

Wing Chun's popularity was low and dropping following the introduction of a plethora of trendy martial arts from various Asiatic countries. Maui Thai, Taekwondo and Jujitsu were much better known and had blended together over recent years as mixed martial arts –

pitching different disciplines against each other in exciting and unpredictable ways. Tia wasn't interested in the macho world of competitive MMA. She'd convinced her dad that the facilities at UCL would be sufficient for her to continue her training because they had a 'parrot' – the wooden pillar with spokes that formed the basis of Wing Chun practice. Judo and Karate had their own societies but everything else fell under the umbrella of the UCL MMAA. Their stand was manned by the usual melee of pumped up boys who revelled in the physical nature of their chosen sport, but Tia's attention was drawn to the short, stocky, ginger girl shouting at the top of her voice.

'Come and sign up for beginners classes in kickboxing,' she cried, like a costermonger selling her wares. The girl's clothes were almost as loud as her booming voice. She wore an outrageous outfit of red paisley print leggings and a custom painted T-shirt depicting a graffiti-enhanced Marilyn Monroe. Tia instinctively gravitated towards her, as she was the only other female anywhere near the table.

'D'you wanna sign up for the beginners class?' the redhead called out enthusiastically as she watched Tia looking through the pamphlets scattered across the display. Her cockney accent was authentic and strong and Tia suspected this girl was even closer to home than she was – East or possibly South London floated into Tia's limited mental map of the capital.

'No it's okay. I was just looking for a class schedule.' Tia smiled and relaxed a degree; thankful to be speaking to the first female she'd met in two days.

'What type of class you looking for?' The loud girl eyed her up and down, appraising the tall, thin frame suspiciously. Surely she should be looking for the netball team? Then she grinned approvingly at this waif who looked as much out of place at the stand of a martial arts club as she did. 'You sure you don't need the beginners class - you look like anyone stronger will break you in two!'

'No.' Tia said looking at her shoes and fighting her usual urge to run away and hide from this overly forward girl. Instead she choked it down and smiled. 'Do you have a Wing Chun class?'

'A what class?' There was no subtlety in the incredulity in the redhead's voice. 'What's that then?

'It's Chinese,' Tia replied as if that explained everything the girl needed to know.

'Well I've never heard of it! You'll have to talk to Henry. He knows all about that fancy shit! He's not here today but if you come along to the gym on Thursday evening you can ask him if he can help. He runs the MMA and I help him. Although really I do all the work, he just takes the credit. What's yer name in case I see him?' She pulled out a campus map and marked a huge X over the site of the gym.

'Tia. Tia Hall.'

'Well Tia, I'm Ashley Rivers. Straightforward kick boxer, me! Comes in handy down the pub when some drunk dickhead gets a bit fresh. Know what I mean?' Her laugh was genuine and infectious.

Tia didn't know, but she could guess. She'd never hit anyone other than her instructor and sparring partners in a totally controlled environment. The local pubs and clubs in Bromley had been off limits to Tia and her friends. Their social life was limited to the odd house party whenever parents were out. Nursing her drunken friends was the extent of her meagre experience with boys or alcohol. At no point could she recall having to repel the advances of anyone - unwanted or otherwise. They were all too scared of her dad!

'So you any good?' Intrigue had replaced Ashley's shock that this thin, caramel, wallflower even knew what MMA was.

'I guess you'll see on Thursday if you're there.' Tia smiled broadly and carried on walking hurriedly through the cloisters, keen to explore her new world.

Chapter 2

Vologda, Russia - August 1968

Political tensions had been mounting steadily across the USSR since the Americans had dropped the atomic bomb on Hiroshima. At that time, the two countries had been fighting for the same cause - to free the world from the Nazi tyranny whose fascist regime was at odds with both the capitalist West and the communist East. But after two decades and a war in Korea, Russia had started to distance itself from its former ally and begun to amass weapons and manpower on a scale it deemed necessary to preserve its political ideology. The Americans had responded in kind and the escalation of arms spiralled out of control.

The Cold War had required the press-ganging of thousands of Russian troops as part of the Warsaw Pact. This was ironic in the sense that the term cold war came from the lack of fighting that actually took place despite a build up of infantry on a scale not imagined in the 50-year history of communism. Even though the Soviets had sustained huge losses during the final years of the Second World War, by 1968 the Red Army was the second biggest military machine in the world - and the biggest in terms of actual recruits.

Boris Rubikov had no intention of being recruited.

He'd seen his three elder brothers give up their dreams to fight for a political dogma that made no sense to a 16 year old with aspirations to make his fortune by whatever means necessary. He was not going the same way as they had. Socialism worked, he thought, if everyone cared as much about their neighbour's welfare as they did about their own. Rubikov knew that wasn't true - and it certainly wasn't his perspective. His brothers had doubted the Stalinist ideology also - and two of them never returned home as a consequence. The rumour that made it back to his hometown of Vologda was that they had been sent to the salt mines; their punishment for speaking out against the conditions in which the conscripted soldiers were forced to live.

Boris vowed that he wasn't going to end up in the army or the mines. He'd watched and learned as one by one the teenage boys from his town left to become another notch on the bedpost of war. On the day that notice was given of the impending Army Recruitment Division's arrival in the city he began to formulate a plan. He needed to avoid the press gang and not get caught doing it.

There was no point running - the draft squadron only arrived after setting up roadblocks and scouting groups around the perimeter of whichever city or town was next on their expanding list of targets. When you're collecting men like grains of sand on a beach, the scale of the personnel required to complete this lockdown was immense but not a problem. Untrained rookies could not be allowed to outsmart the might of the army, so every effort was taken to ensure they left with one hundred per cent of their targets accounted for, one way or another. The containment task provided a useful training activity for the rapidly increasing numbers of army privates, including identifying those with the stomach to turn a gun on their own countrymen if required. If you tried to dodge the draft, you risked being shot on sight. The commanders couldn't afford to bring too many dissenters or potential deserters into the fold - morale was low enough already and those who did speak out were either silenced or shipped out to Siberia.

Boris had seen one of his best friends gunned down in the woods only a year earlier. He knew he would need to be more creative in his attempt to stay alive and out of an unwinnable war.

Inspiration came to him less than a week before the tanks and trucks rolled into town.

He'd been sitting for days on the wild grass banks outside the ruins of the Russian Orthodox Gorne-Uspensky Convent, praying for divine intervention. The white-walled buildings of the Assumption Church and St Sergius chapel, built in 1590, were the oldest and most famous in Vologda. The classical onion-topped towers whose black cupolas soared towards heaven looking like overturned hearts engorged with evil blood.

Throughout his youth Boris had spent hours playing inside the cramped, disused bell tower behind the cathedral, climbing the ropes of the hammerless bells whose chimes once drew the faithful to the various church services. He remembered how sometimes he would swing in an arc wider than intended and graze his knees along the rough stone walls. By the time he was fourteen he'd grown so tall his outstretched arms could reach both sides of the circular room. Arms that were so powerful he could have chimed an entire change sequence on his own, even though the heaviest bell weighed 4 tonnes. It would have required the full weight of his body to set it in motion to deliver its low bass peel but the Red Army had evicted the nuns in 1924 leaving it now in disrepair.

It was Wednesday afternoon when he noticed the discrepancy in the building's structure for the first time. As he sat contemplating impending disaster in the form of a military convoy, the shadows on the walls of the belfry stretched widely with the setting sun. From his current vantage point on the gently sloping bank he thought how much bigger the bell tower looked from the outside than he remembered from being inside, and it suddenly dawned on him that the external walls were rectangular. The spherical walls of the inside could not possibly butt directly up against the rear of the cathedral, as he'd always believed they had. A vague feeling of surprise quickly gave way to growing curiosity - viewed from outside, the inside of the tower would need to be egg shaped for the two walls to have a physical contact point, and he knew better than anyone that it wasn't.

A plan began to form in his head.

Scrambling to his feet, Boris ran down to the spot where the belfry met the cathedral walls. Walking carefully along the grass verge he counted the paces needed to get from the outside rear wall of the church to the spot level with the front entrance. The building was made of huge cut stones, hundreds of years old. He used his fingers to span the width of the doorframe to give him a rough approximation of the thickness of the walls. Then he counted the number of steps required to walk directly from just inside the entrance to the opposite point of the transept behind the sanctuary, where he'd assumed the tower had adjoined the church itself. He had to be careful with his counting as he manoeuvred around the disused altar, which was in the direct path needed for his comparison. He wrote a few numbers on the palm of his hand and left the church, heart pumping. At home he drew a rough sketch of the building and checked his calculations and measurements six or seven times before he was comfortable he'd got it right. Assuming the thickness of the wall was uniform all the way round the church, there was a cavity between the sanctuary wall and the belfry approximately three feet deep and at least as wide as the bell tower. He was no architect, but he assumed it was to soundproof the inside of the church against the noise of the bells. That was enough of a gap in which he could hide, and where no one would ever think to look, as he was fairly sure no one else realised this gap was even there.

The next day he returned desperate to put his plan into action but the walls were made of stone! How was he supposed to cut through 8 inches of solid rock in three days? As his mind contemplated the futility of the task, his eyes registered detail that only prolonged staring at one spot allows. At the base of the wall, there was a patch of what looked like rising damp about 18 inches in diameter. How could that be? The floor of the cathedral was as solid as its walls. Damp came from the earth - not impervious rock. Taking a rouble from his pocket he began to scratch at the darken portion. The walls were unpainted behind the sanctuary screen and the stone colour variation was minimal. The damp patch started to flake relatively easily. After just a few minutes a type of clay-based plaster had been removed from the surface, revealing a scree of small rocks and stones. Without its chalky cover the patch was more noticeable, but it still just looked like damage to the stone. Tracing an outline of the crumbling section with the coin he realised a stone block, 18 inches square, had been left out of the construction, level with the floor, and the gap filled with a makeshift shingle repair.

He wasn't surprised to find a hidden alcove behind the wall, just big enough for a man to stand and turn with tucked in arms. If he lay down on the floor it was difficult to roll sideways, especially at the centre where the curve of the adjoining bell tower left the narrowest gap, but it was just possible. The gaps on each side were wider, almost like two tiny triangular rooms separated by a short corridor.

For three days he prepared his hideout, taking water and food in quantities small enough to hide under his shirt. He rehearsed replacing the stones in the gap from the inside, smoothing them over with a homemade plaster so only a hand-sized patch of unplastered stone remained - enough to let in some air to the self-constructed prison that would be his home for three days. Each evening he re-covered the tiny opening and placed an old wooden stool in front of the breech just in case anyone ventured into the abandoned ruin.

On the Saturday night before the convoy was due to arrive he left home for the last time with his final supplies and a few clothes folded into a small backpack. He knew he wouldn't be able to go back home after evading the army, so he said his silent farewells to his parents, who were unaware they would never see him again.

As he began climbing over the rusting fence that ran around the convent perimeter a voice he recognised called out to him from behind.

'Boris!' It was more like a hiss – a theatrical whisper that echoed in the cold night air.

Boris froze, clinging to the fence. Had the convoy arrived early? He turned to see two boys running towards him in the darkness. Both of the boys were in his class at school. One was a good friend; the other was a scrawny rat who'd frequently gotten Boris into trouble with his teachers over the years.

'What are you doing here?' Boris asked, dropping back to the ground to meet them.

'What are you doing here, Boris?' The rat replied. 'I've been watching you for the last three days and you've been here all the time. What have you got hidden in there?'

'I don't have anything hidden in there?' Boris thought about the meagre supplies stashed in the alcove that would just about feed him for three days, never mind two more.

'Is this where you're going to hide?' the rat asked, convinced he was getting close to the truth, as his own sense of self-preservation drove him forward despite the growing anger in Boris's eyes.

'Keep your voice down!' Boris looked around frantically, praying that no one was close enough to hear them. If the guards did think to look here with anything more than a cursory glance, his makeshift clay wouldn't be sufficient to avoid detection.

'Is there room for us? The second boy spoke in a quiet voice, instinctively understanding Boris's concerns.

Boris did the calculations in his head. It wasn't just a case of physical space, it was about the volume of air inside the cavity. Two people might just survive inside the wall if he widened the air hole a fraction. It would be cramped and virtually impossible to lie down but they could alternate sleeping arrangements. Three bodies would suffocate them all before the end of the second day. Boris shifted his eyes from left to right, indicating to the second boy that three was too many. Vasily Denisov understood his signal immediately.

As Boris began to climb back up the fence, the rat moved in behind him ready to follow. Boris glanced over his shoulder and saw Vasily pick up a broken section of fencing pole that lay on the ground. Boris pivoted on the fence so he faced the rat and aimed a steel toe capped boot straight into the side of his head. From behind, Vasily swung a huge arc with the metal pole and caught the rat on the other side, right across the temple. Bone shattered as the boy dropped to the floor and blood began to run from his ear over the muddy ground.

'Quickly, we need to move him and cover this blood.' Boris said, jumping down from the fence.

Vasily was almost as tall as Boris, with much more powerful arms. He lifted the rat over his shoulder as though he were a sack of coal. The two boys ran through the darkness towards the woods. This would be one of the first places the convoy would search for deserters and the rat would be found quickly, but dead men can't talk. Vasily put the body in a shallow ditch and the two boys covered it with as much bracken and foliage as they could find.

They exited the woods in the opposite direction, towards a small farmstead just outside the town. Inside the barn they collected cow dung into a small discarded hessian grain sack, washing their hands clean of blood and manure in the water trough.

When they got back to the fence, Boris emptied the dung onto the damp ground. The smell would distract the dogs from the pooled blood and mask their own disappearing scent as they climbed back over the fence – a measure Boris had forgotten to take before Vasily and the rat showed up.

They had just finished bricking themselves inside the wall using the remoistened clay when the draft team arrived in town.

Boris and Vasily hid in Assumption Cathedral as the other teenagers lined up to receive their call-up orders. The draft team checked the municipal buildings and wooded areas across the town. They found the body on day two and crossed one less recruit off their list. There was no urgency to find out who was responsible. Whoever it was, was almost certainly heading for the army now anyway. By the time they searched the abandoned church the clay had dried and there was no obvious sign of the false part of the base of the wall unless you looked really closely. The poorly trained conscripts searching the building just saw continuous solid stone.

The boys lay on the floor of their prison for three days in silence and darkness; Boris hadn't dared use a torch in his preparation, as even the smallest shaft of light would reveal his hiding place inside the gloom of the cathedral. They tried to move as little as possible but needed to manoeuvre around each other every few hours to relieve the cramping muscles in their limbs. They ate the food Boris had brought with him when they felt faint with hunger and drank only when they could bear the thirst no longer. The smell of the piss-pot was difficult to ignore despite their efforts to keep its contents to a minimum.

As Vasily slept, Boris tried to relieve his aching muscles when he could no longer stand the pain of sitting with his legs drawn up to his chest. He rose to his knees in his allotted triangle and silently tried to discover the true extent of the sloping sides of his black cave. As he inched his way around the cavity with his fingers he found what felt like a wooden block inside a cloth sack wedged into the topmost point of his triangle. It must have been left there by whoever had originally created the crawl hole in the wall. He imagined some forgotten band of thieves or smugglers putting their perfect hiding place to good use - who looked for stolen property in a church? It was too dark to see what he'd actually found, but he swore to himself that the package had not been there when he'd first slid into the gap on his stomach and had a few glimmers of reflected light available. He used whatever it was as a pillow when it was his turn to sleep and clung to it possessively while he was awake. Even before he discovered what it was he knew it was his good fortune that it had been on his side of their hideout.

After three days the Army Recruitment Squadron left Vologda three men short of their expected haul. One of the three was now lying on the mortuary slab waiting for a funeral date; the other two were added to a list of boys to be shot on sight and whose parents assumed they'd been drafted.

Chapter 3
New York, Friday 28th July 2012

Huge campaign posters for the New York Senate elections lined the Park Avenue office walls like ghetto-fencing propaganda. The smiling, instantly recognisable face of Harry Whittaker Jr. looked down on everyone in the expansive open-plan room, making them seem small. The photo showed his hair with just a touch of grey at the temples, designed specifically to convey wisdom, maturity and a lack of vanity. A PR specialist had carefully chosen his open-neck shirt and casual sports jacket from an off-the-rack range at Ralph Lauren. Photo shoots were the only time he wore shop-bought clothing and the shirt had sold out in hours. His right hand gripped his left elbow and his visible watch was a mid-range Tag Heuer - aspirational but not elusive to his multitude of voters. Even his name was re-crafted to convey a sense of honesty and down-to-earth integrity. He'd been christened Henry after his father in traditional fashion but to the world he was known as Harry to avoid confusion with the older, renowned hardball lawyer who believed unemployment was a personal choice. He kept the Jr. after being assured it invoked trust through his heritage.

In spite of his privileged upbringing and his father's conservative Republican views, Harry was a Democrat, dedicated to delivering a fairer deal to a nation with the biggest divide of wealth in the world. He tried to put his politics into practice at every visible opportunity. He carefully selected his aides to reflect the exact cultural, sexual and ethnic diversity of the world's most famous city - a difficult mix to achieve. His overworked staff loved him and he looked after them. Amid the chaos of re-election fever he'd made sure they had access to a TV today so they could watch the opening ceremony of the Olympic Games in London. It was a gesture that had reduced the current Friday-afternoon work rate to zero but he didn't mind. He knew they would more than make up for it in a few weeks on election night itself.

Harry's father had been a formidable man who commanded the attention of everyone he met. He'd grown his New York law practice through some of the most difficult times in history following the Second World War, specialising in corporate litigation and contract law. Dutifully, Harry had followed him into the family business after graduating from Harvard a year earlier than was usual. Although Henry had built one of the largest and most respected law firms in New York, Harry had never really felt at ease or fulfilled during his 13 years as a corporate lawyer. After meeting his wife, he'd given up his partnership to stand for election to the Senate and had now served the city as one of their senators for over twenty-five years. His efforts alongside Mayor Giuliani following the attacks of September 11th 2001 meant he was unlikely to be removed by election in any foreseeable future, no matter what his politics were. Images of him on the backboard of a fire truck unravelling a hose had been screened around the world whilst his competitors fled to the safety of their suburban mansions.

Harry's seventh campaign was in full swing, with Election Day only three weeks away, but he was struggling to focus on voter profiles and campaign statistics. His 24-year-old son, Henry Jnr, had declared that, instead of following in his father's footsteps and going into the family law practice, he'd signed up to study for a three-year PhD in biochemistry - in London! This now presented the family with no end of security problems thanks to the wealth of his wife, Constance.

Constance's grandfather, Aaron Rosenberg, had been the founder of Blue Star Pharmaceuticals, which now sat in the top ten non-technology companies in America. The Whittaker family still lived in

Aaron's ten-bedroom colonial-style mansion in Washington DC; the home in which Constance had grown up.

Rosenberg had begun his retail empire in Philadelphia just before prohibition, in a small run-down shop marketing a newly emerging category of medicinal tonics and gadgets. Without the prop of alcohol, more and more people looked for alternative methods of lifting their overworked spirits. His rapidly expanding stores had been some of the first in the state to sell Coca Cola, and Aca Candler, the tycoon who had bought the rights to the iconic soft drink and turned it into the world's largest brand, had been a personal family friend.

Even though she was the majority share owner of a company currently valued at $62bn, Constance Whittaker worked for free as an art historian at the National Art Archive, part of the Smithsonian museum in Washington. Her holding amounted to 36% of the business, and her son Henry had a 15% stake held in trust until his 30th birthday. Until then she had voting powers for his share, but she left the running of the business to her older half-brother, Richard Colefax.

Richard had been just 4 years old when his mother died; almost 7 when their father David had married her mother, Caroline Rosenberg; and 9 when Constance was born. He'd been devoted to his half-sister as a child, fiercely protecting her from the envy her wealth created. Now she trusted him implicitly to run a business that an army of lawyers ensured he could never legally make a claim to under the terms of her grandfather's will. Family was one thing; bloodline was something completely different. His personal stake was limited to the share options he earned as part of his annual compensation package.

Harry and Constance had met at a fundraising dinner whilst he was still a lawyer in his father's firm. She was 12 years his junior, still full of the ideologies of youth and just returned from London after graduating from the Royal Academy of Art. He'd been impressed with her enthusiasm and dedication to making the world a more beautiful place to live in through her passion for art. In an uncharacteristically shallow moment she had been impressed with his muscular torso, honed through years of rowing and horse riding. He reminded her of Michelangelo's David - her vision of male physical perfection which she'd fallen in love with on a trip to Florence. Their wedding had been one of the biggest society events of the decade and both had felt extremely uncomfortable with the sheer extravagance of it all.

They'd come a long way since then. Harry looked at one of the photos on his desk of his son, Henry, taken at his graduation from Harvard only a few weeks ago. He was tanned and smiling, standing next to Jennifer, the beautiful, 25-year-old blonde who'd been his constant companion for the last three years, and who was currently waiting outside his office. It was one of the rare occasions on which the boy looked happy, but then life had thrown a whole series of difficulties at him because of their wealth. Difficulties that most children didn't, and shouldn't have to, contend with. Jennifer certainly seemed to have made a difference at first but now things were unravelling again. He pressed the intercom.

'Asked Jen to come in please, Sarah.'

Jennifer Hawley came into the office dressed as if she were there for an interview. She wore a black fitted Chanel suit and black kitten-heel Jason Wu pumps. Her long blonde hair was tied neatly in a low ponytail that fell across her right shoulder. A faint trace of makeup just enhanced her flawless skin and bone structure but her features were set in an unreadable poker face. She looks as if she still works for the FBI, Harry thought. He hugged her, kissing her gently on both cheeks.

'Thank you for coming in to see me Jen but I'm sure you can guess what it's about?' If only she would smile, he thought, she would genuinely be the most beautiful woman in the world.

'I assume you want to talk about our move to London?' Jennifer couldn't shake her efficient manner, even with a man she'd known so well for over three years.

'I just want to know if there is any way we can talk him out of this?' Harry asked.

'Why would you want to do that?' Jen understood why Henry's

parents took such control of his life but they rarely factored what he wanted into their plans. He was a grown man but they still treated him like a little boy who needed to be protected. It infuriated her that Henry often seemed happy to let them.

'You know why, Jen. It's hard enough keeping him safe here in the States, especially since he got the court injunction last month preventing anyone from accessing his whereabouts via his Verichip implant. How are we supposed to protect him when he's thousands of miles away and essentially invisible?'

It had been ten years since the last kidnap attempt, when Henry was 14, but to Harry it might as well have been yesterday. A whole series of security protocols had been put in place after the second botched snatch when he was 12, and they'd actually saved Henry's life the last time, but no measures on earth had been able to save him from his own recklessness.

'Well I take care of that now.' Jen reminded him. She was more than capable of protecting Henry if ever the need arose again. It was, after all, what she'd trained for.

Her friends and impoverished family hadn't understood why she'd wanted to join the FBI, when she could've had a glittering career as a model or actress. They never really noticed the personality trait that required her to always be in control. To Jennifer it was as essential a part of her life as breathing. She'd developed subtle methods of influencing people to get her way and others just assumed she had high expectations and deserved to have them met. But Jennifer had joined the FBI because she loved power, in all its forms - power over men, power over situations and the rush of the physical power needed to maintain her gruelling training regime of Krav Maga and triathlons. It helped keep her body at the peak of its physical perfection and cleared her mind to focus on the goals she'd set for herself to get to the top of this last bastion of male dominance. Every time she took down one of her male colleagues in training she felt no remorse at crushing their ego, only a surge of adrenaline that left her hungry for more.

In a cruel twist, however, Jennifer had discovered that there are some things even the most gifted and beautiful people in the world can't control. A freak accident during a routine exercise had caused her to take a mistimed blow to the head that had severed part of the retina behind her right eye. The surgeons had managed to repair most of the damage, but she'd failed the mandatory sight test and been forced to resign from the FBI only months after qualifying as an agent top of her class.

Then she'd met Henry Whittaker at a Varsity martial arts competition.

He'd been her salvation from the despair of failure and the threat of return to childhood poverty. He'd brought her into his exclusive world and allowed her to exercise her need for control over others with complete freedom and support. He almost seemed to enjoy it, complying with every request without question. For the last three years she'd worked tirelessly to ensure that everyone in his formidable family loved her – well, almost everyone!

Harry continued to voice his frustration with his son and the situation he was putting them in.

'Not only did I find out about this plan from my brother-in-law because my own son forgot to mention it to me but my wife is convinced Richard put him up to it to stop him taking over as CEO at Blue Star. She's furious that she won't see him for months, she's not speaking to Richard and our home life is in turmoil. Surely *you* can't be happy with this move, away from *your* family and friends?' Harry asked. He knew it was unfair to take his concerns out on Jen, as he so often did, but he wasn't done trying to get her on side just yet. 'You were there when we agreed a clear career path before his graduation; 2 years experience at the law firm before taking over Blue Star as CEO.' Harry chopped the air in front of him into imaginary segments with his hands trying to emphasise his point. 'Richard has known this was the plan for years so I don't even understand why he's suddenly so worried! He's due to retire in a few years anyway. I guess he thought it would buy him some more time if things got put back another three years? God knows he's getting through money fast enough with that lazy-arsed wife and daughter of his.'

'It must be hard for him being part of one of the richest families in the world and yet legally only being seen as an employee as far as the company is concerned.' Jennifer could certainly relate to that.

'Richard has done well out of the situation. Henry was raised knowing it was his destiny to take over both of his grandfathers' businesses. Most men would love just one of those opportunities but he seems determined to blow off both. He doesn't ask for our opinions or our advice and he doesn't seem to care about the consequences, especially to himself or you. How do you put up with him?'

'What do you want me to do, exactly?' Jennifer was already suspicious of Harry's unexpected request to see her today. For the first time in three years, he was asking about his son's motives rather than his schedule and she scanned his face for clues to a hidden agenda. Why was he so desperate for Henry to stay in America? It wasn't like he urgently needed to work to earn a living.

'Look, I know why he's angry with us! Ever since the accident....' Harry paused momentarily as the words jarred in his throat. He still couldn't bring himself to mention it. 'Since school he's taken every opportunity to treat our rules and our wealth with indifference. He ignores our requests because he knows we will bail him out of difficulties, no matter what he does.'

'He thinks you don't trust him,' Jennifer said. 'That's why he got the court injunction.'

Harry played with his Mont Blanc pen, habitually clicking the lid over and over.

'He gave us no reason to trust him. He was reckless with his own safety, dodging his bodyguards at every opportunity, and finding reasons to avoid seeing us. Just last week he gave away the bespoke Rolex divers watch, which we gave him as a graduation present, and he doesn't even know who to.' The acts of defiance were trivial but unrelenting. 'And now he plans to avoid working and his family responsibilities yet again with another three years of study. He is going to drag you all the way to London, which no doubt he's happy for us to pay for - leaving all of your family and friends behind. Surely that must upset you too? Did he even ask your opinion?''

On some level Jennifer could understand Henry's rebellion but she would never actively encourage it. It was important to her to maintain the illusion of harmony with his parents – for their sake.

'No, of course he didn't, but I made a commitment to him and to your family and I intend to honour that, sir. He's been given a grant to study but obviously that won't cover the security provisions you wanted to take to protect him.' Jennifer looked down at the 2-carat flawless diamond on her third finger and rubbed it subconsciously. 'He is important to me and I won't abandon him. I don't think he would last long anywhere in the world without me to look after him, despite what he thinks.'

'Sadly, I know you're right.' Harry picked up the second photo of his wife and son on his desk. It had been taken on Henry's third birthday and the bodyguards were visible even then. 'Sometimes I think we should have handled things differently but at least you coming into his life was one good thing to come out of the whole mess.'

Despite three failed kidnap attempts Henry had continually shunned the safety measures his parents desperately tried to enforce. As a teenager he'd abused everything in his life including his own body. He'd been expelled from grade school for fighting and then from prep school for drinking and smoking. Sneaking out at weekends and taking part in extreme sports such as bungee jumping and cave diving, without a care for his own mortality, had been normal behaviour. He'd even abused his extensive martial arts training by getting involved in illegal street fights that had often left him with multiple injuries. Each cut and broken bone seemed like a penance to be paid for the wealth he had been born into that riddled him with golden chains. Things had gotten so bad Harry often wondered if the boy might fail to make it to adulthood, either through his own actions or someone else's. But the events that surrounded his 18th birthday had changed him profoundly. The accident that had left him with numerous physical and mental scars and he'd withdrawn from his huge social circle, limiting his friends to less than a dozen. He began to focus on his studies and his sport; turning his anger instead into indifference for everything his parents gave him. They might control him financially but he was choosing his own path despite their intrusion and they would foot the bill because they were too scared not to. Henry knew that they would comply with his requests for fear of him going off on his own anyway and it was the only power over them that he had. He lived how he wanted and his parents did what they could to wrap him up in extremely expensive cotton wool.

Jennifer usually ended up as the mediator between Henry and his parents, just as she would be today.

'He's has been a kidnap risk since the moment he was born. Its not really surprising that he trusts no one given the on-going ring of security that surrounds him. It's all he's ever known. Sometimes I think he even doubts *my* intentions, although I don't think I could have made my feelings clearer from the start. He believes he can live a relatively normal life in London, where no one knows who he is and he can forget about what happened.'

Harry shrugged his shoulders. He wasn't sure he agreed. A seven-hour flight was no deterrent at all to a determined criminal. The trust fund set up under the terms of his great grandfather's will would make Henry a billionaire in his own right by the time he was 30. That was a pretty good incentive.

'I know he was reckless and arrogant as a teenager but nobody deserves to have that happen to them. We weren't there when he needed us and now I just want to keep him safe.' Harry sighed and slumped back in his chair. He'd never even considered the consequences of bringing a child into Constance's family at the time of their marriage. It wasn't just their wealth that was extreme; the whole family were one of the most recognised in the country, outlasting 4 presidents and their first families in terms of media attention. How did royal families deal with this threat all the time?

'The effects of the accident have all been properly contained.' Jennifer reminded him. 'No long-term damage was done to the family or the business.'

Harry paused and collected his thoughts, almost forgetting that Jennifer was in front of him. He wasn't sure he agreed but he sighed in defeat. Yet again Henry's happiness had been a secondary consideration to his safety.

'Maybe some time abroad will help him finally figure out what he wants in life. God knows it can't be anything we could buy him! There's nothing left to try. Is everything ready in London?'

'The flat in the Barbican is already set up with all the modifications you asked for. Your agent purchased the property below and the apartment has been converted into a two-storey condo with its own gym. We will be able to continue our physical therapy training together and you know it calms him down so much when he's practising his martial arts. The whole place has been soundproofed and the security has been increased to your team's specifications. Domestic staff, university personnel and his medical practitioners have all been thoroughly vetted, although he has refused a security detail so it's just me going with him. His car and phone all have trackers and the lawyers have the Verichip re-activation request ready to go before a judge at a moment's notice.'

Jennifer looked down again at the ring. She was grateful for all the measures the Whitakers had put in place. It would make everything so much easier. The soundproofing was necessary for more than just overenthusiastic sparring sessions. She wasn't going to tell Henry's father about the nightmares she had to listen to almost every night. The less he knew about their life together the better.

Chapter 4

London, Thursday September 25th 2014.

Tia turned into the Main Quad of UCL from Gower St, walking past the porter's lodge towards the famous portico building. The Corinthian columns and apex roof reminded her of the ancient Greek gymnasiums, which literally meant school of bodily exercise. Her sports bag swung gently over her shoulder, tapping against her hip in a rhythmic pattern matching her pace. She hadn't explored this part of the campus yet and the tranquillity of the gardens made her feel as though she'd been transported to a different era. The atmosphere in this small part of the college was very different to the modern, frantic pace found elsewhere on site. On her left, the world famous Slade School of fine art occupied the north transept of the original university building, which had been outgrown several times during its history. Politician and social reformer, Jeremy Bentham, founded UCL in 1826 just before he died at the age of 84. True to his lifelong dedication to reform he left his body to science and asked that his taxidermied remains be put on public display in the South Cloisters of the original building. Unfortunately for Mr Bentham, the taxidermist had struggled with the preservation of his head. Instead a wax effigy that made him look permanently intoxicated topped off his hay-stuffed skeleton. A look that he would definitely not have approved of but which generations of students had adopted as their role model!

The sports facilities were easy to find, sited next to the Bloomsbury Theatre, part of the newly renovated Student Union. Everything had been upgraded considerably over the past few years to accommodate and entice the increasing number of foreign students. With one of the best engineering departments in the world, University College had forged strong links with China and the Far East and its sports focus reflected this specific cultural diversity, just as it seemed China adopted more traditionally Western forms of sport.

Tia arrived at the gym just before 6pm. The large, well-equipped room was on the second floor of the sub-basement next to the bigger and much more popular weights gym. It was windowless and cold but these conditions were ideal for encouraging high levels of cardio activity to ensure you kept warm. Tia needed a coach or sparring partner who knew enough about Wing Chun to allow her to practice. She had high hopes that the significant Chinese contingent of students would stay true to their own sport

As she entered the main sports hall the smell of stale body odour, so familiar in gyms, was still noticeable, despite the efficient new air conditioning system. That was a good sign! At least the fighters here trained hard enough to work up a sweat rather than the static macho muscle flexing she'd witnessed in many less athletic establishments.

'You found it okay then?' a voice called from behind her.

She turned to see the redhead, Ashley, land a sidekick to the right thigh of her partner. He flinched and went down onto one knee as she walked over to greet the rare new female that she still didn't believe would last more than tonight.

Ashley looked Tia up and down, just as she had on their first encounter, and again wondered how someone so tall and so thin could possibly look either graceful or menacing on a fight mat.

'Yes, but I'm still having to use the map.' Tia smiled and waved the folded paper Ashley had given her.

'Well this is the Student Union building so you'll be able to get here blindfolded before long. The changing rooms are over there. You just put a quid in the locker, but you get it back thank god!'

Tia changed into her black cotton trousers and collarless black shirt and came back out into the main gym. Whilst personal security had been his main objective when taking her to that first lesson Stephen Hall had also wanted his daughter to compete, possibly to Olympic standard. Sadly Tia had discovered early on that whilst she was an exceptional practitioner, gaining promotion through the grades quickly and enthusiastically, her shy personality crippled her with stage fright when it came to competitions. She excelled when fighting to gain her belts and knew she could defend herself if she needed to - which so far she had not experienced. She just didn't see the attraction of fighting someone just for sport, to see who could win, especially with rules devised to limit the aggression that could be unleashed. Martial arts had been developed in a different era - one without guns - where hand-to-hand combat was a way to preserve life, not a spectator sport. The woman who created Wing Chun did so to protect her community from marauders, not to attract ticket holders. Tia's first and only attempt to compete to please her father had culminated in a broken collarbone and a vomit-covered opponent. She felt that same feeling surge through her as she looked around the room. Ashley was waiting for her by the water dispenser and was surprised by the very different uniform Tia was wearing.

'Henry!' she shouted at the top of her extremely loud cockney voice as Tia walked over. 'Its the skinny chick I was telling you about!'

Tia flinched at the label but decided now was not the time to be over-sensitive about her body. Her uniform had been specifically chosen to hide her lack of curves and she hated having attention drawn to her appearance. She was nervous enough as it was and didn't want to stand out any more than she already did by making a scene. Her aggrieved thoughts bolted from her mind as she turned to identify Henry.

Across the room, a tall athletic man turned his attention from pinning various notices onto a large corkboard. His hair was dark and dishevelled, as though he had recently been fighting in the street rather than in a well disciplined club. He was wearing the more familiar

41

white cotton trousers and wraparound tunic, tied with a black belt. He was older than the other people in the room and Tia assumed he must be a lecturer rather than a student. As he walked towards them and smiled she noticed his teeth were just a little too perfect and as soon as he spoke his American accent explained his dental work.

'Hi, I'm Henry Whittaker. Ashley said we might have a new girl turning up. I run the MMA club. What's your name?' he said, holding out a hand that looked as if it had been manicured.

'Tia Hall' she replied shyly, unable to fully look him in the eye and only just catching the tips of his fingers as she shook his hand limply. She could feel the smooth, glasslike surface of his nails - definitely manicured! Probably gay! She instantly chastised herself for being so quick to apply a label when she was still indignant about the one that had just been pinned on her. She couldn't stop herself hoping it wasn't true. Where had that notion come from?

'Well Tia, Ashley said you were looking for a Wing Chun class? At least that's what I guessed she meant. It was difficult to understand the actual words she used. Is that right?' He laughed as he pushed his fingers through his hair and it fell into a more groomed style that framed his face perfectly. Tia thought he wouldn't look out of place in a boy band, albeit one that had been around for ten years.

'If there's no class I just need to try and find some sparring partners. I saw there was a parrot here so I assumed someone must practice with it.' She pointed to the Dalek-like structure on the far side of the room that looked more like a medieval torture device than a sports aid. It was about 6 feet tall with padded, extended arms. It didn't look as though it had seen much use and Tia's hopes of fulfilling her promise to her father were beginning to fade. He would be mad! She knew he would insist on her returning twice weekly to Orpington to continue her training at home if the facilities here were insufficient.

'Well we have a few experts as it happens but no women I'm afraid. Have you trained against men before?' The tone of his question implied that he didn't have high expectations regarding her ability. Tia could sense the mist of indignation forming around her temples.

'I was the only woman in my club who remained past the age of 7. Not many little girls like getting punched in the head.' Over the years she had watched young children come and go, not just girls, as they realised Karate was much less demanding physically than Wing Chun.

'Well I can match you up with some possible partners, but let's see what standard you are at - your uniform is not telling me much!'

'No, we don't have the same requirements to wear our grading on our belts - gives the opposition a bit too much info!' Tia flushed at her unusual display of bravado and instantly dropped her gaze to the floor again. 'Do you know Wing Chun then?'

'Not specifically, but I think I can hold my own for a few minutes. Mixed martial arts is about pitching different disciplines against each other so I should be able to read a few of your moves.'

He stood confidently in the middle of the padded floor matting and beckoned her towards him with a curl of his finger and a smile that made her want to run all the way back to the familiar middle-aged trainer she'd left in Orpington. She felt her stomach flip and she became temporarily disoriented.

'Now show me a basic head punch,' he said as he danced lightly on the tips of his toes, prompting her to come forward.

Her hands began to shake a little as she moved into position. Instantly she felt as if she were back on the competitive stage that had resulted in an injury, which had taken 3 months to heal. An injury that might have turned her off training forever if that had been an option for her father. She was convinced he would prefer to lock her in the basement of their house for eternity rather than let her out into the world unable to defend herself.

'Its okay,' Henry coaxed teasingly, his smile once again disorientating her. 'I won't hit you back just yet, I promise!'

For a brief moment Tia saw a flicker of pity mixed with amusement in his face! He thinks I'm a novice playing with a new fad, she thought to herself, and was overwhelmed by a desire to knock that grin straight off his pretty-boy face. She steeled her legs, pulled the weight back into her shoulders and locked her core as she moved towards him. If he has any clue about Wing Chun, she thought, then prancing about like the sugar plum fairy is not going to help him. She could tell he was expecting a slow arcing swing from her right arm by the way he held his guard. He was already in trouble.

Wing Chun is primarily about speed - specifically short sharp forward propulsion pummels with the forearms. Punches are thrown in a lightning fury that grinds your opponent into exhausted submission with their unrelenting frequency. As she launched her initial attack he barely got his arm into a defensive position before this fury rained down on him. His assumptions about her had caused him to let his guard down. She slowly forced him backwards across the matting with the ferocity of her attack, which focused almost entirely on his upper body and head. She kept her feet on the floor to maintain her balance, because in truth he'd left her a little weak at the knees and that was not something she'd experienced before. Her legs weren't operating at their normal optimum output and she didn't feel comfortable adding any kicks to her onslaught. However the speed of her punches was drawing attention from the others in the room as a small circle gathered to witness Henry Whittaker getting pounded on by a girl. As he reached the edge of the mat Henry recovered his composure. The instinct he had crafted through Krav Maga kicked in and he quickly identified her current weakness. As she continued her volley of uppercuts with her powerful arms he took her down with a hook from his right leg that left her sprawling across the floor.

'Whoa Tiger!' he said, rubbing his temple with one hand whilst offering to help her up with the other. 'I said show me a punch to the head, not batter my brains out!'

'You don't fight using single punches in Wing Chun. It's all about fluidity and speed of movement. That's why we use the parrot.' She looked at his hand for a second and then ignored it, jumping to her feet on her own. When she was fighting without an audience Tia's confidence was boundless. 'And what was that move you did to me? You didn't say we were going for take down. I barely used any pressure or force but I can't help the speed - its instinctive now.'

'Well I practice Krav Maga mainly which is more defensive and instinctive, and to be honest I just wasn't expecting such a frenzied first move. I'm sorry, I guess I assumed you wouldn't be as good as you obviously are. Let me get the training pads and I promise not to take you down again.'

Over the next half an hour Tia disappeared into a world of jabs and lunges and chops that felt comfortable and familiar to her. Henry's encouragement was genuine and constant. It wasn't really sparring because he wasn't returning her shots, but it felt good to let off some of her pent-up energy. She was only vaguely aware of the glances she was getting from the gym users more used to slow brutal slogging and throwing than the speed of this new display.

'Not bad for a girl,' Henry teased as they finished the session 'I reckon your performance will be pretty impressive against someone who actually knows Wing Chun. I'll put a notice up for you. If it's written by me then the guys will know you're serious and not just a little girl keeping fit masochistically.' With that he disappeared into a small office, closing the door behind him.

'That *was* pretty impressive.' Ashley came up behind Tia as she towelled herself down. 'Not many people surprise Henry, but trust me, there's nothing quite so satisfying as just kicking a guy in the nuts when he's getting on your nerves.' She laughed so loudly she tipped her head back and Tia noticed a small faint scar, about two inches long, running under her jaw.

Ashley caught her staring and quickly turned away to search her rucksack for her constantly beeping phone. As she scanned the illuminated screen her mood and demeanour changed instantly. She slammed the cover closed and roughly threw the phone back into her bag, swearing under her breath.

'Sorry love… gotta go.' she said without looking up.

After a perfect evening of fighting and almost making a new friend, Tia found herself standing alone in the freezing cold gym.

Chapter 5

Auvers-sur-Oise, France - 28th July 1890

Rene Secretan sat at a table in the Poachers Inn on the Rue Boucher pretending to look out of the window at the River Oise. In fact he was straining his ears, desperately trying to listen to the conversation on the next table. The three men - a farmer, the town butcher and the gamekeeper from the Chateau - paid him no attention as they drank their way through the second carafe of local red vin-de-pays. They were engrossed by the unfolding tale of the artist's shooting, which had spread quickly throughout Auvers.

Rene was 16 years old, the son of a wealthy pharmacist, visiting the town from Paris with his older brother Gaston. He was an arrogant and troublesome outsider, just here for the summer and of no interest to the locals. He sat alone nursing a glass of the same cheap local red wine. The replica Buffalo Bill hat he'd worn every day since arriving last month was pushed down onto the side of his head, his curly blond hair just protruding underneath its brim. It was his prized possession, purchased after watching the world famous travelling rodeo circus two months before in Paris. Its distinctive shape and the outrageous fringed outfit that came with it were the only means by which the locals had come to recognise him. Most thought he looked ridiculous but his father was an important landowner so they kept their opinions to themselves.

The same few details were being repeated over and over. The Dutch artist staying with the Ravoux family at the Auberge had shot himself up by the wheat fields and everyone in the village had an opinion as to why. New information was scarce and rumours of Van Gogh's mental state were rife. Few people were aware of what had actually happened which only served to heighten the gossip. The police had this morning commenced their investigation and so far had little to go on. No one appeared to be able to add much detail that was of any use, but this didn't temper the speculation. Conflicting eyewitness accounts contradicted the story the artist himself had told as to his location, heightening the intrigue, but no one was prepared to swear by their testimony other than Arthur Ravoux.

'His brother, Theo, arrived in town from Paris at midday today,' the butcher explained. 'He's at the Auberge with him now. The Gendarmes arrived and tried to tell Vincent that he'd committed a crime by attempting suicide and threatened to arrest him but he didn't seem to care what they thought. Said it was his body to do with as he wished.'

'He shot himself,' said the farmer disapprovingly, shaking his head. 'God will not look favourably on him. Suicide is a cardinal sin. If he dies I can't imagine Abbot Tessier will allow him to be buried in the churchyard.'

'I doubt he will even allow the funeral to take place in the church,' added the barmaid, joining the conversation as she put more wine on the table and poured them each a glass. 'He'll end up outside the church wall if he dies.'

'The police can't find anything up in the wheat fields,' the gamekeeper added. 'That's where the artist says he was but they can't find the gun or any trace of blood. He says he dropped the gun there, and it hasn't rained for weeks so where's the evidence? Arthur Ravoux says he can't find his pistol that he kept in a box under the counter of the Auberge. The police believe the artist took it but it's not in the Wheatfield's or the lanes that run past the Chateau. I helped with the search myself this morning. Also, all of his materials are missing. He left the Auberge just after lunch with his easel, canvas and paints and had nothing in his possession when he got back that evening. They haven't found any of his things.'

'How could he have the strength to hide them or even carry them that distance with a bullet in his stomach?' asked the butcher.

'How did he have the strength to climb down that steep hill past the Chateau at all? It's at least a mile back to the Auberge, how did he manage that without leaving a trace?' The gamekeeper had worked on the estate since he was a boy and he knew just how difficult getting down that hill was, even for a healthy fit man.

'If you ask me he's a raving lunatic,' the barmaid volunteered unkindly. 'Who shoots himself in the heart to commit suicide if they're serious? When he didn't die straight away, why didn't he just shoot himself again in the head? That is the question they should be asking, my friends.'

Rene silently agreed that these were indeed the questions the police should be asking. His concern was growing as to why they weren't. How long would it take for them to start to enquire as to the whereabouts of the missing items, especially the gun?

His brother Gaston came into the inn and sat opposite him. He was 19 and much more sensitive and quiet than his extravagant younger brother. He preferred music and art to shooting and drinking and was deeply saddened by the news that Van Gogh had been injured. But his loyalty to his family reputation was stronger than his feelings for an acquaintance he had known only a few weeks.

'Father has replied to my telegram and he's demanding we come back to Paris immediately. He doesn't want us to get involved or stay in this place with these events going on. We need to take this opportunity and get out while we can. His carriage is on the way. We must leave tonight.'

Rene just nodded and left his money on the table for the waitress as they left the inn.

As they approached their father's summerhouse he saw her standing to the side of the doorway. She held her head up high and stared at him defiantly as they walked towards her.

'Rene can I speak with you?' she asked.

Gaston gave Rene a suspicious glance as he left them to go inside and pack.

Adeline Ravoux was pretty. Her long curled blonde hair was tied back in a ribbon like his mother's. He still couldn't believe she was only 12 years old; she looked much older and made him feel childlike, which he hated.

'When do you leave?' She asked bluntly without any formalities, her voice suggesting a confidence she didn't feel inside. If she could create the right impression maybe this boy would tell her more than she already knew. She had to protect her family and the rumours about her father and his gun were already getting out of hand. It was no secret that Vincent hadn't paid his rent yet, offering his paintings in lieu of actual money. Her father had been vocal in his anger and many in the town knew this. Rene Secretan could help her stem the gossip, of that she was certain.

'How do you know we're leaving?' he asked quizzically. They'd only met a few weeks ago when her father had proudly shown him the rare gun he kept under the counter at the Auberge. She'd been listening from the doorway to the kitchen and had made him nervous, warning him that the gun was unpredictable, as though he were a baby playing with a rattle. Rene was an excellent marksman who knew everything about guns and he didn't need a little girl to make him look foolish. The memory made him blush uncontrollably and he dropped his gaze to his shoes.

'The artist told me the truth of what happened yesterday so I guessed it wouldn't be long before you ran away with your little secret. I promised never to reveal a word of it and I wanted to make sure that you never will either.' She'd carefully thought out that sentence so it wasn't strictly a lie. God would not be mad with her but this boy might be if he guessed how little she actually understood. All her instincts told her that this arrogant aristocrat was involved somehow but she had no idea how – yet! All that mattered was that her father must not be blamed for these events.

'What do you mean?' he asked, nervously shifting his weight on his feet. He tried to look indignant but she just laughed at him. 'Who told you the truth?'

'He told me what really happened and asked me to give you this.' She handed him the unopened letter from Vincent. 'He begged me to make sure you stuck to your story. What did you do to him?'

'Nothing!' Rene stepped backwards, fear etched across his face and instinctively hiding the letter behind his back as if it never existed. What could the mad Dutchman have possibly told this girl to make her so angry?

His shocked reaction, however, seemed to satisfy her and she calmed down. This boy was not about to contradict her father's story. He wouldn't even be in town. Her family would be safe.

'Make sure you say nothing, Rene Secretan! If you do I'll tell everyone you're lying. I will tell them I saw you steal it from us. Whatever you've done – it must never be found. My father's account must be the only one the world remembers. I will not let you damage my father's reputation.'

Rene looked at her as he registered the actual significance of her words. He realised in that moment that she knew nothing about him or what he'd done! She was fishing to find out if he knew something about her father's involvement. Not surprising given the speculation concerning the gun that was spreading through the town, especially as there was only Arthur's word that the artist had confessed to shooting himself. A few people were already asking how Ravoux could have let the gun out of his sight, knowing the mental state of his erratic guest. But her instincts were good. If a twelve-year-old girl could reach such a conclusion, then so could the rest of the world. Rene had to get out of Auvers and away from the evidence as quickly as possible!

The police arrived at the Secretan's summer home in Auvers that evening.

'We need to speak to Rene and Gaston Secretan,' the officer said when the housekeeper answered the door.

'The boys have already left to return to Paris,' she replied.

'May we ask you a few questions?' the elder gendarme asked.

'Come in,' she replied and led them into a small parlour lined on three sides by rough wooden bookshelves. The fire in the hearth was cold and black, but the heat in the room from the hot summer sun was overbearing.

'I have some questions to ask you regarding the matter of the shooting of Vincent Van Gogh. Do you know the man?'

'No, but I heard the news,' she replied. 'Master Rene did not care for him much but he got on well with Master Gaston. He liked to talk about art.'

'We have information from a number of people that Rene would torment him in the street about his appearance and behaviour. Is that true?'

'I believe he may have played a few pranks on him but Gaston wouldn't let it go too far. He put salt in his drink but nothing more serious than that.' The housekeeper didn't like Rene but her loyalty to the family was steadfast.

'We've also been told that Rene Secretan was in possession of a handgun. A small calibre pistol belonging to the Innkeeper. Do you recall the weapon?'

'Yes, he brought it home a few days ago. It was a terrible thing. It would go off unexpectedly and would never shoot straight. Rene is an excellent marksman and even he struggled with it. I wouldn't allow him to bring it into the house.'

'Do you know where the weapon is now?'

'I haven't seen it for days. I assume he took it back to wherever he got it from. It was more like a toy to him, surely not capable of any real damage.'

'Do you know if he gave the gun to anyone?'

'He is always very careless with his things. He leaves them lying around in his rucksack when he's off in the boat or swimming in the lake. If he still had it I assume anyone could have taken it if they wanted to.' The housekeeper started to look worried. 'Do you think he has something to do with this shooting?'

The officer ignored her question and carried on

'Do you know where he was all day yesterday?'

'Yes, they both went fishing down by the bridge next to the Inn. I'm sure there are a number of people who could confirm that. I heard the accident happened up in the wheat fields on the other side of town?' The housekeeper hoped for the first time that the gossip about Rene was true. Again the officer ignored her question.

'Do you have an address in Paris where we might reach these boys if we need to speak to them in the future to find out more about this gun?'

'Yes, wait here and I will get it for you.'

That night, Van Gogh died and Rene and Gaston Secretan never heard from the Auvers Police again.

Chapter 6
Vologda, Russia - 21st August 1968.

The growing political unrest in the Czechoslovakian republic presented Russian Premier Leonid Brezhnev with ideological as well as practical problems. Prague Spring, a series of political reforms, was designed to give control of Czech industry back to the citizens. Moscow was not impressed. If Czechoslovakia returned to a more democratic political system it might not be long before the other Warsaw pact countries followed suit - especially East Germany, who was starting to show signs of economic recovery following the Second World War.

On the night of Wednesday 21st August 1968, 200,000 Russian troops and 2000 tanks marched into the CSSR.

As the Red Army crossed over the border and headed towards the airport, Boris and Vasily dug their way back out of the wall. As they emerged into the gloomy darkness of the church Boris lit a candle and looked for the first time at the block he had used as a pillow.

'What is it?' Vasily asked him.

'It's a wooden Icon.' Boris had seen them on the walls of churches all over Vologda, but none as perfect or detailed as this one. The colours were more vibrant and the amount of gold leaf used on the intricate borders left him in no doubt that this work was special. He didn't recognise the saint portrayed in the picture but the craftsmanship was incredible compared to other works he'd seen which looked dull and cartoonish in comparison.

Boris and Vasily left the church at midnight and immediately broke into the small local library to try and find out details about the icon. They didn't know where to start.

'You check the Russian art section.' Boris instructed Vasily 'and I'll start with local history. Maybe there is something in the books about the convent that might tell us what this is.'

Vasily turned out to be a useful ally. His reading was good and he quickly found out that Russian history was littered with stories of miraculous appearances of icons - considered to be a gift from God to those in trouble. He also found evidence to suggest that the market for such art was growing. As the fascination for the mysterious USSR grew across the world, Russian art, sculpture and jewellery escalated in value – if you could get the work out of the country. Boris knew he would carry it across the border on foot if he had to!

Boris found damaged records from the ancient convent in the local history archives. They had been salvaged before the desecration of the property began in earnest but they were fragile and old. Hand written manuscripts suggested that the Assumption church had once housed 7 Icons but only five of the originals had been found when the convent was commandeered in 1924 and these had been moved to the Vologda Cultural Museum. The manuscripts were in Latin, but a local historian had made extensive notes in Russian on a separate document, which Boris was able to understand.

The written description of the missing portrait of St Sergius, founder of the Russian Orthodox Church, said it was painted in oil, shellac and gilt on a block of wood. It described the clothing in detail, including the colours and flourishes that filled the background. The icon in his hand was faded and scratched from a history that Boris assumed involved being moved from place to place. It had been stolen from the Assumption church many years before, along with a painting of the saviour. Despite having no visual reference to compare, Boris knew in his heart that this was the portrait he'd found. He might never be able to prove it – but he knew! This Icon had somehow been returned to the church, if it had ever even left.

St Sergius, the patron of the convent church, had helped Boris in his darkest hour, presenting him with sanctuary from almost certain death in the form of the hidden cave. Now his image was captured in a priceless work of art that would provide financial freedom from the communist oppression he hated so much and that had seemed determined to condemn him to a life as an exile. As far as Boris was concerned this icon had appeared to him in his hour of need – A lost treasure that had been his salvation.

He had no idea of its value or provenance but it ignited in him an unfaltering belief that through it, the hand of fate had touched him. It was a feeling so compelling he could not ignore it or explain it. It formed within him was an utterly consuming conviction that he had been saved by the miraculous art, which had called out to him from within the hidden alcove and saved him from poverty and the Draft.

Chapter 7

Tottenham, Thursday September 25th London

Ashley Rivers emerged from Seven Sisters station just as darkness was settling over the grey, decaying buildings of Tottenham High Rd. She was unglamorous and unkempt with an anarchic fashion sense and aggressive manner cultivated specifically to keep men at bay. It had worked as a strategy for 10 years, since the night she got the scar on her neck at the hands of one of her mother's many boyfriends. That had been the night she'd decided to learn to defend herself. She felt protected by the anarchic image she'd created and put up with the loneliness it caused. Tonight's unplanned trip home was yet another occasion that reminded her why she'd kept the world at arms length all her life.

It had started to rain during the 20 minutes she'd been on the Underground and people were running for shelter in the doorways of the kebab shops, off licences and barbers that were still trading. The betting shops and pawnbrokers that provided the locals with a dubious source of income were closed and few made use of the ATMs. Benefit day and cash-in-hand paydays were not until tomorrow so many were left with just the change in their pockets. The traffic was at a standstill. Buses were gridlocked and the occasional pointless blast of a horn added to everyone's frustration. Only the shopkeepers loved the rain! A stranded pedestrian with no waterproof coat was more likely to give in to an impulse to eat fried chicken or get a cheap haircut just to get some shelter.

She pulled up the hood of her thin, customised Primark parka and turned left off the main road towards Broadwater Farm. Her hair was cut short and dyed bright orange, both the product of her own hand. The colour was almost as loud as her booming voice and her bold, mismatched clothes. Now, cloaked in her hooded coat in the darkened street, she became invisible. Not many 23-year-old women would feel safe walking alone on the badly lit pathways of the notorious council estate at any time of the day, and certainly not after nine o'clock in the evening.

Ashley Rivers was different. She'd grown up on Broadwater Farm where it was not unusual for girls much younger than her to be seen wandering aimlessly round the streets looking for something to stimulate their mundane lives, even if it was trouble. Fear was the biggest enemy of the weaker sex in this area. If you looked frightened you became an instant target; act tough and you just might stay on your feet, in every sense. Although Ashley was a proficient kick boxer, even she knew that wasn't enough against a gang or a gun. You had to look confident and unafraid whilst maintaining the highest levels of vigilance. Then, just maybe, you'd be left alone in favour of easier or better-looking pickings. Her own safety, however, couldn't be further from her mind at present and only her instinctive behaviour forced her to adopt the routines she'd developed over a lifetime. Yet again trouble at home was dragging her back past familiar scenes that were a million miles from the grand visage of the college she had literally fought to get into.

The concrete blocks of flats, once notorious after the riots of 1985, still housed some of the poorest residents in London. Despite the poverty, the community had attempted to brighten up their environment with four-storey-high wall murals commissioned by the council. These dubious works of art looked vibrant and alive during the day, but at night the colour disappeared from view. The life was drained from the streets as the oppression of the densely clustered buildings returned.

She turned onto Silver Street and re-read the text from her brother calling for help. They'd grown up witnessing first-hand the troubles that inevitably followed when you were plagued by despair and addiction, and yet again she was on her way home to deal with a mother who still hadn't learned to cope with either.

She could smell the stale beer even before she got the key out of the lock of the battered and faded front door on the tenth floor of a building with no working lift. The galley kitchen on her left stank of days-old takeaway leftovers that were still scattered across the small worktop, spilling into the sink.

'Matty!' she called out to her 14-year-old brother who'd sent her the distress text not 40 minutes earlier. Matt came out of the bedroom they'd shared for 13 years, until she'd moved out just over a year ago. It was the larger of the two bedrooms and contained a double bed, with a single bunk above, and a two-door wardrobe that was older than she was. It was the same room that Matt still shared with Connor, the 22-year-old wayward middle child who was currently out working at his second job - at least Ashley hoped he was if the family was going to eat tomorrow.

'They're in there.... pissed again!' he said raising his eyes in resigned despondence. 'I think she's hurt herself.'

'Who's they?' Ashley asked, opening the living room door and knowing roughly what to expect.

Her mother was passed out, asleep on the sofa with her head buried in the lap of a boy she recognised from Connor's class at school. The floor was littered with crushed cans of Tennant's Super and the room stank of cigarette smoke. Dog ends had fallen out of the overflowing ashtray, leaving burn marks on the threadbare carpet. How she had survived living with this woman for 22 years? A smeared line of blood had dried across her mother's forehead but the injury was obviously new.

'How did she get in that state?' she asked rhetorically, really not wanting to know. The knowledge wouldn't improve her mood.

The boy obliged and didn't reply - he just shifted his gaze to the half-empty bottle of own-label vodka on the small table next to the second-hand sofa. Traces of blood still crusted onto the corner of the cheap metal frame where her mother had clearly banged her forehead in a drunken fall.

'Did you bring that round here?' The accusation was clear. Yet again Ashley was looking for someone else to blame for her mother's increasingly wayward behaviour. The 40-year-old woman stirred briefly and looked up.

'Alright love?' she managed as her eyes rolled backwards in their sockets and closed again involuntarily. Ashley couldn't tell if it was concussion or she was just suffering from another night of extreme alcohol abuse. A visit to the hospital was out of the question. Social services didn't need to be given any more reasons to take Matt into care because of an unfit mother.

Patricia Rivers had grown up in the 70s, the middle child in a family of five kids who lived in the tenements of Hackney before the gentrification process started. She had always been rebellious and at 16 had found herself pregnant after a trip to Margate on which she'd forgotten to establish formalities from her one-night stand, such as his name and address. Her mother had thrown her out of the cramped, ground-floor three-bedroom Victorian conversion and Haringey council had immediately rehoused her in an already run down, purpose-built flat that was half the size. She then bounced from one accident to another, each time falling briefly on her feet surviving on benefit after benefit. Social workers came and went. Some insisted she gave her three children up into care to be quickly followed by replacements who fought relentlessly to get them back home with their mother.

Patricia didn't do drugs, a common time- and money-consumer in Tottenham during the 1990s, but she did like to drink - particularly vodka – Neat. But she didn't like to drink alone, and so Ashley had got used to coming home from school unsure as to who exactly she would find in the 10th-floor two-bedroom flat that had quickly fallen into disrepair inside as well as outside.

In this instance the boy on the sofa caught up in the latest binge event was Eoin Driscoll, an Irish traveller whose family had squatted in a condemned Victorian slum near Edmonton eight years ago and never moved on. Eoin's uncle, Mickey Finnegan, was notoriously bad news and Ashley had always assumed that Eoin was cut from the same cloth.

'She asked me to get it!' he said, picking up the vodka and swigging deeply. 'What am I supposed to say when she's letting me...?'

'Letting you what? What the bloody hell are you doing here in the first place?' Ashley shouted drawing the worst possible conclusions from his unfinished sentence. 'She's nearly 20 years older than you! That's disgusting! Ain't you supposed to be married by now?'

'Get lost! I'm not ready for that sort of responsibility!' Eoin tipped the bottle up again as though the action itself proved the truth of the statement. 'I came to see Connor. He said I could crash here for a couple of days till my uncle calms down and lets me come back home. Don't worry - I'm not screwing your mum!'

'But you come round here and think she's gonna look after you? Look at her - she can't even look after herself.' She looked at the empty plate that sat virtually licked clean next to where the vodka had been. 'I bet she didn't cook whatever it was you polished off there?'

'No... Matt cooked it when he did his own.' The embarrassment was evident as the words came out of his mouth.

'You came round here so my 14-year-old brother could cook you dinner? What was the vodka? The price of entry? Not a bad deal seeing as you look like you've drunk half of it.'

Eoin didn't reply. Ashley would freak if she knew he'd been staying there for the last three weeks and that Matt had either cooked or collected his dinner virtually every night.

'So what *are* you doing here then?' Ashley was fuming that neither boy had even attempted to clean up Patricia's wound.

'Had a row with my uncle and he threw me out.' Eoin didn't want to elaborate. Any half-truthful explanation would make the fiery redhead even angrier. Facing her temper, however didn't even come close to the fear he felt just thinking about what his uncle would do to him if he found him again. He'd broken their agreement, dissolved their partnership and he knew Mickey would never forgive him. He certainly wouldn't welcome him back home any time soon.

'And you think that's a good enough reason to come round here and live off my mum?'

Eoin stayed silent. Now probably wasn't the time to mention that if he hadn't been here there would have been no money to pay for any dinner, no matter where it came from. Connor had moved into his girlfriend's flat and taken his wage packet with him, just as Ashley had done a year ago.

Patricia Rivers and her son existed on the bread line and the alcoholic didn't even understand the potential consequences. Eoin wasn't the smartest person in the world, but he knew that Matt would be in a foster home in less than a week if he moved out and Connor didn't come back. Ashley should know better than anyone that her mother was incapable of supporting her family in any way at all.

As the oldest of the three, Ashley had become a babysitter at 9 years old, a cook at 11 and the main breadwinner at 14, so she knew a lot about early responsibility. Any thoughts of enjoying a normal carefree teen existence had disappeared when she got a job in Berwick Street Market selling vegetables. Every Saturday afternoon she had been able to double her pay just by 'watching' the stalls for the weather worn costermongers who needed a livener in the local pub. The unofficial overtime became her salvation. She gave her pay packet unopened to her mum who promptly gave it back to her with a shopping list and fake ID. She used the cash from the extra effort to fund first her kickboxing lessons and then evening classes to get the A levels she had missed out on after leaving school at 16.

Ashley was bright, but time to study had been a rare commodity. It had taken her four years to do what most people managed in two - but then most 16 year olds didn't have to look after two younger brothers and an alcoholic mother. She had eventually taken on part time work in three different establishments - one paycheck had been spent on her brothers, making sure they had clean clothes and a packed lunch every day. The second she used for herself and her mum, buying food and clothes from the charity shops, and the third she put into a secret bank account, saving to pay for the day she would give up her jobs to become a full time student. Coupled with her student loan and maintenance grant, she was just about surviving.

'So Connor said you went to Uni,' Eoin tried changing the subject in an attempt to placate her. 'What you doing there then?'

'Psychology and Art,' she couldn't resist replying, and felt her chest inflate slightly with pride as the words came out, but she quickly pulled herself back down to earth. 'But I'm not gonna sit here and talk to you about it! You need to get the fuck out of my house and stop sponging off my mum and brothers.' She wasn't going to be side tracked, that was clear.

'I'm not a sponger!' Eoin snapped. That was one insult too far from the girl who had no idea how bad things currently were with her family. 'Who'd you think is paying for the food they're eating this week. You don't seriously think she's got any money left till tomorrow do you?' Eoin might have been poor but he was proud, and he worked hard at his low-paid jobs to earn his keep and for three weeks he'd been paying theirs as well. He was filling the financial void in her family, leading the life she'd left behind, but with no hope of escape. Not that he was stupid! If the circumstances had been different he may have had a chance. If he hadn't been sucked into the damning influence of his uncle's profession he might have done better at school. He was bright and sharp. He didn't miss an opportunity if it presented itself and he survived off his wits. Living in Patricia Rivers' house while Connor stayed at his girlfriend's was a sweet little opportunity given he was currently homeless and in hiding!

'I don't care what you're paying for! I don't want you coming round here, plying her with vodka. How do you think it feels for Matt seeing his mum in this state?' Ashley buried her guilt under a barrage of accusations. Blaming someone else was easier than dealing with the mess she'd left behind to pursue her own dreams. She went into the mould-infested bathroom and found a ball of cotton wool, doused it in the vodka and wiped it over the cut on her mother's head.

Startled by the searing sting of the alcohol, Patricia lifted her head suddenly and retched. Eoin jumped up just as vomit covered the battered cushions, instantly overpowering the cigarette smells and adding to the multitude of stains.

'Now you can bloody well clear that up and help me get her into her bed!' Ashley screamed! 'It's your fault she's in this state! With your crap vodka that's most likely drain cleaner!' She grabbed his arm as he backed away from the mess left in his wake and rotated his wrist through an unnatural angle. 'If Matt rings me and tells me you're still here tomorrow I'll come back and throw you over the bloody balcony!'

As his muscles tightened all the way up his arm, Eoin remembered the last time he'd seen Ashley. She had been kicking the legs out from under a drunk in the local pub after he pinched her arse.

Chapter 8
Moscow, March 4th 2008

The Hotel Moskva, the most luxurious in Moscow, had been the product of a mistake. Stalin had signed the building plans exactly in the centre of the paper without realising he was supposed to make a choice between two alternative facades. The architect, Alexey Shchusev, afraid to point out the error to the cruel dictator, simply constructed the two wings in the different styles - an image immortalised on the label of the Latvian vodka, Stolichnaya, which Boris Rubikov drank for breakfast every morning.

Built in 1935, before the Second World War the hotel was filled with works of art and rich decorations produced by some of the greatest Russian artists of the day. More than 70 years later Boris had chosen it as his home for this very reason, then defiantly set about filling his own apartment rooms with priceless European art, reflecting the on-going conflict between his loyalty to his mother country and his belief in western values.

The privileged view from his penthouse overlooked the length of Red Square. Stalin himself had once looked out of these very windows, according to the hotel records. On the right stood the Kremlin and the Spasskaya Tower, with its giant ruby star and the red walls that many assumed gave the square its name, just visible in the morning gloom. At the far end, the world-famous multi-coloured domes of St Basil's Cathedral dominated the vista that few foreigners had seen first hand for many years until the fall of the Soviet Republic. The huge GUM shopping centre, the former Russian State department store facing the Kremlin, was an architectural echo of the changing times. The ceremonial reopening of its central doors onto Red Square during its centenary in 1993 saw the start of the invasion of Western fashion houses and American clothing shops, replacing the utility outlets and trading stalls that reflected communist oppression and scarcity. The familiar bread lines that once stretched across the square had been replaced by a slowly growing queue of tourists. Boris considered how little the physical view had changed in over a hundred years but how radically the culture it represented had altered, politically and economically, more than once.

His ghostly reflection in the glass of the window held his attention for a moment. The figure looking back at him had also changed considerably over the last four decades. He was the same height as he'd been when he and Vasily had crawled into the cramped space between the church wall and the bell tower in Vologda, but his frame was much bigger. 40 years of weight training and physically hard work had added over 40 pounds of muscle - there was no way he'd be able to hide in the secret alcove today.

His wife, Natalia, came into the living room with his glass of vodka, as she did every morning. She was ten years younger than him and still beautiful. He had seen that even when she was wearing her factory smock, her face smeared with engine oil grime. Now her blonde hair was set and her make-up was perfect - exactly how a millionaire's wife should look, he thought.

' Are you ready for your meeting?' she asked, handing him the crystal glass.

'This will be the greatest day since our babies arrived,' he said, kissing his wife gently on the top of her forehead. 'You know the Americans have been right all along - capitalism really is the way to go - democracy, maybe not so much! Look at the tourists down in the square; it's not even 9am yet and they are desperate to spend their money. This would have been unimaginable only a few years ago. Natalia, today *we* will write the next chapter of history - for Russia and for us. Our fortunes will continue to be good – I am sure of it.'

Since his escape with Vasily from Vologda, the Soviet government had spent billions of roubles fighting the Americans without firing a shot and Boris had made a fortune providing the cloth for uniforms that never saw combat. Now he would earn billions from both nations selling them the oil their countries need to survive into the next millennium.

He finished the remains of his vodka, set the glass on the mantelpiece above the fireplace and looked up at the wooden icon that hung on the most prominent wall in the room. His fortunes had changed dramatically since this noble work of art came into his life, not once, but twice.

To Boris this was not just a work of art; it was a unique item with a significance that no one except Natalia and Vasily would ever understand. An item he would never let go again.

'You know I didn't really understand it's importance when I sold that painting to the art dealer in Vologda. All I knew was that it had saved my life and allowed me to start my business and obviously that eventually led me to you,' he reminisced. 'It was only after the second time I found it that I realised how closely it was bound to my own fate.'

Unable to return home after dodging the draft, Boris and Vasily had used the money to purchase a train ticket to Kiev, a week's stay in a cheap hotel and a hundred bales of cotton and wool. Over the years, as Russia became increasingly free of the dogma of communism, he had expanded into manufacturing denim and importing leather and silk and Vasily had kept him safe as he had on that first night.

He'd met Natalia in one of the factories he employed to produce his bales of material. She had worked on the production line but occasionally helped in the accounts department and was as clever as she was beautiful. He had introduced himself as Alexandre Yeltsof. A name he had used since avoiding national service and leaving home. Today, Alexandre Yeltsof was not a draft dodger from Vologda but a respected businessman from Moscow - a dead man's identity that had served him well for four decades.

Natalia and Boris had built their fabric empire together, but his love was not fashion - it was money, and more importantly the things it allowed you to do. During the 1980s, as Perestroika opened up more and more opportunities for those prepared and able to take them, he had diversified into property and coal. Now his latest venture looked likely to set him apart from the mainstream investor community and earn him a place amongst the Russian financial elite.

'Do you remember the day I found the icon again?' he asked his wife.

'Of course I do. That was the day you purchased the Spetzform Plains.' She straightened his tie affectionately and cupped his face. 'The day I thought you may have ruined us for good, but my heart told me to trust you, as ever.'

'When I saw my painting in that art gallery in St Petersburg I knew it was a sign. The dealer wanted a hundred times the amount I'd sold it for thirty five years earlier, but it was a small price to pay for something that has allowed me to generate a hundred thousand times what I received for it.'

He'd never told his wife that the price to re-purchase his beloved icon had not been any form of currency and had ultimately not been paid by him but by the greedy gallery owner who had foolishly tried to inflate the asking price he wanted from the notorious businessman. He had not needed Vasily Denisov, his brutal head of security, to reason with the man that day. He had been more than capable of securing the painting with his own hands.

'Andrei certainly didn't understand your superstition. I've never seen a man so angry when you told him you'd purchased thousands of acres of Siberian wasteland. This morning he will be glad you never listen to him'

'That is why he is a lawyer and I will be the billionaire.' Boris puffed out his chest involuntarily, recalling how remorselessly Andrei

Kaspov had chastised him. 'I knew as soon as I bought the icon home that whatever deal came my way next was one I would seal on the very same day. It was a divine sign sent from God to guide my actions again and here we are; about to break ground in Siberia and form our new company. The biggest in Russia.'

Natalia pulled on the cuffs of Boris's shirt and inserted the mother of pearl cufflinks from Cartier that she had bought him for their 20th wedding anniversary.

'The geologists reports certainly had Andrei running with his tail between his legs when they estimated the size of the oil field,' she laughed, remembering the day the report had been brought to them. The projections suggested the field was the second largest ever discovered.

That had been three years ago and today, Boris would officially become the chairman, CEO and majority shareholder of his newly consolidated company - Vestock Industries. After liquidating around twenty of his other businesses his focus would now be on producing the largest flow of oil Russia had ever seen. And all completed under a legitimate return to his own name. No one was interested in his unpatriotic past any more.

'Do you want me to come with you?' Natalia asked, already knowing the answer and for which she had spent the morning preparing.

'Of course, lyabov moya. We built this business together and I want you there to share in the rewards. When the drills start up this morning the whole of the Soviet Union will know your real name and my investors would all rather talk to you than to me. The Wall Street journal has sent a journalist to cover the story. Let's show the Yanks that there are some Russians who can beat them at their own game.'

He held open the arms of her mink coat and eased it over her shoulders before she could refuse. When the heads in the hotel lobby turned as they walked through to their waiting car Boris knew they were not looking at him.

As they drove past the Bolshoi Theatre he allowed his thoughts to drift for a second to the other development that he hoped would materialise today. He'd tried hard to focus on his business deal over the last three days, but a phone call from Vasily, who was currently working in Paris, was distracting him incessantly. Please let this other news be favourable today, he whispered to himself. He needed to unlock this puzzle if his fortunes were to be maintained. For all he had seen over the years, that belief was the most unshakeable.

The inaugural meeting took place at 10.30am in Andrei Kaspov's office in a large glass building just outside the historic city centre. They watched the oil field's ceremonial ground-breaking on CCTV as Boris signed the paperwork formally recognising his latest venture under his newly restored name - a legitimate phoenix sprung from the ashes of some extremely suspicious, but now defunct, enterprises and their fictitious owner. A shift from landowner to oil producer. Alexandre Yeltsof had been a vicious entrepreneur; Boris Rubikov was a globally significant business owner and philanthropist.

Even as the drills bit into the ice and rock Boris was restless. With the paperwork out of the way all he could now think of was the phone call he hoped would come through soon.

'Are you okay, dear?' Natalia asked, sensing his distraction.

'Of course! Why wouldn't I be?'

'I have known you long enough to know that you have something else on your mind. The deal is signed and still you are pacing like an expectant father. I haven't seen you like this since you found that painting again.'

'Some things have a value to me beyond their mere cash worth!' he said smiling. 'Like you!'

The phone on his lawyer's desk rang just after midday.

'It's for you,' said Andrei, recognising the voice of the security chief that terrified him. 'Shall we step outside?

'No, it's okay. Tell him I will call him back from my office in half an hour.'

Thirty minutes later Boris picked up his Milcode-encrypted telephone on a line that he knew was secure. The political climate in Russia might be changing but some of its practices would remain for a very long time. In Moscow, only a fool put his trust in the State telecoms system.

'What did you find out?' he said without any formalities, as his call was answered immediately.

'He died in Paris in 1957.' Vasily reported.

'That is the same year as his second interview with Victor Doiteau. It must have been just before he died.' Boris could feel his heart rate climb a fraction. He would not allow himself such hope just yet. It was too soon to speculate about a dying man's confession. 'Did you find out what happened to his estate?'

'The will was executed by the in-house lawyers of Swiss Re, in Paris in 1957. He was on the board of directors before retiring when it was still The Swiss Reinsurance Company of Zurich. It was difficult after more than 30 years, but I have managed to obtain a copy from their archives.'

'Did you have trouble with their security?'

'Not as much trouble as the night security guard will have when trying to walk in the future.' Vasily knew that this detail would be of no consequence to his employer. A necessary inconvenience of getting what he wanted.

'And is there anything in it?' Boris was becoming impatient.

'It is difficult to say.' Vasily knew Boris wasn't going to be happy with what he'd learned so far. 'An item was left with someone in London, with instructions to be handed to the proper authorities at an appropriate time. I have no idea when that time is or whom it was left with. I think it was intentionally vague. It was almost a footnote in a lengthy document that essentially left everything to charity. If you weren't so convinced about this man's identity I would never have picked up on it. I doubt any other person would give it a second thought.'

'Does it say what the item is?' Boris could hardly contain his excitement at this discovery.

'No, it just says he passed over a letter concerning the disposal of property held in trust for a third party and that no claims may be made against this property by the deceased's estate. Nor does it name the recipient, just that he handed over instructions personally to them when he was in London. It reads as if the sole purpose of its inclusion in his will is to prevent anyone claiming it once it's discovered. He's basically stating that whatever it is, it's not his!'

'When was he in London?' Boris could feel his spirits deflating as his anger rose.

'I don't know.' Vasily only had a small consolation to offer. 'He visited London often when he worked for Swiss Re, several times a year. He could have taken the letter at any time. I have tracked down his secretary and she is still alive. She started working for him when she was 18 years old and gave up her career to be his full-time assistant and carer when he retired. She became the main trustee of his charities and sat on numerous boards in his place, even after he died. She never married and is almost 90 now. Maybe she will be able to help us. She may remember when he went and whom he visited. What do you want me to do next?'

'She worked as his PA and carer for 15 years and gave up her chance to be a mother to look after first him and then his charitable endeavours.' Boris was unable to comprehend such dedication to another person without a return on that investment, but he understood obsession. His had developed over more than forty years as apparently had hers. 'That is not the behaviour of an employee, that is devotion. She was clearly in love with him. Women in love do not destroy their memories. Find out her address. I will fly to Paris tonight.'

Chapter 9

London, Friday October 3rd 2014.

Tia woke early and stared at the white painted ceiling of her tiny bedroom. She'd enjoyed her first two weeks of freedom even though it hadn't been exactly as she'd imagined. A twinge of loneliness jarred her as she started her birthday alone for the first time ever. The feeling dissipated as her phone rang just after 7am and her parents sang 'Happy Birthday', maintaining a 19-year tradition even at a distance. She promised them she would be home at some point in the evening for present giving and felt a bit sad that this was her only alternative to another night in her room on her own.

She walked out of Goodge St tube station just after 8.45am and crossed over Tottenham Court Road, down Torrington Place and turned left into Malet place, waving to the security guard sitting in the cubicle that controlled access to the college. She was one of the only students whose name he knew, at the request of his superior.

Tia was proud of her university's heritage, especially the engineering department, which had developed considerably since the 60s. It had originally been a 9-storey, uninspiring brick block, housing mechanical, chemical and electrical engineers. The securing of a government military contract saw the addition of the naval architects and during the 1980s the growing field of electronics had led to the addition of two extra floors, paid for by major corporations keen to benefit from the world-class research into optical fibre communications.

Central to the development of all the innovations within the last thirty years was the growth of the cutting-edge computer science department. Precision control and mathematical modelling had allowed developments such as the 3D baby scan and the fMRI scanner used in hospitals around the world.

Two weeks into her course and Tia could see why the reputation was justified. Her assumption had been that she would go through a gradual transition process from schoolgirl to undergraduate over the course of the first term. The reality was seven hours of lectures every day except Wednesday, starting with at least two hours of advanced maths every morning at 9am sharp. The equations and concepts covered during those intense sessions were necessary to make sense of the logic and coding covered in the programming courses. Miss the maths and you may as well stay home for the rest of the week. In her first week Tia had already clocked up 15 hours of extra-curricula computer time! - Not surfing the web or chatting on Facebook like so many of her peers, but on a blank white screen typing C++ code directly to the developer program in the same way that Bill Gates had done when he'd written his famous MS-DOS program years before.

So far she'd already taught her computer to play itself at tic-tac-toe; a programming feat that had been a term-long module just 25 years ago and that was now covered in one lesson. She loved her time in the computer labs, working on her programs and investigating the infinite resources available to her online. But lectures proved to be a bit lonely because in this particular year Tia was the only girl in her class of 45 students. Having been to an all-girls grammar school she was not familiar or comfortable with engaging boys in conversation about anything other than endless loops and syntax.

As her Friday morning three-hour maths session finished at midday, Tia headed for the Old Refectory in the middle of the main building. She was lucky! She bought a tuna salad and Glaceau Vitamin Water from the self-serve counters and got the last empty table in the room - Friday was obviously not a day for serious study.

Ashley hadn't slept well for the last week, her mind overwhelmed yet again by her disastrous family. Matt was still too young for her to just wash her hands of their impossible mother, even though on the surface he was functioning better than she was at present. He shouldn't have to cook and clean for an alcoholic parent because she was incapable, and definitely not for whatever waifs and strays she or Connor bought in off the street. Matt had been evasive all week about how things were at home and Ashley was finding it difficult to concentrate on her studies.

Eoin's accusations about money kept repeating over and over in her head. She didn't even know if he'd moved out yet. Maybe she'd been a bit hasty in her threats. If Matt were taken into care she would have to give up her college education and move back home to look after him. She only had this final year to go before she could start earning a proper living and take care of them again. As long as Eoin didn't provide Patricia with alcohol it might not be such a bad arrangement. At least he had a job.

She didn't even look at the contents of the sandwich she selected from the chiller as she scanned the room for an empty seat.

'Mind if I join you?' she asked Tia, spotting her sitting alone nursing three empty chairs.

'No. Was everything okay last week?' Tia was delighted to have some female company at last.

'What do you mean?' Ashley could feel the hackles rising on the back of her neck at the unwelcome concern.

'Well you got a message and rushed off pretty quickly.' Tia flushed with embarrassment at her obvious intrusion. She played with her salad, staring at the plastic bowl. 'You looked a bit upset and I haven't seen you at the gym all week. Henry didn't know where you were so I assumed it must have been important. It's none of my business if you don't want to talk about it.'

Ashley sighed deeply. Her family problems weren't Tia's fault. Friends were rare in her life and whilst this skinny mouse hadn't made it past acquaintance yet, she knew it wasn't fair to vent at a relative stranger.

'Sorry, yeh! Family trouble back home. Just had a to sort a few things out.'

'Is everything okay now?'

'It should be by the weekend' Ashley said unconvincingly. 'You're lucky you've got no brothers and perfect parents who don't cause you grief!'

Tia almost snorted with indignation at the thought of her overprotective father who'd sheltered her from life, being described as perfect. This was followed immediately by a pang of guilt at the expression of disloyalty. She felt her usually undetectable blush rise up her face as she turned to see if Ashley had noticed her reaction. She had!

'So what's up with your parents? Don't give you enough pocket money?' she said unkindly before immediately feeling sorry again. The involuntary burst of sarcasm wasn't deserved. She knew she had to learn to control any public display of self-pity about her family's issues or she'd have all sorts of intrusions into her life and she'd seen enough social workers over the years to know that never ended well. Her mother might not be perfect but she couldn't let Matt be taken into care. If that ever happened Patricia really would have nothing left to live for!

'I'm sorry,' Tia said, sensing the resentment in Ashley's tone. 'I guess I just didn't realise how sheltered I'd been until I got here and spent time surviving on my own. The last week has been harder than I thought it would be. It's pretty lonely. My flatmates don't seem to be in much, and when they are they're usually drunk so I haven't really spoken to many people yet.'

'Well at least your parents give a damn about you. And at least you know who they both are.' Ashley softened her expression and began eating the sandwich, which was the only thing she could afford on her current budget. She understood how Tia was feeling. She hadn't had time for friends when she was growing up and now just accepted her isolation as normal. She knew lots of people, but no one well enough that she would call them on the phone. She hadn't let anyone into her life since coming to university other than Henry, but that was different, that was always club stuff. 'So what did you think of the MMA club?' she continued, trying to lighten the mood.

'It was great. Henry really put me through my paces and he's found me a training partner who is very good! I guess I'd got a bit used to my normal sparring partners.'

'Oh he just like showing off in front of new members! He's a bit weird to be honest.'

'In what way?' Tia couldn't suppress her interest.

'Well - I've known him for almost two years and I don't think I've ever seen him talk to anyone else outside the club or his department. He lives in some fancy City apartment and must socialise with people outside the Uni because he never comes to any events. Not even to the Student Union! I know this first hand! I've asked him out hundreds of times and he's always said no!' She laughed out loud and the tension in the air dissolved instantly.

'Yes he is a bit hot!' Tia added smiling shyly 'Even I can tell that and I know nothing about men, except where to kick them so they don't get up again!'

Tia's expression softened and her eyes dipped slightly to the right as if hiding a forbidden secret she didn't know she had.

'Oh my god! Have you got a crush on him already?' Ashley was laughing out loud again.

'No way! I'm just saying he is very good looking!'

'Who's very good looking?' Henry had walked in unseen and was standing behind Tia's shoulder. She turned with a start and felt her cheeks return to their increasingly familiar warmth. He wore immaculate Armani Jeans and a Ralph Lauren jumper over the top of a blue Oxford shirt. He smiled and sat at the table without waiting for an invite.

'My maths lecturer!' Tia stumbled, regretting the words as they came out.

'Now I know you're lying!' Henry laughed, opening his bottled water and taking a pill box from his bag. 'There is no such thing as a good looking maths lecturer at this university.' He emptied today's contents from the seven-day dispenser onto the table and swallowed the multi-coloured tablets one by one. 'Vitamins!' he added, as if they needed explaining.

Tia looked at the pile of pills. She'd seen lots of photographic evidence from her father's various drugs arrests in the past. He'd often discussed cases with her in the belief that if she saw the worst of human nature and could recognise the different prescription drugs and illegal narcotics she would know how best to steer clear of problems. She could tell the difference between ecstasy, speed and Coproxamol. They're not all vitamins, she thought to herself.

'I didn't think you knew where this place was.' Ashley teased, punching him playfully on the arm. 'You've never ventured further than the gym or your stinky lab. Or is it just because they don't serve foie gras and venison here? I don't even know how you get in and out of your building, I've never seen you walk anywhere.'

'That's because I'm magic.' he replied avoiding any elaboration. 'I came to find Tia.' He turned and looked her directly in the eyes and his smile returned. Tia's gaze dropped to the floor and Ashley tried to stifle a smirk. Henry wouldn't have expected that! The redhead didn't know much about his background but she knew he was extremely rich, as did most of the women in the college. It wasn't unusual for girls to sign up for combat classes they had no desire or ability to attend in the hope of meeting him. Unfortunately for them he had no interest in beginners unless their intention was complete dedication to fighting. Tia's shyness and total oblivion as to his status were obviously new to him and her love of her sport was as strong as his.

'I just wanted to let you know I've found someone else who can help us with your coaching,' he continued, undeterred by her avoidance of eye contact. 'He's studying medicine and was on the national squad back in China with a pretty good reputation. I think you've got the potential to represent the college in female tournaments so he'll be able to help get you ready. We've never had a girl good enough to compete so I want to put a proper program together - diet, cardio and technique. I might even learn a bit of Wing Chun myself.' His enthusiasm was complete.

'I don't do competitions,' Tia said urgently. She didn't want that humiliation ever again in her life. Henry reached over and took her hand, holding it gently.

'Tia, by the time I'm done with you, you'll be showing your skills off to whoever will watch!'

She felt his fingers brush along the back of her hand. He spoke with such confidence that for a second she almost believed him. Something had just popped inside her stomach - a feeling she had never experienced and couldn't explain.

'Come over to the club tonight and we'll get started. Unless you have plans with the hot maths lecturer?' he laughed.

'I can't tonight. It's my birthday and I promised my parents I'd come home for the weekend.'

'Your birthday? Well that's much more important. Go home tomorrow!' Henry insisted. 'Come down to the club tonight and I'll take you both out for a celebratory dinner after. I've got a class at 6pm but I'll book a table for 8.30.' He stood up without letting go of her hand and Tia flushed again, but before she could turn down his invitation out of sheer embarrassment, his phone rang.

'What?' he said, answering it curtly. 'Okay I'll be there in about an hour!' He put the phone in his pocket and shrugged. 'Women! See you tonight?' he exclaimed, smiled again and left the girls at the table. Tia felt disoriented.

'Hang on.' Ashley laughed. 'Let me just wipe that drool off your chin for you, shall I?'

'Oh my god was it that obvious?' Tia's face was on fire - surely this time it must be visible! 'I'm such an idiot!'

'Only if he were privy to the previous conversation, which he wasn't! And I can't believe he's invited us to dinner after refusing all my previous requests to come out! You must be *really* good at Wing Chun to have impressed him that much!' Ashley put her hand on top of Tia's wrist and her smile faded for a second. 'But I do have to warn you, I've only ever seen him with one woman and she looks like a supermodel.'

'Is she his girlfriend?' Tia asked, desperately trying not to sound too interested.

'I dunno, I assumed so.' Ashley thought back to the only time she had seen Henry outside of the college. 'I met him by chance in a bar in Covent Garden last term. I'd done some security work for the owner and had been to pick up my money. They were there having dinner and he introduced her as Jennifer. I always thought he was gay because he never noticed women but he said she was the guiding light in his life! To be honest, she was that beautiful it made sense why he doesn't look at anyone else. He didn't say she was his girlfriend but she never took her eyes off him - even when he went to the toilet! She was wearing a rock on her left hand so I assumed they must be engaged. I don't think she has anything to do with Henry's college life, though, because she hadn't met anyone from his course or the club and kept asking me all sorts of questions about how I knew him and who his friends were. She seemed a bit disappointed when I said I didn't think he had many, or even any, and that we were friends because I didn't give him a choice in the matter. She didn't laugh at my joke and I thought she was a bit stuck up. I doubt he has much fun with her and he clearly doesn't tell her anything about his college life! When he came back from the bathroom he paid the bill and they left. I think he was embarrassed.'

Tia had regained her composure and made light of the situation.

'Maybe he just didn't want to talk to you?' she smiled. 'What do his parent do?'

'I've got no idea, he never talks about them.' Ashley hadn't thought it was unusual before because she never spoke about her mum either, but she doubted Henry had similar reasons to be embarrassed by his family. 'They must be really loaded though, cos he lives in the Barbican where it's like £1000 a week rent.' She had no idea how far off the mark she was.

Tia shook her head and frowned.

'My dad would lock me up if I came home with a 26-year-old American man.' she said, trying to play down her interest. 'And I dread to think what he'd do to Henry!'

'Why is your dad so strict?' Ashley felt a twinge of jealousy - what must it be like to have someone always looking out for you rather than having to look after everyone around you yourself?

'He's a policeman! He grew up in Brixton during the 70s and 80s and saw the worst of people, he says. Violence caused major conflict in his family and he's dealt with some of the toughest criminals in England since he started his career. Most parents fill their children's heads with stories of princesses and fairies. Instead he fills my mind with graphic tales of what I should avoid! It's a wonder I'm not scarred for life!' she grinned.

'So are you going to blow your parents off this evening and come out with us? I feel like I have a duty to help celebrate your birthday and chaperone you from the delicious yank at the same time. Plus I could do with a decent meal' she added, looking forlornly at the curling sandwich.

'I'm not sure my dad would sanction you as a chaperone,' Tia laughed out loud for the first time in a very long time and could feel the excitement already - her first proper social event - there was no way she was going to miss this. 'But I guess I could go home in the morning.' Her parents would understand - if she actually told them.

Tia found it difficult to concentrate in the gym that evening and her new training partner was landing blows she would normally contain with ease. The end of the session couldn't come soon enough, and when it did Tia ran for the showers.

Henry was ready and waiting for the girls as they came out of the changing rooms. Ashley was in her usual explosion of mismatched colours, teaming purple leggings with a hand-knitted jumper made from odd balls of wool. Henry raised his eyebrows and wondered what The Ivy would make of her. As he considered changing his booking to a less formal restaurant Tia came out behind her and he forgot all about Ashley's clothes. She was in a short pale-pink shift dress - the first time he'd seen her in anything other than jeans or her uniform - and wearing just a touch of make-up. She looked stunning in her simplicity and he knew she would fit right in at any top restaurant. No one would even notice what Ashley was wearing. Ashley smirked at him staring at Tia and he looked away.

'It's a 10 minute walk to the restaurant.' he said feeling a little flustered but recovering instantly. 'Is that okay? A cab will take forever on a Friday night in the West End.'

'Fine,' both girls replied eagerly.

The evening was one of the best Tia could remember, not that her frame of reference was extensive - or even existed. She and Ashley got on so well she felt as though they had been friends for years and Henry was obviously at ease eating in expensive restaurants. He handled the waiters with expert flair and they clearly all knew him well. The maître d' even came over and asked him how his parents were.

He made sure the girls were given guest menus without the pricing. He didn't want them to feel awkward this evening. He ordered their food and selected a bottle of champagne that cost more than Tia's months rent - not that they would know.

'I don't drink,' Tia said, putting her hand over the top of her glass as the sommelier tipped the bottle.

'Just try one glass,' Henry encouraged. 'Just so we can raise a toast to your birthday.'

'Okay just one - then can I get a bottle of Perrier and some lime?' she asked, feeling like a child again.

'So, 19 today?' Henry said, sipping the champagne. 'I wish I was 19 again. Oh to do things differently! I wouldn't let my parents tell me what to wear this time, that's for sure.' He laughed and looked down at his immaculate designer clothes that screamed expensive from every stitch but that would have better suited a middle-aged businessman than a twenty-something student.

Tia suspected he wasn't entirely joking as a tiny crack in his impenetrable exterior started to form. For the first time she noticed the sadness flickering in his eyes – an emotion he usually kept very well disguised if it were genuine.

'I'd kill myself if I had to go back to being 19 again!' Ashley joined in, laughing at a prospect she found in no way funny. 'Unless I could chose a different family who didn't cost me a fortune and try to ruin my life every minute of the day.'

'I think they teach parents how to annoy their kids at some secret class,' Henry added, pouring another drink for Ashley. 'Are your parents okay?' he asked Tia.

She thought for a moment. Tia knew her parents were overprotective and that it was annoying, but she'd always assumed that the situation was unique because of her dad's job. Maybe the three of them weren't so different after all.

'My mum is fine but my dad can be a bit scary at times. But I wouldn't change them I guess. At least I have a bit of freedom now.' She looked up just as Henry's eyes turned downwards to the floor and again, for a moment, they seemed filled with sadness. She said nothing.

The evening flew past - much too quickly for Tia, who was just starting to relax. Ashley was clearly used to alcohol, even if her entire consumption in her life to date cost less than her 4 glasses of Bollinger. Tia noticed that Henry barely touched his glass, allowing Ashley to drink the majority. He ordered two brandies and a cappuccino for Tia. Ashley didn't notice when Henry switched her empty brandy glass with his. They sang as the waiters bought out an exquisite hand-crafted chocolate cupcake with a candle. As the other guests turned to see whom the celebration was for Tia was sure she noticed a few diners staring at Henry and whispering to their companions.

Tia felt happy with her tiny fledgling social circle. Her two new friends obviously came from worlds that were poles apart and yet seemed completely at ease in each other's company. She sat not quite in the middle of their circumstances, but not really understanding the problems that either existence brought with it. All she could tell was that both of them were as lonely as she was - for very different reasons. Just maybe they could be there for each other.

She allowed her mind to drift to future social possibilities as they made their way out of the Ivy just after 11pm. A taxi was already waiting for them and she felt a surge of disappointment.

'I've paid him to take both of you home.' Henry said. 'I've had a great night. Sometimes I forget what it's like to really laugh out loud. Biochemistry is not known for its comedic value.'

'Are you not coming with us?' Ashley asked.

'My lift is here,' he replied nodding towards a bright red Porsche parked on the opposite side of West St. As Tia turned towards the car, the driver door opened and the tallest, blondest model figure she'd ever seen stepped into the road.

'Are you ready, Henry?' she called across the street in a distinctive Washington accent.

'Meet my guardian angel,' Henry said through a softly forming smile. He kissed them both on the cheeks and crossed the road.

'Is that her?' Tia asked when he'd gone and they were safely in the cab

'That's the one!' Ashley said. 'Told you she was a model!'

Chapter 10

Temple Bar, London, 27th May 2014.

Torrential rain pounded the surface of the River Thames as art dealer Philip Charlesworth and his secretary Serena Holdsworth stepped out of Temple Station onto the Embankment. It had been the wettest May bank holiday in years and was showing no signs of getting better any time soon. He was not dressed for the rain or the Underground. The train had been busy, forcing him to stand for the short journey from Victoria, and at 5'3" tall this had required an uncomfortable stretch to reach the overhead handle. The combination of body heat and rain-soaked umbrellas had raised the humidity to uncomfortable levels; perspiration marks were starting to appear on his purple Anthony Sinclair shirt and his handmade brown suede shoes were soaked through to his socks. His overgrown blonde hair was starting to look greasy as sweat beaded across his hairline. Serena's skirt was too short and her silk stockings were dappled with rain spots and mud. She'd been complaining about her 4-inch heels crippling her feet since they walked out of the Mayfair Gallery and her hangover from a night out with friends was not helping. Serena was almost 6ft tall and in her heels she towered over Philip. As they'd hurried through Berkeley Square she'd made him feel ridiculous. It was her fault they couldn't get a taxi. She'd forgotten to book one and then it had started to rain so he'd made her totter at high speed down to Green Park station. Her bad habits were the reason they were late for one of the most important meetings of his life and he was silently making her pay. He'd have gotten rid of her ages ago if her father wasn't such a valuable customer.

'I can't believe we have this awful weather today of all days!' he said in his distinctive plummy voice, which he had learned to exaggerate over the years. Most of his clients were foreign, predominantly American, Chinese and Russian. They took his accent as a sign of breeding and heritage, which in many respects it was - but this wasn't necessarily good.

'How common to turn up for the reading of my father's will using public transport!' he commented without looking at Serena. His father, Cecil, had passed away two months ago and finally the gallery that had been in his family for three generations would be his to control. He was tired of carrying out his father's old-fashioned instructions. The man had no vision and had refused to retire. Cecil Charlesworth cared for the art first and the deal second. Philip would change that. His new generation of clients would see him as their investment broker, not just an art critic. Around the globe, individuals were amassing wealth way beyond the budgets of museums and galleries and each of them felt they had a right to adorn their personal houses with the greatest works of art ever created. And who was he to deny them this pleasure? The occasional loan of a major work to a national gallery for a limited-time tour just boosted ticket sales for the gallery so really everyone was a winner - except maybe the ordinary art lover who couldn't afford to travel the world for the occasional glimpse of a favourite work. There were other beautiful things in life to look at, Philip thought. Like trees and flowers!

'That was awful!' said Serena, the 27-year-old debutante who had just experienced her first journey on the London Underground, despite growing up in Eaton Square in Chelsea. 'I can't wait for summer. How do people do this on a regular basis? The Mayor clearly needs to issue more licenses for taxis.' She removed a small bottle of hand sanitizer from her Mulberry handbag and rubbed a blob of gel into her palms. Thank god she had tied her long brunette hair into a ponytail today.

'Rain just turns black taxis into gold dust and gridlocks the streets!'

Philip raged, putting up his rarely used umbrella as they walked through the gardens towards the Inns of Court. 'How is one supposed to go about their normal business in the rain? I can't believe you forgot to book a proper car in advance!'

'Your father refused to use private hire companies, and most of the local ones have blacklisted us anyway. He was rude to all of them about how much they charged to go a couple of miles.' Serena recalled how Cecil had insisted on walking everywhere and was grateful she had rarely been required to go with him.

It didn't surprise Philip that ultimately his miserly father had been the cause of his lateness and therefore his bad mood. He deserved every penny that was coming to him after putting up with the old fool for so long.

The solicitors of Young, Jacobs and Harding had held offices in the Inner Temple for over 150 years. Now only the senior partners and their personal staff worked from here. The bulk of their business was done in a bespoke new office just behind the recently opened Shard building at London Bridge on the 'other' side of the river. Their client list was impressive and the waiting list was extensive. They dealt with some of the largest settlements deaths, births and divorce had to offer.

Philip and Serena arrived just after 2pm at the Regency buildings, a stone's throw from the Supreme High Court itself. An efficient-looking, middle-aged PA showed them into a book-lined office that smelled of musty paper and leather polish. The chairs were antique but very well cared for, although designed to discourage sitting for too long - time is money, as they say. Another, younger but equally austere-looking woman appeared immediately with Earl Grey tea in a bone china teapot and matching service. A strainer rested in its own receptacle next to a saucer of sliced lemons and tongs sat alongside the sugar bowl. Serena had spent her last two years of compulsory education in a Swiss finishing school and knew exactly how to deal with the tray placed before her.

William Harding, 65 and the youngest of the senior partners, came in as soon as they were settled and got straight to business.

'Your father was a dear friend, as well as a valued client,' he began, looking with disappointment at Philip. He's a shadow of the man his father had been, he thought to himself. Before Cecil's death he hadn't seen the boy since his mother's funeral and he couldn't suppress the belief that Philip would probably destroy in 5 years what it had taken his forefathers 75 years to build up. He had no time for this longhaired self-centred philistine and had much more deserving benefactors to attend to. He would get through this formality quickly and politely.

'As you know, his will was lodged with us some years ago. The terms are fairly straightforward, as you, Phillip, are the only direct heir. He has made a few minor bequeaths to members of his staff and a few charities but the business and the flat in Hans Crescent are both left to you.'

William Harding pulled out a second envelope and a small package from the pile of documents in front of him. He adjusted his glasses and thought about how to begin.

'We do have another matter to cover which is rather unusual. It concerns elements carried over from your grandfather's instructions following his death in 1974. In addition to the items owned by Cecil Charlesworth himself, there is also a letter and a package, which were left with us under the terms of Andrew Charlesworth's will. Since your grandfather's death, using funds from a significant deposit made to us by him, we have been paying the annual rental on a safe deposit box at the Zurcher Kantonalbank in Zurich. Financial provision was made to cover this cost for a minimum of 60 years up to 75 years. The letter was not to be opened until the minimum time was up. I believe your grandfather's intent was for your father to deal with this matter following his retirement but he never actually gave up work and so his death means the unopened instructions now fall to yourself. Funds exist to maintain this arrangement for at least another 10 years as per your grandfather's original instruction but that decision is ultimately now yours as the minimum term is up. I have no idea what is actually in the box and you would need to make arrangements to investigate that for yourself, or we can continue to fund the rental as requested until you are ready to follow this up. Now your father has passed away the decision to continue to act on these instructions falls to you, Philip.'

'Open it.' Philip said curtly.

The old solicitor opened the sealed envelope, yellow with age, and removed its contents. Inside was a letter, which he read aloud.

'Andrew.

It has been my pleasure to work with you for a number of years and have come to regard you not just as a businessman of integrity and honour but above all, a friend. I write this in the hope that you will do what you feel is right, not for yourself or for me, as I will be long gone, but for the good of the art world we both love so much. The funds I sent you should be sufficient to maintain the safe deposit box for at least 75 years allowing for steady inflation and interest rates. After that time, please arrange for the retrieval of the contents of the box from the Zurcher Kantonalbank and for them to be taken directly to the appropriate authority. I believe they will then know what to do. I am not proud of my actions in this matter, but they were done with the best of intentions and under direct instructions from the person affected the most.

R'

Harding looked mystified by the cryptic and unbelievably short instruction. It said nothing more than he already knew from the Andrew Charlesworth's original will. He was used to dealing with legal documents that spread over dozens of pages spelling out precise orders and preventing unwanted misinterpretations. He opened the enclosed package, which contained an elaborately tooled key and an 8-digit account code as expected.

'That's it. I'm afraid I can offer you no further insight into what this means. You will need to follow up on this bequest at your own convenience. Our instruction was merely that this document be passed down unopened through the family line until the funds were exhausted or the matter was dealt with.' Harding showed no sign of disappointment at not finally uncovering what the 65-year-old document referred to. He was already thinking about the trust fund he was drafting for the new-born son of the Duke of Naples.

'Who wrote it?' Philip asked. 'Who is R?'

'I don't know I'm afraid' replied Harding. 'It was left as part of your grandfather's estate and that is the only reason it now resides with us. I have no idea what the box contains. There may well be nothing in it.'

Philip thanked the lawyer for his time and took the letter and key as they were shown out of the library. He studied both items carefully as they walked along the oak-panelled corridor and out into Temple Square.

'What do you think is in there?' Serena asked, unable to contain her curiosity and excitement at having been present during the unveiling of something so mysterious. '65 years! Maybe its some treasure looted by the Nazi's?'

'I have no idea.' Philip glared, glad to be leaving such an old-fashioned, lifeless building and praying she was wrong. If it was, its provenance would be instantly restored and the item returned to its rightful owner – at his expense. 'We need to get back to work, but I want to get on the first plane to Zurich in the morning. First class of course, now I determine the travel policy!'

The rain had stopped when they emerged back onto Embankment, and they both instinctively looked up and down the rows of traffic for an empty black taxi.

'Serena?' a voice called from the other side on the road.

Serena turned to see a tall, stunningly beautiful blonde crossing towards her.

'It's Jennifer,' the woman said as she caught up with them.

90

'Jennifer Hawley. We were at Roedean together for a year while my father was working at the embassy in London. Do you remember me?'

'Yes!' Serena replied frantically scouring her memory cells, which weren't currently in the best of shape. It had been another heavy night last night, which was one of the reasons she'd forgotten to book a taxi. 'What on earth are you doing here?' She let out a high-pitched squeal of delight, hoping enthusiasm would suffice in place of actual recall.

'I'm living in London again at the moment, in the Barbican. Do you work here?' Jennifer turned towards the buildings of the inner temple.

'I've just been to the reading of my boss's father's will. Goodness I'm so sorry, Philip, this is my friend Jennifer Hawley. We were at Roedean together whilst Jennifer's father was working in England. She's American.' Serena had spent years perfecting the art of using the smallest fragments of information about social contacts to suggest ties that were often as flimsy as cobwebs.

'Yes I gathered that from the accent,' Philip said and held out his hand, utterly besotted, and handed her his card. This woman would look much better behind his reception desk than the airhead standing opposite her.

'I'm sorry to hear about your father, Mr Charlesworth. I hope the reading wasn't too traumatic.'

'We've got a mystery to solve in Zurich,' Serena blustered, unable to contain her excitement. Philip cast her a glare that killed any chance of elaboration instantly.

'It was bearable Miss Hawley, thank you. I see it as my duty to carry out his final wishes, whatever they may be.'

Jennifer recognised the sign of a topic terminated and changed the conversation.

'Is your family still in Eaton Square?' she asked turning back to Serena.

'Yes. Daddy has retired now so the parents are usually off on the boat somewhere but the rest of us still have to earn a living.'

Jennifer looked at the Versace coat and Manolo Blahnik shoes and guessed that Serena's salary wouldn't even cover her dry cleaning bill. The tell-tale redness around her nose suggested an expensive cocaine habit had also developed over the years. She clearly had no concept of what earning a living actually entailed.

Serena had already given up trying to remember her school friend - satisfied that this beautiful woman who lived in the Barbican and wore Chanel suits was impressive enough to join her circle.

'Do you have time for a coffee?' Jennifer asked.

Serena looked dolefully at her boss. He was too engrossed in his thoughts about the mysterious box and key to worry about his useless PA. In fact he could do without her wittering for the next few hours.

'Yes that's fine!' he muttered. 'Just get back in time to book my flights.'

The girls walked up to the Strand and headed for the Savoy.

'So how have you been?' Jennifer asked as they settled into the elegant lounge sofas and sipped at their black coffees.

'Not bad.' Serena replied. 'Daddy threatened to cut me off after art school if I didn't get a job or find a husband to keep me - so here I am. Answering two phone calls a day for an idiot who knows nothing about art!'

'He must know something, surely!' Jennifer said incredulously.

'Well yes, he can tell the difference between a Monet and Vermeer, but most of the business has traditionally focused on finding and developing new artists. His father was responsible for launching the careers of some of the best modern artists of his day, but Philip hasn't got a clue about potential. All he's interested in is what will make him money. I could bring him in so much business but he wont let me near the clients, even though I'm the one with the fine art degree. Anyway, enough about my boring boss - what are you up to? ' Serena hoped that something Jennifer revealed might prompt a memory - memory loss was becoming far too common an occurrence for her liking.

'Well I came back here two years ago after an accident at work meant I had to give up my dream job. I live with Henry Whittaker.'

92

Jennifer placed her hand casually on the table, flashing the diamond that had unlocked so many doors in her life.

'Shut up!' Serena gasped. 'Blue Cross Henry Whittaker whose scrummy dad is the senator of New York?'

'That's him. He's doing a PhD in Biochemistry at UCL and I came along for the ride.'

'Oh my god! That must be fabulous!' Serena looked in awe at the woman who would now be her new best friend. Oh the shopping expeditions they would have, especially as she appeared to have little else to do while her boyfriend studied atoms.

'So what is this secret mystery you mentioned?' Jennifer was intrigued at the snippet of information she'd been given. 'That sounds like fun. Will he let you go with him to investigate?'

'I doubt it. I never get to do any of the good stuff even though I'm the only one who is actually qualified in art!'

'Aren't you booking the flights? Just make sure you book two tickets so he has to take you with him,' Jennifer replied. 'Where is the gallery? Maybe I could find something for our apartment? Henry would love that.'

Serena knew she would burst with pride if she managed to bring Whittaker business into the gallery. Philip would have to take her seriously then.

'It's at 50 Mount St in Mayfair, not far from the American embassy. Here's my card. We should have lunch one day when you're free.'

I'd love that.' Jennifer stood up and retrieved her coat. 'But I have to go now I'm afraid. I have to pick Henry up from the university.'

'Good idea! We must get together when I get back from Zurich and I can tell you all about the mystery; assuming its worth telling of course. I'll call you in a few days and we can make plans. Do you have a number?'

'Of course.' Jennifer handed her a plain white card with her name and mobile number printed in gold leaf. As they left the hotel the skies opened once again. 'Lets do cocktails next week!' Jennifer called as she ran towards the red Porsche parked in the side street, leaving Serena to search for a cab.

Chapter 11

London, Wednesday 15th Oct 2014.

Most of Tia's classmates had left the computer labs long ago. She liked working here on a Wednesday afternoon because it was quiet. For those who played team sports, Wednesday afternoon meant competitions against other universities, either home or away, but even a home match was twenty miles outside London at the university sports grounds in Shenfield so the college emptied early.

It was nearly two weeks since her birthday and whilst Tia had seen Ashley almost every day since, Henry had been elusive, confining himself to his office at the gym whenever she was there. Her training was going okay, but she couldn't help feeling that something had bothered him that evening. His mood had changed so quickly once his girlfriend turned up and he hadn't even introduced her. Maybe she'd been jealous at not being invited. Tia tried to put him out of her mind, but it was difficult knowing she had to see him three times a week for the rest of the year. She hadn't planned for her first crush to happen so quickly and it had caught her unprepared to deal with the fact that he was clearly not available.

At present, however, she was struggling with the code she was writing to control the programs of a washing machine and it demanded her attention. It was the type of code that most people didn't even realise existed - buried inside the microprocessor that controlled the settings on most household appliances. Once written and in production the code was effectively hard wired and couldn't be changed so there was no room for error.

Something was wrong with the timing of the spin cycle. The computer-based simulator on which she was working would not stop after the correct number of rotations and appeared to be stuck in an endless loop from which clothes may never be recovered. It was her own fault. The brief had been to write a simple program to rotate in only one direction and Tia had tried to make the simulated drum reverse intermittently, like the machine her parents had at home. It had taken four hours to iron out the bugs but she would never let the problem beat her.

She looked at the clock on the wall of the lab. Almost 9pm. She'd been in the building for over 12 hours, stopping only for a very quick lunch! Ashley had asked her to come to training but her assignment had to be in by the end of the week and she couldn't miss her first important deadline. She pressed send and officially submitted her first project as an undergraduate. She felt proud and tired and in need of food.

She put on her coat and checked her valuables following the routine her dad had insisted on setting: keys in her inside coat pocket; phone (in a separate pocket); money - in two places! One small note in the most accessible place that could be handed over quickly if necessary and the rest in a pocket sewn into the base of her bag by her mother; cards in the main inside pocket with all pins committed to memory. Ashley had asked her why she bothered with the concealed pocket, and she'd explained the statistics that most bag thieves, especially males, took out the money and credit cards and threw the bag away within minutes of stealing it so they couldn't be caught with the evidence. Chances were good that you would get your bag back - plus whatever they failed to discover in the hard base. But her father's instructions had been clear - if she was mugged her priority was to try to keep some concealed cash and her keys so she could get home - everything else was replaceable and should be handed over! Failing that she just had to walk into any police station - the ride home would be quicker than a taxi - but the ensuing confinement to her room for her own safety would last longer than the expiry date on any of her cards.

Tia walked out of the college into Malet Place past the empty security hut. The guard had gone home and the night patrol was off on their rounds. She was still following her father's obsessive rituals when it happened.

No one was around, as she turned right in front of the engineering building onto Torrington Place. It was quiet now that the shops were closed and the daytime throng of students were long gone. The street was deserted.

Her fighter's intuition suddenly sensed the subtle change in air pressure and flow that were caused by the close proximity of another person. She felt a hand on her left shoulder.

The stale breath on her neck informed her that her attacker was immediately behind her, using his body to shield his actions from possible passers by and oncoming cars. Her heartbeat accelerated. She'd never walked home alone this late before. After the gym, she usually walked to the station with Ashley and the road from Camden to her halls was always busy. In her four weeks of freedom she'd never yet felt any fear on the streets but her instincts started pulsing manically.

The stoned, drunken youth hadn't expected any resistance when he'd assessed his target – young, dark female, alone in the dark side street, hand not on top of the strap of the bag over her right shoulder. But from his vantage point he couldn't see that she was holding her the strap of her bag with her left hand, which was stretched in front of her body under her jacket.

The strap slid off her shoulder as he pushed her violently with his left hand as he made a grab for it with his right. Her grip instantly tightened and the main section of the bag stayed pressed against her side, causing the guy to rock forwards. Tia switched hands as he pulled harder and she twisted to the right on the ball of her back foot, pulling him towards her and trapping his hand in the twisted strap, like a handcuff. In an instant she brought the heel of her left palm up sharply over her right shoulder, crushing his jaw upwards. A thin line of blood ran from between his lips and she assumed he had bitten his own tongue. She stared into his eyes, which were glazed and unfocused and he didn't seem to have registered the pain. Her fear was replaced by an instinct for self-preservation that she'd trained for years to develop. Adrenaline surged to every muscle in her body and primed them to react again.

Gary Duggan was a street kid, used to fighting his way out of scuffles if necessary - instinct of a different kind took over and he no longer saw a young meek female - just an adversary who needed to be put down. Gary had no discipline, no control just blind fury at having been taken by surprise and injured by a girl. He tasted the blood as it filled his mouth before spitting it onto the floor as he momentarily refocused.

He pulled harder on the strap, trying to free his right hand and swung wildly with his left fist, aiming for her face. The force of his tug pulled her further round until she face to face with him. Tia's reactions were trained to be quicker! She raised her right forearm and blocked his punch before continuing her direction of travel fluidly to force his arm backwards and into his own body. As he struggled to maintain his balance by pulling harder on her bag, Tia raised her left leg and connected her flexed knee with his groin before stamping down on his trainer-covered foot. Tia felt tiny bones give way underneath her boot as she heard a yell from behind her.

'Oi!' cried a female voice not more than 10 yards away. 'What do you think you're doing?'

Ashley appeared on the right hand side of the guy and her kick onto the cap of his knee was stomach churning as more bone ground down on top of bone. He instinctively released his grip of the strap, freeing his hand and allowing Tia to move backwards - but she didn't. Instead a short punch to the nose dislocated the cartilage and blood covered Ashley's jeans.

'Oh for god's sake!' she moaned as Duggan hit the floor and

covered his head defensively. 'These were new!'

Gary crawled to the side of the pavement and pulled himself to his feet, limping rapidly towards the side turning. A sole passer-by crossed the road to avoid involvement and his sudden presence shocked Tia to a halt.

'You okay?' Ashley asked noticing how badly Tia was trembling, despite having inflicted some serious wounds on her attacker.

'Yeh - just a bit shaken!' Tia was struggling to catch her breath. What had she been thinking! How was she going to explain this?

'Have you never hit anybody for real before?' Ashley put her hand on Tia's shoulder to calm her down.

'No. My only fights have been sparring matches and grade exams, but my dad won't let my trainers go easy on me. I guess I've just developed an instinct. I never really thought about the damage I could do for real.'

'Well at least he hasn't got far to crawl till he gets to the hospital! I doubt he'll be admitting to the doctors that he just got his arse kicked by a teenage girl!' They both laughed nervously as they watched him slide round the corner into Chenies Mews and out of sight. Tia felt the adrenaline reduce slightly in her veins. Then reality hit.

'Oh my god - if my dad finds out I've been fighting in the street I'll be back in Orpington before that guy makes it to UCH.'

'Don't worry about it.' Ashley linked her arm through Tia's to steady her. 'Lets go get a drink to calm you down and we can work out how to wipe the footage from all the CCTV cameras' She smiled as she pointed to the two visible cameras pointing straight at them from different directions.

Tia felt faint and her knees sank slightly.

'Don't worry.' Ashley laughed. ' I'm joking! No one looks at the film in those things unless asked and I don't see anyone round here being nosey so unless you're planning on telling him yourself he'll never know!'

They crossed Tottenham Court Road and turned right into Goodge

Street heading straight to the Draft House pub. They were far enough away from the scene of the drama not to be found if the guy did indeed tell the doctors or the police of his assailant.

Ashley went to the bar and bought two Kopparberg Pear ciders and two tequila chasers.

Tia sipped at the cider but left the shot in front of her as if it were poison.

'Come on, drink it,' Ashley urged. 'It'll make you feel better.'

'No, I don't like the smell of tequila. And I've never drunk it before.'

Ashley just couldn't understand how this beautiful girl could possess such different personas. She had just witnessed that Tia was physically strong enough to inflict injuries even to a young man yet she was terrified of upsetting anyone or letting herself be truly free to make mistakes.

'Look - you're worrying about your dad making you go back to suburban safety, but if you're not prepared to give things a go then you might as well be in your fluffy pink bedroom letting life pass you by. I don't really like alcohol but you've just kicked the arse of a small time mugger and this will calm your nerves. I don't think he'll pick on women quite so readily in the future so you've probably just saved a few people from a horrible experience.'

'Do you think so?' Tia knew she was right, the only thing that really stood between her fears and her much longed for freedom was herself.

'Of course - I bet he thought you'd be a cakewalk! Now he's getting crutches!'

'Well technically you did that to him!' Tia laughed nervously.

' I meant so he could walk back to look for his balls - god knows where they ended up after you kneed him.' Ashley picked up the two shot glasses and handed one to Tia.

Recalling the ferociousness of her reaction to her assault, Tia closed her eyes and swallowed the tequila in one go.

'And my bedroom is not fluffy or pink!' she retorted as she flinched at the sour taste. She quickly took a long draught from the bottle of cider and let the fear of what she'd just done to another person slowly subside. She'd had no real idea that she was trained to inflict that type of injury on someone in a real fight and instinct had got the better of her. As she considered the scale of damage it was possible for her to exact, without ever realising she was capable, her fear and insecurity started to rise again.

30 minutes and 4 shots later Tia was unable to stand up.

'Come on babe - we need to get you home,' Ashley coaxed, but Tia slid down the chair onto the floor under the table and passed out.

'You need to get her out of here,' the barmaid shouted across the tiny room.

'Okay I'm trying!' Ashley shouted back at her, realising she'd made a serious error of judgement. Even if she could get her into the street, there was no way Ashley could drag her all the way to Camden, and no taxi was going to stop to pick up an unconscious, drunken teenager likely to vomit at any moment. She pulled her phone from her pocket and made a call to the only person she knew who owned a car.

'Henry? I need your help!'

Henry arrived 20 minutes later in the same red Porsche Jennifer had used to collect him from the Ivy.

'What did you do to her?' he asked Ashley disapprovingly as he moved the table and lifted Tia into his arms. 'You know she doesn't drink.'

'I thought it would do her good. She was just attacked by some druggie and I think the severity of the beating she gave him frightened her more than the thought of any danger to herself.'

Henry's motivations were torn for a second between wanting to get Tia home and wanting to go and look for her attacker. He knew that was pointless as he carried her out of the pub.

'Open the passenger door. Here's £20 - you'll have to grab a taxi and meet me at her halls. You won't fit in the back and I can't put her to bed on my own!'

It was just before midnight when they finally managed to get Tia out of the bathroom, where she'd thrown up twice, and into her bed.

'I'll sleep on her floor tonight,' Ashley said, letting Henry out of the communal corridor. 'I'll call you in the morning.'

As Henry pulled out of the car park his thoughts were consumed by how badly things might have turned out for Tia if she hadn't been able to defend herself. Something about her kept clawing at his subconscious, relentlessly reminding him of her existence every few hours. He thought he'd learned to ignore any feelings of concern for another person. He couldn't protect them. He'd kept everyone at a distance for so long he'd forgotten how it felt to really worry. It was too painful, and his life was too dangerous to bring another person into it that wasn't prepared for the consequences. As he turned left past the entrance security camera he had no idea that he would be back in less than 12 hours.

Chapter 12
Meulan, France – February 1905

Fascination and speculation into the death of Van Gogh had grown over the last fifteen years and in turn so had interest in his work. Gaston Secretan often spoke about the latest painting or drawing that Theo Van Gogh's widow, Jo, had put up for sale. Theo had died just six months after his brother and she had a son to support. Vincent's work was her lifeline and so far she was doing a better job than her husband at promoting her brother-in-law's work. She'd translated all of his letters into English and developed an aura of mystery around Vincent's life, and his sudden death. The intrigue and speculation slowly gained attention from collectors around the world, especially America, and Jo made the most of it. Many of the paintings were of places the Secretan brothers knew well in Auvers. They had worshipped in the church that Vincent painted only a few weeks before he died and had often walked past the buildings and fields he'd immortalized on canvas.

Fifteen years seems like a long time, especially when you are young. Even single summers appear to go on forever when you are happy and carefree. As you get older it feels as if time starts to accelerate. That was certainly the experience of Rene Secretan. His youthful, carefree days had been over for a long time but he was always grateful for the life he'd been able to live. He'd excelled in his sport, representing France in shooting competitions, and at 21, had started a promising career as a banker.

The brothers never discussed the events of that summer - not even with each other. Gaston hadn't asked Rene what Adeline Ravoux had wanted with him when they found her standing outside their house on the night the artist died. Gaston knew if it were important then Rene would tell him. His brother didn't share his sentiment and was thankful not to have to explain a secret he could never disclose while his family were alive. Not now, after so long.

The decision to find Adeline Ravoux had been made quickly once the plan was devised in his head. The idea itself, however, had been the result of years spent looking over his shoulder, waiting for his secret to catch up with him. He very much doubted he would ever find true peace unless he did something to change his circumstances. The letter Adeline had given him had been concealed in his bedroom behind a painting since he arrived back in Paris on that fateful July evening. Rene could speak to no one else about his nightmares. No one else would understand.

He wondered if she would remember him and their agreement to maintain her father's story. Even if she did, would she understand his need to be rid of his fifteen-year burden? More importantly, would she agree? He'd thought about her final words to him every day since he left Auvers in such a hurry. He was 31 now, athletic and successful - a far cry from the awkward and petulant teenager she'd known for only a few weeks. Time had moved on but he had left part of his immortal soul in that provincial town and he needed closure, with or without her. If she wouldn't agree to help him he had other ways of setting things right.

It had taken the detective that Rene hired several weeks to track her down to the cafe that her father now ran in Meulan, just northwest of Paris, less than 20 miles from the Auberge. The Ravoux's found Auvers intolerable after the artist died. The rumours and speculation about the gun, it's whereabouts and security had been too much for Arthur. He was a simple man and didn't like the attention the artist's death conferred on him. The family had moved within six months under a cloud of unspoken accusations.

The journey from Paris was tiresome and draining. Rene was driving his father's new automobile, and despite it being capable of 25mph he had twice found himself stuck behind the more familiar horse-drawn carriages doing less than 5mph. The steering on the Daimler was heavy and took all of Rene's concentration and strength to keep it on the unsurfaced road. His companion was an artist, burdened down with two trunks and a large wrapped package necessary to complete the task Rene had assigned to him. The painter was an old man of few words and was struggling to remember the story they'd agreed to tell her despite going over his lines all morning. His talent was very specific and clearly didn't include acting even though he was a master of deceit.

It was just after 11am when he walked into the small cafe on Rue Bouger where Adeline lived. Rene had often wondered if adulthood had produced the beauty he'd predicted when she was 12. He was not disappointed. She was polishing glasses behind the counter and looked almost exactly like the portrait Van Gogh had painted of her; the one he had seen briefly in the Auberge and hoped she still had if his plan was to succeed.

She clearly didn't recognise him.

'Adeline Ravoux? Do you remember me?' he asked as he stood at the bar in his tailored suit and felt hat. He was a businessman now; a far cry from the leather-clad would-be cowboy that had terrorised the locals in Auvers so many years ago.

'No monsieur I am sorry. Do I know you?' she replied looking at the most respectable man she'd seen at the cafe in a long time. He was clearly a Parisian. As she spoke, however, a Parisian prompted memory flickered like a pilot light. Could it be? His appearance had changed but she recognised that voice. He was less fearful than the last time they'd spoken but still had the underlying arrogance of a man who usually got what he wanted. 'Rene?'

'Indeed, mademoiselle. It has taken me a long time to find you, but

I come seeking your help. Can we speak alone inside your private quarters?'

Adeline looked behind her towards the kitchen area. Her father was away for the day, looking for a new chef in Paris. Her sister Germaine was now working at the hotel opposite and wouldn't be back for hours. The cafe was not officially due to open for another hour but Adeline didn't like being here on her own and always opened early on days like this, hoping someone would come in to keep her company.

'Of course,' she said warily, leading him through the small door behind the bar into a dingy, cramped sitting room. He was the one person she'd hoped never to see again, but curiosity meant she needed to hear what he wanted from her. 'Please take a seat and I will bring some coffee.' She returned to the bar, locked the front door and went to the kitchen to brew some espresso.

Rene was delighted. On the wall above the fireplace hung the two paintings Van Gogh had given to the Ravoux's as a token of his appreciation for their hospitality. The 'Town Hall on the 14th July' was a sad depiction of the Bastille Day celebrations, devoid of people and an echo of the divide the remembrance instilled in rural communities throughout France. The single line of coloured lanterns did not shine as intended and made the building look like an abandoned hotel. The other painting was the focus of his attention. 'The portrait of Adeline Ravoux' was vibrant in its multiple shades of blue punctuated by her blonde hair held back with a ribbon. It had been painted in a few hours as she sat for Van Gogh fifteen years ago. She was facing sideways, but it was clear to see that she looked more like the portrait now, at 27, than she had when she was twelve. His search for Adeline had uncovered that Van Gogh had actually painted two other portraits of her, but this was the original that she had posed for, which he had given to her as a gift.

Adeline returned with the coffee pot and two cups.

'To what do I owe this pleasure, monsieur?' she asked, setting the tray on the small low table in the centre of the room. She felt drab in her work clothes compared to his immaculately put-together attire and it certainly didn't feel like a pleasure.

'I must ask a big favour of you Adeline.' He looked serious and concerned. 'Are you still intent on keeping the artist's secret?'

'Of course, I gave him my word and I have to think of my father. The locals made life very difficult for him after you left Auvers.'

'Then we need to act swiftly. I need you to come with me to the house of Dr. Gachet before a discovery is made that could reveal our secret and cause a reinvestigation.'

'What do you mean?' Adeline moved to the edge of her seat as her cup began to shake.

'Before you came to see me at my father's house after the shooting I climbed into the doctor's garden and hid something there. Its discovery would be catastrophic, especially for your father, who has been almost the sole author of the accepted truth about the events of that night.'

'What did you hide?' she asked, only too aware of how vehemently her father had publicly supported the artist's words that he had shot himself.

'You know what I hid there. It's the secret you swore me to protect; the one that could be very difficult for your father to explain if it were found. I chose the location because Gachet was the only person in Auvers who knew the artist prior to his arrival. It made sense to me at the time to let him take the blame for hiding it, although now I realise discovery could only make the situation worse as he wasn't in town that day. I must revisit the garden and undo my mistake, for both our sakes.'

'Why now, after so many years? And why do you need me to come with you?' Adeline picked at her nails nervously as thoughts of that summer in Auvers returned after so long. 'You promised me you would not contradict my father's story.' Her family had moved to escape the speculation. Her father had been the only person in the town with a handgun rather than a shotgun and it hadn't been seen since the artist died. Many of the locals believed it to be the weapon the artist had used to shoot himself, and its discovery would be catastrophic. How would her father ever explain its location - especially if it had been buried? The single biggest question that still remained after all these years was what had happened to the gun.

'I've heard a rumour that the doctor is to open his home to the public so they can view his art collection. Vincent's reputation is growing and the doctor has many of his painting and drawings, as well as those of many other artists. New pathways are to be built around the garden and I need to ensure the hiding place will not be discovered.'

'I still don't understand why you need me to accompany you. You are a respectable businessman now. Surely the old doctor will welcome you into his home without me.' Adeline was not eager to return to the village at the centre of events that had turned her life upside down.

'The doctor will remember you. He knew you for many years. He came to your Auberge while the artist was dying. I have never spoken to him.' He looked at her more closely, drawing her in with his eyes, pressurising her to accept. 'Besides, I need to you keep him busy while I check the gardens. The locals might have turned a blind eye to a 16-year-old troublemaker climbing over a wall, but not to a 31-year-old man they don't know. '

'I can't leave the cafe unattended,' Adeline pleaded, torn between her duty to her father and the oath she'd made to a dying man. 'And how will we get there?'

'My friend is outside. I have borrowed his car. He will remain here and look after your premises. We can drive to Auvers and be back within a few hours, before anyone else gets home. This is important Adeline. Will you come with me?'

'Does your friend know how to run a cafe?'

'He owns several in Paris!' Rene lied. 'How else do you think he can afford a car?'

'Very well, but I must be back before my father or there will be trouble!'

You have no idea how much trouble, Rene thought.

Adeline went to her room to change and put on her hat and coat. While she was gone Rene and his companion moved the trunks and package into the sitting room and hid them behind the threadbare sofa. Within half an hour Adeline and Rene were on the road, heading east towards the town where they'd first met.

Dr Gachet looked old and frail beyond his 77 years. His small house was filled with the art of Cezanne, Manet, Pissarro and Renoir, all of whom had been treated by him at some point for various psychological disorders. Each one of them had presented him with a token of their gratitude that together now amounted to one of the most important collections of impressionist art in the world. The portrait that Van Gogh had painted of him whilst in Auvers took pride of place in the main entrance hall. Rene could see why people would want to come and visit this impressive collection, even in so cramped a space.

Feigning a need for air after the uncomfortable twenty-mile drive, Rene signed the visitor's book and left the doctor proudly showing Adeline round the house. He walked through the back door in the kitchen, into the potting shed and out into the garden. Everything was still as it had been 15 years ago when he'd climbed over the wall in the dead of night. The stone footpath along the far side of the steeply sloping lawn was made of flagstones that had seemed enormous when he was a 16-year-old youth, scared for his life. Now they were not so imposing. They were surrounded by thousands of tiny stone chippings he hadn't noticed in the dark. Moving the third block from the end was simpler than it had been the last time he was here. Nothing had been disturbed. Everything was just as he had left it. His task took less than a minute and he made sure it looked as if nothing had been disturbed. He levelled the flagstone and kicked the chippings back into place. The truth was now in God's hands. He would decide when the time was right for it to be revealed.

As he and Adeline took their leave, Rene shook hands with the old doctor, who failed to notice the traces of soil under the gentleman's fingernails.

They arrived back in Meulan just after 6pm. Rene's companion was sitting behind the counter smoking a pipe. The café was empty.

Adeline immediately checked the cash register in a panic. There were 30 francs in there.

'Monsieur, you must have been busy,' she said, holding up the cash. 'This is our best takings since we arrived in Meulan. My father will be happy.' She took the notes up to her bedroom to keep them safe, and to change back into her work clothes before her father arrived home. He would never know about her trip back to Auvers.

While she was gone the two men loaded the trunks back into the car.

'Here is your package,' Rene's companion said, handing him a freshly wrapped parcel. 'I hope it turns out to be worth your investment. I consider 30 francs plus my fee to be a lot to pay for this.'

Rene walked back into the sitting room to say goodbye to Adeline. He looked up at the two paintings hanging above the mantelpiece and thought to himself, 'I am sure it will be worth every centime one day.'

Chapter 13

Barbican, London; Thursday October 16th 2014.

'Where the hell have you been?' Jennifer shouted before Henry had even walked through the front door. 'It's past midnight and you said you weren't going out!' She came out of the open-plan kitchen into the marble-floored hallway of the Barbican flat, triggering the automatic mood lighting as she moved. Her stiletto heels tapped in furious time to her shouting.

'I wasn't!' Henry replied, already feeling guilty for having left without leaving a note or a text. He did owe her that at least. 'There was a small emergency!'

'What emergency?' Jennifer was livid. 'I go out with an old friend from school for one night and you disappear! How do you think I would explain that to your parents?'

'What are you so worked up about?' He couldn't believe the ferocity in her voice. He'd only been gone for just over an hour. 'You can't have been home more than forty minutes yourself! Why didn't you just text me?' He moved past her and headed straight for the master bedroom, leaving a trail of his outdoor clothes and shoes as he went. Let her pick them up! She did nothing else all day.

'I did text you - three times in half an hour!'

As if on cue Henry's phone beeped and 3 messages and a missed-call alert came through one after the other.

'Sorry Jen, but you can't hold me responsible for the phone signal. I only went to give someone a lift home!' He removed his jeans and underwear outside the bathroom door keeping his back towards her.

'Was it those girls again? What are you doing hanging around with them anyway! They are virtually kids.' She caught him by the shoulder and spun him towards her, staring resolutely into his eyes so she wouldn't be distracted from her tirade. He pulled away and headed for the shower.

'You sound like a jealous housewife!' he shouted into the air in front of him. 'They are members of my martial arts club - the darker girl is brilliant. You should see how fast she moves. I think she could even take you down with a bit more practice.' He knew that would piss her off!

Jennifer laughed. In three years Henry had never managed to get the better of her and she doubted the skinny waif had even beaten him yet. She'd been taught numerous forms of martial arts by some of the best instructors in the world and had moved straight onto the next once she'd defeated them.

'You just need to be more considerate,' she said without following him into the bathroom. 'What would I say to your poor mother. Don't you remember what she went through last time? Would you really put her through that again?'

'Did you check the GPS signal on the trackers you had put in my phone and the car?' Henry came back out of the bathroom and looked straight into her brilliant blue eyes, daring her to lie.

'I checked the phone and car just before you got in,' she confessed. 'And you know I can't track the other chip because of your dangerous injunction!'

'So you knew exactly where I was and that I was okay? All this drama is just for attention isn't it?' A mixture of anger and pity danced across Henry's eyes as he looked at the golden-haired goddess he had to share his life with. 'Well it won't work on me I'm afraid babe! And just out of curiosity, I didn't realise you had any friends? Certainly none that lived in England.' The bathroom door closed in her face as the hurtful comment sunk in.

'There's a lot you don't know about me!' Jen shouted through the soundproofed door.

Jen knew she was beautiful, and indulgent teachers and university professors had provided her with enough advantage over the other students to ensure she always got her own way. She'd used this to continuously graduate top in her class. She had then repeated the pattern on her instructors at Quantico with the same outcome but it consistently failed with Henry Whittaker. His passive indifference often devastated her but she couldn't walk away. He wasn't with her because of how she looked, so she didn't have the same hold over him as she'd had with other men and it drove her insane.

Henry woke up just after 7am. The sun cast a thin yellow frame of light round the blinds at the bedroom window. The white silk bed cover and crisp white sheets had migrated south to the floor, but the temperature was comfortable. He opened the blind and stared out at a bright blue sky and a fifteen-mile view – a perk of living on the 17th floor of the Barbican Tower in an apartment that technically belonged to his mother's company.

The room was decorated in white but it would have taken someone a few moments to realise. The peaceful ambiance was shattered by his clothes and books, which were still strewn across the furniture and floor. His parents might have him in golden handcuffs when it came to paying the rent but they couldn't dictate how he chose to live.

Today was Jennifer's 28th birthday and she was spending the day having her hair and makeup done, ready for the evening. He often told her she would look good in a plastic bin liner but she'd never given it a try. It would have seriously impressed him if she had, but she wasn't really big on humour.

Of course he didn't mind what she did with her time - she could do whatever she pleased. She thought she had control of him and he was happy to let her continue thinking that. Surely his parents must be getting fed up with the boring snippets of information she fed them on a regular basis about what he was up to - which was nothing! He knew

Jennifer was thoroughly bored with their life in England, and that it frustrated her, but she knew the situation. He hated the fact that nearly 8 years after his trouble, his parents still couldn't find a way to trust him. Consequently, he found every means possible to hack them off without actually breaking the law again. Treating their multi-million-pound apartment like a squat was just one of the ways. He didn't actually blame his parents. He couldn't really blame anyone but himself. He hated to think about the awful night that was responsible for his current self-imposed prison sentence, albeit in a beautiful apartment studying a subject he loved.

For the next hour he and Jennifer tore into each other in their purpose-built gym. A morning ritual that had commenced on the day they first met. After once again being forced to concede defeat he left her on the running machine and headed back upstairs to his bedroom.

He picked up his phone and dialled the call return.

'You up yet?' he asked.

'I am,' Ashley replied in a whisper. 'But I don't think she will surface for another couple of hours. She really meant it when she said she'd never drunk in her life before.'

'Was she okay after I left?' It hadn't really surprised Henry that Tia was the first person he'd thought about when he woke up. He'd met very few genuine people in his 26 years and Tia was by far the most beautiful, even though she had no idea herself.

'Well apart from the time she puked in the bin and nearly all over me she's been fine. Good job this is not the first time I've slept on the floor looking after a drunk.'

'Yeah sorry Ash - just didn't think her dad would like it if some 26-year-old guy spent the night in her room. Do you think he really is as bad as she says he is?'

'Dunno, I've never met him. I don't think she's physically afraid of him. But while he controls her finances he controls her!'

'Well I know what that feels like!' Henry said almost to himself then bit his lip in frustration at bringing his painful memories back into his head so soon in the day.

'I've got a lecture at 9am. Do you think she'll be okay to leave alone by then? I can't miss this class again or they'll chuck me off the course.' Ashley didn't seem to notice his mood change.

'Yeh she should be fine. Program my number into her mobile and leave her a note to call me if she needs something when she wakes up. I don't need to be in until ten and hopefully she'll be awake by then.'

He put the phone down and went into the bathroom. He rejected the sunken bath in favour of the walk-in double shower. The 12-inch showerhead made the water feel like tropical rain pounding his body, relieving some of the tension that thinking about his past always seemed to produce. He had long ago resigned himself to never being completely guilt free - no matter how much therapy his parents paid for or how hard Jennifer kicked him around.

He wrapped a towel round his waist and walked wet footprints through the flat to the kitchen. Jennifer was still in her sweats cooking pancakes and making coffee. As he walked up to the central island and sat on a high stool she just looked indignantly at the trail of water he was leaving behind him,

'Breakfast in bed?' he asked sarcastically, as she piled the pancakes onto a plate.

'You do realise I'm not your servant don't you? ' She said, knowing the water would remain there until it evaporated or she cleaned it up. The cleaner wouldn't be back until Monday. She handed him the pancakes and a mug of freshly brewed coffee. 'I've eaten, and after your behaviour last night I don't want to make myself sick!' she replied equally rudely.

'I'd look after you if you were sick,' he laughed as he went back towards the bedroom with his plate and mug. He turned and smiled smugly 'Have fun having your hair and nails done all day. I can survive for one day without you. Enjoy your birthday.' He disappeared into the bedroom and kicked the door behind him. He knew better than to get too near her while she was in this mood.

Jennifer checked carefully that he had closed the bedroom door and did her usual first sweep of the apartment. First the visual check - All the devices were still in place. Her laptop showed they were all still working. She was fairly certain he knew they were there; he just didn't seem to care. Next a content check. As usual, there was no material to review apart from a call to the red-haired girl a few minutes ago. Apparently the skinny waif had a hangover! What a shame.

She paused for a second to reflect on the first call he'd made in two weeks that wasn't to her or his parents. That was good! A call to that particular girl today of all days would work to her advantage. It was an unexpected bonus that she'd called him the night before also, and that his car tracker would show he'd picked her up just after 11pm and taken her home. Once his parents got going they would find plenty of evidence of their son's betrayal.

Jennifer knew it wouldn't be long before she got the financial settlement she was due from this dysfunctional family and then her real life could begin.

Chapter 14

Paris, July 2008.

La Bourget Airport operated exclusively for private aircraft and was the busiest of its kind in Europe. It had been the first airport built in France and the crowds had cheered Charles Lindbergh in the 'Spirit of St Louis' when he landed after his 33-hour flight across the Atlantic on the 21st May 1927. Some years later Hitler followed suit on his one and only visit to Paris, but hadn't been afforded the same welcome.

Boris touched down in his private Cessna just after 7pm and checked into the George Cinq, where Vasily had booked the Suite Royale. He threw his hastily packed overnight bag onto the Louis XIV armchair, ignoring the 17th-century French masters on the walls. His head of security had never seen him dismiss artwork of this quality so readily, even though he'd stayed here before. Whenever he arrived at a hotel he always took a few moments to take in the craftsmanship his money was paying for. He would only ever settle for the best. It seemed to re-inspire him, reminding him of how far they'd come from their hole in Vologda. Vasily's comprehension of the importance of their mission intensified.

'She lives alone a few miles from here in the suburbs near Versailles,' he began, believing his boss would be keen to get started.

Boris stopped him with a wave of his hand. He knew they wouldn't make progress tonight.

'An 89-year-old woman is unlikely to entertain strangers at this hour. I doubt she'll even come to the door.' He picked up the phone and called for room service from 'le Cinq' restaurant, deciding to swap his traditional evening Vodka for a bottle of Montrachet Grand Cru Chablis. Tonight he would celebrate the finer things that had already come into his life. Tomorrow he would focus his efforts on the dirty business of maintaining his fortune and his future.

Chaville was a small suburb southwest of Paris nestled between the Bois De Meudon and the Foreit Domainale de Faussess Reposses. Cecilia Roux had bought her modest two-bedroom house with its small but immaculate garden after her employer died in 1957. She'd only been 39 at the time and had worked for him for 7 years as his secretary and 14 years as his personal assistant once he retired. It was not a long time by some standards but he had no family and had left her an annuity that was sufficient for her not to have to work again. Instead, at his request, she'd spent the rest of her working life running the children's home she'd helped set up in his former house. He'd donated his remaining wealth and property to establish a school for orphaned boys who had been excluded from normal education due to poor behaviour. He never said as much, but Cecilia suspected he felt he had much in common with these wayward urchins, and but for the fortune of birth into a wealthy family, such would have been his lot in life. She had dedicated all her time and effort to his project until she retired 10 years ago. Few of her friends remained alive, but sometimes the orphans she'd helped to care for would come and visit to make sure she was okay.

Cecilia wasn't expecting visitors when the doorbell rang, but her 'boys' didn't always make an appointment. The two gentlemen who blocked her doorway, however, were unfamiliar, and she doubted they had ever missed a meal in their lifetime.

'Madame Roux?' the taller of the two men asked.

'Yes. Do I know you?'

'My name is Boris Rubikov. I would like to speak to you about your former employer at Swiss Re.'

'I have not worked for them for 64 years.' Cecelia didn't move from the doorway. Something concerned her about these gentlemen with strong foreign accents and brutish manners. They wore heavy leather jackets and gloves despite it being the height of summer. The morning temperature was already into the 80s.

'We are particularly interested in the time you spent caring for him at his home on Rue Balzac in Paris.' Boris moved forward as he spoke, forcing the frail old woman to retreat into her own hallway. 'I suspect a woman of your training would have been meticulous in maintaining his diaries and journals and I would be very interested in finding out about his trips to London in particular.'

'I have not kept anything from that time' Cecelia insisted. 'This is a small apartment. I could not keep all his journals, there would be no room.'

'Well I'm sure you won't mind if my colleague and I have a look around?'

Vasily came in behind Boris and closed the front door. He gripped the spinster's wrist and felt one of the fragile bones snap under the pressure. She opened her mouth to scream but a silk handkerchief forced into her throat blocked any sound. Her breathing became strained and her legs buckled beneath her, causing her to fall. Vasily caught her elbow and manoeuvred her roughly into the living room to an upright armchair. He didn't need to restrain her; she didn't have the strength to move while she was gagged.

The Russians worked systematically through the small building. They checked bookshelves, the desk, a small bureau filled with writing materials and an old typewriter and various cupboards. In the bedside cabinet of the master bedroom Boris found a single journal. It was made of fine brown leather with the instantly recognisable LV monogram embossed across its surface. Inside the cover was a small removable notebook with gilt-edged pages. The date at the top of the first page was January 1957. The contents were sparse but recorded details of the 1956 interview with the journalist, Doiteau that Boris had already read and that had been the catalyst for his quest.

'This is his last journal,' Boris said, showing it to Vasily. 'It's a refillable cover and I'm guessing the previous editions will be stored somewhere safe to protect the pages.'

Vasily continued to search the bedrooms as Boris looked through the handwritten notes that were over 50 years old. The writing was spidery and slanted, clearly the writing of an elderly person with an unsteady hand. Boris was not familiar with French and couldn't recognise a single word. Vasily would have to take care of the translation later.

'I've found them!' Vasily declared from the small loft. 'She has also kept his desk diaries, but this could be a problem.' He handed Boris a cardboard box containing about thirty notebooks similar to the one in the leather cover. The Russian wondered how a man could fill a whole book documenting his life. Surely he'd had better things to do with his time. He assumed the books covered a year each, much like a diary, which meant there were 30 years of memories to translate and decode. This could be more difficult than he suspected given the illegible handwriting and unrecognisable language. He tried to calculate the estimated time to translate the books, assuming each one took a few weeks. At best he should have them done within a year. He could possibly have them done quicker using an interpreter, but the contents of these works were for him alone to know. He was in no rush. Other trophies could sustain him for a while. He turned to carry the box down to the living room when Vasily called him back.

'Boris,' he shouted down from the eaves. 'Let me pass you the next box.'

Boris looked quizzically up at his henchman.

'What next box?'

'The next box of journals.'

Boris turned the box in his hands round so the front label was in view; on the white-typed label were the dates. Feb 1903 - July 1908. He nearly dropped the box and its contents on the floor. The time span was less than six years, which meant each journal covered about 2 months!

'How many boxes of these are there?' He wasn't sure he wanted to know.

'There are another 12, plus about 3 boxes of diaries.' Vasily said. 'There is nothing else up here.'

Boris did the calculation in his head and cursed out loud. At his predicted rate the time required to translate the journals was now nearer a decade! They had no idea when the banker had taken the letter to England. It would be like searching for the proverbial needle in a haystack. Maybe the old woman could narrow the search for them.

The two men brought the boxes of journals and diaries down to the living room and laid them on the table in front of the old woman. The expensive notebooks were all written in the same spidery hand, which was in stark contrast to the neat calligraphic print in the functional appointment books. It was easy to see which she'd written and which had been written by her employer. There were significantly more journals than there were appointment books so the difference in the level of detail would be immense. He'd started writing his journals long before he'd been afforded his own secretary.

Cecilia tried to stand, reaching instinctively to protect her cherished memories and the reputation of her employer, but Boris knocked her back into the seat. Her heart rate accelerated rapidly and her breathing weakened still further.

'I need you to tell me when he took the letter mentioned in his will over to England,' Boris said, running his gloved finger around the secretary's frail neck. 'I know you were present at the reading of his last testimony. You've been almost single-handedly responsible for ensuring his last requests were adhered to. What was it the letter referred to and who did he give it to?'

Cecelia remained motionless, her eyes lifted to the ceiling saying a silent prayer of thanks for her wonderful life.

Vasily began to read from one of the 'appointments' diaries slowly translating each entry to Boris. They were written in her neat French hand and easier to understand than the journals.

Cecilia could feel her vision blurring and her consciousness slipping away. She'd spent her life trying to protect his secret, as she'd sworn she would do. Let them read his appointment books, she thought, they give nothing away on their own.

Boris turned back to the old woman and removed the handkerchief from her mouth. Her breathing eased a little but all colour had drained from her sunken cheeks. He knew he did not have long with her.

'How often did he travel to London?' Boris attempted to narrow the search periods down as he stared at the mountain of books.

Cecilia kept her lips tightly pressed together, suppressing a weak smile. This Russian would never understand the lengths a man with a lifelong secret of terrible consequence would go to, to protect his lie. The journals were written in Occitan, not French, and barely anyone used that language anymore. She doubted they would even recognise it. Good luck with your translations, she thought, they will keep you busy for years.

Cecilia had lived a good life, thanks entirely to her benefactor and only love. She was old and her time was nearly up. There was nothing this brute could threaten her with that made her afraid. She knew her patron had been excessive in the amount of detail he'd included in his journals, burying his past in words. Interest in his life had grown over the years concerning his relationship with the Dutch artist. Even she didn't know the exact details despite reading the books hundreds of times since his death. Whatever secret he had wanted to protect, whoever it was he had entrusted with the knowledge of his story, they would not discover it from her. They might find a name buried among the pages. And if they did, it would be years before that knowledge would be any use to them at all. Her beloved had been cleverer by far than this thug, and his plan would take more than threats of violence to uncover. What threat can you make to a woman desperate to return to the only man she had ever truly loved.

Boris watched Cecilia's pupils contract as she focused on a mark on the ceiling of her living room. The lines around her eyes pulled together, stealing themselves ready for battle as he tested her resolve. He knew she was never going to betray him. A woman in love determined to afford protection, whether it was for a child or a man, would never be broken.

'Pack the books into the boot,' he ordered Vasily.

As his head of security carried the volumes out to the car, which had been rented using a false name, Boris covered his gloved hand with the damp handkerchief. As his fingers pressed against her mouth and nostrils he could feel her lamentable struggle as she swallowed her final breath. He pulled the dining chair onto its side to make it look as if she'd fallen. That would explain the broken wrist when she was eventually found.

Rubikov was confident he'd be able to work out the details from the diaries himself. If it took him another ten years, so be it. He *would* eventually discover what secret Rene Secretan had taken to his grave.

Chapter 15

Tottenham, London. Thursday Oct 16th 2014.

Eoin Driscoll had completely forgotten about his 9am booking this morning. He'd also forgotten Ashley's threats as to what she'd do if he didn't move out. He hadn't been in a fit state to remember the conversation at the time and although she'd rattled him a bit it hadn't been enough to make him go. Five pounds a day lunch money had been the price of Matt's silence. As long as Eoin looked after Patricia at night, leaving the teenager free to get on with his PS2 conquests, he'd be safe. Eoin didn't mind. Watching her was the easiest job in the world in exchange for somewhere to sleep. She'd fallen asleep on the sofa again last night, leaving her takeaway curry and half a bottle of vodka unfinished on the table. He'd demolished the remains of her dinner and alcohol, before drifting into a vacuous stupor and dreaming of when he could afford a flat of his own.

Now it was 7.00am and he'd woken up hung-over and feeling awful. How could he mess up his first important job before he'd even left the house? He swore at his own stupidity as he went in search of paracetamol and water. Stan had lent him a suit that was two sizes too big in the chest and an inch too short for his thin, 6'2" build, but it was better than nothing and certainly better than anything he owned. He brushed his teeth three times and stole one of Connor's shirts in a bid to look more presentable. He used a baby wipe to clean his shoes and a black magic marker to hide the scuffs as best he could. He couldn't afford to lose this job. It was bad enough that he'd been forced to flee his uncle's house and crash in a flat with virtual strangers. Thank God

Connor had let him have his bed, which thankfully he'd managed to crawl into it at some point last night.

Eoin had worked as a bike messenger at Elite Courier services for 5 years, since leaving school at 16 with no qualifications. From Thursday to Sunday he supplemented his pitiful day job by working the nightshift for a mini cab service. He would ferry the drunk and disorderly back home after the drinking establishments of Tottenham threw them out. His best customer was the daytime cab driver whose car Eoin rented every weekend for £30 a night; the same man who promptly handed the cash back in fares for the inebriated late-night trip back to Edmonton from whichever pub still allowed him in.

The bike work was mainly in the City and his knowledge of that part of London was pretty good now. He would take documents from one building to another - often distances the clients could have walked themselves in the time they waited for him to turn up. But lawyers and bankers would do no such thing. Not even their secretaries or mailroom staff would stoop so low! Once a week he would also make a number of special personal deliveries for his boss, Stan Meaney. The contents of these packages were white, but not made of paper and the traders who received them always tipped well. Today, however, was different! This was the first time they'd given him a job in a car, in the West End. He couldn't afford to screw it up. The package he was due to collect was too big and too valuable for a bike and Stan had given him his personal Mercedes to carry out the drop. It was a new customer and Eoin understood exactly how important this business must be, because Stan got angry if anyone so much as looked at his car, much less wanted to drive it. Stan had made it clear he wanted to give the job to someone else but Eoin had been asked for by name, so if he screwed it up the client would know who to come after. He'd even taken Eoin's bike from him as collateral when he arrived to pick up the car last night. Stan had been in a foul mood as he'd emptied everything from the back box of the moped into the boot of the Mercedes, including his 'special' traders packages that needed to be delivered straight after the Knightsbridge drop.

Fortunately, in a rare moment of clear thinking, Eoin had parked the car in Grosvenor Square at 6.30pm last night and got the underground back home. The area around the American Embassy was sufficiently well protected by CCTV to safeguard Stan's prized possession and a boot load of contraband. He couldn't leave it overnight on the Broadwater Farm Estate and expect it to have four wheels the next day. He guessed that it would be quicker to get the tube back into town during the rush hour anyway. That decision now gave him another couple of hours' grace in which to sober up. He knew he shouldn't be driving while he was still intoxicated, but the one thing guaranteed to upset Stan more than damaging his car was missing a booking.

He arrived back at Grosvenor Square just after 8.30am and fed the parking meter up to the maximum 2 hours. He wasn't taking any chances with the car being towed just because the package he was collecting wasn't ready. He turned left into South Audley Street and was at the gallery in Mount Street a couple of minutes later. He was fifteen minutes early. Hopefully they'd be impressed enough to use him again.

He rang the bell and a plummy voice he could barely understand answered sleepily.

'Can I help you?'

'It's Eoin Driscoll,' he said, suddenly conscious of his own Irish accent. ' I'm from Elite Courier Services. I've got a booking to deliver a package.'

'You're early! You weren't due until 9am,' stated the voice, clearly annoyed. 'Philip isn't here yet but you can't stand out there like a vagrant, so you'll have to wait in the kitchen.'

The door made a clicking sound as the internal bolts slid back inside the metal doorframe. An immaculately groomed brunette towered above him in her impossibly high red-soled heels.

'You're not what I was expecting,' Serena Holdsworth said rudely as she looked him up and down in disgust and moved aside to avoid any possible contact. Thank god she'd made it into work early for once after a very late and restless night. 'My friend suggested I use you yesterday. She's obviously not met you personally from her description but every courier in this area has blacklisted us so I had no choice! Did you remember to bring the white gloves?' Serena had panicked at lunchtime yesterday when she realised she'd forgotten to book a proper art handling company. After the taxi fiasco before the will reading she couldn't afford another mistake to be exposed.

'What?' Eoin asked absentmindedly, no one had mentioned gloves. He walked into the gallery showroom and began looking at a painting on the pillar in the middle of the room, wondering if it was round the right way. He scanned the walls, which displayed about 25 works of art of varying sizes. All had plaques with elaborate descriptions about the piece and the artist, which was just as well because he couldn't make out the subjects in any of them. There were no price's on display on the basis that if you had to ask, you can't afford it, which for Eoin included just about everything.

'Oh never mind, I bought some in Fenwick's last night just in case.' Serena shrugged in frustration at his lack of attention. She walked over to her curved corner desk and took out a brand new pair of white cotton gloves from the top drawer. ' You wont actually be touching the painting directly but I need you to look the part. If Philip asks, you need to tell him you work for an art handler's, not a courier company, or he'll send you away and you wont get paid.' She didn't mention that she would have been fired for sure this time if Jen hadn't been able to suggest a courier that could help.

Serena's desk was on the left, towards the back of the room, and a large highly polished walnut sideboard took up most of the right hand side of the gallery. In the furthest corner a spiral metal staircase led to a small mezzanine floor out of the glare of the sunlight, used for exhibitions of upcoming talent.

'Oh my god have you actually been to sleep in those clothes?' Serena said, noticing the creases in the shirt as she walked past him. She flinched as a waft of stale vodka with a hint of curry hit her.

'Probably got more sleep than you, love,' he replied cheekily, having instantly recognised the bloodshot eyes and red raw nostrils. They were familiar signs of artificially fuelled adrenaline among the punters he picked up from the nightclubs in Tottenham. Make up can cover a multitude of sins, he conceded, but that didn't extend to the whites of your eyes. 'At least my nose will still be intact this time next year!'

'Unlike your liver if your breath is anything to go by,' she retaliated. At least she'd been on time for work this morning after her night out had been cut short. She'd expected to meet the elusive Henry Whittaker, but Jen had left unexpectedly in a taxi just before midnight. Not to worry though, she'd get to meet him today. Serena's customary powdered nightcap, alone in her bedroom, was confirmation of her growing addiction but she consoled herself with the thought that at least she was doing a better job of covering up her bad habits than this guy was.

'You need to get rid of that smell of vodka. The client you're delivering the painting to is not the type of man you want to insult by turning up drunk.' She opened her Gucci bag and threw him a packet of chewing gum. 'Mr Yau is a very important Chinese businessman who deals with problems personally, if you understand my meaning. If anything should happen to his painting because you were over the limit you might need to consider a change of address - for about 25 years. Go and make coffee and wait until we're ready for you. I can't have you visible from the street. God knows what the neighbours will think and I have a very important client visit to prepare for.'

'Fine by me. I could do with a brew!' he replied following her through the mirror-panelled double doors at the back of the gallery. They entered a small hallway with an office on the left that looked as if it may once have been a storage cupboard, a kitchen to the right and another office straight ahead whose door was closed.

'Don't touch the bone china!' Serena said ushering him into the kitchen. 'Use one of those promotional mugs. They are so ugly I don't know what Philip was thinking when he ordered them. He was clearly more interested in the company's rep than their products, and trust me she looked just as cheap.'

Eoin wasn't paying attention to her moaning. He was more interested in the full-length mirrors in the double doors, which, despite their opaque appearance on approach, were actually windows from the other side. Two-way glass! He'd never seen it before. So this was what the cops used in their interrogation rooms! He childishly put his hand on either side to study the difference. Serena's irritation levels rose as she watched him playing with the means by which her boss kept an eye on her.

'What are these for?' he asked. 'In case the debt collectors turn up?'

'The mirrors make the gallery look bigger and reflect the pictures on the pillars back into the street. And the glass means Philip can see the counter vault and when his appointments arrive from his desk in there.' She pointed to the office with the closed door.

'Why didn't he just get a camera installed?' Eoin said.

'There are cameras. But if an important client comes in he likes to greet them personally. The camera screens are on my desk so I can open the electronic doors, so he wanted to be able to see the shop front at all times.'

'So what's a counter vault?' Eoin asked.

'None of your business! I don't have time to answer your silly questions. You just wait here and whatever you do, don't come into the showroom. God forbid my customer should smell you!' She left him to make his own tea.

Philip Charlesworth was running fifteen minutes late when he collected his usual vanilla mocha from the Mount Street Deli. Being late was rare for him, but what did it matter - he was the boss now! His father was no longer here to bully and criticise him. He was excited and buoyant and his unusual good mood took the barista by surprise. Today was set to be an exceptional one. If all went according to plan this would be the single biggest day's turnover in the firm's history. That would show his miserable father just how competent he was. What a shame he wasn't here to witness it first hand. Maybe at last he'd have been proud of him.

The Charlesworth family had owned the Lenister Gallery for over 75 years and he was a fourth generation art dealer charged with two key types of business transaction. The first was showcasing new talent at small intimate exhibitions to an invited audience. Recent graduates from the Royal Academy and up-and-coming foreign artists were the most common exhibitors. The turnover at these events was modest and the work was often dull, extolling the virtues of artists, who often had more anger than talent, to clients who had more money than sense. The second activity was far more interesting, brokering deals for major works of art worth millions to a client base of less than 50 collectors worldwide. His father had never let him take on this work while he was alive and Philip was revelling in his first few months of success.

The shop floor itself was largely used just for show and for the use of the exclusive Mount Street address. The more expensive art on display wasn't original - the humid conditions in the listed building could never be allowed to come into contact with the genuine articles, all of which were stored under museum conditions in the climate-controlled vaults that had been custom built in the extensive basement that ran the length of several of the neighbouring shops above. Most of the works on site were unsold items from collections of up-and-coming artists whose shows had recently completed in the gallery. Nothing was worth more than five figures currently but they all showed promise and once in a lifetime you might discover the next Damien Hirst or Tracey Emin.

When his father died, Philip had taken over the main office but still hadn't got round to converting his old one back to the storage cupboard it had been. After today he could afford to take on a proper assistant, who could look after the new talent, leaving him free to focus on brokering the important deals to wealthy new clients.

As he waited for his syrupy coffee he stared across Mount Street toward the doorway of his empire. The art handler ordered to deliver a painting by Chagall should be waiting for him as long as Serena had made it into work on time! He'd known as soon as his father had employed her that they'd made a mistake - but she looked good, moved in the right circles and was the daughter of one of his oldest clients. Even after two years, she was finding it difficult to adapt to working life. She'd spent four years studying history of art at the Slade and continued to behave like a person without employment. Partying till 3am was her norm and she was often still in bed at 9am when she was supposed to be opening the gallery. As he crossed the road he could see there was no one in the doorway, so either the delivery company was late or Serena had been early for once. He'd drilled her incessantly over the last week to ensure she understood just how important today was and that he absolutely would fire her if things went badly, no matter what the consequences. It was the first time the company had two deliveries in one day and he'd never trusted a third party with this task before, but today he was prepared to make an exception because he had a more important delivery to attend to himself.

Serena had assured him the art handler had been booked. The Chagall was worth just over £1.4 million and demanded respect. He'd purchased it on behalf of his client at a recent Christie's auction and his fee of 10% would add £140,000 to the day's accumulator. Strict transportation measures had to be taken to deliver the painting, as it wouldn't be insured once it was outside his premises. The GPS tracking device in a state-of-the-art metal carry case was a requirement of his policy. The buyer was staying at the Mandarin Oriental Hotel, less than 2 miles away in Knightsbridge and he was leaving for China that afternoon. Once the painting was physically handed over its protection and insurance were no longer the gallery's concern. By all accounts, Mr Yau had the resources to take care of his own possessions more than sufficiently and he was the only other person who had the code to open the case.

Philip enjoyed delivering the paintings himself. He liked to watch his client's reactions when they saw their purchases for the first time up close and in private. He revelled in their praise and gratitude for finding them exactly what they'd been looking for. But today he had a second work of much greater value that had to be delivered before 11am. He hoped this single deal would not only add more to his turnover than last year's entire return, but would exceed anything his father or grandfather had achieved during their safe, unadventurous careers. He could follow the delivery of the Chagall from door to door on his phone, while he attended to one of his wealthiest customers. If it strayed 10 yards from its expected route, or if the packaging was disturbed, the police would be notified instantly.

It was almost 9.15am when Philip arrived at the gallery.

Serena sat at her small desk and watched him cross the road on the screen in front of her. She activated the door lock from the control panel built into her top drawer. Few customers came in off the street without an appointment and today she had secured her first introductory meeting, but she wouldn't be telling Philip unless it was successful.

Philip didn't expect his clients to come to him. Most of his brokering deals were conducted over the phone or in the five-star restaurants of every major city around the world. In his ten years' experience, under the tutelage of his father, he'd learned not to question his customers about the source of their excessive wealth. Few could afford his services on a pay cheque, not even the CEOs of many of the Fortune 500 companies. He'd become fluent in Russian and Mandarin as the global economy and wealth moved east. Third-world gangsters legitimised their fortunes by investing in Western culture and property that continued to multiply in value, even during the numerous recessions.

'Is the art handler here?' he asked Serena, who jumped up to take his coat.

'Yes, he arrived early so I hid him in the kitchen. He looks a little bit rough.' Serena's eyes dipped to the left as she lied to her boss.

'I don't care what he looks like as long as he gets that painting to Mr Yau before 10am. I'll just go and check his security clearance and then I'll send the paintings up from the basement. I need you to put the first one in the safe and lock it, then leave the second one in the counter vault until I come back up. Do you have the inkpad and card?' Serena took two items from her top drawer that she'd purchased yesterday along with the gloves and handed them to him.

Philip headed into the kitchen and didn't bother with any introductions.

'Did your employer give you the security code?' he asked Eoin. 'And may I see your driving licence? Did he explain you would need to complete a fingerprint card?'

'Yes - 76524AH' Eoin replied as he handed over the plastic card, completely unaware as to why such extensive measures were necessary for a package going less than 2 miles. This must just be what art handlers do.

Philip put the inkpad on the worktop and manoeuvred Eoin's fingertips into place to produce a complete set of prints. He handed him an alcohol wipe.

'Okay, clean your fingers and put on your gloves while I check the paperwork and packaging. I'll call you out when it's ready to go and you can get your car. It shouldn't take you more than 15 minutes to get to the hotel and you've been booked into the loading bay. Were you made aware that this case is being GPS tracked?'

'Yeh Stan told me not to divert from the route at all or there'd be hell to pay!'

'Trust me, it would be worse than hell if you crossed this particular Chinese gentleman. You, your family and the owners of your company would all be considered legitimate targets for revenge. He knows your name should you decide not to deliver the package as agreed and that would be a big mistake for all concerned. And obviously these will go straight to the police.' Philip waved the fingerprint card in the air, hoping his scare tactics would sink in. He wondered if the poor boy had any idea what would really happen to him if he didn't turn up. The police would be the least of his worries. He reassured himself that even if he had an inkling of its value, trying to dispose of the asset at anywhere near its true amount would be virtually impossible for someone like him. Effectively to Eoin Driscoll, given the circles he undoubtedly moved in, this package was worthless in comparison to the trouble that would rain down on him if he crossed the intended recipient.

Eoin picked at a bunch of grapes in the fruit bowl above the fridge as Philip put the fingerprint card into his pocket and disappeared into his office.

Back in the gallery Serena was waiting in front of the walnut sideboard. Eoin watched through the two-way glass as she opened the door on the right hand side and removed what looked like a large metal briefcase. She attached a cable to the side of the case as a picture on the wall above sprung into life and a computer screen filled its frame. She waited briefly as the screen flickered before lifting the case onto the floor. Nice arse, Eoin thought, as she bent over to open a door on the left and moved the case into what was evidently the safe, built into the mock antique furniture. The electronic voice from the screen said something but Eoin couldn't make out what. She then shut the door and spun the door handle, which he guessed was the concealed combination lock. She pushed the right-hand door back into position just as her phone started to ring. She disappeared from his view as she went to answer it and Eoin could hear the muffled mechanical sound of chains turning on spokes and the soft whirr of an engine seemed to be coming from below him.

A minute later Philip came out of his office and without acknowledging Eoin again went over to the safe.

Serena was still on the phone. Philip frowned at her and opened the right hand door himself. He removed a second package almost identical in size to the one in the safe. Both were made of grey moulded metal that looked seamless apart from black rivets that formed a studded border round the middle of each case.

Philip put the case on top of the sideboard and plugged the same cable into a slot at the back. The framed picture lit up again, and Philip punched some numbers into an on-screen keypad. He waited till the screen went blank and a voice message confirmed that GPS tracking had been initiated. He then checked his phone and punched something into the screen.

Eoin returned to the kitchen to the bowl of grapes and his tea. He didn't hear the front door open, or see the person who came in. He could hear Philip start to talk quite loudly and assumed he was on his phone.

'I'm afraid we are closed at the moment.' he heard him say.

From his hidden position in the kitchen he wasn't close enough to hear the muted sound of the silencer as the .22 calibre bullet tore through Philip's temple, but there was no mistaking Serena's brief scream before it was unnaturally halted mid-breath.

Eoin froze momentarily before dropping under the worktop. He crept to the edge of the kitchen door and peered round the frame. Through the mirrored doors he could see the gallery owner lying on the floor, blood pooling rapidly under his head. It was several minutes after he heard the front door slam shut before Eoin dared venture out into the main gallery.

Philip Charlesworth lay on the ground with the left side of his forehead spread around him. Bone and brain matter were splattered over the sideboard and floor, and blood was running toward the kitchen over the smooth marble tiles. Serena was slumped in her chair behind her desk with a single bullet hole through her left eye.

'Route commenced,' a voice announced from behind him. He turned abruptly, shaking and in shock. The screen on the wall showed a map with a dot, which began to blink green, and then turned red.

'Planned route deviation detected,' the electronic voice told him as a phone beeped from inside Charlesworth's pocket. Visions of a murderous Chinese gangster and the police gouged at Eoin's eyes. He was 21 and virtually unemployable, but he was streetwise and smart enough to realise that the only person other than the two dead bodies who could officially be traced to this building today was him!

As his panic escalated he thought about his limited options. He couldn't contact his uncle, even though he would probably know what to do. Mickey would use this as leverage over him for the rest of his life. He couldn't contact the police as he had a boot full of Stan's packages that would earn him ten years in prison on their own. Stan wouldn't hesitate to let him take the blame for the contents of his car. He'd probably even claim Eoin stole it if it meant protecting himself. But this was murder, not just theft! It wouldn't be long before somebody was coming after him one way or another. As the thought of threats to his safety swirled around his head another problem came to mind. He pulled down the blinds of the shop window and realised there was one person who now potentially had as much to lose as he did. If the Triad or the police traced his last known address through the courier company he wouldn't be dragged into this on his own. He wasn't sure if they would help or leave him to his unthinkable fate, but their own had just become horrifically bound up with his.

Taking his phone out of his pocket, he called Ashley.

Chapter 16

Meulan, France November 1905

Harry Harronson sipped his favourite Legal le Gout 1851 Grand Arabica French coffee and smoked his third Gauloise cigarette of the morning. He'd been introduced to both brands in Paris, where he'd been living for the last year. In that time he'd rarely ventured outside the city centre but now he was watching the cafe on the corner of Rue Gambetta from the Salon of the Hotel Pinchon in Meulan. He hoped his trip to this small Paris suburb might change his fortune and reputation and finally allow him to return home to America as a success.

The town was not on a main route into the capital so traffic was light. The occasional horse and carriage sporadically blocked his view of the entrance to the rundown cafe, but not enough to disrupt his surveillance. At night he maintained his vigil, switching to a Beau Sejour Becor, Saint-Émilion Merlot that was better than anything he'd tried back home. He stayed hidden inside the small salon, avoiding the pavement terrace and the cold November temperatures.

Harry spent his time in Paris dealing in impressionist art, which was just starting to gain in popularity in Washington and New York. The acquisition of major works had eluded him since his arrival in Europe and he felt sure the local dealers were making things difficult for him on purpose. His client base was small but growing due to the increasing momentum in manufacturing and retailing in the States. Millionaires appeared to be created daily and one strong deal would set him up for good. He was confident that this would be that deal.

His companion at the hotel was an artist known only as 'Le petit pere, Sam'. Meeting Sam a few months ago had been fortuitous for Harry. Sam had information that could bring a handsome profit to a man who knew its value. It seemed the cafe owner, Arthur Ravoux, had owned the Auberge where Van Gogh had died fifteen years earlier in strange circumstances. Even though the family had sold up and moved on less than a year after Van Gogh's suicide, interest in his life, death and work had increased so rapidly the inn still bore the name Auberge Ravoux. The new owners seemed more than happy to make the most of the premise's notoriety.

Over the last three days Harry had learned the routines of the cafe owners and their regulars. He knew when the father Arthur-Gustave Ravoux would be out and the daughter, Adeline, would be left in charge.

Sam had told him about her already. She and her father had been present when Van Gogh died. The younger sister had been there too, but as she'd been only 2 years old at the time would be of little value. The family had known the artist for the last three months of his life and this girl was apparently the subject of a portrait in various shades of blue, not seen since he'd given it to her after its completion.

Of more interest to Harry was the painting titled 'The Town Hall in Auvers, 14th July 1890'. The scene, painted from the roadside in front of the Auberge, showed a sad and forlorn attempt to celebrate Bastille day and was a unique perspective of a moment in the artist's history, and possibly one of his last ever creations. Sam's information suggested that the artist had given this work to Arthur Ravoux in lieu of rent and that it currently hung, unframed, above the mantel in their tiny parlour.

It was fifteen years since the artist committed suicide, and interest in his work was gaining momentum in Paris. There was a steady stream of his art coming onto the market in a carefully constructed campaign by his sister-in-law to keep Van Gogh's legacy alive. He'd been an exceptionally talented and visionary painter, even if the world had not seen this when he was alive.

Some of the works were currently selling for hundreds of francs in Paris and Harronson felt certain the uncultured Ravoux's would know nothing of this development.

An artist had told Sam about the two works only a few months ago and confirmed they were genuine. Apparently the artist had visited the family with a young Parisian banker who had also been in Auvers at the time of Van Gogh's death. Although the banker had only been a teenager at the time he claimed to have seen the artist paint these very works and knew exactly which ones Vincent had given to the family. He'd refused to tell Sam why he'd visited the cafe with the banker, just that he had seen the two works with his own eyes. He'd explained that the two paintings hung in the living room of the cafe owner's private quarters and the hot, humid conditions within the building were causing the paint to flake at a rate faster than would be ideal.

Harronson had already agreed a sale for the 'Town Hall' with two members of Van Gogh's family and he was waiting for them to arrive from Amsterdam. Despite not yet owning either painting he'd struck a deal that would set him up financially for the foreseeable future. They would pay him fr1000 for one of the paintings and he would keep the second to take pride of place when he opened his gallery in New York. His buyers would be in Paris in less than two days. Harry needed to make his move before then. If they turned up and approached the Ravoux's directly he would lose his sale, his painting and his gallery.

Arthur Ravoux was tired. He was 57 years old and having to work hard just to exist. This exhausting pattern was showing no sign of changing any time soon. Trade was slow. Rural life was declining in France as more and more people gravitated towards the cities and the industrial northern towns. He could tell his first customer of the day had money as soon as he walked through the door.

'Good morning,' Harry said, emphasising his American accent. 'Would you be the owner of this establishment?'

'I am sir,' Ravoux replied coming out from behind his counter and offering his hand. 'I am Arthur Ravoux. What can I get you?'

'My name is Harry Harronson. I am an art dealer working on behalf of the Van Gogh family in Amsterdam. I am led to understand you knew the artist, Vincent?' He handed his host a card.

'I did indeed, monsieur,' Arthur said. He never tired of telling his story now it no longer affected his business and he wasn't blighted by rumour. 'I was with him when he died.'

'I believe the artist gave you two paintings while he was staying with you? I wondered if it would be possible for me to view these?'

Arthur thought for a moment. The works hung on the wall in his living room and he'd never given them a thought; never considered that they may be of interest to anyone else.

'Of course, sir. Follow me.' He led the American out to the tiny parlour, where the paintings were the only items on the small walls.

Harry's skill at poker helped him conceal his excitement as he viewed the two masterpieces for the first time. The town hall was clearly a Van Gogh. It was painted in the same distinctive style as the painting of the church, which he'd seen at an exhibition in Paris a couple of years ago.

The portrait of Adeline Ravoux, however, captivated Harronson. He instantly recognised the girl he had been watching for the past three days. She looked almost exactly like her portrait, despite the fact it was painted over fifteen years ago when she was no more than 13. He moved closer to the fireplace to study them in greater detail.

'Mr Ravoux, have you always displayed them above this mantelpiece?' he asked.

'Since we moved here, yes. Why? What is wrong?'

Harry pointed to the right hand corner of the town hall painting.

'Can you see how the paint has started to flake and dry out?' He pressed a finger against the surface and specs of dried oil came away on his fingertip.

'What does that mean?' asked the cafe owner.

'These paintings need to be kept in special conditions with controlled temperature, light and humidity. They will not last more than a few years if you keep them here.'

'I can't afford to have then stored,' Arthur said, concerned about the possibility of incurring a cost that would wipe out his week's takings.

'Well as I mentioned, I represent the Van Gogh family in Amsterdam. They are setting up a little museum of the artists work in his hometown. With your consent they have authorised me to purchase these works on their behalf.'

Arthur looked up at the two paintings that had hung in his living room for fifteen years, a constant reminder of the tragedy that had befallen his guest and caused his family to abandon their business to get away from the suspicion and the questions. The paintings had been given to him in lieu of rent the artist couldn't afford to pay and now he was facing the same dilemma. What could they possibly be worth to someone else? - Especially the one of his daughter, who was unknown to anyone other than her immediate family and friends.

'How much?' he asked, intrigued as to how this gentleman knew the paintings were even here.

'I'll give you twenty francs for them both!' Harry chanced a low bid.

'Twenty francs each and they are yours!' Ravoux replied. That was more than two whole days' takings and these paintings would pay next month's rent.

'You have a deal, Mr Ravoux,' Harronson said, trying to hide his delight at the bargain he'd struck. 'Just out of interest, has your daughter's portrait always hung here as well?'

'Yes, why?' Arthur prayed the American wouldn't change his mind about buying the painting of a peasant girl.

Harry looked more closely at the portrait. The condition of the paint didn't look as bad as the flaking on the town hall. In fact it looked as if it had been stored in a different location to its neighbour. Harronson couldn't explain a sense that something wasn't quite as it should be but the painting was clearly of the woman he'd been studying all week; the woman who was currently in the cafe tending to customers.

'No reason.' He said softly and shrugged to himself. The provenance was unassailable. No person other than the subject herself had ever been in possession of this work.

Chapter 17

Bloomsbury, London, Thursday 16th October 2014

The cognitive psychology lecturer was facing the electronic screen displaying a large cross section of the human brain. He was explaining the function of the various lobes to a half-empty class - a typical scenario for the first lesson of the day. Ashley Rivers sat at the back of the tiered lecture theatre listening to the detailed descriptions of neural pathways, synapses and neurotransmitters. She could do with some serotonin right now after a complete lack of sleep on Tia's uncomfortable floor.

The habit of sitting near an exit was instinctive, in case she had to escape quickly to deal with whatever new domestic dispute hit her family on any given day. Her concentration today, however, was on keeping her eyes open and she wasn't really paying attention. What must it be like to own a car like Henry's, she mused, allowing her mind to wander. Or even any car?

Her phone vibrated in her coat pocket interrupting her thoughts. The call was from a number she didn't recognise so she rejected it, sending it to voicemail. Five seconds later the phone started to vibrate again. A second rejection followed by a third attempt to contact her usually only meant one thing - trouble at home, again! Maybe it was a neighbour or someone from Matt's school, which was why she didn't recognise the number. Silently gathering up her bag and textbooks, she left the lecture hall unnoticed via the back door and pressed the call return button.

'Who is this?' she demanded as the phone was answered on the second ring.

'Ashley is that you?' came an Irish voice that she recognised but couldn't place.

'Yeh. Who wants to know?'

'It's Eoin. Eoin Driscoll'.

'What's wrong with my mum?' the accusation was immediate and clear as she jumped to her usual conclusion that the worst must have happened. He could have no other reason to call her. 'What have you done to her? How did you get my number?'

'Matt gave me your number in case of an emergency. Nothing is wrong with her!' he replied warily before quietly adding, 'Yet!'

Ashley felt an intake of breath fill her lungs involuntarily.

'What's that supposed to mean? Are you threatening my family you little piece of shit?' she quickened her pace out of the psychology building onto Bedford Way, her head swimming with possibilities but not sure in which direction to head.

'Not me Ash, but this is an emergency and I need your help or someone else might hurt her.'

'Who?' she asked.

'I can't talk over the phone.' The urgency in Eoin's voice was bordering on panic.

She didn't know him well but she knew he was usually more laid back than was good for him. Now he was clearly in distress and not making sense. '

I'm in deep shit Ash, I need you to come and meet me - now!'

'I'm in class you idiot! I can't just up and leave!' she lied; she wasn't interested in whatever mess he'd gotten himself into.

'Look this isn't a joke. I'm in big trouble and unless I can sort it quickly it's likely to spread back home! I'm supposed to be delivering a package to a hotel and the person waiting for me is dangerous. Things have gone badly wrong. I can't make the delivery and he's gonna come looking for me any minute and it won't be to ask questions!' Eoin was trying to instil his desperation without mentioning the two bodies in the room with him. He didn't want her to

144

call the police!

'What's that got to do with me? Why should I be worried if trouble turns up on your doorstep?'

'Cos it ain't my doorstep, Ash!'

As swiftly as the words came down the line realisation overtook her - he hadn't moved out. Whatever trouble he was now in, whoever was looking for him, the trail led right back to her mum's flat. If someone wanted to find him they were going to start there. What if Matt was home alone? He wouldn't know what to do and he was too young to defend himself. Even if her mum were home she'd be unlikely to offer much resistance. Ashley knew of Eoin's uncle by reputation. His criminal activities were often reported in the local newspapers, although no jury had actually convicted him of anything more serious than petty theft. He was too smart to do any actual dirty work himself but everybody knew the truth and that was one battle she didn't want landing on her family.

'Where are you?' she asked, calming her voice and trying to stem her anger. Years of dealing with an alcoholic mother had taught her that getting irate at this point wouldn't help anyone and would just prevent her from thinking straight.

'I'm in Mayfair at an art gallery. Lenisters. You need to get here in the next 20 minutes. I don't know what to do! I need to get into a locked computer urgently and you're the only person I know who could even turn one on.'

Ashley considered her options. If she helped him, he would most likely pull her into some illegal or dangerous crime; if she didn't and something happened to her family she could never live with herself.

'Text me the address - I'm getting in a cab now.'

Ashley hailed a taxi almost immediately and collected her thoughts as she sat in the back heading west on the 10-minute journey to Mayfair. Why would someone like Eoin even be in a Mayfair coffee shop, never mind an art gallery? What could he possibly be doing that he needed access to a computer. She remembered Connor had once mentioned that Eoin was brilliant at something but she couldn't remember what it was. She had no idea about computers…she'd never owned one and had to use the communal terminals in the library to type up her essays. She could just about open Windows and Office. She had no clue how to do anything else - but she knew someone who did. She dialled the number.

'Hello?' came the groggy reply of someone clearly still in bed with a hangover.

'Tia, it's Ashley!'

'What happened last night? How did I get home?'

Ashley prayed Tia was sufficiently recovered to be able to get dressed without throwing up again.

'Look, I'll tell you later, but right now I need you to do me a massive favour. Do you have any software for getting into someone else's PC without their password?'

'Maybe,' Tia replied warily, sitting up in bed and rubbing her eyes. 'Why, what's happened?'

' I'm not sure yet and I can't talk over the phone! I just need you to get dressed, I'm gonna call Henry to come and pick you up, so be ready in 10 minutes.'

Henry was almost at the Christopher Ingold Chemistry building in Gordon Street when his phone rang.

'Rivers, you are becoming a pain in the ass.' he chided as he answered.

'Henry I can't explain now but I really need you to go and pick up Tia and get to Mount Street in Mayfair as fast as you can.' The words tumbled out of her mouth so rapidly he could barely comprehend them.

'Do you suddenly think I'm your personal taxi service, you cheeky bugger?'

Ashley lowered her voice to a whisper as fear started to strangle her vocal chords

'Seriously Henry! Please just trust me and get her there as fast as

146

you can. I don't know anyone else with a car and Tia is in no fit state to get there on her own. I doubt she even knows where Mayfair is and I really need her to help me.'

Henry opened his mouth to object but his words stalled. As his brain processed the difference in Ashley's strained voice he realised she wasn't messing around. Whatever trouble she was in, it was serious - he could hear it in her frightened whispers. He'd known her for almost two years and he'd never seen her afraid of anything or anyone, to the point of foolishness. She'd never asked for help for herself, not even when she should have. He had an idea about the dire financial situation she was in and helping her out wouldn't have even registered on his monthly accounts, but she'd never asked for anything and he wouldn't insult or embarrass her by offering help. Now, the fear and panic in her voice was real and immediate. Henry knew this wasn't the time for questions.

'I'm on my way.' He said as he accelerated past Euston station towards Camden.

Just before 10am Ashley rang the bell at Lenisters Art Gallery, shouting for Eoin to open the door. It took him a few moments to find the emergency exit button on the wall to release the deadbolts that had reset automatically after the killer left the building. As Ashley walked into the gallery she felt the bile rise in her stomach as she scanned the bloody scene that lay before her. The gore around Philip Charlesworth's' body was starting to dry out on the cold tiles, changing colour rapidly.

'Holy shit Eoin! What have you done?' Ashley was no stranger to blood but she'd never seen a man missing the side of his face before. Instinctively she began to back away from the Irish traveller.

'What? I didn't do this!' he cried. Her initial reaction confirmed his primary fear. Any rational assessment of the situation would suggest that he was to blame for this carnage when the police eventually turned up. At least that would be their initial assumption and he didn't have time for delays. There was much more at stake than just a stolen painting. He was in a building that could only be opened from the inside and both its tenants were dead. The only way anyone could have gotten in was if one of the now-deceased persons had let them in. That meant they both had to have been alive when he arrived. He couldn't claim he found them like this when there was no physical way to get into the building; and then the questions would be asked as to why he hadn't phoned the police straight away. He was in shock. His nervous system wouldn't move on from processing that at least he was still alive. Despite his frequent brushes with the law he had never considered his own mortality, but today he had been saved by two-way glass. The murderer hadn't seen him behind the mirrored door and had no idea that he'd left a witness behind. Eoin knew as soon as the trace on that painting disappeared then so would any trail leading to the killer and he would be left to take the blame.

'Then what the hell happened?' Ashley looked at the brown congealed mass that was splattered all over the walnut sideboard and her thoughts flew to the flat in Tottenham. As she walked further into the room, past the central pillar, she caught sight of Serena's body slumped in the chair behind the desk, her remaining eye wide open and still showing the fear that had clearly been her final emotion. 'Oh my god another one! Shit Eoin, have you called the police?'

'I can't. Not yet!' He was pacing up and down the small gallery, swinging wildly between shock and panic.

'Why the hell not - there's two dead bodies here!'

'Think about it! - I'm the only person inside a place with electronic deadbolts on the door. Whoever it was that did this must have been known them or at least have been expected or she wouldn't have let them in. Although when I arrived I think she was still doped up or hung over from last night so maybe she just didn't check properly? But the point is I'm in here already - how do I explain how I got in and didn't get shot? Plus there's another problem - bigger than this!'

'What on earth is bigger that two dead bodies?' Ashley said.

' I didn't see who it was that came in, but whoever he was, he took a package that I was supposed to be delivering. The dead guy was getting it ready for me.'

'So he shot them and stole a painting! That just gives him a motive. You clearly haven't stolen the painting or you wouldn't be hanging around. The police will see that you were just the first person on the scene. You're just a witness Eoin, call the bloody police!'

'It's not that simple. If that package doesn't arrive at its destination soon the Chinese guy who' s expecting it to be delivered is gonna think it's me that's stolen it. He won't know what's gone on in here. He knows who I work for and I don't think he'll have the same patience as the police or worry about details like it wasn't me! Besides, by the time the police get here and get to the point of realising it wasn't me it'll be too late.'

'What do you mean?'

'The dead geezer told me this Mr Yau was proper trouble. I guess he's some sort of Triad bigwig. He's gonna come after me when I don't turn up and the first place my firm will send him will be your mum's'

'You bastard, Eoin!' Ashley cried, punching him on the left temple with a limp blow that betrayed how quickly the fight in her had been replaced by panic. 'I told you to get out of there three weeks ago. Why didn't Matt tell me?'

'I've been paying for everything to keep him quiet, ain't I?' Eoin at least had the grace to lower his gaze in remorse. 'The owner said the painting has a USB tracker in. I thought if we can track the killer on the computer and let Mr Yau know where he is, he can go and get his painting back and that might stop him from breaking your mum's front door down.'

Ashley put her head in her hands and thought. She knew that phoning the police was the sensible thing to do. But Eoin was right - if this Chinese man really was that dangerous then they just didn't have time to be detained and deal with a barrage of questions right now.

They could explain everything later, and nothing was going to help these poor dead people. Their priority was to stop the body count rising.

'Okay, well if the package has a tracking device in it - there must be something in here that can track it. Where's their computer?'

'I think it's that picture behind the sideboard. That's what he was pressing just before the gunman came in and shot him.' He pointed up at what looked like a small framed print of Jackson Pollock's Autumn Rhythms mounted on the wall.

Ashley flinched as she navigated her way carefully around the congealing blood, careful not to step in it. She touched the glass and it lit up in the recognisable blue of a Microsoft Windows screen, immediately requesting a password.

'Shit! You got any idea what it might be?' She knew the question was stupid.

'How would I know - I've never been here in my life before!'

'Okay - well hopefully help is on its way.'

Tia was waiting for Henry outside the entrance to Ifor Evans halls. The panic in Ashley's voice had coursed through her like a shot of adrenalin, banishing her hangover. She'd thrown on her jeans and a clean T-shirt and had almost thrown up again while brushing her teeth. Brushing her hair and tying the laces in her trainers had been a struggle but she'd been ready in under 10 minutes. She put on her jacket and locked the door. Henry pulled up just after 10am and Tia got into the Porsche for the second time in twelve hours. She put her laptop on the floor in the foot well and fussed over her seatbelt to delay looking at him. Has anyone so bedraggled and foolish ever gotten into such a beautiful car? She thought.

'How's the head?' Henry asked trying to suppress a smile at her embarrassment.

'Pounding!' she replied, recalling his presence last night and feeling mortified that he'd witnessed her in the worst state of her life.

'How do you people do this for fun?'

'You get used to it, eventually,' he laughed, punching the car into first gear. He pulled out of the gates and made an illegal right turn onto Camden Road, ignoring the police car to his right held up at the oncoming red lights. He accelerated sharply into the left turn onto Eversholt Street and Tia rocked sideways in the passenger seat.

'Well your driving's not helping!'

'Sorry, but Ashley sounded really scared. That's not like her at all. Did she say anything to you?'

'She said she couldn't talk. Just asked me to bring my software for getting past computer security systems. One of my dad's tech guys gave me a copy to practice with on my own computer. My dad would go nuts if he knew I had it!'

'Well any excuse to floor the Porsche is good enough for me!' He tried to make light of the situation, then suddenly realised she may throw up over his custom leather seats.

They arrived at the gallery just before 10.15am. Henry left the car parked illegally on a single yellow line immediately outside the front door. He could watch it from the window! His diplomatic number plates would deter any over-enthusiastic traffic wardens so close to the American Embassy. His father being an American senator did have some uses. As the central locking clicked into place on the car Eoin let them into the gallery.

'What happened?' Tia exclaimed as she entered the showroom. She'd seen plenty of crime-scene photos in her life when peeking through her dad's work, but not two real dead bodies up close and still warm. She felt she should be recoiling in horror and was a little surprised at herself that she wasn't. Instead her mind was filled with a multitude of questions that she doubted anyone present would be able to answer. Henry showed no reaction at all, as if there were no scene on earth that could shock him.

'I don't have time to explain who this idiot is!' Ashley nodded towards Eoin. 'But my mum could be in trouble. I need you to get into

151

that computer and see if you can track the package the killer took. We have to find him and get it back to its owner before all hell breaks loose.'

'What happened here? It looks like Hell already broke loose,' Henry asked as Tia stepped over Philip's body to get to the computer.

'He says he doesn't know who it was,' Ashley said, not allowing Eoin to speak. 'But whoever did this took a case containing a painting belonging to a mad triad godfather, and this idiot has my mum's flat as his last known address. Apparently the case has a GPS tracker built in and its current whereabouts should be on that computer, assuming he's not deactivated it yet.'

'It's protected by a simple windows password.' Tia was already inserting a disk containing a police-modified version of the trinity rescue kit into the drive on the side of the screen. 'This program will automatically log me into his administrator account. I can't get his password but I can overwrite it with a new one,' she explained to her bewildered audience. Two minutes later the desktop came up. Tia first checked the email program, as she'd seen her father's experts do when they were handed a new laptop to crack.

'Apparently the package was due to be delivered to a Mr Yau, over from China and staying at the Mandarin Oriental. He has a flight back to Beijing at 4pm this afternoon and needs to check the painting in through customs early. Well clearly that's not gonna happen!' she said paraphrasing a message out loud.

'Is there any software that looks like it might be a GPS tracking program?' Ashley leaned over her shoulder to watch her work. Tia called up the list of program files.

'Yes there's this one. OpenGTS.' She clicked on the icon on the desktop and a map of London opened on the screen. 'It's a web-based program so it can be accessed from any Internet device that has the login details and tracker code. It's showing two live traces. One is red and currently heading west on the M4 and the other one is green and...' Tia stopped dead.

'What is it?' Eoin asked, more concerned as to how far away the painting already was.

'The other one is still here! Apparently right in front of me!'

'Yeh!' Eoin leapt over to the sideboard, remembering the sequence of events from less than an hour ago. 'That's right! The bloke went down into the basement and sent something up first in this thing. He called it a counter vault.' He pointed at the deep-brown walnut door on the right of the sideboard. 'It was the same sort of case as the one the killer took. The secretary took it out, plugged it into that screen for a couple of seconds and then put it in here!' He tried the handle of the identical door on the left of the sideboard but nothing moved.

'It's an integral safe,' Henry said from the window where he was watching his car. 'My parents have one like it at home. The sideboard must be concreted into the floor. The walnut veneer is just for show. I'm guessing the casing is probably 3 inches of solid steel. Some of the work in here must be worth quite a bit. What's your name, by the way?' He looked directly at Eoin.

'This is Eoin Driscoll.' Ashley said, still not allowing him to be acknowledged; as if enforced silence would make it feel like he wasn't there. 'It's his fault we've been dragged into this. He's my brother Connor's friend who's been staying at my mum's flat.' Ashley turned and glared at him 'And when this is over he'll be staying at Whipps Cross hospital for a few weeks!'

'Listen Eoin,' Henry said, ignoring her threats. 'What exactly did they do before the gunman came in?'

'He went into his office, and the girl stood here by the sideboard. First she opened this door and took out some sort of large metal case and put it in that safe. Then her phone rang and she went to answer it. A few minutes later he came back in and took a second case, almost exactly the same, out of the same door. The cupboard made a weird noise, like chains rattling when the door was closed.'

Henry tried the right hand door and it opened to reveal a large oblong space that had a small gap almost the whole way round.

'It's like a dumb-waiter lift system,' he explained. 'There must be a vault in the basement that's climate controlled where the originals of these works are kept. The inner steel casing runs right down into the foundations making it impossible to dislodge and the pictures come up in the lift system. Any larger works are probably kept at an auction house or art handlers before being transported but these are obviously less than a metre in any direction and without their ornate frames many paintings are actually quite small, especially impressionist ones. I wonder what it was she put in there.' He pointed at the safe.

'The painting you were due to deliver was a Chagall purchased by the Lenister Gallery at auction on behalf of Mr Yau for £1.4m last week at Christie's,' Tia interrupted, still reading through files on the computer. 'Payment has already been made into the gallery's account.'

'Is that all?' Henry asked. 'Doesn't seem like a painting someone would kill two innocent people for.'

Ashley looked at him and rolled her eyes incredulously. Did this rich yank have no grasp of reality? He obviously hadn't visited the pawnshops of Tottenham lately.

'Are you serious?' she asked. 'I know loads of people who would kill for much less than that.'

'It's not the amount paid by the legitimate buyer that's important with art theft.' Henry tried to explain. 'Art is only ever worth what someone is prepared to pay for it and the minute a painting's provenance is disrupted it loses most of its value.'

'What the hell is provenance?' Ashley asked.

'It's the chain of ownership and custody,' Henry replied.

Ashley still looked confused. The painting had been stolen; who cared about proof of ownership? Surely they had more important things to worry about right now. Henry could sense that she didn't understand how this was relevant to their current situation.

'A painting can be quite easily copied, so you have to be able to show evidence of where you got the work from and what you paid for it to prove that it's the original.' Henry explained, recalling the lecture his mother had given him on a trip to her gallery. 'It's like a chain of command for evidence. Once a painting is stolen, the chain is broken and the thief has no way of proving it is genuine without a huge amount of work so its value drops massively. The market for stolen art is tiny and requires extremely precise contacts. Most is stolen to order. If there's another crime like murder attached to the theft then the painting becomes virtually worthless as a buyer could be accused of being an accomplice. A thief would somehow need to alter the proof of ownership to legitimise the stolen painting which is extremely difficult and expensive to do.'

'Like money laundering?' Ashley said.

'Sort of, yes.' Henry said. 'And for £1.4m it would be easier, cheaper and safer for the buyer to just bid at the auction.'

'But they've clearly taken the painting Eoin was due to deliver so someone must have been prepared to pay for it.' Ashley still couldn't understand why they weren't already following the tracker.

'But it doesn't make sense.' Tia started to apply her logic to the facts. 'Charlesworth obviously had two things to be delivered this morning; the missing case and whatever is in there.' She pointed at the blood-spattered safe. 'It's reasonable to assume he would have sent Eoin on his way before sorting out the second one, which I guess he was going to deliver himself. If the painting for Mr Yau was the more valuable, why entrust it to a courier you've never used before. Surely that would be the one you would take yourself? We need to find out what is in that second case!'

'Why?' Ashley still wasn't following. Tia continued to develop her theory.

'Based on the execution style of these murders the killer must be a professional. Two shots, two dead bodies. He obviously didn't realise Eoin was in the building or he would never have left him alive as a potential witness. Therefore we can assume he didn't know that there were two packages being delivered from here today.' She looked round at the silent group and hoped they were following her logic.

'Pretty soon the murderer is going to realise he's got the wrong case, especially if it was stolen to order. It won't take him long to work out that there must have been a second drop being made today by someone else. He may also assume that collection was imminent as the wrong painting was out of the safe and that maybe the courier was already in the building and he missed them. I suspect whatever is in the safe is the more valuable of the two. So what if the killer has taken the wrong case and decides to recover the correct one? Eoin wouldn't just have a triad boss looking for him.'

'Check her purse!' Ashley almost shouted the instructions at Eoin as she pointed to the dead woman. The increasing gravity of their situation fell into place. They didn't just need Mr Yau to recover his own painting now. Somehow they had to deal with the murderer himself.

'What? Why?' Eoin didn't want to go near her.

'You said you thought she was still high on something or drunk when you got here so she must have a system.' Ashley had seen plenty of functioning drink-and drug-fuelled women before in the nightclubs she'd worked in and they all shared a common trait; they all suffered from occasional memory loss. 'Being a PA, even in Mayfair, doesn't pay for Louboutin shoes and Gucci handbags so she's obviously some sort of society girl who likes to party. I bet the silly cow has written the combination down somewhere in case she has a memory lapse. They all do it - it's the only way they don't end up behind bars or disowned by their families.'

Eoin leaned over the dead woman's body and took her Gucci bag off the back of her chair. He emptied the contents onto the top of the desk. The contents included an iPhone, a Tiffany key ring holding 3 keys, a Louis Vuitton purse, Chanel makeup and No 5 atomiser and a pale pink Smythson's address book.

He picked up the purse and emptied the various coins, store cards and credit cards onto the counter. Henry came over to help and they each went through scraps of paper checking for anything that might be a code for a safe. Eoin switched on the iPhone and was amazed that it had no pin code.

'She probably couldn't remember it when she was drunk and in need of a cab, so easier to leave it off.' Ashley explained. Her mum never used the pin code on her ancient phone either.

Eoin went through the various search functions, contacts and apps but found nothing that looked like a safe code, only phone numbers. Ashley bent down, shut her eyes and grimaced as she put her hand into the pockets of Philip Charlesworth's jacket. She pulled out his phone. This one was locked. She closed her eyes and tried to imagine what a twenty-something PA with a poor memory and some sort of bad habit would do with important information. She walked over to the desk and picked up the baby-pink leather address book with their signature pale blue pages. Who owns a paper address book these days?

'Check under Lenister Gallery,' she said, handing it to Henry. 'Maybe she's written it down.'

'Nothing!' he replied, thumbing quickly through the pages. 'God she knows a lot of people!'

Eoin searched the various pots and holders on her desk and found a pile of business cards edged in gold in front of the phone. Next to the phone was a flat screen monitor with a card tucked into the screen showing the name of a security company specialising in video surveillance.

'There's a security system on her desk.' He said noticing the terminal for the first time. 'Maybe we can get a look at the bloke entering or leaving the building?'

Henry leaned over the desk to take a closer look.

'Open the drawer.' He said.

Eoin opened the top draw to find a small control panel with 4 buttons labelled camera1 to camera4. The main power switch was flicked upwards.

'Its been physically turned off.' He said.

"Why would someone do that?" Henry asked, incredulously, 'today of all days!'

'Try Philip Charlesworth,' Eoin suggested, staring at the business cards in the holder next to the security screen. 'She called him Philip.' Instinctively the four of them turned towards the male body under their feet. At least they now knew his name.

'Yes - there's a 5-digit number here. Too short for a phone number!' Henry read it out.

'7-4-2-3-6,' he said as Tia carefully aligned the barely visible Roman numerals that surrounded the ornate knob on the safe. The door swung forward with a click.

'What sort of idiot would completely invalidate state-of-the-art security by writing down the code?' Tia asked. Her dad always said the weakest point in any password-protected system was the people. She reached into the safe and removed the aluminium casing.

'That's the same as the one I was supposed to take to the Chinese bloke.' Eoin shouted across the room,

'There are no email or diary details of a second drop this morning anywhere on the computer but whatever is in this case has a tracking device also,' Tia said, continuing to check the gallery email whilst transferring the files to the flash drive on her key ring. It might take her a while to check things properly and she suspected they didn't have much time before the first tracker was deactivated. 'I guess he was going to take this second package himself but I've no idea where to. And given that he was happy to entrust a £1.4m painting to a courier he'd never met before, whatever is in that case must be worth considerably more.'

'A lot more!' said Ashley staring down at Charlesworth's phone still in her hand. 'Most people have a crap memory, which means they can't remember more than one set of digits, so they use the same numbers for all their security and pin codes. Basic psychology! The first four digits on that safe combination were the pin code for his phone. He's got a lot of messages and voicemails from people he obviously knows but there's a text sent this morning to a foreign mobile with no name against it and no history. It was sent at 9am today and I assume its about this second case but it's only three words long… estimated price, £50m'.

Chapter 18

Mayfair, London. Thursday October 16th 2014

The occupant of the most expensive suite in Claridge's hotel was not calm, but years of self-control hid the mental turbulence completely. Events of the last few weeks had become increasingly worrying, especially after the private analysis showed alarming results.

The Guest knew they were accurate; they'd carried out the chemical tests themselves. Every possible permutation of scenarios had been considered, and the way things looked right now it wasn't possible to imagine a favourable outcome to the meeting due to start as soon Charlesworth arrived.

The Guest had initially had no idea why they'd been contacted by Lenisters and asked to get in touch urgently. The family hadn't used that gallery for many years. The calls had gone unanswered after being screened by an army of receptionists and secretaries in a long chain of gatekeepers, but Charlesworth had been persistent. He'd used every contact in the galleries records to get access to various phone numbers. In the end he'd resorted to a phone number found in his fathers personal letters to get his aggressive message to its intended recipient

Philip Charlesworth hadn't even worked for his father, Cecil, the last time the Guest had met him at the Royal Academy summer exhibition over 15 years ago. He'd clearly had no eye for talent but could sniff out the investors who had money with expert precision. The unexpected contact six weeks ago had been worrying. Only certain people, and very few art dealers, had access to this unlisted number. Cecil had been one of them, but it had certainly not been entrusted to his arrogant son. Lenisters had been removed from the approved list of brokers after Cecil's death in March.

Philip's claims had been dismissed out-of-hand initially, but the broker was too confident. The possible consequences of his assertions were unthinkable if they were true. The Guest had eventually listened, carried out tests themselves and agreed to meet.

The Guest had broken all of their usual travel protocols by bringing the package into England at considerable risk to themselves and the priceless work. A web of lies had been spun to provide plausible cover if anything went wrong. The insurance companies wouldn't pay if anything went wrong but the Guest was willing to take the risk.

It was almost 11am and he still wasn't here. It was less than a few minutes walk to the Mayfair hotel from the Mount St Gallery and he hadn't even called to say he would be late. His father would never have conducted business like this. There was no option but to sit tight. A potential scandal of this magnitude could not just be dismissed in a fit of pique at being kept waiting.

Some art was just too important.

Chapter 19
Mayfair, Thursday October 16th 2014

Ashley and Eoin both stared at the metal case, shocked by the potential value of its contents. Neither of them had ever seen anything worth even £5000 so something in excess of £50m was beyond their comprehension. Even Stan's Mercedes probably wasn't worth as much as the case itself.

'I don't believe it!' Henry was struggling to make sense of the brief text on Charlesworth's phone. Unlike the others he'd grown up in a world where friends had art of that value hanging on their living room walls. 'My mother is an art historian at the Smithsonian in Washington and no way would a work of that value be dealt with directly by a gallery as insignificant as this. She works with paintings worth millions of dollars every day and they are dealt with almost exclusively by the top 3 auction houses.' He omitted to add that she also owned one of the most extensive private collections in the world. 'Even if a work of that value did somehow end up in this gallery's possession, no way would it be dealt with off the books. They would need detailed proof of where it had come from to preserve its value. Are you sure there's no purchase history or documentation regarding the seller?' he asked Tia.

'There's no mention of anything worth that sort of money anywhere on this computer. The painting doesn't exist other than in the GPS tracking program so I assume that's purely for security purposes or habit and it's actually the case that's being tracked, not the contents. There's no invoice or receipt for anything even close to that value in the inventory files and certainly no details of a potential buyer or seller. It could be an empty case for all we know but I doubt he would have locked it in the safe if it was.' Tia spoke as she continued to search the deleted files buried deep in the computer's archive memory.

Henry frowned. Galleries like this acted as brokers for major works, not sellers as they did with new artists. They bought and sold on behalf of their clients, under their instructions. The art they acquired probably never left the auction house until it was purchased and even then would be stored in off-site, security-patrolled buildings owned by an art handler, not minor showrooms in central London. The dealer would bid as a representative of their client in an open auction and take a commission for their efforts but never normally take possession of the physical art unless their client requested it. Yet here was a single anonymous buyer of an unknown work in a huge deal being engineered by an experienced art dealer from a reputable, if small, gallery. With no paper trail of any description on the computer, the only alternative he could think of was that Philip Charlesworth was actually the seller of whatever was in the case, not a broker at all. If he owned the painting and could prove it, then there might not be an electronic trail. If it weren't for the two dead bodies, Henry wouldn't believe the case contained anything at all.

'What the hell sort of painting is worth £50m anyway?' Ashley asked, still unable to comprehend anything being worth that amount of money unless it was made of bricks and mortar and set in hundreds of acres.

'Quite a few,' Henry replied. ' The Card Players, by Cezanne sold for $259m in 2011. The co-founder of DreamWorks sold a Jackson Pollock for $140m in 2006. Bacon, Picasso, and Van Gogh - they all sell for multi-million dollar deals when they come up - but it's rare! Most of the premier works are in galleries and museums and unlikely to ever come up for sale. It's even rarer that a gallery like this would sell a work of that magnitude. They usually specialise in new artists or specific purchases. If that valuation is accurate I can't believe

Sotheby's, Christie's or Bonham's is not handling it. '

Another thought suddenly occurred to him. If his idea was correct then this could be a major breakthrough in the art world. His breathing increased and he started to feel a tingle of exhilaration he hadn't experienced for years.

'If there is no provenance or record of purchase then maybe this is already a stolen or lost painting?' He blurted as fast as he could speak.. 'The Nazis removed a huge amount of valuable art from various museums and galleries during the Second World War and sometimes a piece surfaces again unexpectedly. If Charlesworth has found one of these stolen works he couldn't possibly hope to sell it. Legally, the painting would simply be restored to its rightful owner but most institutions now pay a finders fee as an incentive to ensure its return. Sometimes up to 10% of its value as a reward. Maybe that's who he was taking the painting to. It would explain why someone else might try to steal it if they knew what it was, especially if there was no record of it being here. £5m compensation is a lot of money for whoever gets it back to the rightful owner. And unlike the theft of Mr Yau's painting, this one's not tainted with murder because it looks like no-one knows its here. If the cases hadn't got switched as we suspect, the police would just find two dead bodies and no stolen art. The text on his phone would mean nothing. The GPS trail would die as soon as the case was destroyed. It's actually a brilliant plan – steal a stolen painting and then claim you found it. I don't remember reading about a painting of that value going missing so it can't be a recent theft. Believe me my mum would know if it had and I wouldn't have heard the end of it.'

Henry began to examine the case more closely. The casing was large - the size of a suitcase but squarer and only about 5-inches thick. He lifted it up onto the top of the sideboard and turned it round, surveying it from all sides. It was heavier than he'd expected and made from a grey moulded metal. It appeared to be riveted with dozens of black studs all the way round the outside edge where the bottom and top halves joined. There was a leather handle and a digital number pad next to a small glass disk. On the side was a USB port - clearly the method by which the GPS tracking was enabled. There were no other markings on the outside to show that it was the property of the Lenister Gallery but Eoin confirmed it was exactly the same as the one he'd seen Philip preparing just before he'd been shot.

'Well I think we need to sort out the shit we are in first,' Ashley said, her thoughts returning to her family back in Tottenham. Given everything she'd just heard there could now be a professional hit man looking for Eoin as well as a Chinese gangster. Her family were her priority. She needed to do something. 'Whatever is in that case is probably the reason these two are dead. Either Yau is coming after Eoin or some maniac gunman is. What are we gonna do?'

'The GPS signal is currently in Windsor and has been stationary for a few minutes.' Tia refocused the group, scribbling down the GPS co-ordinates just in case the device became deactivated. 'I think the thief has got to his destination so we need to act quickly. Once he removes the contents from that casing we won't be able to track him any more. Fortunately he can't just destroy the case without damaging what's inside but I have no idea how long it will take for him to pick the lock. It looks pretty sophisticated, but it's the only lead to a murderer.' Her hangover was already forgotten and she'd now switched back to her usual fully focused mode. The logical side of her brain kicked into action, recalling everything she could remember from her visits to New Scotland Yard. What deductions could she make without jumping to conclusions or inventing evidence that wasn't there? Despite the devastation of death at her feet her nerves were tingling with excitement and for the first time in her life she felt like she was doing something important. They didn't have time to wait for the police. The GPS signal could disappear at any moment and the trail would go cold. She knew she could do whatever was needed to track this killer. She felt as if she had a purpose – one that was illegal, but important! Maybe her work today could help solve a double murder. That would make her father proud!

The thought suddenly hit her like a cricket bat.

Her father! Oh god, why hadn't she thought!

'Listen, we have to get out of her now!' she announced in a panic.

'Why?' asked Eoin as if leaving the building would mean finally facing the reality of the situation he had wandered into by chance.

'It's my father!'

'What's he got to do with this?' Henry asked.

'Nothing yet…. but I suspect he will have in the next few minutes.'

The three of them looked at her, puzzled. What was she talking about?

'He doesn't think I know,' she explained, already starting to pack up her software and flash drive. 'But he's had a squad car check on me every day since I started at Uni. When he finds out I'm not in class he'll start looking for me. It won't be long before he is running background checks on Henry and his car once he checks the traffic cameras outside the halls.'

Henry felt a flash of fear tear through his stomach.

'What do you mean background checks and a squad car? Who is your dad?' There were things he didn't want anyone to know, Tia least of all.

'He's the Assistant Commissioner for Special Operations with the Metropolitan Police.' She didn't notice the colour leach from Henry's face as she continued to press them out of the building. 'He's probably tracing your car at this very moment. We can't be caught in here - Eoin can explain why he's here - we can't. I've got everything from the hard drive on my memory stick,' Tia explained. 'I've deleted the trace on this case and there's no other evidence on here that this painting even exists. That should buy us enough time to try and track down whoever has the first case.'

'The guy just shot 2 people!' Eoin said incredulously. 'What are we gonna do when we find him? Ask him nicely to give it back?'

'No, we trade,' Tia explained. 'I've got a plan as to how we do that without getting killed but you're going to have to trust me. It won't be long before he discovers what's happened when he opens that first case - or worse, my dad arrives and catches me in the middle of a double homicide!'

Tia wiped the screen with the sleeve of her jacket to remove her fingerprints. She knew she would have to confess to her dad eventually but they didn't need to leave physical evidence as well.

'Bring everything you've touched with us,' she added, deciding they would deal with evidence tampering in due course. She was going to be grounded forever, even if they managed to escape jail.

'I just need to get something.' Eoin announced leaning over Charlesworth's body. He put his hand in his pocket and pulled out the card containing his fingerprints. 'Don't want that left lying around.' he said as he put the card in his back pocket.

Henry returned the contents to the secretary's bag and handed it to Tia.

'If he was going to track Eoin on his trip to the Mandarin Oriental, I'm guessing the GPS software will be on his phone.' Ashley said handing it to Tia also. 'Eoin, where's your car?'

'Grosvenor Square. But I can't take that – it's not mine. Stan will kill me!'

'And what exactly do you think will happen if the Chinese Mafia catch up to you? Or Tia's dad apparently!' Henry asked.

'Good point!' Eoin said taking the car keys out of his pocket. 'Come on Ash, you'll have to navigate!'

Before they left the building Henry handed Ashley the case.

'Why are you giving that to me?' she asked, flinching as though her skin had been burned by the touch of the £50m case.

'If Tia's dad is tracing my car and we get stopped after leaving a gallery I can't have a painting in the boot! I'd never explain that away, especially as I can't open it. They have no idea what car you're driving or that you're even here yet. Hopefully it will take them a while to find out that Eoin was booked and what car he used so you have a bit more time'

Eoin and Ashley left the gallery first. They crossed the road and turned right into South Audley St heading in the direction of the American Embassy. Ashley couldn't believe she was carrying a possibly stolen £50m work of art through the most intense coverage of CCTV geography in the world. When they reached the Mercedes she threw the case into the boot as though they were radioactive and ran to the phone box opposite.

Henry climbed into his Porsche, with Tia beside him. He opened the glove compartment, took out a small electronic device and plugged it into the cigarette lighter.

'What's that?' Tia asked.

'It's a GPS signal jammer,' Henry explained as if it were the most natural thing to have in a car glove compartment.

'Why do you have that?'

'It's a long story, but lets just say my parents are as paranoid about what I get up to as your dad seems to be about you.' He turned to her and gave her a cheeky wink. 'Fortunately I'm a bit more used to dodging their efforts than you are! I don't keep it plugged in all the time or they'd get suspicious if my car was constantly off the grid, but there are times when I don't want her knowing where I go! And I'd say this is definitely one of those times.'

He started the engine, which purred into life. As they turned left into South Audley Street and immediately right towards Park Lane he pulled a road atlas out from behind his car seat and handed it to Tia.

'Hopefully you know how to map read?' he said and headed down towards the A4 at Hyde Park Corner and out towards Windsor in pursuit of a killer.

Chapter 20

New Scotland Yard, London. Thursday Oct 16th 2014.

Stephen Hall had been at his desk since 7am. From his window he could see the famous rotating-wedge shaped sign four floors below him marking the entrance to New Scotland Yard. He'd already attended his weekly meeting with each of the divisional commanders and had just finished discussing budget requirements for the following year with his Director of Forensic Services.

The Metropolitan Police Service covered the entire Greater London area - all 32 boroughs. It's fifty thousand staff and five thousand volunteers protected a resident population of over 8 million people and a GNP of £600 trillion. It took a lot of money to protect that much collateral and managing budgets was one of Stephen's key responsibilities these days. He felt more like an accountant than a policeman.

Stephen Hall was the Assistant Commissioner for the specialist crime and operations directorate, which covered areas such as homicide, sex crimes and tactical support. He often thought it was ironic that his strategy to avoid gangs and guns when he was growing up in Brixton had led him now to the very job responsible for their covert surveillance.

He was the highest-ranking black officer in the country, in a police system that had less than 5% of its employees coming from ethnic minorities. Only the recent appointment of two female black deputy ACs had diverted attention away from him, for which he was extremely grateful - professionally and personally. 25 years ago such moves would have been unimaginable. Like his daughter he had seen prejudice move with the times, removing barriers and opening doors to unprecedented opportunities. He had been kept away from notoriously racist forces and stations to ensure he didn't let a moment of anger ruin his carefully structured promotional path. It had worked - Stephen Hall's self-control was impeccable. Not a foot wrong in 30 years. That was about to change.

He checked his watch. It was now nearly 11am and he was starting to feel anxious. He hadn't had a communication from the local Camden squad car to confirm Tia had made it to college and was safely inside the Engineering Building. The favour had been agreed with his colleague, the Assistant Commissioner for Territory Policing. For the first term, the local police would check on Tia each day until she was settled into a routine.

His staff were all aware of the reason behind Stephen's tactics for maintaining his vigil over his daughter. They knew about the serial killer he'd eventually apprehended when Tia was just four. Maurice Madison had only been close to her for a few terrifying minutes, but with 7 child murders attributed to him Stephen hadn't been prepared to take any chances. Tia fortunately couldn't remember the events and had no idea what lay behind her father's obsession with her safety. He and Frances had agreed she should never be told. Her confidence was already fragile enough. His team understood why he felt the need to have her watched constantly but weren't necessarily in agreement that the measures were for the best. They all secretly thought that Tia should be allowed to grow up and live her own life, but none of them was about to tell him this to his face. He was one of the best officers in the country, but his daughter was his blind spot. Many of them had known her since she was a little girl, when he had been a rising star within the force. She'd spent many holidays wandering round the various offices learning about their work - especially the computer and forensic labs that she found fascinating. However, whilst they felt his overprotective nature was extreme they understood it and were all only too happy to play their part in making her new independence as risk free as possible. In fact, many thought the more they could do to allay his fears about her safety, the more likely he was to give her some breathing space. One or two even secretly wished they could get a daily update as to the whereabouts of their loved ones first thing every morning.

Stephen Hall's daughter was actually a particularly valid subject for extra vigilance even now, and not just because of her dad's cautious nature. He had been responsible for the apprehension of dozens of notorious criminals including 3 terrorist bombers, not just the serial killer who'd threatened her. There were any number of interested parties who would make the most of an opportunity to hold her to ransom, or just take bloody revenge, if the chance ever arose and they found out who she was.

So for Stephen Hall, any break in her normal routine was a matter of concern to him. He didn't usually take the call from the squad car himself. He was happy for his secretary to relay the message when he was next free - but it had never been later than 10am. He checked the despatch boards for Camden to see the location of the nearest squad cars. Maybe they had to attend an actual police emergency, he thought to himself.

He gazed at the silver-framed photo on his large, well-ordered desk. It was his favourite photo of Tia with her mum on her first day at Newstead Woods School for Girls, in her bottle-green skirt and sweatshirt. It was one of the top three state schools in the country and they had been so proud of her when she passed the entrance exams.

Ever since she was born, Stephen had promised himself that his little girl would not have to go through the same hardship he'd suffered, fighting to stay in school while the race riots in Brixton in the early 80s raged around him. He'd alienated a lot of friends and family at that time. Brothers and cousins, who felt he should stand by them and fight against the oppression they were suffering at the hands of the police, refused to speak to him - some even to this day. But Stephen was clever. He knew the only way to beat the system was to join the system and change it from within. So far he'd been doing a pretty good job, despite the help he was unknowingly getting from above. He'd excelled in all the roles he'd been given and had won the respect of nearly everyone he'd worked with over the years.

So when he asked Camden police station to have a car drive by his daughter's hall of residence at 8.15 each day to check she left on time and was okay they were happy to oblige. A mobile squad car might as well be there as anywhere else.

The phone rang shrilly on his desk and disrupted his thoughts.

'Hello,' he snapped - his anxiety evident.

'It's the Camden patrol car, sir,' said Madeline Fox, his secretary, over the intercom. He could tell from her voice the news was not something he would want to hear. 'I think you should take this call yourself.' She transferred the call over to his phone.

'Assistant Commissioner Hall? Its officer Packham, sir, from Camden police force. We seem to have a bit of a problem, sir,' the speaker's voice was hesitant and he was clearly nervous. Stephen suspected he had delayed making this call for some time, contemplating his best course of action. It wasn't going to be good news, he could tell.

'Thank you for calling officer Packham.' Stephen tried to put the constable at ease to help speed up the story. 'Do you have a whereabouts for my daughter?'

'We don't know exactly, sir. She didn't come out of the building at her usual time. She'd been regular as clockwork every other day so we weren't sure what to do. We couldn't sit there all day waiting if she had a day off so we've been doing sweeps of the main road. We figured we would see her walking to the station once she actually left.'

'So where is she now?' The story wasn't doing anything to help Stephen's growing concern, which was always on maximum potential when it came to Tia. Ever since that first threat he'd lived on edge. Very real fears of a revenge attack guided every action he took regarding her safety; and the threats had been numerous, if not always serious, over the years.

'That's the problem.' There was a long pause; the pause of a man who has to deliver the worst possible news to a father; a father who just happens to be one of the most senior-ranking officers in the force.

'Well?'

'We caught sight of her driving off in a red Porsche Targa, at about 10am.'

'Did you follow her?'

'We couldn't. We were facing the wrong way and sitting at a set of lights. They turned right out of the side turning and went in the opposite direction. By the time we'd turned round they were out of sight. He was driving pretty fast and we lost him.'

'Did she arrive at college? Did you check with the university gatehouse security officers in Malet Place?' The head of university security had worked with Stephen for several years and was only too happy to put extra checks in place to log her arrival each day. The police network extended far beyond the current employees of the Met.

'Yes sir, we did. That's why we waited to call you in case the guy was just dropping her off.'

'Guy?' Stephen demanded. 'She was in a Porsche being driven by a guy? What guy?'

The air in the room went cold. The officer had expected the inquisition and had been warned by his CO not to make the call until he had more details. The delay in response told Stephen all he needed to know. The driver was clearly not a choirboy!

'Er, that's the problem sir!'

Stephen was rapidly losing patience and nerves.

'Get on with it for god's sake!'

'Well we ran his number plate. His name is Henry Whittaker; he's a 26-year-old American post-grad student currently doing a PhD in Biochemistry. College records show that he is the President of the Mixed Martial Arts Society and is a qualified instructor in Krav

Maga.'

'26!' Stephen yelled down the phone, unimpressed by the other achievements. 'Does he know she's only 19?'

'I don't know sir, but there is more you should know.'

Stephen couldn't speak! What could possibly be worse than a 26-year-old yank leaving his daughter's halls in the morning, driving a Porsche, with her in tow?

His office door opened without a knock and Andrew Hatcher, head of Intelligence, came in. He indicated to Stephen to put the phone on speaker. He held up a file of papers, suggesting he'd already been briefed.

'Its okay officer,' Andrew said into the microphone. 'I've got the full details here from my counterpart at the FBI.'

Packham let out an audible sigh - he did not want to be the one to deliver this news.

'He has a suppressed arrest sheet in the US,' Andrew said, laying the papers on the table.

'Oh my god, what did he do?' Stephen turned them round and started to read through a pile of emails.

'Well he was never convicted according to his visa application form, but there was a flag against him because of his involvement. The details I could get are sketchy but it seems he had some sort of a fight with a drug dealer when he was 18.' Andrew paused in anticipation of the expected explosion. 'There was a car chase and it ended up with his 17-year-old girlfriend being killed but it's been pretty comprehensively buried.'

Stephen bit his lip and sat back in his chair. His office was lined with the accolades and awards received over an exceptional career. Arranged in chronological order, they told the story of a journey through personal challenges and professional successes that only the truly dedicated and talented ever experience. He had faced gunfire, racism and extreme fatigue, but in an instant Stephen was completely cut off from his environment, his achievements and his training.

Emotions he had not experienced for 15 years surfaced into consciousness.

How had he missed this? Before Tia had even received her A-level results Stephen's team had completed background checks on all the main college faculty staff, including the management team at the hall of residence. How had he overlooked the sports department and the martial arts instructors? He had been the one who'd insisted she maintain her training regime at the college and he'd led her straight into the path of a drug user apparently responsible for the death of a young girl. The tips of his fingers started to go numb as the voice on the phone resumed telling the story.

Officer Packham relayed what he'd learnt so far as Stephen started to take notes, as he'd been trained to do. Slipping into autopilot he demanded licence details, number plate, visa application number - everything they had discovered so far. As he wrote he switched on his computer, logged into the immigration database and called up the passport details for Henry Whittaker III. His photo was four years old and showed a tanned, fit, good-looking male with hair cropped underneath and worn long on top. He looked assured, confident and slightly arrogant in the way only rich people do. Home address showed as Washington DC. Stephen could see why any woman would find him attractive. So why was he currently driving his 19-year-old daughter around London? Madeline was already waiting when he got off the phone.

'It's probably nothing,' she said as she took a seat and prepared to take instructions. 'Maybe they've just gone for coffee?' Even as she said it, she knew that until he found out where Tia was and who she was with, this was far from nothing.

'The boy is an interesting one,' Andrew said cautiously. He had already done a basic search based on the details given to the secretary.

'He's not a boy!' Stephen was choking down anger and fear, trying to stay calm. 'He's a 26-year-old man. A man who somehow got his girlfriend killed over drugs and covered it up. Do you think I want him anywhere near Tia?'

Andrew looked out of the window and tried to empathise. He wasn't sure how to behave in front of a man he had never seen lose his temper before but who was clearly struggling to maintain control and any rational sense at this moment. In his heart he knew he would never want his daughter in this position, even if there was a simple explanation. He turned back to his notes, deciding to stick purely to the facts for the time being.

'His Father is Henry Whittaker Jr. - US senator for New York. His Mother is Constance Whittaker, née Colefax. She was the sole heir to the Blue Star Pharmaceutical business when her mother died and, with her son's trust fund, is the majority shareholder. Her current personal worth is roughly $22 billion!' Andrew paused briefly to let this news sink in.

'That makes him one of the biggest kidnap risks in the world.' Stephen knew exactly what that meant and the stakes escalated. Kidnapping was part of his directorate's responsibility. He was well aware of the security protocols in place at the most expensive schools in America. Most of the fees paid by parents were to cover the costs of running what in effect were luxurious fortresses; such was the extent of the threats received by these families.

'There have been three attempted kidnaps, according to his police file.' Andrew was loading new pages onto his laptop, pulling together the fastest profile he'd ever delivered. 'They all happened before he was 14. Nothing since, so I guess whatever measures they put in place worked.'

'Was he there all night?' Stephen couldn't stop himself voicing his biggest concern out loud. Andrew had already anticipated that question.

'I've checked the traffic cameras outside the Hall of Residence. He turned up just before 10 am and left again 2 minutes later with Tia.' His eyes shifted slightly to the left as he knowingly omitted to add that he had been there the night before just before midnight and had stayed

176

for about half an hour. Until things became a bit clearer he didn't think Stephen needed to add that to his concerns just yet. He took silence as a sign to continue.

'He lives in a penthouse flat in the Barbican which is owned by the Blue Star Corporation. He had a history of bad behaviour when he was younger. Got expelled from two private schools, had a stint in rehab for drug and alcohol abuse and you know about the dropped charges involving a drug dealer. Since then he appears to have been a model citizen, although it looks like his parents keep him on a tight financial lead. He has been here for just over two years living off his parents money.'

Stephen stood up and began to pace behind his desk. If someone had asked him to put together a profile for the worst imaginable person that Tia could have brought home to meet him this would be pretty close to the result.

'He has a first-class chemistry degree from MIT and a postgraduate law degree from Harvard,' Andrew countered, trying to balance the character description to ease the stress each new snippet was obviously causing Stephen. 'He hasn't put a foot wrong in 8 years according to his university application and visa papers. He is here completing a PhD in Biochemistry, specialising in DNA identification methods, at UCL and is president of the Mixed Martial Arts association. I assume that's how they met.' Everyone in his department was aware of Tia's Wing Chun achievements.

Stephen sat back down and tried to regain his composure. The man was the worst possible character he could imagine! No work ethic and apparently no consequences to any of his actions! Mummy and daddy were always there to bail him out. The irony of his thoughts didn't even occur to him.

'And where are they at the moment?'

'I have my team checking the traffic cameras and we're trying the GPS on his car. Fortunately it's pretty distinctive, and luxury cars come with tracking devices as standard. It's a requirement of the insurance. We should know in a few minutes.' He paused and drew a nervous breath. 'You know it could be perfectly innocent don't you?' Andrew felt it was his duty to try and reason with his boss. 'They could just be doing a karate thing'.

'At 11am in the morning when she has lectures?'

Andrew's assistant, Sam Ainslie, senior officer within the forensic computing division, interrupted the conversation.

'We've located his car!' he said standing tentatively in the doorway. 'It's parked outside 50 Mount St, Mayfair. We can have a squad car there in ten minutes given the traffic. Do you want us to get someone to go and check she is okay?'

Stephen had a reputation for taking decisive action under extreme pressure. He had made life-or-death calls in the face of danger both to himself and the public he was paid to protect. This was personal. It was his baby girl; his only child. He rubbed his eyes and temples in a circular motion, a habit he'd developed at school when he was trying to work out a complex equation or formula. It helped him think. Here were three of the Met's top law-enforcement officers sitting in his office worrying about the whereabouts of his teenager daughter. He could not justify this use of their time just because Tia went to a martial arts club with a former wild child, even if she was a target for a potential revenge attack. Every fibre in his body wanted to run out of the building across St James's Park and Piccadilly as fast as his not-so-young body would carry him but he had been trained by one of the best police forces in the world to focus on the evidence and evaluate the risks. Tia would be furious if he turned up and she was actually just having coffee. She probably wouldn't forgive him for such a violation of her privacy and the freedom to live her life that she wanted so badly. She was an adult now. The throbbing in his veins started to subside as the rational arguments put forward by his well-meaning and straight-thinking team sunk in and calmed his nerves.

His perspective cleared enough to override his heart and go with the advice coming in from his head.

'Yes, get someone just to drive down there and check everything is okay. No need to approach them.'

Andrew smiled to himself. He had worked with Stephen for more than ten years and knew him well. He respected him enormously and knew he would see sense before doing something he might regret, seriously damaging the trust Tia placed in him. Sam was already onto despatch giving instructions.

'A squad car is on its way, Stephen. They will be there in less than ten minutes,' he confirmed, repeating the information coming through on his headphones.

'I'd have wanted to go down there if it was Alice,' Andrew confided quietly. He knew he'd have gone through the same emotional turmoil if he'd been told his daughter was with a man like Henry Whittaker.

'I'll get some coffee sent in.' Madeline got up from her seat as the tension in the room started to dissipate.

The coffee arrived two minutes later, the same time as Henry's GPS signal disappeared from Sam's screen. He couldn't hide the surprise on his face and Stephen could feel his shoulders tighten again.

'I don't understand,' Sam announced to the room. 'The car has just vanished from the grid.' He pulled the mouthpiece up on his headset and punched in the number for dispatch. 'Is the patrol car there yet?' He asked before repeating their response to the room.

'They've just turned up but the Porsche has gone.' As he spoke the others became aware of the colour draining from Sam's face. He was listening to further information from despatch that was visibly affecting his experienced reactions. He disconnected the call and pulled the headset from his ears. He stared at the table for a second before raising his eyes to meet the stares of his superiors.

'Another call just came into despatch.' Beads of sweat had started to form on his forehead. 'Someone just called in from a phone box in Grosvenor Square reporting gunfire in Mount St.'

Chapter 21

Mayfair, London. October 16th 2014.

Eoin was waiting in the Mercedes facing the gated gardens of Grosvenor Square as Ashley ran back towards him from the phone box. He glanced nervously over at the American Embassy on the opposite side of the gardens, convinced that every security camera they possessed was currently trained on him. Ashley checked the surrounding area before climbing into the passenger seat.

'I can't believe you've got us all involved in this, you stupid prick!' she shouted, desperate to vent some nervous energy as she started to contemplate the ordeal her mother might have to endure if they failed. She had no idea what a Chinese gangster might be capable of, but she knew what she would do if someone had stolen something from her worth £1.4m, or even 1% of that value. Plus, she'd seen first hand what the killer was capable of if he ever found out that Eoin had been in the building.

'How is this my fault?' Eoin sounded like an injured child pleading with his mother for comfort and support. 'I didn't kill them. I'm just a courier in the wrong place at the wrong time.' He didn't mention the drugs in the boot of his car that had stopped him from phoning the police.

'No. The wrong place is you living at my mum's when I told you to get out! If you'd done what I said then she wouldn't be in danger and I wouldn't be sitting in this bloody car with you!' She threw her bag onto the floor and jerked the seatbelt strap across her body, roughly jamming the clasp into its holder.

'Well I'm glad you're involved.' Eoin said, without really thinking about the words coming out of his mouth. He stared resolutely ahead and turned the car out of the parking space onto Park Street.

'What?' Ashley screamed, furious at his attitude. He turned and looked at her, halting his manoeuvres for a moment, and his shoulders dropped in despair.

''Well if you weren't here, I'd basically be buggered! I would either be facing a mad Chinaman or a copper alone - either way I doubt I'd be able to talk my way out of it that easily.'

'Why didn't you just call the police and tell them the truth? If you'd done that straight away maybe they could have got to the Chinese guy before he came after you?'

'I was too scared to come out straight away. I couldn't tell if the gunman was still there or not. I hid in the kitchen after I heard him shoot the girl and I could only see him when he moved beyond the pillar in the centre of the room. I figured he couldn't be working for the Chinese man; why kill the gallery owner when I was on my way to deliver a painting he'd already paid for. He had to be there for a different reason. I didn't realise what was in the other case!'

'Well then why didn't you call someone else? I don't have a clue what to do if we catch up with this guy! He's a professional hit man for god's sake!'

'I didn't know who else to call. If you hadn't rung back I would have had to call my uncle and then I'd never work again.'

'Well I'm glad we're doing all this to save your illustrious courier career!'

'I don't just mean I'd never work as a courier again, Ash! I mean I'd never work at all again! He dishes out punishment and asks questions after! I know it's not much of a job, but I'm not like you. I ain't got anything else going for me and it would be even harder to find work with two broken legs.'

'Well let's just see if we actually make it through this first shall we? Get a move on! We need to get to Windsor and pray this guy is still there.' Ashley got the phone out of her bag and dialled Tia's number.

In the Porsche, Tia's phone started to ring and Henry immediately took it from her. He looked at the name and answered the call as they passed the Natural History Museum.

'We can't talk on these phones.' He'd spent his life being briefed on what to do if he ever found himself in an emergency and needed to be tracked. Now he was putting all that advice into reverse. 'If Tia's dad is tracking my car you can bet he's tracing her phone and mine. Meet us in the car park of the Windsor Leisure Centre just off the M4.' He hung up.

'Take the SIM out of the phone and switch it off,' he told Tia, handing her phone back to her. 'And mine too. That should be enough to stop any trace for the time being.'

'Shouldn't I throw the phones out of the window?' Tia asked. 'That's what they do in the films.'

'That's just for added drama! I'm guessing at some point we may need to be traced as I have no idea how we deal with an armed gunman if he doesn't want to negotiate.'

'How do you know all this stuff?' Tia was impressed by his knowledge of surveillance.

'Let's just say this is not the first time I've had a run in with the police! I picked up a few tips from my dad's security team as well, especially how to avoid them. The families of New York senators have a high collateral apparently.' He decided his kidnap vulnerability was on balance the more palatable story.

'Your dad's a senator?' Tia gasped in awe, like a teenage boy band fan, instantly regretting her childishness. He must feel like he's babysitting a kid, she thought.

'Yes. So I know a bit about what it's like to have someone examining your life under a microscope. Although in my case it's not usually my dad - it's the press!'

Tia had a thousand questions formulating in her head but didn't have the nerve to ask any of them, although the stares from some of the guests at the Ivy now made sense. She wondered how much of this Ashley already knew. Henry's family or his past wouldn't intimidate her.

'How are you getting on with that GPS app on Charlesworth's phone?' he asked, changing the subject.

'I'm already in,' she replied, pleased with herself and feeling like she'd regained a tiny bit of her dignity.

'That was quick! How did you do that?'

'The code was the same as the phone lock.' Tia confessed. 'His secretary obviously wasn't the only one with a poor memory. My guess is she probably set it up for him. How is this still working if you've got a GPS jammer plugged in?'

'The jammer blocks a transmitted signal at a certain frequency so it's only blocking the one in the car. That's why we can't use our phones because they would still be traceable. Hopefully the police don't know we have Charlesworth's phone yet. Good work though, girl!' Henry smiled for the first time since arriving at the gallery, patting her knee gently. Tia blushed and returned to playing with the phone.

'My dad said most people are predictable with codes and passwords. Apparently they are the weakest link in any security system and it's all biometrics now.'

'Well lucky for us this murderer wasn't more knowledgeable and didn't know how to get into the gallery's computer and shut down the trace.' Henry moved into 4th gear as he pulled onto the Hammersmith flyover and sped up towards the Chiswick roundabout. 'Where is the case now?'

'It's still in the same location it was when we left the gallery. We have to hope he hasn't just taken the painting out and left the case behind. I'm not sure what our next move would be if we just found an empty case.'

'That's a strong possibility.' Henry said. 'If he is a professional then I guess he knows it's the case that is traceable. He'll want to get rid of it as soon as possible and transfer the painting to another carrier. The only thing on our side is that he has no idea Eoin was in the building and discovered the murders immediately. He probably thinks he has a few hours before the bodies are found and the trackers are activated. That's our only advantage at the moment. I suspect by now he has opened the case and realised he's got the wrong painting, although he may not actually know what art he was collecting. Our best hope is that he is now waiting for further instructions from whoever he is working for.' Henry went quiet for a few moments as he collected his thoughts. 'What I can't figure out is how someone knew Charlesworth had that painting at all. We've only got a single text to go on and that might have nothing to do with that case. If it weren't for the two dead bodies I would just assume the text meant he'd sold his entire business to someone. Even then it would be overpriced. In fact, it doesn't really make sense that someone like him would have a painting of that value at all! Everything else in his gallery was six figures or less. I'm guessing the painting destined for the Chinaman was the most expensive deal he'd had until he came across this £50m one. I wonder what it is.'

Tia tried to stay focused on her plan to intercept the gunman. She had barely spoken for the entire journey, her entire attention wrapped up in Philip Charlesworth's phone.

'At some point we are going to have to make a physical trade,' she said at last as they approached the Windsor turn off on the M4. 'That will require both paintings being in the same place at the same time and that gives us a few problems.'

'What specific problems would they be?' Henry could think of at least six.

'Think about it!' Tia said. 'He's an armed killer and we are four untrained students with no weapons! What if he decides to just take both paintings and shoot the four of us! That's what I'd do if I were him. The painting he has would be a £1.4m bonus that whoever he's working for effectively knows nothing about! We need to figure out a way to get his painting away from him before we hand over the second one.' Tia tried to sound confident in her plan

'Well you're the smart one!' Henry teased. 'Any ideas?'

'Maybe!' she replied.

Henry pulled into the leisure centre and parked in the middle of the busiest section of the car park between two Range Rovers, which provided cover from the security cameras as they got out and headed towards the car park entrance. Windsor was a royal borough and the surrounding vehicles blended well with his Porsche. A few minutes later Eoin pulled up in the Mercedes and Tia and Henry got in.

Eoin pulled out of the car park, following the directions shown by the tracker on Philip Charlesworth's phone.

Tia checked the details she'd remembered as soon as they were on the main road.

'Eoin, you said Mr Yau was staying at the Mandarin Oriental, is that right?

'Yes. He said that if I didn't take the painting straight there he would cause me all sorts of problems when he hunted me down.' Eoin sunk back into the seat, reminded of the fate he'd been threatened with.

'Okay so that means he should be approximately ten minutes behind us if he's taken the bait' Tia said, getting more animated.

'What do you mean, taken the bait.' Henry looked at her nervously. 'What have you done?'

'None of us is qualified to recover that painting on our own, but from Eoin's description I suspected Mr Yau would be more than capable.' Tia said, scrolling through the messages on Philip's phone. 'So when we left the gallery I sent a text from this phone telling him to leave immediately and head towards Windsor. I said I would phone with further instructions in 40 minutes. I've just been trying to figure out what those instructions should be but I think I've got a plan that should work.'

She pressed the green button.

The phone was answered almost immediately.

Chapter 22

Knightsbridge, 16th October 2014.

The Mandarin Oriental Hotel was built on one on the most expensive pieces of real estate in the world. Opposite its entrance stood the exclusive Knightsbridge shops of Harvey Nichols and Harrods. To the rear of the hotel, the vast expanse of Hyde Park afforded beautiful green views to those who could afford the most expensive suites. Cut off from the constant sound of traffic the occupants could have been overlooking a tranquil country estate rather than the violently beating heart of London.

Zhang Wei Yau didn't suffer from stress or worry, but he hated being made a fool of. 'Arbre Bleu' by Marc Chagall, purchased through the Lenister Gallery, was not the most expensive work he owned but he had been waiting for this piece to come up for sale for a long time and £1.4m was not a small sum of money.

But it wasn't about money - money was easy to come by. It was about respect! Anyone who was brave or stupid enough to disrespect him by taking something that was legally his would find out just how a humble Chinese businessman rises to the top of his field in a land of 900 million people.

He looked at his watch for the twentieth time that day. It was already past 11am. Charlesworth had told him the painting would arrive soon after 10am. He had been briefed on the security measures that had been put in place. He'd been given the details of the courier and his company and Charlesworth's secretary had confirmed that the case would be GPS tracked all the way to his hotel via a predefined route.

Yau had wanted to send his own men to pick up the case, but the gallery owner had refused the offer, explaining that he would not be in the office until after his flight had departed. He had assured him that arrangements were sound and that everything was in place for the transportation.

A short, stocky man came into the living room of the top floor suite and waited until Yau faced him to speak.

'We need to leave in 30 minutes if you are to clear customs in time, sir,' he said in heavily accented mandarin.

'I don't need to clear customs if I don't have my painting!' Yau barked in reply, picking up the phone and taking a card from his inside pocket.

He dialled the number for the Lenister gallery, punching the buttons hard as his anger continued to climb. If the courier had not left yet he would have to take the painting directly to Heathrow and meet him there. The phone rang for about a minute before the answering machine announced that the showroom was currently closed and enquiries would be dealt with as soon as someone was back in the office.

As he hung up, a text came through from Philip Charlesworth's mobile. He read it quickly, fighting every urge in his body to ring the man straight back.

'Is the car out the front?' he shouted at his security chief.

'Yes. Your luggage is loaded and my men are waiting for you.'

'Good we need to head towards Windsor as quickly as possible.'

The two men left the room and headed down to the lobby, and within a few minutes they were passing the Victoria and Albert Museum heading west.

Yau kept his hand on the mobile phone in his pocket for the whole journey. As they passed under the M25 he could stand it no longer. No-one told him what to do.

He was reopening the text from Charlesworth when his phone

started to ring and those very same details appeared on the screen as an incoming call.

'Where is my painting?' he shouted angrily into the phone.

'Mr Yau?' Tia tried to sound as grown up and confident as she could.

'Who is this? Where is Charlesworth? Where is my painting? He said delivery would be before 10am. My flight leaves in less than four hours and I'm already on my way to Heathrow.'

'As I said in my text, there has been a problem with your delivery Mr Yau. Its been stolen and Mr Charlesworth and his secretary have been murdered. I'm afraid I'm going to have to ask for your help if you want to see your painting at all!'

Chapter 23
Victoria, London . Thursday October 16th 2014

A car was waiting outside the entrance to New Scotland Yard in under a minute. Andrew had been on the radio to his team before Sam even finished relaying the message. Patrol cars were already on their way to Mount Street to secure the area and he was now briefing the detectives assigned to the kidnap division.

'Henry Whittaker is the sole heir to the majority shareholding of a $62-billion-dollar company and his car was in the vicinity of reported gunfire.' His brief was efficient and conveyed the urgency felt by all three of the senior team. 'We have to treat this as a possible abduction until we can confirm the whereabouts of the car. We need to get this right first time. Don't overlook anything.' He paused to allow the news they had just heard sink in. 'Also, Assistant Commissioner Hall's daughter, Tia, is potentially with him.'

Stephen sat in the passenger seat in silence, allowing his team to do their jobs regarding first response. The driver put the blue light on top of the unmarked car, which sped down Birdcage Walk towards Buckingham Palace. The traffic on Park Lane divided like the Red Sea as they blared down the right-hand lane before turning into Grosvenor Street. Officers were already taping off both ends of Mount St when they arrived.

'I want every shop owner in the street questioned in the next ten minutes' Andrew was still issuing orders when their car pulled up in the space that had been occupied by Henry's Porsche not fifteen minutes ago. 'We need to establish if anyone else heard anything and where the shots came from.'

'The caller didn't give any details as to the location.' Sam was continuing to gather information via the phone and his laptop. 'They just said that two shots had been fired from inside a building. They didn't give a name and hung up when the operator tried to question they further.'

'Was it a male or female?' Stephen asked, speaking for the first time since they'd left the Yard. His concentration was on forcing his mind to stay calm. He knew that panic now would be a bigger problem for Tia if she needed his help and he was not about to let her down again.

'Female, with a strong London accent.' Sam spoke as he continued to tap information into his laptop. 'The telephone box has already been cordoned off so we can get prints.'

'Any sign of the Porsche on the traffic cameras yet?'

'Not yet. It's so busy at this time if day. We won't get any flag until it's picked up and analysed on a Congestion Charge camera with number plate recognition. Even then it will only give us a rough direction and will still take time to process. We've prioritised the feeds from all entry points within a mile of here and have gone back 20 minutes. We should get something in the next 15 minutes or so.' Sam could feel the adrenaline course through his fingers as he worked. He had been one of the best Detective Inspectors in the Met and missed being close to the action now he was confined to a desk.

Stephen and Andrew got out of the car and went into the Mount Street Deli, which was the busiest shop in the street coming into lunchtime. They summoned the owner from behind the counter, ignoring the queue and discreetly holding out their badges.

'Did you see a red Porsche parked outside just now?' Stephen asked in a tone harsher than he would normally use but the owner was left in no doubt as to the urgency of the question.

'Yes. They left about fifteen minutes ago. Two kids by the look of them!'

'Did you see which way they went?' Stephen continued.

'No, we've been rushed off our feet all morning. It's cold and people want coffee. I haven't been out from behind the counter since 7.30am.'

Stephen looked around at the queue of customers; they were all staring up at the menu boards on the walls behind the counter - none of them was facing the street.

'Did you hear anything in the last fifteen to twenty minutes that may have sounded like gunshots?'

'Gunshots?' The expression on the shop owner's face was enough to confirm he had no idea what Stephen was talking about. Several customers in the queue turned towards the street, apprehensive and expecting to see trouble in progress. A couple involuntarily backed away from the windows.

Sam came into the coffee shop followed by the constable who'd been the first to arrive.

'All the shop owners have been questioned apart from two. No one claims to have heard anything.' He was already starting to think that maybe this was a false alarm. If this was a badly timed prank the perpetrator who would feel the full force of the Met's capability in tracking them down once the facts were known.

'Which two buildings?' Stephen asked.

'Number 37, looks like it used to be a dry cleaners.'

'That was Mario Acosta,' the coffee shop owner volunteered, still listening to the conversation. 'He closed down about 6 months ago and moved back to Sicily.'

'And Number 50,' Sam continued. 'The art gallery opposite.'

'That's Philip Charlesworth. He should be there! He was in here this morning getting his usual coffee and I haven't seen him go out since.' The shop owner moved closer to the window as he spoke, trying to see what was happening. 'What's going on? Is he in trouble?'

'I don't know. But I need you to write down the names of all of your regular customers who have been in here in the last half an hour.'

192

The three policemen went back out into the street and ran across the road to the Mayfair gallery. Stephen pushed hard on the front door, but it wouldn't budge. He moved quickly out of the doorway and pressed his face against the window, cupping the sides of his eyes with his hands. The venetian blinds were drawn and angled to protect the art from the damaging effects of the sun, but inside he could just see a male, lying in a pool of blood on the floor. In an instant his loyalties divided. As a father he wanted to ignore the scene that he was looking at and find Tia, but as the Assistant Commissioner for policing he knew this was more important. He mouthed a solitary prayer that his conflicts were in no way connected and slipped into his professional mode.

'Get the door open - now! We have a man down inside,' he barked at Andrew 'Get more back up here immediately! I want CCTV footage from all the premises in the street!'

'This is a metal-framed door with bolts built into the frame, sir.' Andrew was already running his fingers around the frame to check the tightness of the seal. 'There is no way we are breaking this down without taking the wall out.'

'Then break the bloody window!' Stephen shouted. 'We have a wounded man inside!'

Frenzy erupted on the exclusive Mayfair street. Sam and the driver came over with a battering ram from the car and the toughened glass eventually shattered into the gallery as they took out the first pane. Stephen climbed through the breach and activated the emergency exit button on the wall letting Andrew and Sam into the building. He then went to check for vitals on the body. He didn't need to - the man had a severe gunshot wound to the head. The bullet had entered through the front of his forehead, almost in the centre of the face, and exited just behind the ear at the base of the skull judging by the bone area that was missing. Whoever shot him was tall; noticeably so. As he knelt down to feel the cooling wrist in an attempt to gauge a rough time of death he spotted the woman behind the desk.

'God! There's another one! Check her pulse!'

Andrew ran over to the desk and bent down to look at the stunning brunette, slumped backwards in her chair, with a single bullet hole through her forehead. Her facial features seemed fixed in the scream she had tried to expel when she died. 'She's gone!' In his experience the congealing pool of blood suggested she'd been dead for a couple of hours. 'When did you say the call came in?' he asked Sam.

'About twenty minutes ago.' Sam was already documenting the findings at the crime scene so he could brief the forensics team. They all knew not to touch anything.

'It looks like she's been dead at least an hour! Whoever made that call couldn't have just heard shots! Why did they wait so long to call it in?' Andrew knew no one in the room could answer his question but he worked best by talking aloud.

Outside three more police cars pulled up alongside the pavement - this time with sirens blaring and lights illuminating the fashionable street. The kidnap team were joined by two detectives from homicide who already knew they were superfluous and were there just to carry out the routine checks given the senior nature of the officers already on site.

'Find out who they are.' Stephen said - an instruction already in progress. Within 15 minutes the forensics teams had equipment laid out ready to begin the detailed fingertip examination of the premises.

The most senior team ever to preside over a single crime scene gathered in the small kitchen and began an initial debrief on what they'd discovered so far.

'The man is Philip Charlesworth. He owns the business and his family have been art dealers for over 75 years.' Andrew began, reading from his rarely used notebook. 'The woman is his secretary, Serena Holdsworth. She's worked here for two years since her graduation from the Slade and is the granddaughter of Lord Astell, the newspaper owner. This is going to be a nightmare! The press are like starving vultures when it's one of their own.'

'Could any more high-profile kids be involved in this?' Sam said as his usual gallows humour helped him cope with the scene he had just walked into. He swallowed hard and skipped a breath as he suddenly realised who he was talking to. 'Sorry!' he mouthed silently. Stephen understood the mechanisms by which people dealt with shock and just nodded as Sam went back to the mahogany desk to resume his CCTV checks.

All three officers knew the coverage of this event would be global. Astell's family would do whatever was within their considerable power to ensure the killer was apprehended. They couldn't afford to make a single mistake. Fortunately their collective experience meant that none would be made.

'Is anything missing?' Stephen asked Andrew.

'It doesn't look like anything is missing from the gallery. We're just checking the computer but most of the real stock is in the vault in the basement. The door to the basement has a security code so we'll have to wait for the company that installed the equipment to get here and override the access codes before we can check that, but it doesn't look like anything on the shop floor had a value high enough to kill for!'

'How did the killer get in? We had to smash the window. Somebody must have let them in. Where are we with the CCTV footage?' Stephen continued to drill his team through the protocols.

'The CCTV for the premises has been deactivated. It looks like it's actually been switched off from inside.' Sam called them back into the gallery and took them through his rechecks of the control panel in Serena's desk drawer, but there was no mistake. The whole system was physically shut down. The screens on her desk were blank and the recorder had stopped at 9.25am. Sam began to replay the footage he did have. He rewound the recording on triple speed until Serena arrived. 'The secretary arrived for work at 8.30pm and there's a youth in a suit arriving at 8.45am. The diary on her desk suggests he's a courier booked to take a painting to a Mr Yau, who's staying at the

Mandarin Oriental in Knightsbridge. Charlesworth arrives just after 9.15 and he's carrying the coffee from the shop opposite, which ties in with what the owner told us. Then the tape stops.'

'So there is no recording showing the courier leaving?' Stephen asked.

'No, there's nothing else after 9.25, although he wasn't due at the hotel until 10am and it's only 5 minutes away.'

'Well he's not here, so we have to assume for now that he either left to make his delivery after the security system was shut down or he's the gunman. This looks like a professional hit. Two shots - two victims - both headshots. I can't imagine a professional would leave a witness to just walk out the door.'

'I don't believe he'd leave footage of his arrival on this system if he was the courier. Why switch it off and not erase the previous 45 minutes? We need to assume there are two possibilities. A second person might not have realised the courier was here if he was in the kitchen. It's two-way glass in these doors. The killer might not have been able to see him, and if he wasn't expecting anyone else to be in the building why waste time looking around?'

'Unless the courier was the killer! We need more footage. What about other shops and offices? Everyone round here must have some form of security.' Stephen instinctively checked his phone in case Tia had contacted him. He prayed she hadn't been close when this happened.

'Judging by the camera angles on the outside walls, the only one that has a partial view of the front door is the antique shop opposite. An officer has secured their system. We are just pulling the files off their computer now. Should be a few minutes or so.' Sam could barely keep up with the flood of possible evidence.

'Anything else from the computer in here?' Andrew hadn't realised the print behind the sideboard was a PC screen until Sam switched it on.

'There're two things of interest so far, although I've only had time to check recent file activity and his email. The email chain with Mr Yau confirms that the courier was delivering a Chagall purchased last week for £1.4m from Christie's. The commission transfer for £140,000 cleared the day after the sale. It all looks pretty legit.' Sam clicked back to the home screen and pulled up the control panel. 'The second thing is a bit more concerning. At 10.15am someone loaded a program file onto the computer and changed the password to get into the system using the same program that I've just used - exactly the same file, which was developed specifically for us! They also accessed the email program and a GPS tracking program but there's no live trace showing at the moment. It could be that the transmitter has been deactivated or whoever accessed the system turned it off, but it will take me a while to find out when the last trace was running.'

'So we think whoever did this accessed their computer? It's unusual for a gunman in a busy Central London building to hang around in case someone has called the police?' Andrew tried to sift through the logic in his head.

'I assume they used a silencer,' Sam pointed out. 'No one in the street heard any gunshots.'

'So who made the 999 call?' Stephen added to the growing pile of questions as the officer arrived with the CCTV files from the antique shop.

The team worked quickly and effectively - the laptop was uploaded with the last three hours of footage from the morning. Unfortunately their security system was also antique by current standards. It had five cameras but only one recording device. The officers watched as 30-second images scrolled through a two-and-a-half-minute loop. The cameras covered the back door and both floors of the shop as well as the street. The camera angle captured only half of the door to Lenisters and for only 20% of the time. The officers watched as a youth in an ill-fitting suit was let into the shop at 8.45am, which concurred with the gallery footage. It failed to record the arrival of Philip Charlesworth or anyone else in the estimated time frame. Successive 30-second vignettes showed the street was filled with commuters and residents rushing to work until just after 9am but no one paid any attention to the gallery. The officer who had retrieved the footage fast-forwarded the file another frustrating 30 minutes in which nothing of significance was recorded. The camera angle wasn't wide enough to even show the Porsche arrive and park just to the right of the shop front. Then Stephen's world turned upside down.

As the tape timer turned to 11.09 a tall willowy figure was captured leaving the building. Stephen knew immediately who he was looking at - and so did his team.

'It looks like we really do need to find Tia now!' Andrew said, knowing this was now about to be the worst day of his career.

Chapter 24

Joseph Colthart sat on the only chair in the crowded basement of a closed down retail unit in St. Leonards Rd, Windsor and laid out the tools he'd brought with him to complete his assignment. His Crombie overcoat and silk tie, which had blended him seamlessly into the Mayfair street this morning, were discarded and draped carelessly over a dusty box. His sun-damaged, pockmarked skin and unkempt black hair aged him beyond his 39 years. He was tall, fit and completely lacking in empathy. His chosen profession would have been foreseeable had he been assessed for psychopathy as a child growing up in Zimbabwe but his parents had attributed his animal experiments to intellectual curiosity rather than cruelty. Even if he'd been diagnosed it was unlikely he'd have been deterred, such was the pleasure he gained from his work.

The premises he'd chosen had previously been an Oxfam charity shop, unable to cover the soaring rent in an area marked for gentrification. It was an unremarkable corner unit on a parade of uninhabited shops waiting for a developer to take over the entire block and revive the less fashionable end of the royal town.

The ground-level shop floor was completely empty, with whitewashed windows on two sides and a mounting pile of uncollected post. The glass front door led onto the main road and a paper notice gave details of the charity's nearest alternative collection site. In contrast and out of view the downstairs room was still exactly as the previous tenants had left it, with stacks of boxes full of unwanted jumble and piles of junk. There was a tiny bathroom at the foot of an unusually steep flight of stairs that led up to a small hallway at the back of the shop and the wooden side access door.

Joseph had chosen this location for a number of reasons based on years of experience. Primarily, there were no neighbours to notice any strange comings and goings, and the units were being marketed by the estate agent as a collective group so a visit from a random buyer was highly unlikely; secondly, it was close to where he was due to meet his client once he'd extracted the contents from the case; and most importantly, the separate side entrance was fenced off and not visible from the main road. The door lock had been easy to pick and had taken him less than 30 seconds to get through.

The large metal case was balanced carefully on top of an old display cabinet filled with costume jewellery. It was custom made to carry stretched canvas paintings without their decorative frames and Colthart could tell immediately that the gallery owner had been the victim of unscrupulous misinformation when he bought this container. The casing itself was made with the highest quality composite metal. Cutting through it would have taken days and almost certainly have destroyed the contents inside. Next to the handle was a digital combination lock with a small glass disc that required a thumbprint in addition to the 6-digit code to deactivate the lock. Joseph also knew that this model had a relocking system that would trigger additional bolts from an independent system if the incorrect code was entered too many times. These electronic gadgets were no doubt key selling features highlighted by the salesman to an unknowledgeable customer, but they were all virtually useless because, like most safe's, the lock had a mechanical override system that made it possible to bypass the main locks if you knew what you were doing. Primarily used only by the manufacturer, it would probably take him about 3 hours to deactivate the case this way - 2 if he was lucky but this wasn't his primary expertise.

Using two picks that looked like dentists' scrapers he flipped the glass thumbprint reader out of its surroundings, careful not to damage the connection wire that might trigger the relocking mechanism. As he worked he glanced intermittently at his mobile phone. Charlesworth had been 15 minutes late arriving at the gallery and now his carefully timed schedule was off track. He knew he would receive details of his final destination, once he confirmed that he'd acquired the item he'd been paid to steal, but his client wasn't used to being kept waiting. It wouldn't be long before they lost patience and that was never good for business.

Underneath the glass disc was the mechanical means by which in 128 patient minutes of 'jiggling' he was able to lift the lid back on its hinges, revealing the contents inside its foam moulding. The painting was smaller than he had expected without its frame. It took a second or two for his brain to register that what he was looking at could only be described as bizarre. He was no art lover, but he'd been told he was collecting an impressionist portrait. His knowledge was limited but a bride and groom floating in a tree above a plate full of fruit was stretching the description of portrait a bit far, even by modern art standards. And in the bottom left corner the signature read Marc Chagall.

Something had gone wrong!

He sat staring at the contents of the metal case for what seemed like hours. Joseph had not worked for this particular client before and another booking just became extremely unlikely - or any other booking unless he could figure out what had happened.

His instructions had been simple. He'd been told to arrive at the gallery entrance at precisely 9.15 am and not a second before. He'd get a text once the internal video surveillance system was switched off. Once he'd rung the bell he should then wait for no more than 90 seconds for the door to be opened. If it wasn't he needed to walk away and repeat the exercise every 10 minutes precisely until he was inside. He knew the CCTV cameras in the antique store opposite were on a rotating loop so he had to time the 30-second windows that he needed to avoid carefully, both for entering the building and when he left, allowing for some margin of error. He'd watched Charlesworth enter the gallery 15 minutes later than expected, at 9.15 and had to wait a full 10 minutes before approaching the front door. His first attempt had been unsuccessful because the secretary was on the phone so he'd circled south into Berkeley Square and the text had come through. At 9.36am the door had been opened electronically as expected. Charlesworth had the case on the sideboard, ready for transportation, exactly as he had been briefed. He knew the tracker had been activated but he had plenty of time before anything untoward was discovered. His client had seen to that.

Dealing with Charlesworth and his secretary had been his immediate priority. He hadn't wasted time with rope and gags - especially when there were two of them. It was much simpler to just take them out with a silenced revolver before they could activate any secret panic alarms. He knew his client would not object to adding murder to this particular theft - fewer loose ends. Besides, it was his reward to himself for carrying out the job; his favourite part of any operation. Watching the life disappear from a creature's eyes as the bullets tore through brain tissue and bone had fascinated him as a boy growing up in Harare. He'd started out torturing wild animals before claiming his first human victim. The boy had been breaking into what he thought was an empty house when 13-year-old Colthart shot him in the side of the head. Over 25 years he'd perfected his craft and marketed his talents to an elite, powerful and growing client base.

Colthart had been in and out of the building in less than 5 minutes. Once the gallery door closed behind him, he knew there was no way to get in without a key. No one would discover the theft until the cleaners turned up that evening, by which time the contents would be in a different county to the casing - possibly even a different country.

Now he sat on the wooden chair and collected his thoughts. He couldn't understand what had happened. Everything had been exactly as he'd been briefed by his colleague. How was he going to break this news to their client? He had the wrong painting.

He jumped up from the seat and punched the side of the display cabinet, shattering the real glass all over the glass jewellery and spattering it with blood from his lacerated hand. The heavy case rocked awkwardly on top of the frame and he caught it before it crashed to the floor. He sighed and felt a twinge in his stomach he had never experienced before. He took a handkerchief from his coat pocket and wrapped it round the small but deep cut on the palm of his hand.

Joseph was clear about and comfortable with the fact that he was a violent sociopath who felt no remorse when hurting people. Possessing these traits also meant that he recognised them in others. So he was well aware that this particular client was ruthless and cruel, even by his standards, and more than capable of hurting others. Joseph knew they had access to unimaginable resources but wasn't entirely sure why they paid him so handsomely to do jobs he was convinced they would prefer to carry out themselves - just for fun! Now he had to contact them and tell them their plan had somehow gone wrong.

He tried to recall the scene again to identify the mistake but knew it didn't really matter. It was the wrong painting and that was all they would care about. He couldn't put it off any longer. He had to make the call. He took out a pay-as-you-go phone from his pocket and dialled the only number in the memory.

His client answered on the second ring, obviously waiting for news they had been expecting for over an hour.

'Have you got it?' they said impatiently.

'I'm no art expert,' Joseph explained, aware that any normal person would be experiencing a racing heart and profuse perspiration at this stage. He wondered what that must feel like. 'but this is not the painting you thought it was going to be.'

———

Two hundred yards away, in the Costa Coffee at the other end of St. Leonard's Rd, Tia was defending her plan. They could lose the signal at any moment. Time was rapidly running out and they'd needed to do something now.

'Tell me again why Ashley had to go on her own?' Henry said.

'She volunteered!' Tia replied facetiously. 'Seriously, we need to make sure the painting is still in the building and not just a discarded case before we give a Chinese gangster our actual location. I've pulled up the floor plan of the building from the estate agent's website. There is a small basement with a separate toilet, which is where I suspect he will have taken the case to deactivate the tracker or remove the contents. All she needs to do is knock and verify that someone is there then let Yau's men deal with the thief. Once she confirms they're still there she'll send a text to Yau with the actual address and then get out of sight. I've told Yau he has about ten minutes to get his painting back before the police arrive following our tip off. If everything goes to plan, he gets his painting, the killer gets arrested and we don't have to confront either of them directly.'

Henry stared at her, willing his not-insignificant intellect to catch up to hers. She had set in motion an unbelievably dangerous plan without consulting any of them but he couldn't come up with anything better. Her brain had mapped out scenarios and tactics way beyond the obvious, like a chess master. The sheer brazen nature of her idea had shocked him. Where did this waif-like teenager learn to think like that? Her dad may be head of the police but she had a bright future as a master criminal if she chose to follow it!

'What if the killer takes out Yau's men and gets away before the police arrive!' Henry said.

'I thought about that and there's nothing we can do if that happens. At least Yau won't go looking for Eoin as he'll know it wasn't him that stole his painting so we'll be one bad guy down. We've got no way of contacting the killer so we can't negotiate with him directly to give him back the painting he wanted. We'll just have to wait and see what happens and hope he didn't know who Eoin worked for. Yau sounded confident his men could recover the painting. I did give him the option of leaving it to the police but it seems he doesn't have that high an opinion of my dad's team! He wanted to deal with it himself and they are ready when Ashley gives the signal. Now all we can do is pray.'

Eoin came back to the table with three cappuccinos and sat down in the vacant seat.

'I know it's a risky plan, but we are not equipped to deal with this murderer on our own,' Tia continued. 'At least not while he has a gun and is clearly an expert in using it. No amount of martial arts training is going to help us against a bullet. I've been through all the possible permutations of interactions we could have with the killer and none of them come out favourable for us. We came here to make an exchange but we don't actually need to give him the painting he was after - all we need to do is enable Yau to get his painting back. Our thinking in the gallery was flawed and fortunately it works in our favour. '

Eoin looked up from his coffee, desperate for some good news right now. He couldn't control the feelings of guilt raging through his brain at the amount of trouble he'd dragged these two complete strangers into. Tia noticed his expression and tried to explain her thinking to them both.

'This killer clearly had no idea you were in the gallery or he wouldn't have left you there.' She tried to reassure him. 'Unlike Mr Yau, however, he doesn't know a courier was booked to collect a second case, or which courier company you worked for and now has no way of finding out given the only other people who knew are both dead. He can't go back to the gallery either as my dad is probably searching for fingerprints personally as we speak. My plan is banking on Yau's ability to carry out the threats he obviously made to Charlesworth should his painting go missing. Well it has gone missing, and all we need to do is verify that it's where we think it is. If it's not, then start thinking of a new plan.' Tia smiled to hide the anxiety that her racing heart was creating. She had no idea if this was going to work but it was her best guess.

'But seriously, what if it isn't there! You've already told Yau roughly where we are!' Eoin was almost crying at the thought of the imminent arrival of the Chinese gangster he'd been hired to deliver to and failed.

'If it isn't there then we are no worse off than we are now - except that Yau knows someone else stole his painting. I haven't told him where we are; I've told him where the painting is. As far as Mr Yau is concerned I am just an innocent eyewitness caught up in a theft that went wrong and with access to the tracker. As long as Ashley can confirm it's still in that building Mr Yau seems more than willing and capable of retrieving it himself, I hope!'

'And once he's got his painting he will have no reason to start searching for a courier that didn't even take possession of the art, leaving Ashley's mum in the clear.' Henry said, clearly impressed.

'Well his incentive is a bit more than just getting his painting back.' Tia added with a grin. 'According to my Internet search he is wanted in Taiwan under suspicion of the murder of a factory owner. I simply told him the truth of what happened at the gallery this morning and pointed out what conclusions the police might reach when they eventually realise it is his work of art that has been stolen. Revenge is a powerful motive for murder in their eyes. If, on the other hand, he could get his painting back and say that the courier delivered it on time as expected then both him and Eoin would be off the hook - they could corroborate each other's stories.'

'But what about the phone call you made from Charlesworth's phone to Yau? The police will be able to access the phone records. Why would someone contact him from that phone if he had nothing to do with it and had received his painting as planned? It couldn't have been Charlesworth - he was dead.' Henry pushed his hair back out of his eyes, certain he'd found a flaw in Tia's argument.

The teenager thought for a moment, running the scenarios through in her head.

'Eoin will just have to say Charlesworth gave him his phone so he could call Yau when he arrived at the hotel! It's not great, but right now it's all we've got. Besides, worrying about who made a phone call could be the least of our worries if the killer gets away with Yau's painting, because as of now we can no longer see where he is!'

She turned the phone to face them – the signal had disappeared from the screen.

Chapter 25

Egham, England, December 2011.

Boris's business was growing, but not without cost. He'd made many enemies over the years and the move to England had been a necessary step to protect his family from rivals in the increasingly violent Russian Bratva. At his new home in Egham, on the edge of Berkshire, he could run his empire relatively free from the fear of reprisal waiting outside his front door. Boris could look after himself but he couldn't be with his wife and children all the time. He had powerful allies but the fragmented nations of the former Soviet Union were locked in permanent battle for dominance, politically and economically, and corruption was endemic. Money bought power, and power ensured survival. The wealth that derived from the blood on his hands tainted the treasures on his walls. He needed something new to inspire him. His unfaltering, almost religious, belief that his good fortune was intrinsically linked to his love of art grew stronger. But where was the fun or the skill in buying at an auction? Anyone with enough money could do that. His joy came from the careful planning and patience that only a true master can employ. Even his new home was an architectural masterpiece, practically stolen from the bankrupt conferencing company he'd bought it from for a fraction of its value. At the height of a recession, cash is king.

He knew his wife loved her new home. She had never felt comfortable living in a hotel, even if it was the best her homeland had to offer. Over the years they had bought many properties in different countries but had never settled for more than a few months in any of them. The assets always felt like business transactions rather than somewhere they could re-establish roots for their family. Staying in Russia had not been an option if the children were ever going to have a normal life. Despite the challenges he'd faced, his business was growing. The oil field proved to be as fruitful as expected, even if the cost of extraction and transportation had increased significantly. His business was taking care of itself and his thoughts were filled almost entirely with his primary pursuit.

Boris had spent the first year after stealing the journals from Cecilia Roux in a permanent state of anger and frustration. It had taken Vasily months just to work out what language the banker had used to write his lifelong chronicles and then more time to learn the Occitan dialect from the south of France. He knew, just as certainly as he loved his wife and children, that the diaries held the key to a prize that would radically alter his future.

It was almost ten years since he'd first read the interviews that Rene Secretan had given to the journalist, Victor Doiteau, in 1956, and then again in 1957. The release of the film 'Lust for Life' had prompted the banker to finally speak out about what he had called the inaccurate and incompetent investigations by the police in Auvers almost 60 years before. He'd been an old man when he decided to break his silence and speak to Doiteau, but was a credible witness even after so many years. The underlying tone of his assertion, that Van Gogh had not been in the wheat fields on the day of the shooting, hadn't received much media attention, but it had convinced Boris that Rene Secretan knew more about the death of Van Gogh than anyone realised. From the first moment of reading what amounted to a contradiction of the accepted version of events he knew this Frenchman was hiding something more than just the geography of the shooting. When Vasily had obtained the copy of his will from his former employers, confirming the existence of a letter that had been left with someone in London, Boris became convinced there was more to the suicide than anyone believed. On the day after the shooting two peasant eyewitnesses had placed Vincent down by the river but they had been ignored in favour of the artist's personal version of events, voiced emphatically by Ravoux. Now a distinguished gentleman had corroborated them. Rene Secretan either knew something or had something that could potentially rewrite the accepted history of the death of the most famous impressionist artist ever.

Van Gogh had been a prolific letter writer and public interest in his communication with his brother, which had been painstakingly translated by Theo's wife, Jo, had been critical to developing the intrigue and fascination with his life and his work. What if the letter Secretan had taken to London were a signed confession of the truth by the artist himself, or maybe the whereabouts of the missing gun? Boris didn't know what secret the banker had spent his life hiding, but he knew in his very soul that it was significant enough to change history. And he knew that the answer lay in those diaries.

The lawyers of Swiss Re had prepared the will in 1956, just over a year before Rene had died at his Paris home. The only change from the previous draft, which had been in the file along with the executed version, had been the addition of the letter, left with someone in London. All other terms of the will had remained the same. His secretary had her annuity and now his house was a school for orphaned boys in Paris.

Boris had concluded that whatever the envelope contained, the covering letter at least had to have been written in the final years of Rene's life, so when they'd started the process of translating the diaries they began at the end and worked their way backwards.

For the last three and a half years the two men had painstakingly worked through the journals in reverse chronological order. It had taken them a year to find a trip to England that held promise. It had not been recorded in the appointment diary kept by Cecelia and Boris wondered if she'd even known he'd gone there.

The trip was detailed in the journals covering 1949. The slivers of information seemed to fit with what they were looking for.

'He visited only three places during his two day visit,' Vasily had informed Boris. 'He stayed at the Goring Hotel in Belgravia and had appointments at an unspecified address in Bond St; the London branch of his former company and the Reading Room at the British Museum.'

Vasily had researched each of the establishments in detail. If this was the visit they were looking for then he'd narrowed the search.

'There were a number of art galleries on Bond St in 1949, mainly surrounding Sotheby's and the Fine Art Society. Most of them have gone now and been replaced with retail shops. We may never find the owners if it was one of them. One still remains and another moved to bigger premises in Mount St in 1974. I suspect the only way we will find out if this is where he went is to actually visit the galleries and speak to the owners.'

Boris knew they did not have enough yet to make a trip worthwhile.

'Even if we visit these establishments, we have no idea what we are looking for. We can't just turn up at a London gallery and ask to see a letter left with them over 50 years before. Whatever it is that Rene Secretan is hiding, the clues we need are in these journals. A man as influential as him does not keep such a detailed account of his life in a foreign language for no reason. He has buried his story in millions of words so that one day it may be discovered and our job is to find that story. Until we know what he has hidden we are blind. We must continue our translations and trust that God will lead us to the truth that we seek. He has never failed me before.'

Vasily was sceptical. They had no idea what they were looking for or if it even still existed. He voiced the concern that had been at the back of his mind since their quest began. 'You know they could have already executed the instructions in the letter. There could be nothing left to find.'

'If that were the case,' Boris replied 'I believe news of their discovery would have made headlines... globally. Whatever secret Rene Secretan is hiding, its impact on art, and even history would be enormous. You've read the interview with Victor Doiteau! Secretan practically admitted that Van Gogh did not commit suicide. Whatever he is hiding I will find it. And if it is what I suspect, it will be the greatest addition to my collection ever.'

Three and a half years after they had started the task of translating the journals, Vasily had finally reached the last two books covering 1904 to 1905.

In 1905, Rene Secretan had visited the home of Adeline Ravoux in Meulan. As soon as her description appeared in the February entry Boris knew this was what he had been looking for. Secretan had not actually used her name. He had simply described her as the girl in blue, but Boris knew enough of Van Gogh's work to understand the reference. He cursed his decision to start at the end of Rene's life and realised the banker's compulsion to write down his life story had started with this visit. Impatience had prolonged his search, but his dedication would be rewarded now, he knew for certain. The journal entry finished with a simple sentence that confirmed to Boris this event was the trigger - '*it has been put right*'.

According to the journal, Rene had driven to Meulan with a friend by the name of Francois Farabet. His companion had looked after the cafe owned by Arthur Ravoux while Adeline and Rene visited the home of Dr Gachet, the celebrated homeopath and art collector, in Auvers. The details of the visit were vague, and Rene did not seem to have a purpose beyond simply viewing the physician's collection. This made no sense to Boris - why would he need Adeline Ravoux to accompany him just to look at some paintings? He was a respected businessman. He would not need a waitress to afford him an introduction.

The journals gave no hint as to what it was Rene was hiding, but Boris knew that this was the catalyst.

A month ago, Boris had despatched Vasily to Paris to find out what he could about the companion, Francois Farabet.

Natalia was out when Vasily arrived back in Egham after four weeks in France undertaking extensive but frustrating research. The two men went into the study where the Russian Icon now hung above the antique desk. The walls of the room were lined on three sides by rows of books acquired by the interior decorator Natalia had employed to redesign the former stately home. None of them had ever been read. The French windows on either side of the Icon looked out onto the estate. No other building was visible from this vantage point.

'So what did you find out?' Boris asked, opting for the sofa rather than his chair, so he could look as his Icon as they spoke..

'As you know, Van Gogh gave the Ravoux's two paintings before he died. A portrait that he'd done of the girl when she was 12 and the Town Hall on the 14th July.'

'Everybody knows this!' Boris was impatient for some news.

'They were sold to an American dealer in November 1905 for forty francs after he told the family they would not survive the humid conditions in the drawing room above the cafe.'

'Yes, Harry Harronson bought them. This detail is widely known from the interview with Adeline Ravoux herself. Her father had no idea of their potential value at the time. The American was a clever man.' Boris knew he would have just taken the paintings if he'd been Harronson, but with the purchase came genuine provenance, which was worth more than anything to a dealer.

'Look at the journal entry dates. Rene Secretan visited Adeline in the February of that year, nearly nine months before Harronson turned up.' Vasily waited a few moments composing himself to deliver the news they'd been craving for nearly a decade. 'Secretan was educated in the finest schools in Paris and at 31 was already a successful businessman. Do you not think it strange that a rich, educated banker and celebrated marksman, who had represented France in shooting competitions, and who'd known Van Gogh personally, didn't realise their potential value and left without so much as a comment in his tortuous diaries?' Vasily could see that Boris was beginning to understand the implications of the timing of the visits.

'Why did Rene not offer to buy the paintings himself? He knew the family's relationship with Van Gogh. He must have seen them if he spent the entire day with the girl.' Boris knew what he would have done.

'That was exactly my thought when I looked at the dates. It has taken me considerable time to go through all the newspaper articles and references in the Paris Central Library to find the name Francois Farabet. He was almost 50 in 1905, when he travelled with Rene to Meulan. He was an artist with little vision but high skill. Do you recall the name of the man who accompanied Harronson when he bought the paintings from Ravoux?'

Boris thought for a moment.

'The Adeline interview names him only as 'le petit pere, Sam.'

'Yes, and in July 1905 a photograph appeared in Le Figaro taken at the Salon de Automne, Les Fauves art exhibition. It was the first showing of Matisse's Woman with a Hat so there was considerable press interest. In it the artist, Francois Farabet is pictured with his protégé, Samuel Ingres. I assumed this must be the same Farabet who had been with Rene that day. I did more research and found that he died a couple of years later, but he was quite notorious in his day.'

'For what?' Boris asked, his usually controlled breathing gathering pace slightly as the evidence began falling into place.

'He was a master art forger!' Vasily declared triumphantly.

Boris considered the implications of this. An acquaintance of Rene Secretan had potentially been known to the mysterious Le petit pere, Sam. An acquaintance who could have easily told his protégé of the two Van Gogh's that hung in the drawing room of the peasant's cafe.

Boris knew 'The Town Hall in Auvers' had been sold in 1992 for more than $10m to a private collector in Chicago. He was well aware that at the time it would have been subject to every test and scrutiny modern science afforded the sale of such major works, especially since the Nazi thefts. There was no way that painting could be a forgery - it would have made the news around the world. He thought about the other work - the portrait of Adeline Ravoux. Its whereabouts were undocumented for at least 50 years and only very old reproductions served to remind the world it even existed. He had no idea who the owner was. It certainly hadn't come up for auction in his lifetime. It might never have been put through the chemical analysis and X-ray scanning used today. Whoever owned it had clearly had it for a very long time and may not even be aware themselves - after all... who else would know! Boris jumped to his feet and crossed the room to stand in front of his Icon.

'I know what Rene Secretan is hiding!' He declared to Vasily, triumphantly.

Chapter 26
Windsor, Berks. Thursday 16th October 2014

Joseph Colthart held the phone away from his ear, expecting an explosion. It didn't come.

'What exactly do you mean it's not the painting I was expecting?' The heavily accented voice at the end of the phone was too controlled. 'Describe it to me.'

'Well it's hard to describe. It looks like the ghosts of a bride and groom floating in a tree next to a bowl of fruit. There are things all over the place. I thought you said it would be a portrait.'

Silence…

'Joseph… is the signature at the bottom Marc Chagall?' The client should have been more surprised than they sounded. Joseph had already checked the painting.

'Yes, how did you know?' His suspicion and concern were growing

'Do you realise how badly you have screwed up?' The foreigner was cold. Anger not surprise was evident from their tone. Joseph knew that was the worst possible development.

'The case was exactly as you described it. Charlesworth had it out on top of his safe just as you said.'

'Did you see a second case?' The client already knew the answer.

'Of course not!' Joseph could feel the anger biting into him. 'What second case? You never said there would be a second case.'

'Did you not see the courier arrive?'

Joseph had no idea what they were talking about. He'd been following Philip Charlesworth since he left his flat in Hans Crescent.

He hadn't arrived in Mount St until after 9am, and then he'd gone straight to the Deli for his coffee. No one had gone into the gallery during that time.

'No!' As the reply came out of his mouth his mind began running backwards reviewing the scene he'd left behind. 'Who?'

He hadn't expected anyone else to be in the building so he hadn't checked. What an amateur mistake! Everything had happened exactly as he'd been briefed and he'd taken his client's word of what to expect at face value. The only variation was that it had all happened 15 minutes later than planned. The secretary had opened the door without question when he mentioned the name his client had told him to use so he'd assumed he was expected. He tried to recall the layout of the gallery he'd stood in for less than three minutes, searching for something he may have missed. All he could remember was the case, two dead bodies and his own reflection in the mirrored walls. As his subconscious processed this morning's scene his conscious brain registered the sound of the bell ringing frantically from the side door upstairs. Joseph ignored it the first few times it rang, trying to focus on the phone call, but its growing persistence began to add to his concerns.

'What's that?' his client jolted him out of his memory-searching stupor.

'I have to go!' he said urgently, hoping to buy some thinking time. 'There's someone at the back door.'

'Are you sure you weren't followed? Did you deactivate the tracking device?'

'Yes as soon as I got the case open.'

The bell rang again - it was being held down consistently now and would soon start to draw attention from the street.

'I'll get rid of them and call you straight back.'

He ended the call without waiting for a reply. His client rang back immediately but he diverted the call to voicemail. He'd deal with them later.

The bell continued to sound upstairs. Had someone seen him come into the building? He'd parked several streets away but the case he was carrying was large and very distinctive. Maybe it was the estate agent, but she wouldn't be ringing the bell - she had a key. He'd seen the 'to let' sign when he was planning the job and had contacted them to be shown around. She'd told him the premises had been vacant for over a year and assured him that she could get the whole block for a very good price if he was prepared to move quickly. He had moved quickly, but completely without her knowledge.

He went upstairs and looked through the spyhole in the door. A short red-haired girl in colourful mismatching clothes and a parka was bouncing up and down on the spot outside on the pavement.

'I saw you go in!' she shouted as if she sensed his presence behind the door.

He opened the door slowly.

'Oh my god! I thought you'd never answer!' Ashley cried in her loud voice

'Who the hell are you?' he asked.

'I'm friends with Ramon; he said you might be able to sort me out with some gear?' Ashley drew a breath as she'd planned and turned away quickly to get back onto the street. 'But he's obviously given me the wrong address so sorry mate.'

Joseph was too quick for her. He grabbed her arm and pulled her back inside the building.

"Where the hell do you think you're going?' he asked as he pushed her towards the steep staircase. He wasn't taking any more chances today. 'I asked you who you were?' He stood blocking her exit back into the street, closing the door behind him. She needed to send the text to Mr Yau urgently. He was only seconds away, but she might not have seconds. The man in front of her oozed viciousness and Ashley's recklessness took over her common sense.

Holding the doorframe that led into the showroom, Ashley stabilised herself and kicked up high and fast, connecting her solid boot with Colthart's groin. In a heartbeat she made good use of her only advantage – surprise. He hadn't been expecting an attack and doubled over as her steel toecap crushed him and pain seared through his body and his eyes started to stream.

Ashley turned and jumped down the stairs three at a time, locking herself in the tiny toilet at the bottom. The wooden door was not going to protect her, but there were no windows in the basement. Would he go high or low?

She took a chance and dropped to the floor as she hit the send button on the prepared message on her phone.

Joseph recovered and ran down the stairs after her. He licked at the door, but it opened outward due to the lack of space inside the cubicle and the frame held it steady.

He looked around the room and found his gun. He flicked the safety catch off and aimed at the door but stopped himself. He turned back towards the blood spattered across the costume jewellery in the cabinet. Shooting this girl with the same gun he'd used to kill the gallery owner this morning wasn't smart. DNA evidence and bullets would tie the two crimes together. An unnecessary risk just to get rid of a junkie. Today was turning into a disaster. He paced for a few seconds, fighting his natural instinct to shoot indiscriminately at the bathroom door.

'Who the hell are you?' he shouted in frustration. Ashley realised the accent sounded South African.

'I told you. I'm one of Ramon's regulars. I only wanted to buy some coke.' She played the part she'd planned in her head to perfection.

'Who is Ramon?'

'He's my dealer. Aren't you the guy he's sent me to see? I badly need a fix man.'

Joseph returned to the painting. He'd deactivated the tracker and put it back into the case out of sight. He didn't want it seen by anyone who might remember him once the evening news broke. No one had ever seen his face and lived. Were drug dealers using this building? There'd been no sign of any squatters during his reconnaissance. There were no remnants of drug gear on the floor. He needed to get out of here immediately and not leave any more potential witnesses. He'd take his chances with the DNA. It was unlikely to be on any file he knew of anyway. The scruffy addict in the bathroom, who had alerted him to potential discovery, was about to draw her last breath.

His phone rang again. He knew better than to divert them a second time.

"Who was it?' the voice demanded.

'Just some junkie woman after a fix. I'll deal with her in a minute. What do you want me to do with this painting?' Joseph didn't take his eyes off the bathroom door as he spoke.

'That painting was supposed to have been taken by courier to another client.'

'What courier are you talking about? There was no one else in the room and I could see upstairs.'

'Did you check the kitchen or offices?'

'What kitchen?'

'The one behind the mirror doors?'

'I didn't see any mirror doors. You didn't say anything about a kitchen.' Joseph stopped dead - he'd seen mirrors, lots of them, but no doors.

'The back of the gallery had two mirrored doors into the back office. They are made of two-way glass. Anyone in the kitchen would have been able to see into the showroom.'

Joseph was getting agitated but there wasn't enough room in the crowded basement to pace and he started to feel claustrophobic. Nobody had ever seen his face before. He'd always been so careful about that, and now there may be a potential witness who was still alive; someone who could potentially identify him as a double murderer.

'I need to think! Let me get rid of this girl and I'll figure out what to do.'

'Deal with her and get out of there now. Your location's been compromised. Call me when you're somewhere safe.' The line went dead.

Joseph stood in front of the bathroom door and raised the gun. He shot at the lock and the bullet splintered the bolt, its casing and most of the surrounding wood.

As the door swung outwards, leaving Ashley completely unprotected, a second gunshot and splintering of more wood exploded from the top of the stairs. Joseph froze for a fraction of a second, instinctively turning towards the noise coming from the side door. Ashley pulled the toilet door shut and dropped straight to the floor. Joseph shot through the wood at chest height but didn't wait to check if the bullet had found its target. Someone was breaking in upstairs and he was in a basement from which there was no other way out. If drug dealers really were using this place he would be trapped like a fly under a glass. He grabbed the case and fired up the stairs towards the badly damaged door, forcing the intruders to retreat back onto the doorstep. Joseph shot out the light in the basement, plunging the staircase into darkness. The advantage gave him enough time to get to the top of the stairs and into the showroom. He could hear voices just outside shouting but didn't recognise the words. A foreign accent but not the one he was used to. As Joseph turned right into the showroom a short, stocky Chinese man kicked open the door a second time. Joseph fired at the intruder, and the bullet grazed his right arm. Behind him two other men - younger and fitter - began firing into the showroom.

Joseph considered his options in a fragment of frozen time, as he had been trained to do during his years in the Zimbabwean army. He was trapped by three armed men in a shop with no cover. He was guarding a painting that wasn't the one he was supposed to have stolen. The girl in the basement was the least of his worries. As the three Chinese men edged past the top of the staircase towards the showroom door Joseph fired at the whitewashed windows. Glass shattered everywhere and the Chinese instinctively recoiled for a split second. Joseph launched himself through the window, rolling across the broken glass that covered the concrete paving slabs. Bullets ricocheted around him, hitting the metal case, as he pushed his frame back onto his feet in one fluid movement. As he reached down to retrieve the case a bullet caught the top of his left arm and he lost sensation in his fingers. Leaving the art on the floor he ran into the road behind the line of parked cars. Alarms started to go off as a wave of gunfire followed him down the street as people ran for cover and the distant sound of sirens started to wail.

The stocky Chinese man pulled up his coat hood and picked up the painting while the younger men retrieved the casings from their bullets. They couldn't afford to leave anything here if the painting was supposed to have been delivered safely to the hotel as planned. Nothing would be left to tie the three of them to the murder at a gallery twenty-five miles away.

As the sound of retreating footsteps echoed above her head, Ashley came out of the bathroom and ran up the stairs. She looked into the destroyed showroom and her vision blurred slightly as she realised how close she'd come to being shot. She recovered quickly. Her pulse was racing and she felt an intoxicating mixture of fear and adrenalin. As she ran out into the street through the destroyed back door relief surged through her. The main part of Tia's plan had worked and her family were safe. The killer had got away but he would never be able to find them again without access to the gallery records. She smiled as she turned left into the side street and slowed to a walk with the hood of her parka pulled up tight around her ears as three police cars pulled up on both sides of the wrecked corner shop.

There was no one left to explain to them what had happened in that building but the extensive damage would keep them busy for some time.

When she arrived at Costa Coffee, Philip's phone had already received a text from Mr Yau to confirm he'd recovered his painting. He would be out of the country before sunset.

Ashley was breathing hard as she sat in the corner of the coffee shop, watching the drama unfold at the other end of the street and trying desperately to appear calm. She drank the hot black coffee but her hands were shaking as she took them through what had happened. As the words poured out in a hastily recalled frenzy she managed to get to the point where the bullet had torn through the bathroom door less than two inches above her head before she froze mid-sentence. She looked briefly out of the window to a point 100 metres away, where police were beginning to set up a cordon. Without warning she slammed the mug on the table as a new fear began to seep into her racing mind. She stood up suddenly, frantic to get out of the coffee shop.

'We need to get back to the car now!' she said, the panic in her voice evident.

'What's wrong?' Henry had never seen Ashley look so frightened before - not even as she'd prepared to knock on the door of a building occupied by a killer. That had been before she'd seen first hand the damage caused by his bullets.

'Mr Yau might not be coming to look for Eoin any more,' she said, her hands trembling, 'but the killer just got away and I've just remembered a phone conversation he had whilst I was locked in the toilet. It didn't make sense to me at the time because I could only hear his replies.' She didn't wait for their response as she started to jog into the street towards the parked Mercedes. The three jumped up and ran after her. She was impatiently pulling at the handle when they caught up with her.

'What's wrong?' Tia asked again softly as they got into the car,

'The guy didn't realise there were mirrored doors at the back of the gallery. He thought he was alone once he shot those two people but now he's been ambushed less than three hours after leaving the scene, in a building at least 25 miles away. It won't take him long to realise someone must have been inside the gallery to raise the alarm so quickly, and therefore there must have been a witness.'

Tia tried to placate her. They'd already been over this and discarded it as a problem.

'Its okay, even if he's figured out that there was a witness, the chances of him finding Eoin, or you, are very remote. He can't get back into the gallery now.'

'No they're not.' Ashley pulled out her phone and started typing frantically. 'I don't know who he was talking to but I heard him say *what courier?* Someone else knows that Charlesworth was making a second drop this morning and had booked a courier. They may even know who Eoin works for. Yau might have his painting back but we've just swapped one dangerous thug for another, and this time their missing painting is apparently worth £50m not £1.4m. There's no way of dealing with the African without going to the police. And what do we tell them? Someone is after us but we've no idea what for. We took the case from the gallery remember. As far as the police are concerned it was never there. We're back to square one and my family are still possibly in danger again. Our only bargaining chip with either side is the painting in the boot of the car. It's the only thing that supports our story. There's no paper trail that it exists so it's the only physical proof. We have to find out what the hell is in that case!'

Chapter 27

Mayfair, London April 2012.

Cecil Charlesworth was a man of his word, a trait he had inherited from his father and failed to pass onto his son. Integrity had been his greatest asset over the years and it had produced a client base of loyal investors who trusted his advice and treated him as a friend. He had worked for his father at Lenisters for 30 years before inheriting it when he died in 1974. Since then he had expanded the business into new premises and developed an exceptional eye for young talent with potential. His quarterly exhibitions rarely failed to sell out. Despite the growth in the business, however, he had never managed to emulate his father and uncover a major global talent so, coupled with a poor marriage and the bitter disappointment caused by his son, Cecil often felt like a failure.

His unsuitable young wife had died suddenly when Philip was only six years old and Cecil knew he hadn't done his best in raising him alone. Philip had graduated from Kent University thirteen years ago and had still not succeeded in keeping a job for more than a few months. His education at Wellington College boarding school had cost Cecil more than £30,000 a year and the boy had earned less than a third of that amount from the various jobs he'd had so far.

Long periods of time away at school had masked the growing gulf between father and son and Cecil had not really missed him. When Philip was 18, bitter arguments had developed from his insistence on completing a business degree rather than an art history course, adding to those already raging following his failure to secure a place at Oxford or Cambridge. To date, nothing in the boy's life had gone according to Cecil's plan.

Cecil was an only child and had been 48 years old when Philip was born so he had no other heir. When he was home from school and university Cecil had tried endlessly to make the boy understand that the gallery would flounder unless he knew the subject and the client base and their needs,

But Philip's first love was money, not art. He had ambitions of making his fortune quickly in the spiralling financial sector, specialising in the burgeoning dot.com market. He'd made it clear he had no interest in taking over the family business until his father died by which time Cecil knew it would be too late.

After a week as a trainee stockbroker, a job secured as a favour to Cecil by one of his grateful customers, Philip had already cost the firm a small fortune and lost an account. Cecil had taken him out of the company before he was asked to leave. Dalliances into insurance and banking had produced similar results and his father had been left with no other choice than to take Philip on in the gallery anyway, despite his lack of interest and knowledge.

Fortunately Cecil had been able to keep the boy at a harmless distance so far. He had been dispatched to learn Japanese, Russian and Chinese, as the emerging superpowers became the global focus for wealth development. Philip was currently in Japan studying the art industry there, and the preferences that they were developing. The *Vase with Fifteen Sunflowers* by Van Gogh had been the first modern painting to sell for more than an old master when it was purchased by the Japanese company Yasuda Comp. in 1987 for almost $40m - three times the value it had sold for only two years earlier. The sun was very definitely rising in the East.

Despite the setbacks, Cecil was still proud of the way he had developed his father's company since his death. Andrew Charlesworth had started Lenisters, named after his mother's maiden name, in 1934 using her considerable inheritance. Her family had important connections and Andrew had an instinct for new talent. Three years after opening he'd presented Francis Bacon's second exhibition, paving the way for the young artist's breakthrough in 1944 with the shocking 'Crucifixion Triptych'. For almost 80 years Lenisters had been at the forefront of showcasing emerging talent, whilst maintaining a credible income as a broker for auctioned art.

The client base was indeed changing as Cecil had predicted. Today he had his first meeting with a prospective client who had moved to England from Russia just over two years ago. Boris Rubikov had bought the beautiful Savil Court estate in Egham and was rumoured to be one of the richest men in Russia, worth several billion dollars. Securing Rubikov as a client would be the perfect foothold to develop the untapped business behind the former Iron Curtain.

Rubikov arrived just after 10am, accompanied by his head of security, Vasily Denisov. Cecil felt intimidated by their physical stature but his very British breeding refused to allow this to show. He escorted them round the gallery where they were currently showing the final year work of the Camberwell College of Art graduates from 2012.

'Mr Rubikov, welcome to Lenisters. I understand from my friend Maxwell Compton at Christie's that you are looking to invest in British art?' Cecil walked him slowly through the gallery, allowing him to view the work on display. 'Let's go into my office and we can discuss exactly what your requirements are.'

Cecil led Boris through to his office at the back of the gallery. Vasily stood guard outside the small kitchen whilst the two men talked.

'I have to confess Mr Charlesworth, whilst I may indeed look to purchase some new art, my interest lies elsewhere.' Boris settled back into the leather armchair and laced his fingers as if praying.

'So what is it that I can help you with?'

'I've received information from a contact in Paris that you may have come into possession of something from a banker named Rene Secretan.'

'I've never heard that name before.' Cecil knew all of his clients personally and this was definitely not one of them.

'This particular gentleman sadly died in 1957, but I have been led to believe that he entrusted a letter to the safekeeping of this gallery a few years prior to his death. I am very keen to acquire that letter and would make it extremely worthwhile for you.'

'In 1957 I'm afraid I didn't work here. I was travelling around America after completing my studies. The gallery was run by my father, Andrew, until his death in 1974. I've made a number of changes since I took over the business but I have never found anything relating to that name.'

'How can you be sure without checking your records?' Boris leaned forward in the chair, raising his large frame intimidatingly.

'Mr Rubikov, the only real attributes required to run a gallery such as this are an eye for talent and a memory for names. It is about matching tastes with trends and to do that you have to know everything you can about your clients, past and present. Someone who was once a buyer may just as quickly become a seller, either personally or through his estate. If he had been a client of Lenisters then I would know. What is the letter about?'

'It is difficult to be certain. The information I was given was, shall we say, sketchy. But I believe it relates to something Mr Secretan may have taken from a cafe in Meulan that did not belong to him. I am led to believe that it was stolen even whilst the rightful owner was in the room. This stolen painting is of the greatest interest to me and I would be expecting to pay a seven-figure sum to secure the work.'

Cecil Charlesworth smiled at the Russian who obviously thought he was a fool.

'Mr Rubikof, if there a an item worth seven figures in his gallery, or information as to its whereabouts, I would most certainly know about it! One thing I do have extensive knowledge of, however, is the history of art - especially impressionist art.' Cecil leaned back in his seat, his decision to pass this Russian up as a client already cemented. 'I have never heard of a Rene Secretan, but I do know that Meulan was the location of the cafe owned by Arthur Ravoux after he left Auvers. He owned two Van Gogh's, which were legitimately, if foolishly, sold to an American called Harronson in 1905 and have cast-iron provenance. The *'Town Hall at Auvers on 14th July'* and the *'Portrait of Adeline Ravoux'* are both in private collections in America. I know this as I have personally seen them both. The owners are both clients of this gallery and there is no record of the Ravoux's having a third painting, by Van Gogh or any other artist.'

'It is the portrait that I am particularly interested in,' Boris pressed on. 'Maybe I can speak with your clients and make them an offer?'

'Mr Rubikof.' Cecil was tiring of the Russian now. The man had no finesse. 'I am aware of your recently acquired wealth and status within the former Soviet Union, but even your fortune pales into insignificance when compared to the owner of that painting. They are only the second family to have possessed the work since the subject who sat for it. I very much doubt they would be willing to part with it after such a long time.'

Boris knew this man could not help him, but he had already given him a valuable lead.

'Mr Charlesworth, we both know that eventually everyone has their price.' His eyes narrowed and Cecil felt his initial fear return. 'If your client should decide to dispose of the work I would ask that you allow me first refusal. As a gesture of good faith, I will buy the remaining paintings from your current exhibition for my new offices in Canary Wharf. Please let me know if there are any developments.' Boris signed a blank cheque and placed it on the desk in front of Cecil, his fingers lingering longer than was necessary to ensure his message was understood. Cecil looked up the 6'3" monolith and nodded silently as the Russians left the gallery. Thank God Philip had not been here, he thought; he would have been unable to stay silent.

As the two Russians climbed into the Maybech outside the gallery Boris smiled. He was currently assessed to be the 50th richest person in the world. That left a very short list of people above him who might be the legitimate owner of the woman in blue. If his suspicions were correct, when the letter did eventually surface it would inevitably lead back to them. He knew this gallery was somehow involved, even if the current owner was unaware, and he was a patient man. When the time was right, he would be ready to act.

Chapter 28

Mayfair, London Thursday 16th October 2014.

Stephen was finding it difficult to focus on his job. He had two bodies and video footage that clearly showed his own daughter leaving the building after the slaughter had happened. No one in the room was accusing Tia of committing the crime – the medical examiner had confirmed that Philip Charlesworth and his assistant had been dead for at least 2 hours. At that time Tia had still been in her bedroom in Camden. They had no idea what time Tia had actually arrived based on the video footage, which had now been turned into a series of timed-stamped, printed stills showing the relevant events, but assuming she'd driven straight here from Camden they calculated Henry would have parked outside at around 10.15am. Sam pulled Stephen to one side and his guilt was palpable.

'Sir, I think it might have been Tia who accessed the computer.'

'Why on earth would she do that?' Stephen was still finding it difficult to tie these two events together. 'How would she be able to access it? You said whoever did it used a program the same as...' He didn't finish the statement. He could tell from Sam's expression that he wasn't going to like the answers to either of those last two questions.

'She wanted a copy to practice with,' Sam confessed, 'and she is so talented I wanted to help her.'

'It's not your fault Sam, until we find her and get the explanation I have to trust that she thinks she is doing something good or heroic.' Stephen knew his daughter well enough to believe she had a profound sense of right and wrong - but he couldn't forget the American. He had

231

no idea what that guy was capable of. 'Where are we with the phone records for the deceased?'

'We've found no mobiles on the victims so we have to assume someone took them. The woman has no handbag either, which is unusual, so I assume that's been taken as well. There doesn't seem to be anything else missing and the phone companies are pulling the call logs now.'

Stephen went out into the street and found an officer smoking a cigarette.

'You got a spare?' he asked the terrified man who quickly produced a Marlboro Menthol and a lighter. Stephen had not smoked since Tia was born but the hot nicotine sent calming signals to his brain, followed by coughing signals to his lungs. Andrew came out into the street a lit one of his own.

'You know there is a rational explanation, don't you?'

Stephen just looked at his Head of Intelligence. He didn't know anything at the moment.

'All I keep asking myself is what had she been doing here at all, in the company of an American whose parents have clearly bailed him out of some serious trouble in the past.'

News crews had started to congregate at the cordons at the end of the street. 'We had better get someone round to the secretary's family and let them know what has happened before they figure it out from a press photo of the gallery. And get hold of the American boy's parents. He may have been in contact with them at some point.'

Sam came out into the cold street with an update.

'Sir, I've checked the desk diaries. It seems Charlesworth booked a courier to take a painting to Mr Yau at the Mandarin Oriental. He used a courier company from Hackney. I've spoken to the hotel reception and Yau checked out just after 11am. Heathrow have confirmed he just cleared customs with his painting so the courier obviously turned up.'

'Get someone round to the courier's office,' Stephen ordered. 'Find out who they sent and get an address. We need to speak to him urgently.'

Stephen went back into the showroom, sidestepping the array of scientists photographing and mapping every trace of evidence splattered across the room. In the corner the security company engineer was overriding the security codes to the basement doors. It took him 20 minutes to access the staircase inside the main office.

Andrew was the first one down in the basement - his team inventoried every item in the room. Nothing was missing according to the manifest on the computer. Every work of art that should be down here was, and the Chagall had been delivered to Mr Yau as expected.

Upstairs the computer technician was still going through Charlesworth's PC.

'The hard drive has been copied by someone who knew what they were doing. I'll need to take this back to the lab and check the hard drive forensically to see what else they've accessed but it doesn't look like anything has been deleted. The basement and showroom checks show that the only painting due to leave the building today was documented in the sales log as the one purchased for Mr Yau that the courier collected.'

'Have we got hold of Mr Yau yet to confirm he has the correct painting?'

'I've just spoken to him on his mobile phone,' Andrew said, staying one step ahead of his superior. 'He says he checked the contents himself and the painting is the correct one. The gallery accounts show that his funds cleared on the day of the auction last week, so it's not like he's trying to evade paying for it.'

'Something doesn't add up. Two murders, nothing taken and Tia apparently tampering with the PC.' Stephen said. 'We need to find that bloody Yank. His car can't be that hard to locate, even if he has turned the tracker off. People notice Porsches! Get onto the traffic cameras further afield - it's got to show up somewhere.'

'It just did!' Andrew said looking worried as he covered the mouthpiece of his phone, 'It's in a leisure centre car park in Windsor and looks like it's been left there. Staff say neither Tia or Henry are with the car. CCTV cameras don't cover the whole car park and he parked in a blind spot between two bigger cars so we don't know where they've gone from there.'

'I'm not sure if this is significant but I ran a check on Whittaker's family for last known whereabouts,' Sam volunteered looking up from the screen to which he had seemed permanently glued. 'Constance Whittaker flew into London yesterday and is currently staying at Claridge's Hotel. It's literally round the corner from here.'

Stephen thought for a second.

'Andrew, get a team over to Windsor and check out the area and then head over to Hackney to find out what you can about the courier. Sam, you come with me – let's go and have a chat with a billionaire.'

Chapter 29

Staines, Thursday 16th October 2014.

Joseph Colthart pulled off his tie and used it as a tourniquet around the top of his wounded arm. The bullet had cut through the skin, deep enough to be bleeding profusely. He looked conspicuous in just a jumper and shirt on such a cold autumn afternoon and the blood was starting to soak through the wool. His coat was still in the basement of the charity shop along with the rental car keys and the blood from his hand. Fortunately his wallet and phone were in his trouser pockets, a habit he'd developed for situations like this. He'd abandoned the car, which he assumed would have a gps tracker, and was carrying out his rudimentary first aid from the toilets of the London-bound train from Eton Riverside. Somehow he'd managed to keep hold of his gun but he checked the chamber and he was down to his last three bullets.

He tore a strip of material from the bottom of his shirt and wrapped it over the injury. The white cotton quickly soaked with blood but the tourniquet was doing its job and the flow slowed rapidly. By the time he reached Staines his arm was bandaged and covered up and he was wearing a coat stolen from a sleeping lunchtime commuter. He got off the train and headed down towards the River Thames. An unlocked boathouse provided temporary refuge while he planned what to do next.

He'd gone over the events of the last two hours in his head repeatedly since escaping from the gunmen and the arriving police and was struggling to make sense of what had happened. No one had known about the random venue he'd chosen to open the case and transfer the painting, not even the client who'd hired him. How had anyone managed to find him so quickly? He'd only been in the basement for just over two hours - more than enough time for him to unlock the case before the alarm was raised. How had he been compromised? Someone must have accessed the GPS tracking system inside the gallery already. No matter how he looked at it, everything came back to the courier he'd known nothing about. Whoever he was, he must have still been in the building when Joseph left.

This morning he'd left Mayfair assuming the job had been perfectly executed, but vital information had been withheld, seemingly on purpose, and that made him nervous and angry. All of his instructions had come from his client yet they'd failed to mention a courier or a second delivery despite apparently being aware of them both. Again and again he kept coming back to the same question – why?

He made up his mind quickly. He would cut his losses and get out of the country immediately. He no longer trusted the person who'd hired him. His travel bag, passport and an open ticket were already in a locker at Heathrow. He could be on his way back to Zimbabwe within two hours. Good luck to anyone trying to find him then. It wouldn't be the first time he'd put his own security ahead of the job in hand. He felt no loyalty to the clients who hired him and certainly not to those who had compromised his anonymity. His blood was in the basement of the shop in Windsor, and if the police recovered a bullet from inside the building they would be able to match it to the ones used to kill Charlesworth and his secretary. He'd lost the painting he'd taken by mistake and had nothing to show for his efforts. No one, not even his client, knew what he looked like and another job would come along soon. Better to survive and fight another day than face this particular client empty handed.

He switched on his phone and the text came through immediately.

It was a photo message, sent from the only number programmed into the memory.

Joseph opened the text and downloaded the image. As the grainy pixels slowly sharpened he started to recognise the location. As the picture cleared he was looking at an image of himself, leaving the Lenister Gallery, looking away from the auction house security camera as instructed but directly into the lens of this photographer. The time stamp on the photo was 9.40am.

Joseph was stunned. His client had anticipated his reaction precisely. They'd known that if anything went wrong Joseph Colthart would look after himself first. If his face were released to the British police he would never work again. Anonymity was critical in his line of work. Facial recognition technology now used at the airports would make international travel virtually impossible without some form of facial bone-altering surgery or a means of bypassing passport control. Terrorists with huge support networks behind them might be able to achieve this, but not one man operating alone. His own analysis of the security systems in the area had worked against him. In looking away from the known CCTV cameras he had looked directly into the lens of his client. They'd anticipated exactly what he would do and had been ready for him. He dialled the number.

'You've made your point. I had no intention of leaving the job unfinished,' he lied.

'What happened?'

'While I was dealing with the girl in the basement three Chinese gunmen broke into the shop. '

'Chinese?'

'Yes. I had to shoot out the windows of the shop front to escape. I've no idea if I hit the girl or if she's still down there.' He grimaced to himself as he realised that if the girl was still alive she would be the only person ever to see his face while he was holding a gun and not to have died by its use.

'The Chagall was supposed to be delivered to a Chinese businessman. The courier should have left before you arrived but obviously Philip was late for work.'

His client's accent grated on him and he felt like a scolded child.

'Well I suspect he has it now after his men shot at me.' His suspicions were mounting. 'What else did you not tell me?'

'I told you what you needed to know. What matters now is you have to clean up the mess. The mirrored doors in the gallery are not actually mirrors, they're made of two way glass, installed as part of the security overhaul. If the courier was in the kitchen when you fired those shots he would have been able to see you, even though you couldn't see him. If you want to maintain your anonymity then you need to find him and get rid of him. Then you need to find a way back into the gallery to recover the case you should have removed unless you want this photo to be sent to the police. I'm sure they'd love to have your image on file.'

Joseph thought carefully about the way the morning had unfolded. He'd been following Philip Charlesworth, but Philip had been late for work. His client hadn't told him about the courier who must have arrived early. He had never known there was a second painting. Why not?

He looked again at the photo of himself in the doorway of the gallery. From the camera angle he could tell that his client must have been in the Mount St Deli when it was taken, He hadn't told them that Philip was late for work, so how did they know? They had obviously been following him; waiting for the exact moment he left the building to purposely take the incriminating photo. He'd been set up!

'What did the girl who came to the shop look like?' His employer called his attention back from his thoughts.

'She looked like a hippie with no dress sense. Short and a bit chubby. You'd notice the clothes without taking in the face.'

'What colour was her hair?'

'Red and quite short. Why?'

'Joseph you are in trouble. You were followed!'

'How do you know that?'

'It's my job to know everything. She arrived at the gallery about fifteen minutes after you left. I waited in the coffee shop to make sure no one had reported gunfire. Listen carefully - you need to get to a messenger company in Hackney as quickly as possible and get the home address of that courier.'

Chapter 30

Mayfair, London Thursday 16th October 2014

The phone rang in the Brook Penthouse, the largest of the suites at Claridge's, and jolted Constance Whittaker back to the reality of her day. She was sitting outside on the large, granite-stoned balcony looking over the rooftops of Brook St and the Houses of Parliament, drinking coffee and wondering what she should do next. Her shoulder length brown hair bobbed in the breeze and she pulled the cashmere cardigan tightly across her slim frame. It was already 2pm, only three people in the world knew she was here and all three of them were causing her anxiety. She recovered her drifting senses, walked back into the Art Deco living room and located the ringing mobile phone on the French mahogany sideboard.

'Hello' She removed the pearl earring from her ear as she recognised her brother, Richard's voice. He always kept her on the phone too long, normally pressurising her to support his various business decisions.

'Why didn't you tell me you were going to England?' Since Henry's birth Richard's devotion to Constance had started to wane as his frustration with his nephew increased.

'This is nothing to do with the company, Richard. It's a private matter.'

'You've left Washington with only one of your bodyguards. That puts you in breach of your life insurance policy. Do you know what shit will hit the fan for the company if anything happens to you?'

Constance felt her growing annoyance with her brother resurface.

She hadn't seen him for months, since his second marriage to that awful woman. When she did speak to him the only topic was his disappointment with Henry and how unsuitable he was to take over her grandfathers business. Now he was reprimanding her. Clearly he'd infiltrated her security team yet again to know she was out of the country. Time for a reshuffle as soon as she got home.

'Richard if I want to come and spend time with my son then that is none of your business – or the insurance company's.'

'Yes but Harry has told me why you are really there and that is my business. I'm just ringing to let you know that the rest of your security team will be arriving in Northolt in a couple of hours. All I'm asking is that you don't try and dodge them again! Thing about the share price just for once Constance.'

'Richard you really are worse than father,'

'That's why you put me in charge.' He said and hung up. No one else apart from Henry would ever speak to her like that and they both infuriated her.

As she put down the phone it rang again.

'Hello,' said the caller.

Constance again recognised the voice; Jennifer Hawley had been the second of the three to cause her concern this morning. She'd phoned just after 10.15am to say Henry had not turned up at the university.

'Have you found him?' Constance asked hoping at least something had improved in her day.

'No, not yet I'm afraid and his cell phone is switched off and the SIM must have been removed as there is no GPS trace.' Jennifer knew Henry had bought the signal jammer to hide his car's whereabouts when it suited him but she wasn't about to admit that to his over-cautious mother. 'He left here just after 9.30am but never arrived at the Christopher Ingold building. His car's not there and no one has seen him today. I was ringing to check if he'd contacted you.'

As part of the security preparations carried out for Henry's move to

London the Whittaker family had made a sizeable donation to the university in exchange for a parking space near the chemistry building entrance and secret daily reports on his arrival and departure. When the security consultant had explained about the scale of the threat to Henry and showed them the size of the donation the university was only too happy to oblige.

'He hasn't spoken to me for two weeks,' Constance admitted. 'He still hasn't forgiven me for summoning him home for Thanksgiving. Do you have any idea where he might have gone or who he might be meeting?'

'Not really. Maybe one possibility. I'll check it out.' Jennifer recalled the way he had looked at the tall dark girl outside the Ivy and how he'd been late home last night. Did he really think she wouldn't figure it out? He would be sorry if her suspicions were right.

Constance pulled Jennifer back from her thoughts.

'I have to go, Jen. There's someone knocking at the door. Call me as soon as you find anything.'

Constance didn't recall asking for room service, but the Brook Penthouse came with frequent complimentary services that just arrived unannounced. She'd sent the butler away, not wanting anyone else in the room while she was in her business meeting so she opened the door herself.

'Mrs Constance Whittaker?' a tall, black man asked, holding out a badge she didn't recognise.

'Yes.' Access to the penthouse floor was restricted. These men could only have gotten up here with the assistance of the hotel management.

'My name is Stephen Hall, Assistant Commissioner for the Metropolitan Police.'

'Oh my god!' The colour leached from Constance's cheeks and she could feel her muscles abandon their support of her body. Sam caught her arm as she started to fall and helped her into the living room. 'What has happened to Henry?'

'We were hoping you might be able to help us with that,' Stephen said, wondering if she were always this on edge.

Constance regained her composure. The arrival of senior ranking detectives had only ever involved bad news before, especially where Henry was concerned.

'I don't understand. Henry doesn't even know I'm in the country. His girlfriend rang me this morning to say he hadn't turned up at the university and I was just on the phone to her when you knocked. We still haven't found him. When you arrived I assumed the worse.' She knew most people wouldn't automatically assume failure to arrive somewhere on time was a problem, but then most people hadn't spent their entire lives under threat of abduction, either personally or through members of their family. Even though Henry was a grown man, he was still considered one of the top-10 kidnap targets in America, only a few places ahead of Constance herself. Threat assessment had concluded that she was more likely to pay a ransom demand if anything happened to him than the other way round, which made him the more likely risk.

'When was the last time you spoke to your son?' Stephen began his questioning gently. In his experience parents would do anything to protect their children, including telling lies, so watching for her reactions was as important as listening to the words she spoke.

'About two weeks ago,' she admitted. 'I rang him to confirm his flight details back home for Thanksgiving and he said he wasn't coming home because it wasn't a holiday in England. We had an argument and I said some things I shouldn't have and he hasn't spoken to me since. I was hoping to see him whilst I was over here and sort things out.'

'So you haven't told him you're in England?' Stephen had heard about families who needed appointments in order to see each other.

'No but his girlfriend, Jennifer, knows I'm here and she controls his schedule. It's her birthday today and I'd planned to join them for dinner this evening as a surprise.'

'This is the same girlfriend that rang you this morning to ask if you knew why he hadn't turned up at the University?' Stephen's irritation at the American who was possibly in possession of his daughter grew. 'It doesn't sound much like she's in control to me.'

'It's complicated, detective. Henry doesn't have many friends. Jennifer is almost the only person he will talk to. It's difficult growing up when every move you make is monitored either for your own safety or by the press. Sometimes he rebels against his gilded cage and goes off on his own. We've tried our best to make sure he's able to defend himself but it doesn't stop you worrying.'

Stephen didn't reply. He understood that sentiment through more than just empathy. They weren't just the concerns of an overly anxious and worried mother, but of someone who had lived that experience personally and had probably rebelled against similar intrusion herself. The same way that he had rebelled against his family by joining the police instead of the rioters. The same way, he reflected, that Tia was rebelling against him by insisting on living away from home to attend a university less than 45 minutes from their house. He'd done exactly the same as Constance Whittaker in trying to prepare his child for a life without his protection but was struggling to let her go. Was it just human nature to want to battle against your parents?

'Mrs Whittaker, it's essential that we speak to your son as soon as possible.' Stephen decided he needed to play it straight with this women - she was in the same position as him. Her only child was missing. Even if it was voluntary and not kidnap they were still possible witnesses in a double murder. Finding them was his priority. 'Do you have any other way of getting in contact with him?'

'No, his mobile is switched off.' Constance looked at her phone, willing it to ring.

'What about the GPS tracker in his car? Most sports cars have them fitted as standard.' Stephen didn't tell her the signal had disappeared from their radar almost two hours ago. Constance's expression changed.

'Good question!' she said almost to herself. 'Why didn't Jennifer mention that when she called me?'

Constance switched on her iPad and opened a custom built app. She placed it on the table so that the two policemen could see the screen. A GPS map illuminated with a list of locations running down the side. At 11.09 the Porsche had been parked on Mount Street before its trace disappeared off the screen.

'This doesn't make any sense!' Constance zoomed in on the map to bring up more detail. 'Jennifer has access to this system. Now I don't understand her call.'

Stephen was losing track of the heiress's train of thought.

'What doesn't make sense, Mrs Whittaker? Do you know why your son was on Mount Street this morning?'

'No, but Jennifer called me just after 10.15am to say Henry hadn't turned up at college and asked if he was with me.'

'Why is that a surprise to you?'

'Because she could have just looked at this and seen he was in Camden and then at Lenisters Gallery until 11.09am. Why didn't she check before calling me?'

Stephen looked up from his notebook and leaned over the iPad. His finely honed instincts were fizzing. There were no markings on the map other than street names.

'Mrs Whittaker, how do you know that location is Lenisters Gallery?'

'Because that's why I'm in England,' she said. 'I had a meeting planned at 11am this morning with Philip Charlesworth, the owner of Lenisters. He was coming to see me about a painting he'd acquired but he hasn't showed up and it's really quite a concern. Henry didn't know anything about this meeting, unless Jennifer told him, so I'm surprised he was there. She was the only person apart from my husband and Mr Charlesworth who knew I was coming over and why. I told her specifically not to get Henry involved, as he wouldn't have been able to help himself if he thought I was going to have problems. He can't afford any more trouble and he's done so well over the last few years.'

'Mrs Whittaker.' Stephen paused to consider if this was the right time to investigate a possible link. He decided he had no choice. 'Does the name Tia Hall mean anything to you?'

Constance thought for a second. The name sounded familiar but she couldn't quite place where she'd heard it. It must be something to do with Henry. Then it came to her.

'The girl in his Martial Arts club?' It was Constance's turn to look confused but the memory was coming back.

'Yes.' Stephen could feel he was holding his breath.

'Only that the last time I spoke to him she was all he could talk about. He said she had one of the most amazing natural talents he'd seen and he was hoping he would be able to convince her to compete for the university. He hasn't been so enthusiastic about anything or anyone since...' She didn't finish the sentence. 'What does she have to do with anything?'

Sam spared his boss the difficulty of having to explain.

'Mrs Whittaker, we have CCTV footage of your son leaving Lenisters Gallery at 11.09, just before his GPS was switched off. He had Tia Hall with him in the car.' Sam looked at Stephen who signalled him to continue. 'Tia is Assistant Commissioner Hall's,'

Constance turned to the tall black detective, now completely confused.

'So this is not official police business? You're just here looking for your daughter?'

'Mrs Whittaker, this is official police business. We need to find your son *and* my daughter as quickly as possible.'

'Why? What's happened?'

'Henry and Tia were last seen leaving Lenisters gallery this morning roughly an hour and a half after Mr Charlesworth and his secretary were murdered.'

Chapter 31
Ealing, London Thursday 16th October 2014.

'Does anyone have any cash?' Ashley asked as they turned onto the M4 heading back towards London.

'No,' Tia and Eoin replied simultaneously.

'I have about £100, a credit card and a cash card,' Henry said.

'There's a hotel just off the A4 called the Master Brewer.' Ashley programmed the satnav on her phone with the location. 'It's rough, but it's cheap and I'm guessing they'll rent rooms by the hour. Plus we need to eat and think what to do next. If we stop there we may be able to figure out a way to open the case.'

Eoin pulled off the slip road at Ealing and parked on the industrial estate next to the run-down two-star hotel. Henry paid cash for a first floor room overlooking the main entrance. He and Eoin took the case up to the room while the girls went to find them something to eat. They returned about 15 minutes later with petrol-station sandwiches and crisps. No one complained.

'How on earth do we get it open?' Ashley asked in between bites of chicken tikka on white bread.

'I've seen these before. My parents have a couple for transporting paintings between houses but they've always had the combination code so I've no idea how you open one without that.' Henry was still turning the case round hoping for inspiration as to how it might unlock. He'd already tried the combination used for the safe and it hadn't worked. He didn't want to risk shutting down the system by making too many failed attempts.

'It looks pretty expensive,' Tia said. 'The metal looks like a composite which means it will be tough. My dad always talks about the anti-manipulation features that modern digital locks have. You used to be able to just bang the top and knock out the solenoid that moves the pin but now they have relocking systems that trigger a second set of bolts if you try that. You could get through the original lock and still not be able to open the case.'

'Could we cut through it with an axle grinder or laser pen?' Ashley asked, having no idea what the impact might be on the contents of the case.

'By the look of the metal and the thickness of the casing I'd guess that might take a couple of days. The noise would be unbearable and we'd be investigated in minutes.' Henry thought for a few seconds, searching his knowledge banks for other possible solutions. 'There are chemical compounds - acids - that could cut through metal, but they wouldn't stop when they got through the casing and whatever is inside is apparently worth £50m so I don't think we could risk that even if I could get to my lab and prepare some.'

Eoin had been silent for the entire journey and now he just sat on the bed, not eating and not looking at the case. He listened to their fruitless conversation while battling with his conscience.

Throughout his life Mickey Finnegan, his mother's brother, had unrelentingly told him how much of a loser his dad had been. That he'd run off with another woman before Eoin was even born, leaving Mickey to bring up his nephew instead. For 10 years Eoin had been repaying the debt he believed he owed his uncle by perfecting a craft he hated.

His life had always been tough but nothing came close to the day he'd learned the truth. Seven weeks ago a chance discovery had turned his life upside down. He'd been searching his uncle's attic for a long, narrow wooden box that he'd seen as a kid back home in Belfast. As he dug around the junk that blocked his path to the old chest, buried under piles of paintings and books, he found a faded photo album that had been used as a scrapbook. Inside were pictures and press cuttings of an explosion, alongside details of the innocent victims who had been caught in a failed paramilitary attack. Patrick Driscoll had been on his way home from work when an IRA bomb exploded prematurely in a fish shop on the Shankill Road in Belfast. The device had killed 10 people, including one of the bombers and had been the last killings in Northern Ireland before the ceasefire. The album was a shrine to his father's memory that his mother had secretly preserved, hidden from her brother and her only son. He'd always wondered why he'd been given his fathers surname if he was really so bad, and now he knew.

Eoin had been less than a year old at the time and knew nothing of the senseless murders. His father hadn't run off. His parents had actually been married. Mickey had made him pay every day for his father's alleged desertion. For almost 10 years Eoin had paid in physical labour, suffering daily from guilt and fear of turning out like his dad. His uncle had taken advantage of him for his own greed until Eoin learned the truth. That was the day he'd had walked out of their house and taken refuge with Patricia. He never wanted to see his uncle again. He didn't care how mad he was with him or how violent he could be.

As he sat on the bed Eoin thought of his dad's wasted life, taken before his only son had uttered a word in a tragic attack. His father had simply been in the wrong place at the wrong time and today history had repeated itself. He looked at the three people in the room with him, two of whom he'd only known for a couple of hours. They'd put their own lives on hold and at risk to help him in his hour of need. Ashley had actually put herself in the firing line of a gun to protect him and her family. He owed them. He would have to risk their judgement to make sure they had a chance against the killer who would by now certainly be looking for whoever had alerted the Chinese. Slowly he swung his feet off the bed and went out to the car.

He came back a few minutes later with a canvas bag that looked like a Swiss roll, which he carried with him everywhere he went. He gently pushed the girls aside and sat in front of the metal case, spreading the canvas wrap onto the table. Inside was a huge selection of thin flat keys of varying sizes and lengths. They looked like elaborate versions of the type of key found on the side on a tin of sardines. His toolkit also contained a number of picks and ultra-fine screwdrivers normally only used by jewellers or dentists. Eoin picked up two of the fine picks and slid them either side of the glass disc to the left of the digital number pad. As the fingerprint reader came away he used a piece of Blu-Tack from his tool kit to prevent the disc from triggering the relocking mechanism, sticking it to the casing. Underneath where the glass had been was a tiny slot that looked like a traditional keyhole. Eoin selected a tiny flat key from the wrap and inserted it into the slot. He jiggled it from side to side gently, listening for the tell-tale click of the wafers inside moving slowly into alignment. He worked carefully for several minutes before selecting a second and third key and repeating the process. The others watched as he manoeuvred and cajoled tiny discs inside the case into a precise alignment. Half an hour later he twisted the final flat key slowly to the left and the locking mechanism inside the case popped open, pushing the heavy lid upwards on its hinges. He stood back and lifted the lid fully.

'Bloody Hell Eoin!' Ashley cried in a mixture of disbelief and elation. 'Where on earth did you learn to do that?' She looked at him and the pain and embarrassment evident in his face stopped her pursuing the matter further. She knew enough about his life in Tottenham to guess where this particular skill had come from.

'Even the most secure bank vault in the world has to have a mechanical component to physically work the bolts. If you know what you are doing, you can pick any lock in existence. This is just the equivalent of listening for the clicks on a dial of a safe.' He wasn't ready to tell them the truth about how he knew this just yet, but for the last ten years, his uncle had overseen his education in a trade that had run through their family for generations - theft.

Eoin had been taught to pick pockets before moving onto picking locks. By the age of 14 he had been able to get into any school locker within a minute, no matter how heavy the padlock. He'd been forced to accompany his uncle on numerous jobs, often being pushed through impossibly small spaces to open a door or window from within, until he got too tall. It was a testimony to his uncle's dedication to his training and his own inherent skill that he had never been arrested. He'd been able to work his way through entire floors of hotels in minutes, opening the room doors and their wardrobe safes with ease.

Two months ago, however, he'd almost been caught after breaking into a jeweller's on Green Lanes. His near miss hadn't been with the police, but the brutal Turkish owners of the store who'd shot at his head as he ran off into the night. In fear, he'd started to search the attic for the chest with the shotgun he'd seen as a boy. He'd watched his uncle clean the gun at least twice while they were still in Belfast; a gun he'd forgotten about once he discovered the scrapbook.

He'd moved into Connor's bedroom the next day.

He'd never told anyone about his illicit employment and now his secret had been partially shared with a group of strangers. He was sure they would fill in the blanks with judgments.

'That was amazing!' Tia said, sensing his tension and shame. 'My dad always said there was no such thing as an unpickable lock if you knew exactly what you were doing.'

'There isn't,' Eoin said allowing a tiny amount of relief to seep into his muscles. 'But you can't afford to make a mistake or you make the situation worse.'

'So that's what all the fuss is about,' Ashley said, deflecting their attention back to the contents of the case.

Inside was an oil-on-canvas portrait of a girl wearing a blue dress with a blue ribbon in her hair. She sat in profile against a blue background and it was difficult to estimate her age. The clothing and the ribbon suggested a young girl but her features looked older. The dress was old fashioned - Victorian probably - and fairly simple in

251

design. The quality of the light and the brushwork were beautiful and distinctive.

'That looks well old,' Eoin said with no understanding at all as to what he had just released from the metal case.

'It's almost 125 years old to be precise,' Henry said, staring at the painting that had been the last thing he'd expected to find.

'The colours are amazing and it looks so vibrant. It could have been painted yesterday!' Ashley loved the picture instantly. As a psychology with art student she was captivated by the way brush strokes on a canvas could affect how you feel.

'I wonder who she is?' Tia asked. 'And who painted it? It must have been an artist we've heard of to be worth killing two people for.'

'It's Adeline Ravoux and she was 12 years old at the time.' Henry could not take his eyes off her. He lifted the painting out of the case and held it up to the natural light. It looked perfect. Even the signature looked genuine. 'It was painted by Van Gogh in June 1890 when he was staying at her father's Auberge in Auvers-sur-Oise, just outside Paris. It was one of the last paintings he did before he died the following month in the room where this was painted. He did paint two other versions of her without her knowledge. One is in the Cleveland museum and the other is in a private collection in Switzerland, but this was the painting she sat for and the real one hasn't been seen since the 1950s.'

'What do you mean the real one?' Tia asked quizzically. 'How do you know this?'

'Because the American dealer, Harry Harronson, who bought the original directly from Arthur Ravoux in 1905 for 20 francs sold it to my great-grandfather in 1940 for just over $4,000. The original is currently hanging on my family's living room wall. At the average rate of inflation since 1940, today it's worth would be about $80m or £50m.'

Henry needed to speak to his parents. He hadn't been home for two years, but the painting had still been there before for he left for London. Worrying about being traced was irrelevant now; protocols would have already been triggered.

By now the police would have found his car and would know who he was. Once they had his identity there were a whole series of actions that would be put in place to find him - starting with tracing the experimental chip that had been inserted under his skin when he was twelve, after the second kidnap attempt. Micro chipped like a dog! It had been a good move at the time because the third attempt was the only one carried out by people who knew what they were doing and he doubted he would have made it home alive if the police hadn't been able to follow his tracker. Then when he turned 21 he'd obtained a court order to restrict access to the GPS signal it generated. It could only be switched back on by the judicial authorities and only in the event of a genuine threat. His car parked outside the scene of a double homicide would definitely be classified as a credible threat by the judge authorising the release of the signal so tracing him was now just a matter of time.

He took the SIM out of his pocket and put it back in his iPhone. The minute he turned it back on a barrage of voicemails and texts came through, making the rest of the group jump as beep after beep sounded. Most of the alerts were from Jennifer - of course they would be - but she wouldn't be able to help him. She'd been in England the whole time he had been. It was possible his father may have confided in her but he doubted it. They only involved her in issues that related directly to him. He needed to speak to his mother.

He walked out into the austere corridor and rang her cell phone. She answered almost immediately, which was unusual. The phone must have been in her hand.

'Hello. Constance Whittaker,' was all she said. She'd never answered the phone like that to him before. She sounded nervous.

'Mum, it's Henry. I need to ask you something and it's pretty urgent.'

'You need to speak to Harry about that!' she replied vaguely.

Henry paused. What? His mother was talking to him as if they'd never met before. What on Earth was going on?

'Mum it's Henry,' he tried again 'I need to speak to you about the Van Gogh.'

'Harry will know more about that. I would give him a call now; he'll still be at home. Sorry I can't be of more help.' There was a pause. Henry wasn't sure what to say to his mother. It was as if she were talking to one of their staff. He didn't get a chance to speak again. Before he could reply she terminated the conversation, 'Okay thanks for that. Speak soon.'

And the phone went dead.

Something was wrong, but her instructions were clear, call Harry.

Henry dialled his father's private cell and he answered after a couple of rings.

'Hey son, how's London?' His father sounded perfectly normal.

'Dad what's going on?'

'What do you mean?'

'I just called mum on her cell and she spoke to me as if I were a delivery driver and told me to call you.'

'Maybe she was busy getting ready for dinner.'

'Dinner?' Henry was now completely confused. 'It's 11am in the morning in Washington. Why would she be getting ready for dinner?'

'She's not in Washington, Henry. Did Jennifer not tell you?'

'Tell me what?'

'Your mother had an important meeting in London this morning. She was meeting you for dinner this evening for Jennifer's birthday.'

'Dad I don't know anything about that. When did she fly into London?'

'Last night. She had a meeting at 11am this morning with a gallery owner called Philip Charlesworth, it thinks that's what she called him.'

Henry's blood ran cold! He could feel his nerves preparing adrenaline ready for immediate flight response.

'Who?' was all he could manage in reply.

'Philip Charlesworth. I'm sure that was his name. He owns a gallery in Mayfair. He contacted your mother a few weeks ago suggesting he had something she would be interested in. I'm surprised you didn't know she was there, although I think Jennifer did suggest it might be nice to surprise you.'

Henry froze. He'd phoned his mother to enquire about a painting he'd effectively just stolen from the art dealer she was in London to meet. He didn't believe in coincidences, certainly not on this scale.

'Dad I need to know something,' he said. 'Is the portrait of Adeline Ravoux still in the living room?'

'So you did speak to her?' Harry replied, now starting to become as confused as his son sounded.

'No dad. Why?'

'Because she's taken the Van Gogh with her on the company jet. Whatever this art dealer wanted, I know it caused your mother significant concern. As far as I'm aware the portrait is currently in the safe in her room at Claridge's.'

Chapter 32

Mayfair, London. Friday August 15th 2014.

The Maybach 62 saloon pulled up outside Lenisters Gallery just as Philip Charlesworth was closing up for the day. He was standing by the window trying to program the alarm system and was failing. Serena had already left for the evening to go and meet a friend for drinks and he was struggling to remember the code. The owner of a car like that was definitely someone he would want as a client. Maybe they were coming to see him; after all, most of the other shops on the street were already closed. He'd had business to attend to that he couldn't do while Serena had been here but yet again he'd been unsuccessful in completing his phone call.

The driver got out of the car and went to open the back door. He was at least six feet 2 inches tall, stocky with stubble visible even from where Philip was standing looking through the blinds. The man who climbed out of the back was even taller. He was leaner but obviously fit and much better dressed. They made a formidable pair and would not go unnoticed on this most conservative of streets. The taller man made his way towards the gallery, and Philip jolted backwards as though he had been caught snooping. The bell rang but he hesitated, grateful that he had already closed the blinds.

'Can I help you?' he said through the intercom system.

'I would like to speak with Mr Charlesworth.' The voice was foreign, probably Russian or one of those former Soviet countries.

'Do you have an appointment?' Philip asked, knowing full well they didn't. His schedule had declined rapidly since his father died.

'My name is Boris Rubikov. I would like to make a significant purchase which I am sure Mr Charlesworth could see fit to support me with.'

Philip didn't need any further information. He knew exactly who Boris Rubikov was. In his business you needed to know everything there was to know about the occupants of the top-1000 rich list, especially anyone in the top 100. He pressed the buzzer and the front door clicked open.

'Come in, please. I'm Philip Charlesworth. I was just closing up for the evening and my secretary has already left but I'm sure I can help you with your requirements.' Philip guided the two men through the showroom towards the large office at the rear of the gallery, which he had recently redecorated in a taste more in keeping with how he saw the future development of the business. 'Would you like some coffee?' he asked as they passed the small kitchen.

'No thank you,' Boris replied, taking one of the modern leather chairs in front of the glass desk. The room was different to the last time he'd been here and the new tenant of this office didn't possess the same good taste as their predecessor. The art on the walls was brash and violent. Philip noticed him surveying it.

'They're by a new artist, just out of the Royal Academy,' Philip explained as he sat down. 'We've just finished a summer exhibition of his work and I couldn't help myself. I bought the first 3 pieces on the opening night and I'm sure they'll prove to be a worthwhile investment.'

Boris couldn't agree less. Who would want the tranquillity of their home invaded by these monstrosities, he thought to himself.

'My tastes are somewhat more traditional.' He said, taking out a Louis Vuitton Monogram notebook from his leather briefcase and removing a photo. 'I have reason to believe you recently came into the possession of an item that was left in a safety deposit box in Zurich. I have been researching this particular item for many years now and would very much like the opportunity to purchase it.'

Philip turned the photo towards him. He could feel the Russian scrutinising his reaction but he could barely control his features. He stared blankly at a spot on the floor trying to conceal his surprise and rested his hand on the desk to hide the trembling that he could feel inching down his metatarsals. How on earth could this man have possibly known?

'I'm afraid there must be some mistake,' Philip said, the tremor in his voice perceptible even to him. 'This painting isn't for sale. It was purchased by Aaron Rosenberg over 60 years ago and hasn't been up for auction since. I'm sure you're aware that the Blue Star Pharmacy Corporation is one of the biggest private enterprises in the world and I have no reason to believe that the current owners will have a need to part with the work any time soon.'

'Mr Charlesworth.' Boris looked straight into Philip's eyes and Charlesworth could feel the rings of perspiration forming around his armpits and groin. 'I am well aware that Mrs Constance Whittaker believes she has the original of this painting on the wall of her living room.'

'Mr Rubikov, the Whittaker's were very important clients for my father. He has personally seen that painting in their home in Washington.'

'And I can tell you, Mr Charlesworth, that I have proof that the version on their wall at this moment in time is a fake. I also believe that you recently acquired the original as part of your father's will, although I very much doubt he had any idea exactly what was in the safety deposit box in Zurich.'

Philip could feel the beads of sweat forming on his temples. When he'd opened the safety deposit box in Switzerland he'd been devastated. The Whittaker's copy of 'Adeline' had one of the strongest provenances in the world. He'd been crushed to find a worthless copy of such a work. Anything less watertight would have made for an interesting negotiation with the legitimate owner but in this case the painting was unassailable.

And yet here was a Russian billionaire claiming to know that the painting currently sitting in his basement vault was the genuine version. He couldn't begin to fathom how that was even possible given the very famous purchase history.

Charlesworth doubted that Rubikov would make these claims lightly and felt sure that some evidence at least must exist to back up his allegations.

How much would this knowledge be worth to Constance Whittaker?

She'd refused to take his calls over the last few weeks since he'd discovered the contents of the safe.

Could he risk telling her to carry out her own tests?

If what Rubikov claimed was true then Constance Whittaker could discover it easily for herself. She was one of the top art historians and analysts in the world. She had access to state of the art equipment that might prove Rubikov's claim without needing to involve him at all. If her painting really *was* a fake then a test of the paint itself would soon reveal it.

Excitement at the repercussions of this talk overwhelmed Philip. He couldn't wait to get the Russian out of his office so he could make another call.

'I'm sorry for your wasted trip, Mr Rubikov, but I've no idea what you're talking about.'

Boris stood up and leaned across the desk, pulling Philip to his feet by his collar.

'Now you listen to me, you worthless piece of shit!' He bared his teeth and his breath smelled strongly of vodka. 'I know you have that painting. Rest assured that I will do whatever is necessary to acquire the portrait I have been pursuing for over a decade! You'd be a foolish man to stand in my way!'

Boris released the starched collar and Philip fell back into the chair. He knew he'd been captured on the CCTV coming into the gallery so now was not the time for violence. Vasily came into the room and put a gilt edged business card on the table as the two men left the room.

Boris stopped momentarily in the doorway of the office and turned.

'You know there is more than one way for me to skin this particular cat, Mr Charlesworth. Have a good day!'

And they left.

Chapter 33

Ealing, London Thursday 16th October 2014.

Henry banged furiously on the hotel door, temples pulsating and shouting to be let back into the bedroom. Hillingdon was almost 15 miles from Claridge's and it would take at least forty minutes at this time of day to get back. His elevated adrenalin levels attacked his nervous system sending it into an extreme flight state that he hadn't experienced for eight years. Eoin opened the door and Henry pushed quickly past him.

'We need to get back to London.' He started packing the painting carefully back into the case, closing the lid without activating the locking mechanism. 'I've just spoken to my father and I have another problem I have to deal with right now.'

'Yes we do have another problem!' Tia said, realising where he had been and what he'd done. 'If you've turned your phone on that means the police will be able to track us again. They'll find us before I have a chance to get to my dad and explain things.'

'Worrying about being traced is irrelevant now.' He didn't elaborate about his chip, which had almost certainly been re-activated. 'I have to go back to Mayfair immediately.'

'Are you mad?' Ashley said. She was already on edge and anxious to get going in a different direction. 'We can't go back to Mayfair. We've spent all day trying to get away from there. They must surely know Eoin's registration number by now and Tia's dad will have cops all over the place. If that African bloke is still out there then I need to get to my Mum's and make sure my brother is safe.'

Henry ignored her. If his theory was right her mum and brother would be safe for a while. His mother, on the other hand was potentially in danger and he was sure he knew why.

'Eoin, did Charlesworth say anything to you about the second drop being made today? Anything at all about where it was or who he was meeting?'

'No, he just said that he had an important appointment that he had to go to personally, but that he would be able to track me from his phone. I saw the girl put that case in the vault before answering the phone but she didn't say anything either.'

'Henry what's wrong? Tia said touching his arm and feeling guilty for reprimanding him. His manner had changed considerably since he left the room. His normal confidence and assurance had disappeared. She'd only ever seen him laid back and unfazed, but now he seemed to be in a panic. 'You're scaring me.'

'We need to get to Claridge's hotel immediately.' Henry paused and felt a wave of conflicting emotions wash over him but fear was dominant and he held his breath as his words caught up with his thoughts. 'I think my mom is in danger.'

'What's happened?'

Henry was losing track of his own rationale. Ideas were flying through his mind at such an alarming rate his logic was failing to keep them in sequence. This new information was difficult to comprehend. He didn't believe in co-incidences so there had to be an explanation as to why he was guarding a copy of the painting his mother just happened to have brought over to London yesterday. He needed clarity to be able to see the expanding puzzle in full so he tried to explain things to his friends.

'The person Philip Charlesworth was going to meet this morning with this painting was my mom.'

His audience looked at each and slowly drew a collective breath of disbelief as the revelation sunk in. That surely wasn't possible. Inside Ashley felt compelled to break the stunned silence and speak but she couldn't find any words so Henry continued. 'Apparently he contacted her a few months ago and they arranged to meet today. She flew into London last night and my dad thinks she was planning to surprise me by turning up at Jennifer's birthday dinner this evening, which is why she never told me she was coming'

Tia felt her heart sink. She'd forgotten about Jennifer. She blushed slightly as she became aware that she was thinking about Henry and not the impossible coincidence he was explaining and on which she needed to stay focused.

'I can only guess that Charlesworth told my mum he had this painting and somehow convinced her that they needed to have the two side by side to make a comparison.' As the words came out yet another possibility struck him. Maybe this one wasn't a fake after all. 'Van Gogh painted two other versions of Adeline Ravoux without her knowledge. Maybe this is an undiscovered fourth version although it's identical to the original.' He knew he was clutching at straws. That explanation was unlikely and he discounted the option as quickly as it had come into his head – no artist would make an exact copy of their own painting right down to the direction of the brush strokes; certainly not one in the fragile state of mind that Van Gogh must have been in so close to his suicide. He paused for a moment and shook his head, debating with himself, trying to reassess what he actually knew. 'She's bought the original over with her and it's in her room at Claridge's right now. Why would she do that? She knows more about art than almost anyone in the world and has the resources to check his story. She would never have risked moving the painting outside of our house unless she found something that worried her. If he was able to convince her to come to London and bring the portrait with her then there must be more to this that we don't yet know. I need to speak to her urgently, but it sounded like there was someone with her because she was really weird on the phone. I think its possible that she may have been the real target and that someone may already have got to her.'

'How can that be true?' Tia asked, trying to keep pace with the changing scenario. 'Even you didn't know she was in the country.'

But Henry's mind was racing now.

'Well my dad and Jennifer knew, plus my uncle, Richard employs her security team and nothing gets past him so it wasn't a complete secret. Any one of her staff or flight crew could have let it slip. As far as I'm aware my mom had never met Philip Charlesworth before. What if the killer intended to impersonate him and go to her hotel and steal the real one? ' Henry's train of thought continued to jump from one unfounded conclusion to another. 'Eoin, when we first met you said that you were worried about Ashley's family being in danger because you'd been asked for by name for this job. Is that right?'

Eoin looked at the floor nervously. He was the reason everyone was in this mess because he'd taken advantage of his friend and moved into their house.

'Yes, that's what Charlesworth said. That I'd been booked specifically and that he'd given Mr Yau my name and company details so he'd be able to find me. I thought he was just trying to scare me and to be honest, it worked!' Eoin had spent the whole day trying to explain this very point to himself and had so far failed miserably. Why had he been booked specifically? 'I thought maybe he knew about my lock picking talents, but it can't be that. I've never been caught, have no criminal record and only my uncle ever knew what I could do. Some random bloke in Mayfair would never have known that.'

'That's been bothering me too. Why you?' Henry's consciousness was flooded with wildly erratic explanations. 'Charlesworth could have phoned any courier in Central London. Why phone an East End courier company to deliver a package less than five minutes away from a West End office. Usually a specialist art handler would be used to deliver paintings, not a courier service and there must be hundreds nearer than your firm. Even upmarket taxi services could have done the same job. Why ask for you?'

Eoin could only think of one reason.

'It must have something to do with my uncle. He's a thief, and I don't mean like a drug-crazed opportunist. He's an expert.' The words hung in the air.

'Eoin if they wanted you to actually steal the painting they would have told you. I don't think this has anything to do with you or what you can do. I think someone wanted you to do this job because of where you live!'

Moments of silence passed as his conclusion hit home.

'Hang on!' Ashley abruptly realised what he was suggesting and objected. 'He's been living at my mum's house. Are you saying that my mum had something to do with this?'

Henry tried to suppress a smile at the thought.

'No Ash, not your mum... You!'

Embers of anger began to flicker in her eyes again. Tia thought she might punch Henry if he let her get close enough and got ready to step between them.

'You think I've caused all this?' her fiery temper was dangerously close to exploding. 'I nearly got shot because of that bloody painting!'

'No I don't think that at all.' Henry sat at the table and picked up a pencil and paper and tried to draw out the connections.

'I think someone was going to steal from my mum and were setting me up to take the blame. God knows I've done enough bad things with their money in the past for a jury to make that connection stick. It starts with Charlesworth planning to meet her this morning. Somehow he got her to bring a valuable original Van Gogh with her halfway across the world, even though they've never met before. Someone wanted to make sure that I was in or near that gallery when the meeting was supposed to take place.'

'How does Eoin lead to you being in the gallery?' Ashley was lost.

'Ashley, how many people do I socialise with at the college?'

'No one that I know of,' Ashley replied.

'And how many people have I met socially outside of college that you do know of?'

Ashley paused and reflected. She didn't understand. She had explained to Tia only a few weeks ago, on her birthday, that she had bumped into Henry in Soho one night but she didn't know anyone else he'd met. She realised what he meant.

'I only know two people you've met outside college - me and Tia!'

'That's because you are the only two people I've had anything to do with outside of my studies and the martial arts club. I have not had a conversation with another person outside of those two topics apart from you two. I know that's true, because I've made it true. For 8 years I've been in a self-imposed prison, allowing myself only to study and fight.'

'But I only met you a month ago,' Tia protested, not wanting him to blame her.

'And that is why it comes back to Ashley.' Henry drew the connecting lines onto the paper.

'Charlesworth contacted my mum two months ago and arranged this date for a meeting. I didn't know Tia then, but if someone had been watching me and following me the only person they would ever have seen or heard me contact outside of my family was Ashley. She is the only person who has my cell phone number in this country. They would have seen us go out on Tia's birthday. They knew that you would be the only person in London I'd have helped if you'd asked. They wouldn't have known I wasn't with my mum this morning and that I didn't even realise she was here so they set up a situation that would keep me away from the hotel while they went in and pretended to be Philip Charlesworth and stole her original and made it look like I'd killed Charlesworth for blackmailing her. They could easily set me up to take the blame if there is CCTV footage of me at the gallery – a good lawyer could easily make a case for me stealing from my parents after the trouble I've caused them in the past.'

'That makes no sense,' Tia was scribbling furiously on the scrap of paper, trying to maintain her reason and perspective. 'If someone wanted to get you out of the way surely they would have done something to Jennifer. She's your girlfriend after all and in the country all the time!'

Henry looked at Tia and battled with what to tell her. She would never understand the complexity behind his relationship with Jennifer and he didn't have time to explain it properly right now. Jennifer's story would have to wait. Right now he would just give her the facts.

'If someone was watching me and studying my habits they would never have taken on Jennifer,' he said.

'Why not?' Tia could feel herself staring into his eyes, willing him to disown the woman she would love to replace.

'Because Jennifer used to work for the FBI,' Henry admitted, disorientating Tia completely. 'She was a special agent and is more than capable of handling herself and anyone that might try to take her on. She was attached to one of my protection teams after... my accident. That's how we met.' Henry watched closely for signs of acceptance from Tia. Disappointment was etched into her face and he hated hurting her. He knew she wasn't convinced but she didn't probe further.

'So you're saying I was an easy target?' Ashley was furious with him now.

'No, just easier than someone who had been trained by the best in the world to spot signs of deceit and risk. If something bad had happened to Jennifer I'd be the last person she would call for help. In fact she would be processing the reasons as to how it came back to me as they were taking her away. She's protected me for so long it's almost habitual now. She is always at least three steps ahead of every move I make.'

'But I called Tia for help, not you. I only rang you because you had a car and she had a hangover.'

'And that is the bit that I think was just pure luck for whoever planned this. If you hadn't met Tia, who would you have phoned first this morning?'

Ashley was poised to argue back but then just looked at the floor defeated. She had no other friends in the world. She had never had time for friends until she met Henry, and then Tia. There was no one else she could have called.

'You,' was all she could say.

'So what you're saying is someone killed Charlesworth and lured you to the gallery so they could get access to your mother and her painting and then make it look like you orchestrated his murder?' Tia asked.

'Yes,' Henry said, wondering why he hadn't been able to summarise it so succinctly. Tia looked up from her laptop and shouted abruptly into the room.

'I don't agree.' She couldn't believe she was arguing with him but his logic was flawed. 'At least not with all of it.' She added quietly, her embarrassment at being so forthright returning.

'Based on what?' Henry defied her to come up with another explanation, praying that she could.

'Well I agree with your theory about why they targeted Eoin. Someone wants this to look like it somehow ties back to you and as long as the connection from Eoin to Ashley to you could be shown, it wasn't even necessary for you to have been at the gallery. That just makes the connection stronger. But I don't think they planned on going to the hotel to confront your mother. For a start, if your theory was true, why did the killer drive all the way out to Windsor to open the case if he was planning to go to Claridge's as Philip Charlesworth. He would have locked the doors of the gallery and opened the case in there before walking across the road to the hotel.'

Henry had no explanation for that.

'Plus there's more. ' Tia turned her laptop round to face the others. His mother's face was staring back at them from a photo he'd seen in the press only a few weeks ago. She was arriving in New York for his father's fundraising dinner, flanked on all sides as usual by huge, efficient-looking bodyguards.

'You've never told us who your mother is - only your father. While you've been talking I've been running some basic checks on the internet.'

'So?' Henry braced himself for the truth to come out

'Your mother was Constance Colefax before she married your dad. Her mother, Caroline, was the only child of Aaron Rosenberg, who started Blue Star Pharmaceuticals.'

'I've heard of them!' Ashley added.

'Your mother is the majority shareholder of a $62 billion dollar empire. She is the second richest woman in the world!' Tia continued.

Ashley's mouth fell open. She couldn't even imagine what that number would look like written down, never mind as a pile of cash.

'I don't think this is about your mother or her painting. Do you really think that if someone had unbridled access to her they would be worrying about a $50m Van Gogh that you yourself told us would be virtually worthless once it was stolen? Does she ever travel without those bodyguards?'

'No.' Henry started to realise the flaws in his assumptions. 'She's not allowed to go anywhere without at least one of them under the terms of her life insurance. Richard insists on it.'

'Will she have someone looking after her right now given she is one of the biggest security risks in the world?'

'Yes'.

'And when she travels does she have special protocols for making reservations and booking flight plans in place?'

'Of course she does,' Henry said 'All her movements are protected by aliases and alternates. She has a PA just for her travel arrangements, and they have worked for her for 20 years.' An army of personnel worked round the clock to allow his mother to have the feeling of living a normal life. Her Chauffeur never even drove the same route each day when he took her to work.

'Then this isn't about your mother. At least not primarily. If someone knew exactly where she was going to be and when and could get that close to her, they would just go to the hotel, shoot you, shoot the bodyguards and take *her* - not a painting that would plummet in value as they walked out the door! She'd be worth much more than £50m in ransom money. Why bother shooting the gallery owner just because he has an appointment with her, which he never actually made it to. Whoever is doing this doesn't care where she is or what she's brought with her. From what you've just said, I think your mother has discovered the same thing Charlesworth suspected when he contacted her; something that you personally *could* be accused of wanting to take into your own hands. I think he may have wanted to blackmail her or extort a huge finders fee in excess of his 10% commission. Why else would she have entertained his claims and come all the way to England with the painting in tow. I think she knows that the painting that's been hanging in your living room for years is possibly a fake.' She pointed to the metal case on the £49-per-night bed. 'Whoever is planning all this wants that painting, and I think they've set everything up to make it look like you did too!'

Chapter 34

Hackney, London. Thursday 16th October 2014

Andrew Hatcher pulled up outside the controller's office at Elite Couriers and watched as several pedestrians on Lower Clapton Road disappeared into the shadows at the sight of the patrol car. The windows of the surrounding shop fronts were obliterated by posters advertising goods and services aimed at a displaced population. Turkish kebab shops competed with Polish supermarkets and Caribbean hair stylists. Almost every outlet offered international phone cards at huge discounts to call home, wherever home may be.

He went into the run down building and asked to speak to the person in charge.

Stan Meaney came out from a small office to the left of the filthy reception area. He was approaching 60 years old, and despite living in Haringey for almost 50 years still spoke with a strong Belfast accent

'Can I help you?' he asked pulling a Pall Mall cigarette from a crushed pack and pulling off the filter. He lit the cigarette in front of the man who was obviously a copper, almost daring him to try and stop him. His office, his rules.

Andrew produced a warrant card he hadn't used in five years, ignoring the cigarette. He had more important things to worry about.

'DAC Andrew Hatcher, New Scotland Yard. I need to speak to you about a booking you took for a delivery this morning.'

Stan didn't need to ask which booking. It was 4pm and he'd had a feeling something was wrong for the last three hours. He hadn't heard from Eoin all day and the job should have taken less than an hour. Not even a complaint so he assumed the package had been delivered as expected. Now suddenly everyone wanted to know where he was.

'You better come into my office,' he said leading the way. 'What has that little shit done this time? Where's my car?' He sat down in a battered leather chair and pulled an ashtray out from under a file of paperwork.

'I was hoping you would be able to tell me that, sir, assuming we're talking about the same person.' Andrew took out his notebook and began to write his usual meticulous notes. Five years behind a desk wasn't enough to break some habits. 'I need to know who you sent to Lenisters Gallery in Mayfair this morning.'

'His name is Eoin Driscoll.' Stan didn't hesitate. He hated the police but he wasn't getting in trouble for that useless boy. 'I knew I shouldn't have sent him but they insisted. I gave him my own bloody car, what's happened to it?'

'Sir, can you give me the registration number of the vehicle Mr Driscoll was driving?'

Stan wrote his own registration number inside a dried coffee-cup ring on a Post-it note and passed it across the ancient metal desk.

'What exactly was the nature of the booking?' Andrew resumed his note taking, which included details about Stan himself. He couldn't stop himself wondering what dubious activities he'd been involved with in the past.

'Some posh bird phoned up looking for a top-end car to deliver a package to the Mandarin Oriental Hotel. She didn't say what the package was. Paid by credit card.'

'Did she give her name?'

'Hang on; I've got the original booking sheet here. I just had my hand on it. They had never used us before and I didn't recognise any of the info she gave me.' Stan swivelled round in his chair and picked through a pile of papers before turning back with a grease-stained worksheet from the shelf behind him. 'Her name was Serena Holdsworth. She was so bloody stuck up I could barely understand her.

She booked the courier to arrive at 9am sharp, dressed smartly wearing white gloves and with a car, as the package was quite large. We've never had a job in the West End before so I was hoping it might be a nice new earner! Do you know what I mean, inspector?'

Andrew knew. No one would turn down work in Mayfair. There might be a lot of crooks there, but not the sorts who do runners from cab drivers.

'How many drivers do you employ here?'

'About 15 usually although we do have a few casuals we can call on when we're busy. Most of them only do bike work though and don't have cars.'

'Does Eoin Driscoll have a car?'

'Don't make me laugh!' Stan leaned back in his chair. 'He can't even afford a car air freshener. His uncle threw him out of their house over a month ago and he's been shacking up with some old lush on the Broadwater Farm Estate in Tottenham. He's a dodgy liberty taker if you ask me and I wouldn't have sent him if it was down to me. I've got much better drivers.'

'So why did you send him?'

'Because the posh bird asked for him by name. Said that he'd been recommended to her and she would only use us if we sent Eoin. She also had a long list of security checks he needed to complete on arrival. I was sure he'd screw that up and I bet I'm right, ain't I?'

'Do clients usually ask for a specific driver?' Andrew ignored the request to bring Stan up to speed.

'Never had it before. Most of our clients don't even register the driver as a person - he's just a walking advert for the firm who delivers the stuff they're too busy or lazy to take themselves.'

Andrew made careful notes of the questions that were forming as fast as he was getting answers. Why had the courier been asked for by name and who had made the recommendation? Given the person making the booking was now in the mortuary he doubted he would ever know.

'Do you have an address for where he is living?' Andrew knew the Irishman was not going to be much more help.

'What's happened to my car?' Stan was burning with curiosity but he was more concerned about what had happened to his Mercedes and his packages. He hoped to god the police hadn't found them.

'I can't tell you that at the moment sir, but if you can give me the address I'll let you know as soon as we have any word.'

'Well you better hurry up and get in line mate, cos I've just given his address to his parole officer. That's why the worksheet was out.' Stan would kill Eoin himself when he eventually showed up. 'He's just left. The little shit never told me he'd been in prison when I gave him a job, and nor did his uncle.'

Andrew looked at the old man quizzically. He'd never heard of a parole officer turning up at a place of employment before. At least not without an appointment; it was the parolee's duty to go to them, not the other way round.

'What was he in prison for?' he asked.

'No idea. I didn't know he had been. If I had I'd have never given him a job.'

'Did the parole officer show you any identification?'

'Yeh it looked just like a police badge.'

'You said Eoin had just moved. Where did he live before that?'

Andrew was concerned. Broadwater Farm was in Tottenham and came under a different station for police and parole services. Why would they come all the way down here?

'He lived on Meridian Way in Edmonton with his uncle. I think he'd been there since he was about ten.'

Andrew pulled out his radio and called his office.

'Margaret, can you check if a parole officer was sent to see Eoin Driscoll at Elite Couriers today. It's in Lower Clapton Road but I think he'll be with the Tottenham division.' He waited while the secretary made the necessary checks. 'And can you check the record for Eoin Driscoll of Meridian Way, Edmonton.' He added, wondering what the boy had been in trouble for previously. As he listened to the reply he turned to look at Stan and his eyes widened. He repeated Margaret's message to the Irishman.

'Eoin Driscoll has no criminal record! He's never even been arrested before!'

'So who was the bloke looking for him? He had a South African sounding accent and didn't look like someone you'd mess about with.'

Andrew was already a step ahead of Stan in his assessment.

'What's the exact address you said he was living at?' He switched his police radio back on as Stan wrote it under his registration number on the Post-it note.

'Urgent assistance required from any units within the vicinity of Broadwater Farm Estate. Suspect is an I.C.1, white male, dark hair, South African accent, believed to be armed and dangerous.'

Chapter 35

Ealing, London. Thursday 16th October 2014

Henry reopened the lid of the metal case and appraised the painting again. He had to admit he would never have been able to tell them apart. The brushwork, colours and light looked exactly the same as the portrait he'd grown up looking at every day over dinner. He wasn't an expert but if there were differences between the two paintings his mother would be able to tell. He knew some of the chemical tests that she used to check for age and paint composition but she would have to interpret the results. He'd only really paid attention to the science when she'd showed him her lab and hadn't taken much notice when she explained what the results of each test meant.

He couldn't argue with Tia's assessment of the situation though. Of course kidnapping his mother would be worth more to a criminal than a stolen painting if they cold get access to her. The board of directors at Blue Star would vote unanimously to pay any ransom. Their share price would never survive the crash if anything happened to her. Not that Richard would even give them a choice. In her absence, Richard assumed control of voting rights for her shares and Henry's trust until Henry turned 30 in 4 years. That would give him 51% of the shares and enough to sanction the ransom payment without involving the rest of the board at all. He also had to agree that whoever was behind the murders was not responsible for his mother being in the country. She had flown to London specifically to see Philip Charlesworth and to listen to what he had to say. Henry knew he needed to stay focused on that and find out exactly what it was.

'Whatever Philip Charlesworth's reasons for contacting my mother were, they were compelling enough for her to come over from the States and bring the original Adeline with her.' He was unable to bring himself to acknowledge that his mother's version of the painting may not be genuine. . 'If this copy is so important that someone was prepared to kill two people to get it then I need to show it to her. She's an art expert and may even already know why Philip wanted to see her today.'

'You'll never get close to her without being seen.' Tia pointed out. 'If the police know she's in London, which I assume they do by now, they'll have posted a patrol unit outside the hotel and you'll be picked up as soon as you walk through the front door.'

'I think they may have already been there when I spoke to her earlier, Henry said recalling the bizarre conversation. 'Her behaviour was weird and she was obviously unable to talk to me. I thought it might have been whoever was behind the murders, but it makes more sense that the police would have gone to speak to her once they found out she was here. I'll need to get her to meet me somewhere else. We also have to assume that they now know that Eoin was the courier and that he's a potential witness to the murders and obviously everyone will be looking for Tia, but at the moment no one knows who Ashley is or that she was there too. I am going to need you to get a message to my mother to come and meet us.'

'But where can we go?' Tia said. 'I'm sure they'll be watching our accommodation and the college to see if we go back. They may even have traced the tracker for Eoin's Mercedes by now.'

'They won't get anything from that,' Eoin replied. 'Stan doesn't trust the authorities at all. He disabled the tracker as soon as the car left the showroom. We should be okay for a bit but the traffic cameras will eventually pick up the number plate if we go back.'

'There is another alternative,' Tia said hesitantly.

'What?' three voices asked in unison.

'I could contact my dad and ask for his help. At the very least he could get someone over to Ashley's mum's flat to make sure her family are okay.'

Ashley nodded her approval. As far as she could see there was no way they could continue to try to chase this gunman on their own. They were unarmed and would be no use if he arrived at the flat still carrying his gun.

Eoin wasn't so keen. He'd spent his whole life learning how to avoid the police and to conceal evidence to protect himself. They may not think he was just in the wrong place at the wrong time. But he'd spent the last two months looking over his shoulder, checking that his uncle wasn't following him; the last thing he wanted was another person to look out for; one just as vicious and with more to lose.

Henry agreed they couldn't put their own interests ahead of the investigation into the two deaths this morning any longer. Their reason for chasing the killer and not calling the police had felt right at the time – they had to track the case before he cut the trace and disappeared into the wind but there was no excuse any more. In hindsight it was foolish – they should let the police deal with chasing the murderer now. He had something else to worry about. If someone really was setting him up to make it look as if he was behind the murders then he needed to find out why. He couldn't do that if he was locked up in a holding cell. He needed more time to check this painting and see exactly why it was important enough for someone to kill for. A plan was forming….now he needed to execute it.

'I agree we will have to go to your dad soon but first I need to speak to my mum and get these two paintings in the same room so we can try and work out their significance. If someone is trying to frame me then I need to understand why and for what. I can get into my lab at the college without being spotted. I have a key code to the back entrance because PhD students work outside normal college hours. It can't be seen from the street, so even if they have a patrol car outside I think I can avoid it. Ashley, if you can get in to see my mum and get her to come with you to my lab I have the equipment and the chemicals there to examine the paintings.'

Tia nodded her agreement.

'If I go to my dad alone and take him through what has happened, that might give you enough time to get your mum over to your lab and carry out whatever tests she thinks are necessary. I'll try to buy at least an hour and then bring him over to the college. I know he will believe me eventually but we've broken a lot of laws today - we've left the scene of a crime, although technically we did report it and I'm sure the fingerprint analysis in the telephone box will prove that it was Ashley who made the call. We also took their phones and the woman's bag but we needed them to contact Yau. Worst of all we caused a shootout in Windsor that left a shop in ruins but I'm fairly sure none of that can be traced back to us. Mr Yau is not going to be able to prove we had any involvement in the shop attack, other than telling him where his painting was. On the plus side, Ashley can now positively identify the murderer if they ever catch him but maybe I'll wait until they do before we let my dad know that! I'm not sure we need to tell him we took a painting just yet. It was never registered as having ever been in the gallery so they won't be looking for it. But if they have questioned your mum then she may have told them. I'll just say she was meeting Charlesworth without mentioning the second case. Hopefully that will give you the time to check them out with your mum. '

'So!' Henry said standing up and closing the case again. 'Lets go and face the music!'

Chapter 36

Mayfair, London. Thursday 16th October 2014.

The journey back into London was just enough time to plan how to get Ashley into the suite at Claridge's, past some of the best hotel security in the world, including Constance's own bodyguards. The A40 was slowing to a crawl as the evening rush hour headed towards its peak, but they were going against the main flow of traffic until they got to Edgware Road.

'Eoin, drop me at the American Embassy and I'll go back to the gallery,' Tia said looking at her Google map of their destination 'Then drop Ashley at the hotel and Henry in Tailstock square. I think you'll have to leave the car somewhere after that because once they find out the registration number, your car will flag to central control the minute we get to Hyde Park'

As they slowly rounded Marble Arch and headed onto Park Lane past the congestion zone traffic cameras, they braced themselves for their various confrontations.

It was dusk when Tia got out of the car on Park Street. As the Mercedes drove off towards Claridge's Tia walked past the American Embassy and realised she'd never seen it before. She crossed Grosvenor Square and saw the phone box that Ashley had used had been taped-off just as she'd predicted. As she turned into South Audley Street she could see the police cordon still blocking the entrance to Mount Street. Two officers were posted in front of the tape turning cars away and directing them to alternate routes through the Mayfair rush hour. She approached one of the officers, her heart pounding. For the first time in her life she was on the wrong side of the law her father was charged with upholding.

'Officer, I need to get through,' she said as her blush flamed up her neck.

'You can't come through here love. You'll need to go round to the left and through Berkeley Square.'

From where she was standing she could make out a face she recognised standing in the street talking to a crime-scene technician in white overalls. She recognised Sam from her many visits to her father's office. He'd been the one who had given her the illicit software that she'd used at the start of the day. She took her student union card out from her bag and held it up.

'Officer, if you call Sam Ainslie over I'm pretty sure he will want to talk to me.'

The officer looked at the teenager and scrutinised the pass she was holding up in front of him. How did she know the name of the senior officer working on this site? As soon as he registered the photo and name he jumped into action.

'DAC Ainslie!' he shouted down the street, instinctively grabbing Tia by the arm and pulling her under the blue and white tape.

Sam turned toward the commotion and saw Tia with the policeman. He broke into a sprint.

'Tia, what the hell is going on?' he was shouting. 'Your dad is frantic!'

He came over and took the officer's hand off Tia's arm and led her towards the gallery. He pulled out his radio and called Stephen.

'Guv, its Sam. I'm at the gallery and Tia has just turned up.'

Stephen was sitting in the lobby of Claridge's lost in thought. He'd left Constance Whittaker in her room but hadn't left the hotel. Something told him her son would turn up or make contact eventually and he wanted to be there if Tia was with him. He'd left Sam to go back to the crime scene and carry on the investigation, which would take them well into the night.

The lobby guests turned and starred as his loud radio echoed through the marble atrium and news that his second in command had Tia back safely came through.

'Don't let her out of your sight!' he shouted, jumping to his feet and alarming the guests having their pre-dinner drinks. He ran out of the main entrance, into Brook Street and back in the direction of Lenisters. 'I'll be there in two minutes.'

Stephen forgot all of his police protocols as he ran towards his daughter and wrapped his arms around her. The officers working on the street watched as the most professional cop on the force dropped his guard and gave into his own humanity, prioritising his daughter over everything else that was going on around them.

'Oh my god Tia, where have you been?' he could scarcely breathe. 'I've been worried sick.'

'We need to talk,' was all she could manage.

Stephen led Tia back into the gallery where she'd stood just seven hours earlier hacking a PC that was no longer on the wall. The two bodies had been removed but the blood and tissue still clung to the floor tiles and mahogany sideboard reminding her of the devastation she'd left behind. She was visibly shaking as they walked into Philip Charlesworth's office, which was being used as the command centre for the investigation.

'Tia this is a really serious crime scene and we have CCTV footage showing you leaving here at 11am. I'm going to have to ask you questions but Sam is going to have to sit in here with me.' Stephen had no idea how he would make it through an interview with his own daughter but he knew in his heart that she would have an explanation.

'That's okay dad. I'll tell you everything I know, but then I'm going to need your help. I don't think this is over yet.'

Tia began the tale as the four had agreed it should be told.

'Eoin Driscoll is a courier for a company based in the East End. At 8.45am this morning he turned up to collect a delivery he'd been hired

282

to make. It was to take a painting valued at £1.4m to a Chinese businessman in the Mandarin Oriental Hotel in Knightsbridge. The gallery owner, Philip Charlesworth was late getting into work and wasn't ready for Eoin to take the painting. He made Eoin wait in the kitchen while he sorted out the delivery – we also now know that he had a meeting with Constance Whittaker at Claridge's, which is why he needed a courier.'

Stephen listened carefully. Everything she'd said so far he already knew. The name of the courier had been sent through to him just over half an hour ago, along with the license plate of the car.

'Where is Eoin now?' he asked 'I've got officers on their way to his Tottenham address as we speak.'

'Dad, I need you to trust me. I'll tell you everything that has happened but you need to let me take you through this in order or it won't make sense!' Tia couldn't afford to have her train of thought interrupted if she was going to get things right.

Stephen looked at his daughter. He'd expected her to be hysterical and traumatised but she was calm and efficient in her narrative. He didn't speak again and she continued.

'Eoin heard the shooting, but couldn't see the man who did it because of the central pillar in the room. The gunman clearly couldn't see Eoin because of the two-way glass in the back doors. After he left, Eoin realised the killer had taken the painting he was supposed to be delivering to Mr Yau. He panicked. Charlesworth had told him the Chinese man would come after him if he failed to turn up on time. He didn't know what to do, but knew there was a tracker in the case. He called Ashley because he is staying at her mum's house and asked her to help him. He was worried he'd put her family in danger. Ashley is my friend but she's a psychology with art student and doesn't know anything about computers so she called me.'

'How did you end up in a car with Henry Whittaker?' Stephen still couldn't help interject over the man who'd last been seen with his child.

Tia dropped her gaze to the floor and felt the return of her undetectable flush. Her father was the only person who could recognise it and put a hand on her knee.

'It's okay, you can tell me.'

'I had some trouble on my way home last night and Ashley helped me out. I was very shaken so she took me for a drink to calm me down and I had too much. She slept on my floor last night and knew I wouldn't be able to get to her on my own this morning. Not in time, at least. I was too ill and had no idea where Mayfair was or how to get there. Henry's the only person she knows with a car. He picked me up and brought me here.'

'God, are you okay?' Yet again Stephen momentarily forgot his job as his concern for his daughter rose again. Sam took over the questioning.

'Tia, what did you do when you got here?'

'I logged into the computer using your file, Sam and accessed the GPS tracking system. I took Philip's phone and we followed the signal out to West London.'

'Why didn't you call the police?' Her father interrupted again.

Tia hung her head again and bit her lower lip. She knew there was no excuse. She should have trusted her dad and his team. Looking back at the risk Ashley had taken to get the painting back to Mr Yau, Tia knew they'd been reckless. But she also knew that by the time they explained everything, even to her father, the murderer would have gotten away. They had only just made it to Windsor before the trace disappeared. It had been a judgement call and they'd made it together.

'I guess we panicked. I knew from spending time with Sam that once the aluminium case was opened and the tracker was disabled we would lose the trail and the killer would get away. Following that tracker was the only way of finding whoever was responsible for the murders and I knew we only had a window of about an hour or two before he would pick the lock and be gone. We also thought that Mr Yau might go after Eoin, which could have put Ashley's family in danger. He's been living at her mum's flat for the last month. Our only thoughts were getting that painting back to Mr Yau and finding the murderer. I know I should have trusted you but everything was happening so quickly, and to be honest I didn't know if you would believe me.'

Stephen was feeling physically sick as his brain processed the potential consequences of his daughter's actions.

'You went after an armed killer on your own?' He could hardly believe what he was hearing. Had he really instilled such a profound sense of right and wrong that she was prepared to put her own life in danger to bring a gunman to justice?

'Dad, we didn't actually go anywhere near the gunman. On the way out to Windsor I called Mr Yau who was on his way to Heathrow. That's why we had to take Charlesworth's phone. I told him where the painting was and he sent someone to recover his property himself.'

Tia didn't tell him that Ashley had been in the basement with the murderer when Yau's men had arrived, had been shot at and could probably identify him if necessary. Ashley needed to get to Constance before the police started to look for her too.

'So Mr Yau got his painting back?' Sam asked. 'We've checked on him and his flight left Heathrow for China over an hour ago. He was on board and the manifest showed that he checked his painting into the hold under special transfer conditions. Apparently he only just made it.'

'I don't know about that,' Tia lied. 'Once we told him where the case was we left him to it. All he did was recover what was his from the man who stole it. I'm assuming that the gunman got away?'

'Tia, for him to have made that flight this must have happened at least three hours ago!' her father said. 'Where have you been since then?'

Tia knew she needed to stall. Henry needed more time and she couldn't tell him about the second painting they'd taken from the gallery yet. He would have to arrest her for theft and she needed him to come with her to Henry's lab. She put her head in her hands and rested her elbows on her knees.

'I feel dizzy, dad,' she said. 'I need some water.'

'I'll get it,' Sam volunteered as Tia had hoped.

As he left her alone with her father, Tia lifted her head urgently.

'Dad I know I'm getting you into loads of trouble but I need you to help us. Whatever it was the gunman wanted, he didn't get it. He took the wrong painting from the gallery this morning by mistake. While we were in here we found the case he was after. The one Charlesworth was taking to Henry's mum. There was nothing on the computer to say it even existed. No purchase history and no record of it ever having been in the gallery. Eoin saw Charlesworth's secretary put it in the safe and we got it out.'

'How?' Stephen could not believe the things his daughter had managed to do in such a short space of time this morning.

'That doesn't matter at the moment. What is important is I need to take you to Henry to help find out what whoever hired the gunman is really after. Until we know what is in that second case we are all in danger, including Mrs Whittaker. The killer must realise by now that someone was in here when he shot those two people. How else would Mr Yau have been able to find him so quickly? I need you to help me, and worry about all the trouble I'm in after this is over. The killer obviously got away from Yau's men or you'd have him in custody by now. He's messed up whatever he was paid to do so we think he will already be looking for Eoin or he'll go straight after Henry's mum. We also think whoever hired him is trying to make it look like Henry had something to do with it and must still be looking for that second painting. I'll explain why later but for now you need to trust me. I know you should take me in for proper questioning but we don't have time. We need to get to Henry before things get worse.'

Stephen anxiously started clicking the lid of his pen as he contemplated the worst decision of his life. Even as a teenager in Brixton he had lived by his principles and put doing what he thought was right ahead of the feelings and demands of his family, siding with the police instead of the rioters. Now his daughter was asking for his help in leaving a crime scene where she was a primary witness because she believed the danger was still real.

His principles had helped him climb to the highest levels of a career that had previously been almost impossible for someone like him to pursue. He looked at his daughter and felt a surge of pride. How many other teenage girls would go to these lengths to help their friends and assist the police? Their shared principles stood firm. His duty first and foremost was to prevent any further crime. Solving murders that had already been committed wouldn't bring the victims back and any issue still on-going took precedence. If more people were still in danger then that was his priority. Every instinct in his body told him to trust his daughter and work with her. His team could carry on working on the process of gathering evidence here. He had to make one quick decision. Should he involve Sam? It would be easier with his help but he might potentially be putting his career in danger. Stephen might be willing to risk that for his daughter but he wasn't sure Sam was, or even should. Stephen tried to think logically, as he'd been trained to do. If the girl sitting in front of him, telling him this story, was anyone other than Tia what would he do? He would probably take them into custody and question them further and try to establish the facts, by which time he might be too late to prevent further bloodshed. But this *was* his daughter; he knew her better than anyone else in the world. Logic was important, but Stephen knew in his heart that her story was genuine.

As Sam came back in with a glass of water Stephen made the call.

'Sam, I need to get Tia out of here and go to see Henry Whittaker, who thinks his mother may still be in danger. This is your call but I need a favour. If you don't want to get involved then I'll send you off somewhere now and you'll know nothing about it. It's entirely up to you.'

Sam looked at the man who had been his mentor and friend for ten years; he knew the principles that guided him and the consequences of what he was asking him to do in breaking the protocols concerning witness testimony. Yes police work was about following procedures – but it was also about following your gut. He knew he should take Tia back to the nearest police station and take a formal statement. Possibly even arrest her for leaving the scene of a crime, and maybe aiding and abetting a murderer. That's what the 'book' said to do. He had a family to support! But he also trusted Stephen unequivocally. He'd known Tia most of her life. If her instinct told her someone was still in danger then he wouldn't argue. Sam's daughter was only eleven, but he truly believed if she were in this situation then Stephen would do the same for him. He didn't need a second option.

'Where do we need to go?'

Chapter 37

Tottenham, London. Thursday 16th October 2014.

Andrew Hatcher pulled up at the entrance to Wellesley House on the Broadwater Farm Estate and surveyed the proximity illuminated by the flashing blue light of the patrol car. The streets appeared deserted even though it was only just gone 5pm but he suspected they weren't; the calm created a dangerous sense of security for the naive pedestrian. He silently thanked his lucky stars that he hadn't grown up in an area like this. It was getting dark and he was out of place. Policing neighbourhoods like this took sensitivity and precaution, but he didn't have time for either at the moment. He'd already put on body armour on the drive from Hackney and didn't wait for his driver to get ready. As he jumped out of the car two back-up patrols pulled up in formation. An armed officer got out of the back of one in full-body protection and riot gear. He ran over to Andrew and led the way into the building as more tactical response officers followed.

Stan Meaney had given this as the address currently being used by Eoin Driscoll and a file copy of his driving licence, required for their insurance records. A check with the DVLA showed that he was still officially registered as living in Edmonton so Andrew guessed he hadn't been here that long.

He looked at the numbering on the doors. There appeared to be 23 flats per floor and he needed number 213. Typical! He thought. Tenth floor and no working lift!

By the time they reached the top landing he was out of breath and the last to arrive. Sitting at a desk all day had rapidly undone his years of training. He sincerely hoped he wouldn't need to chase anyone today.

Andrew turned left towards number 213 and gave the sign for the armed officers to proceed. No breech was required. The flaking painted wood from the door was splintered and scattered onto the doorstep. Someone had already put a boot to this door recently and not a lot of force had been required.

He examined the door as the armed unit entered the flat to secure it. The feeble Yale lock was in pieces on the hallway floor. He was one of a handful of officers in the Met recently authorised to carry a handgun, a Glock semi-automatic pistol, which he pulled out from his holster.

'Armed policed, put your hands in the air!' The officers' cries echoed through the tiny apartment. He watched as they carried out the sweep he'd been trained to do only two months earlier as the police force slowly increased its armed presence. He'd never expected to have to use this training in the field.

The lead officers kicked open the living room door.

'Police. Is anyone at home?'

Nothing. They tried again.

'Armed police. Come out with your hands above your head and don't make any sudden movements.'

Inside the living room, they could hear a faint moaning. Andrew rushed in to check if anyone was hurt.

Patricia Rivers was lying on the floor with a two-inch gash across her forehead. The stained, ancient carpet was soaked with her blood. Andrew knelt down to check her pulse. Her wound was still open and she was barely breathing. The blood hadn't started to clot telling Andrew this had happened in the last thirty minutes. He looked around the room to check for any other damage. There were no signs of any bullets having been fired and he suspected the woman had been hit with the butt of the gun rather than shot at. If this was the same person who'd murdered the gallery owner and his secretary this morning he'd changed his methods. Leaving a witness without shooting them suggested to Andrew that ammunition may be an issue for whoever was responsible. He pulled out his radio to summon medical help.

'I need back up and an ambulance to 213 Wellesley Buildings on the Broadwater Farm Estate now,' he shouted at the dispatcher. He bent forward and checked her for any other sign of injury. A broken spirit bottle had cut into her left wrist but it was only superficial. Andrew suspected it had occur when she fell.

'Hello ma'am, can you hear me?' he asked her. 'I'm deputy assistant commissioner Hatcher. Can you tell me what happened to you?'

The woman smelled strongly of gin and Andrew suspected it wasn't just a blow to the head causing her unconscious state. Then she muttered something faintly.

'Matt…' was all he could understand.

'Madam, who is Matt? Was he the one who attacked you?'

But it was no use. She was unconscious again.

Andrew started to look through papers scattered across the small table and in the sideboard drawer. Her name was Patricia Rivers. A couple of final demands sat unopened next to the only photo in the room, showing a girl of about 12, a boy of 10 and another boy who was no more than 3 or 4. The photo looked to be about 10 years old judging by the clothes they were wearing. Next to the photo, lying face down, was a cheap certificate frame. Andrew turned it over and found a letter of acceptance to UCL for an Ashley Rivers, to study Psychology and Art. Wrapped around the bottom of the frame was a rosette for second place in a kick-boxing tournament three years ago. That couldn't possibly be a coincidence. Same college and martial arts? There had to be a connection to Tia.

Andrew moved out to the kitchen as the paramedics turned up and he pointed them towards the living room. There was literally nothing in the kitchen. Not even a pint of milk.

The main bedroom was in a disgusting state. He doubted it had been cleaned this year and the bed covers had worked loose exposing the bare mattress underneath. Dirty laundry was scattered across the floor and an empty bottle of vodka stood on the tiny bedside table. How could anyone live in conditions like this?

He finally checked the second bedroom. It was a very different story. Both beds of the double bunk combination were made and the floor was spotless. A small TV stood on an upended crate. Whoever played this old PS2 had to sit on the end of the bed as there was no room for a chair. An old single door wooden wardrobe took up the remaining space in the room. Stephen opened the door to find male clothes in two different sizes hanging from the rail. School uniform for a boy of about 14 years old took up most of the space, along with a couple of sweatshirts and an out-of-date Tottenham football shirt. Jeans for a man of about 6'2" hung underneath a fake Ralph Lauren Polo shirt clearly belonging to someone larger than the 14 year old. There was no one else at home in the flat.

Andrew sat down on the end of the bed. As he watched the out-dated animation repeat over and over on the screen he tried to call the unsettled feeling he had into focus. Something in this room wasn't right. As he watched the little dragon on the screen wait patiently for his life to be restored Andrew realised what was strange. The TV was on! A game was in progress and the cartoon character had died through lack of interaction but the action had not been restarted. Someone had been playing this recently judging by the on-screen request to press the cross to try again. Andrew pulled out his mobile.

Stephen answered on the first ring.

'Andrew where are you? Tia came back to the gallery and has taken us through what happened. We are on our way to the University. What have you found out about the courier?'

'That's good news about Tia,' Andrew said. 'As she's there, can you ask her if she's heard of a Patricia Rivers?'

Stephen passed on the question and came back to confirm that she thought it might be her friend Ashley's mum, but that she hadn't actually met her. The mention of Ashley's name told Andrew it was the same family.

'Ask her if Ashley has a young brother.'

Silence. And then the answer came back.

'Yes she has two. Connor is 22 and Matt is 14. Why?' Stephen asked.

Andrew's hand holding his phone dropped to his side as he looked out of the bedroom window into the street. His thoughts flew back to the solitary word the unconscious woman in the living room had spoken. She had tried to alert him. When the intruder broke into her flat she hadn't been alone, but there was no one else here now. He raised the mobile back to his ear and spoke to his boss.

'Someone has been to the flat. The woman is unconscious with a gash on her head. She'll be okay but I think the younger boy may be missing!'

Chapter 38

Mayfair, London. Thursday 16th October 2014

Eoin coasted along Davies St, barely allowing the wheels of the Mercedes to stop turning for Ashley to get out opposite Claridge's. Ashley watched them drive away across Oxford Street before turning to look at the world famous hotel for the first time in her life. The white ionic columns were backlit by low-hung balls of light and flanked by the grand lanterns that hung on the white stone-slat walls. The song from the musical 'Oliver' floated into her mind and for a second she wondered what it really would be like to own a suite at Claridge's and run a fleet of carriages. Inside was a woman who did and she needed to speak to her urgently.

Henry had given her specific instructions but hadn't had time to explain the significance of what she needed to do. She would just have to trust him. His mother would be staying in the Brook Suite, her favourite, which could only be accessed by those with a security key for the private lift, or by scaling the outside walls. She was going to need help from inside.

Before she could go into the hotel she needed to go shopping. Henry had given her his credit card and directions.

Ashley walked down Brook Street watching carefully for any obvious signs of police activity. She crossed Bond Street and turned right, walking a couple of hundred yards until she came to Smythson's stationers. Garlands of roses and carnations framed the curved white windows and the marble entrance floor lead the way into the brightly illuminated showroom. Recalling Henry's precise instructions, and clutching his PIN-activated Centurion AMEX card she walked in and went straight to the counter. The immaculately groomed assistant showed no sign of surprise at the attire of the red head; even rich people have weird fashion tastes and eccentricities.

'I need a sunflower correspondence card.' Ashley had no idea what she'd actually just asked for but she stuck to the instructions she'd been given.

'Yes madam.' The assistant opened a draw and pulled out a pack of six postcard-sized yellow-edged cards with three simple yellow stems of different heights along the sides. The yellow tissue lined matching envelopes felt like stiffened linen. 'That's £26 please.'

Ashley swallowed and tried to hide her utter disbelief that these small cards could cost so much, but it wasn't her money so she pushed the charge card into the card reader and entered the PIN.

'Do you have a pen I could borrow?' she asked the assistant. She took the black lacquered ball pen and wrote the words exactly as Henry had told her on one of the cards and put it into an envelope. She then printed '*Caroline Rosenberg*' - *Brook Suite* on the envelope, put the rest of the cards in her bag and left the shop.

She walked back towards the hotel and climbed the front steps. On the Broadwater Farm Estate, surrounded by junkies and muggers, she felt safe and familiar; as she entered the opulent entrance hall of one of the world's most famous hotels she wanted to flee. Her heart was racing and she felt intimidated by the wealth that surrounded her but she pushed the feelings to the back of her mind. She needed to get up to that suite.

Ashley ignored the reception desk and went straight to the concierge as instructed. She handed a £20 note to the man on the desk and asked him to call the Brook Suite.

'I have a delivery of sunflowers for Caroline Rosenberg,' she explained.

'We don't have a Caroline Rosenberg staying in the Brook Suite!' Derek Maltby replied snootily looking her up and down, before returning to his paperwork, ignoring the money. The only woman he'd known to have had that name in his 35 years at this hotel had been dead for almost a decade.

'Mrs Whittaker will understand the reference,' Ashley whispered pushing the note closer. Maltby looked up from the list of names he was staring at. Not many people knew the connection between those two names! No one knew that this was the real name of the current occupant of that suite other than the hotel manager and himself. The concierge pocketed the £20 note, dialled the extension and delivered the message. His eyebrows raised and the urgency of the reply was obviously not what he had expected. He listened for a few seconds before calling over a bellboy.

'Can you take this young lady up to the Brook Suite. Our guest needs her to come up immediately.' He looked at Ashley expecting her to go and get her delivery. She just turned towards the lift. 'Where are the flowers?' he called after her. She turned back and held up the yellow card before turning left out of sight,

The walnut-panelled lift climbed slowly to the 7th floor and opened noiselessly into a similarly panelled corridor. The only door visible was already open and an elegant woman stood silhouetted against the cream walls of the room behind her. Outside the door a man dressed like a stockbroker stood motionless and expressionless.

Ashley recognised her instantly; the similarity to Henry was unmistakable.

'Mrs Whittaker?' she asked.

'Yes.'

Ashley handed her the card addressed to Caroline Rosenberg and the two women stood in the hallway for a few brief seconds as Constance read the words Henry had dictated to Ashley.

29th September 1959.

That was all it said. Constance looked at the multi-coloured explosion stood in front of her and smiled.

'I'm sorry, I didn't catch your name?'

'It's Ashley, ma'am,' she replied as if addressing royalty.

'Come in Ashley,' Constance said stepping back inside the suite.

The Brook Suite living room was bigger than Ashley's entire flat in Tottenham. Huge cream sofas were arranged around a pale-pink wool rug on a pale oak floor. The view from the glass-walled window overlooked the most beautiful parts of Central London.

'Would you like something to eat?' Constance asked as if she were receiving a friend for afternoon tea.

'I'm starving!' Ashley suddenly realised she'd only eaten a single sandwich all day - something that hadn't happened for a few years. A man dressed in a tailcoat appeared from nowhere and asked if she would prefer coffee or Diet Coke.

'Got any PG Tips?' Ashley asked. The butler nodded and disappeared into an adjoining room.

As soon as he'd left Constance allowed her guard to drop.

'Oh god! Where is Henry?' she pleaded. 'Is he okay?'

'He's fine. He's sent me to get you, but we need to get out of the building without being seen and he needs you to bring the Adeline Ravoux portrait with you. You need to be really careful - he thinks you could be in danger.'

Constance didn't show any sign of surprise that Ashley knew the portrait was in the hotel. Her priority right now was her son.

'What is going on? I've had the police here most of the afternoon. They told me the art dealer I was supposed to be meeting had been killed and that Henry was somehow involved. The officer I spoke to said his daughter was with Henry. Is that true?' The flurry of questions was halted as the butler returned with a tray that must have already been prepared before her arrival. Ashley ate furiously as they waited for him to pour the tea and leave.

'I don't really understand what's happened either.' Ashley spoke with her mouth full of bread, desperate to get her story out. 'Two people have been murdered and we've got a painting that he needs you to look at. He thinks it's the one that Philip Charlesworth was bringing to you this morning. I've been sent to take you to his lab at the university so he can compare it with your original. He'll explain everything when we get there.'

'Has he spoken to Jennifer?'

'I don't think so,' Ashley replied. 'But he's had the SIM card out of his phone most of the day.'

Constance looked down at her mobile, trying to decide what to do next. Jennifer should have put the protocols into place to activate Henry's tracker hours ago. Certainly once his abandoned car was discovered in Windsor. How had he managed to avoid her all day? If he really had been kidnapped the delay could have been fatal. She excused herself and disappeared into the master bedroom.

Ashley hastily drank her tea, trying not to spill anything in this immaculate room. Constance came out with an aluminium case almost identical to the one they had taken from the gallery that morning apart from black metal monograms across the front - C.C.W. She'd changed into tailored jeans and flat shoes and was wearing her coat.

They were going to the university.

Constance opened the front door and spoke to the huge bodyguard that was still standing outside.

'Adams could you go and bring the car round to the front of the hotel.'

Constance couldn't trust any of her current security detail given one of them was leaking information to her brother. Richard could not find out about this and she wasn't taking any chances that he would, especially if he had more guards en route. As he disappeared in the private lift Constance beckoned Ashley to follow her down the fire escape staircase to the 6th floor through a door that could only be opened from inside the Brook Suite. There was no restricted access to this conference floor and a bank of lifts allowed them to be in the lobby two minutes later. The two women headed away from the concierge desk, where Constance would be instantly recognised, and out into the street. Ashley put her fingers in her mouth and whistled loudly, summoning a black taxi off the street.

'Gordon Square,' she said and they climbed in just as Constance's limo pulled up outside the main entrance to wait for her. Ashley relaxed enough to allow her curiosity to get the better of her.

'What was the significance of that date on the card? How did you know I had a message from Henry?'

'My mother was better known as Caroline Colefax. Rosenberg was her maiden name. On the date you wrote on the card she was still a Rosenberg. It was the date she first met my father,' Constance explained. 'Only four other people in the world know that they met in a florist where he was buying sunflowers for his first wife's grave; myself, my husband and my step-brother, who are both in New York, and my son! Now we use it as a secret verification code. It's how I knew that whatever message you had came directly from Henry Now I need to get to him urgently.'

As the taxi turned left onto Bond Street, Adams ran out of the front of the hotel. He took his phone from his pocket and dialled his employer.

'I've lost her,' he said, expecting the tirade that was now coming down the line. 'She just left in a taxi with a stocky girl with red hair and she's taken the case with her.

Chapter 39

Bloomsbury, London. Thursday 16th October 2014.

Eoin drove past the Christopher Ingold building and noticed the police patrol car parked in the side street to the right of the main entrance almost immediately. He turned right into Endsleigh Gardens and pulled over at the back of the building.

'Pop the trunk,' Henry said, unbuckling the seat belt he'd worn for the first time in a car. He couldn't afford to do anything that would draw attention to them.

'I'll take the painting up to my lab while you go and park the car at least a mile away. Call Ashley when you get back and hopefully she'll be on her way with my mum. You'll need this number to get in the back door then its second floor, third door on the right.' Henry handed Eoin 4 digits on a scrap of paper.

He took the aluminium case out of the boot and turned into Taverton Street. The back entrance to the building was actually the bin store. Behind the huge rancid metal dustbins a keypad entrance allowed unchecked access for a select few trusted staff with the code.

Henry's lab was a fusion of an old-fashioned school chemistry lab with a high-tech bio facility. Racks of test tubes of varying sizes sat alongside modern machinery more likely to be found in a hospital.

He lifted the case up onto the workbench and removed the painting, placing the case on the floor behind him. There was no decorative frame - just the canvas nailed tight over the internal wooden stretcher frame. It looked perfect in every respect.

He began preparing the equipment he would need to carry out the tests he'd watched his mother perform when he was younger and was just developing his interest in science. She'd hoped that the fusion of the science he loved and her passion for art would inspire him and to an extent it had – pushing him further towards science than she'd hoped. Now he studied DNA in the same way his mother investigated brush strokes.

Taking a scalpel from his assembled tray of tools Henry careful scraped some of the blue paint from the side of the internal stretcher frame and put it into a test tube. He added a drop of water and an organic solvent before inserting it into the liquid chromatography-mass spectrometer. Inside, the component compounds of the paint ionised and fragmented and passed through the mass spectrometer ready for detection. As soon as the output was ready the machine would produce a spectrum of the chemicals used in the paint and which his mother could have to analyse. He repeated the process with a sliver of the wooden stretcher itself.

Henry turned the canvas over and, using the scalpel again, cut a tiny fragment of fibres from the back of the portrait, close to where the rusted nails held the material in place. He taped the threads to a slide and put them under the microscope on his desk. He switched on his desktop computer and pulled up a reference list of material samples under microscope analysis. He set the magnification to the exact same level as the reference diagram for cotton canvas, the most common type used in oil paintings.

As he looked through the eyepiece he was surprised by what he saw. The fibres weren't the usual distinctive smooth twisting strands of cotton and didn't match the reference photo. The edges were parallel and more jagged and the strands were thinner. He called up the reference catalogue and began to manually search for a match.

His concentration was disturbed by the alert on his phone. A text came through. Ashley and his mother were just pulling up in a taxi in Taverton Gardens.

He ran down the stairs and opened the back door, checking that no one had seen them pull up. Eoin wasn't with them but he had the code and knew where to go. He hugged his mother, all thoughts of their fight over Thanksgiving forgotten.

'Where's Jennifer?' she asked.

'I've no idea,' Henry replied. 'I haven't spoken to her all day.'

His mother looked worried. Now they had both given their protectors the slip. No doubt all hell would break loose with their insurance companies if they ever found out. Thank goodness Richard would do whatever he could to bury it.

'How has she not been able to trace you or the car? She should have been with you by now. We have no bodyguards and are breaching our life insurance cover.'

Constance was getting angry. This was supposed to be Jennifer's job.

'Well let's worry about that when she turns up. I need you to bring the Adeline up to the lab and work through these tests with me. I've never done a full investigation before, and I only know the science - I need you to check the art.'

The three of them went back up to the lab. The Adeline copy was lying on top of the spectroscope.

'We need to get to work,' Constance said picking up the new Adeline and turning it round for appraisal. It looked immaculate and her instincts were already starting to fire. 'When Philip Charlesworth first tried to contact me about a copy of Adeline's portrait I left him to deal with Alex, my assistant. He told her that it had been left to him through his grandfather's will, and had been in a safety deposit box in Zurich for the last 65 years. He had no idea who'd taken out the box and left custody to his family, but he had the key and the account number so he recovered the item and brought it back to London'

Constance opened her case and took the Whittaker version of Adeline out of its foam surround. It hadn't been outside their family home for almost 70 years, unseen by anyone other than their intimate circle of friends. She placed it on the counter next to the Charlesworth copy and continued to explain the contact she'd had so far with the gallery owner.

'Like you, Charlesworth initially assumed the work was a fake because he was well aware of the provenance of the version in our home. He faxed me a scan of his painting and wanted to know if I was aware of any copies that had been authorised by the Ravouxs because our portrait hadn't been seen on public display for many years. He only knew we had the original because his father had seen it hanging in our living room as a young man when he came to oversee delivery of the Francis Bacon. I simply told him I wasn't aware of any exact copies and thought that was the end of it.'

As she spoke Constance worked swiftly and methodically. She put the new painting under the industrial Infrared Reflectographic Analyser. It was by far the largest piece of equipment in the room and looked more like an oversized photocopier. Henry usually used it to look at layers of tissue cell structures but it would do the job. It would show the different densities of the painting's internal materials, where layers of paint that had been applied on top of each other. It would identify if there was another painting underneath the one that was visible. It was common for canvases used in art forgery to be recycled paintings, especially if the canvas needed to be old. It would also show any grid lines and drawings under the paint that might help determine how the forgery was completed or confirm the practices of the real artist. She placed a film plate under the scanner and moved behind the protective shield at the back of the room to activate the imaging process, instructing Henry and Ashley to do the same. Once she had the X-ray captured she resumed her story.

'Charlesworth then called again at the end of August and his manner was very different. He was much more arrogant and insistent. He told me that he'd taken his work for testing and the results had come back entirely consistent with it being painted at the same time as our original. He said he had a buyer who had documented proof that his version was the real portrait but that he was keen to work with me. I knew exactly what that meant. He wanted to sell me a painting we have owned for over 70 years. Obviously we know Van Gogh painted two other versions of Adeline, but they don't look like this one. One is bigger with much brighter blues, and the other is a square and just of her face. Adeline herself wasn't even aware of the other two according to an interview with her. So it's entirely possible that there could be a fourth portrait, but as you can see, this version is an exact replica of ours.'

Constance studied both paintings carefully and up close. The nails in both frames were intact and original. There were no spare holes or signs that the canvas had been moved in any way. The craquelure on the surface of the paint was similar and both had signs of aging paint, although one had spent the last 70 years on the wall of an air-conditioned Washington mansion, whilst the other had been sitting in a safety deposit box with no exposure to light or air at all. It looked more luminous and vibrant but that wasn't really a reliable comparison given their histories.

'I've got a sample of the blue paint and the wood in the mass spec.' Henry brought his mother up to speed, walking her through the test she'd once shown him how to complete. He shone a UV Wood's light over both paintings but neither showed any sign of repair or alteration.

As they compared fluorescence the spectroscopic analysis of the wood printed out. Constance studied the profile – poplar dating from about 1895 give or take 10 years. It was the right timeframe but not enough to be conclusive - the stretcher could have been used for another picture beforehand. Constance was starting to believe it might be impossible to tell these two paintings apart.

'Charlesworth was absolutely convinced that the version he had was also an original Van Gogh. He speculated that maybe Harronson had either purchased a fake or a second copy from the Ravouxs. The only way we would be able to tell for sure was to have the two paintings side-by-side and make a physical comparison. He was so emphatic I carried out a couple of tests myself. I've already tested the wood used in our version and the analysis came back with a similar profile for poplar, cut in 1900 give or take 10 years. That only just puts it in range for the original, which was completed in 1890. So I carried out IT Reflectographic analysis even though I knew it would only really help if the two portraits were viewed together? What I found was enough to convince me that I needed to take Charlesworth's claims seriously so I agreed to come over.'

She put both the films from the IR scans into the light box, one at a time. The Whittaker version had gridlines printed underneath the oils. It was a technique that Van Gogh hardly ever used. As the second film slid in next to its companion the difference was clear. There were no grid lines on the Charlesworth version. No underlying painting typical of forgeries that required aged canvases - just bold sweeping outlines of the portrait that emerged as the finished work - exactly how Van Gogh usually composed his paintings. The Whittakers looked at each other. Had they really been living with a forgery for all these years?

'There is one last test left to do,' Constance said, her heart sinking rapidly as her beloved work became increasingly suspect. 'I've avoided carrying it out because it would mean taking paint samples from the very centre of the portrait, which may then be noticeable and would leave permanent damage to the surface of the art, but if my theory is correct we only need to test one of these paintings.'

'So what's the theory?' Henry asked.

'The back of the chair is painted in various shades of yellow and you can see that there are a few clear differences in shade between the two paintings. The real Adeline was painted in 1890, when Indian Yellow was still available as a colour, but it was withdrawn by most manufacturers that year, and totally banned by 1910 because of its lead content. The trouble is, we have to test the real painting, otherwise we may just get a false negative. It is really the last resort used by an conservationist because it degrades the surface of the painting, in this case right in the middle of the work, but I don't think we have another choice.'

'There is one other thing I tested,' said Henry holding up his hand to halt her. 'I took some fibres from the back of the one we found in the gallery and the threads didn't look like normal cotton canvas under magnification. I didn't recognise them.'

'Let's have a look,' said his mother.

He showed her the microscope and she examined the sample. As her eyes adjusted to focus on the image she began to laugh.

'What's funny?' Henry asked.

'I read a story somewhere that Paul Gauguin had purchased a huge bail of cheap canvas that he and Van Gogh used instead of cotton. It was very unusual at the time as virtually no one else used it and no forger would ever know to do the same. Those fibres are the same as the material from that canvas bail - jute!'

Henry turned over his mother's portrait and pulled some fibres from the edge. Which ever was the original he was literally pulling it apart, thread-by-thread. He put the new fibres on a slide and put it under the microscope. The fibres where smoother and spiralled in the ribbon like manner that cotton twists into. Constance looked through the scope and recognised the fibres of traditional artists canvas immediately.

As the reality sunk in that their priceless work of art was really a fake, and that they were now in possession of the real Adeline, they didn't notice Ashley studying the films still in the light box.

She was an art student, and knew very little about the science used in testing forgeries. She did, however, have an exceptional eye for detail, no matter how fine.

'Did Van Gogh ever draw on the back of his paintings?' she asked.

Henry and Constance looked at her, not understanding what she was referring to. She pointed up at Charlesworth's real Adeline and traced the path of barely visible lines that they couldn't make out. They looked almost like strands of fine hair that had become trapped under the canvas.

Henry ran his finger along the film and quickly found a faint trace of a straight line, which led to a corner and another straight line. He looked at his mother and then turned over the actual painting, checking the reverse..

'There are two sheets of backing paper on this version of Adeline.' He pointed to the outlines on the light box 'Someone has added a second layer and there appears to be something trapped between the two sheets.

Chapter 40

Bloomsbury, London. Thursday 16th October 2015.

Constance stared at the forged painting she'd lived with since she was born. Van Gogh's work had been her passion for decades. She knew how he held his brush, the length of his strokes and the colours in his palette. The copy was exceptional; the forger had obviously been a talented painter trained in the same Impressionist style as most late turn-of-the-century artists. But now she could see it wasn't the real thing; she'd just never had reason to question its authenticity. The Ravoux's were poor, uneducated hoteliers. They would never have noticed the paintings had been switched because the differences were so subtle.

Still Constance couldn't shake off the nagging feeling that something still didn't make sense in this whole situation. She accepted that her portrait was clearly a copy, but what she couldn't understand was why it had been forged. If the results of these crude and rapidly carried out tests were to be believed the replacement must have been painted a mere ten to fifteen years after the original. At that time Van Gogh's reputation was only just starting to grow. Why would someone want to copy a painting that at the time could have been purchased for a few francs? Forgers at the turn of the twentieth century were copying Turners and Raphael's – not recent Impressionist art.

She thought about the story known to everyone in the art world as to her portrait's acquisition. Harronson had bought the two paintings owned by the Ravouxs for just 40 francs. Could the other one they'd owned be a fake also?

She knew that wasn't possible. 'The Town Hall in Auvers' had been sold less than 20 years ago and would have been thoroughly tested for authenticity at that time. She was too tired to even think about their next steps now. The day had frayed her usually calm nerves to a fringe and she had a sinking feeling things were not going to improve any time soon. She mentally resigned herself to saying goodbye to her beloved Adeline.

'I'll ring my contact at Christie's and ask them if they can store both of these paintings in their vaults until we can get an official verification of authenticity,' Constance said taking her mobile out of her handbag. 'Then we'll need to get the Van Gogh Museum to rule on who owns the original and what we can do about removing the backing paper to see what's behind it.'

'No mum,' Henry stopped her, placing his hand gently on her shoulder. He had reached no such conclusion! Only the three people in this room knew the truth, and potentially whoever was after Charlesworth's case, but they could have no possible physical evidence given he was in possession of both paintings. Constance had immediately defaulted to the view of the professional conservationist that she'd trained for decades to become. She was suggesting they just give away a £50m painting that to the world she legitimately owned and that had most likely been stolen from the Ravoux's in the first place. Henry was much more pragmatic and not prepared to concede to whoever was orchestrating today's events. 'Don't talk to anyone.'

He breathed deeply, as her expression suggested she would take some persuading. He picked up the portrait he'd been carrying all day and held it up for them both to see. His mouth pursed as his plan crystallised in his mind.

'As I see it, no one other than Charlesworth, and possibly his secretary, knew this painting even existed. His reputation would have been at stake if he'd been caught attempting to sell a forgery, especially of such a well-known work. I suspect he used different labs to carry out any paint and wood sample tests to prevent one individual institute from working out what he'd found. That's if he had any tests performed at all. After the day we've had today, and from what you've just told us, my gut is telling me that Charlesworth only really considered the possibility that this version might be the real one when someone else made a ridiculous offer for it and claimed to have documentary proof that it was the real one! I suspect it's the same someone who has obviously gone to a huge amount of trouble to get it and who will stop at nothing, including murder, if that's what it takes. He may just have been taking a huge gamble in calling you, to see how you reacted when you saw them together. It hasn't taken a lot of work for you to be convinced.' He ran his hands over the frameless painting, resisting the urge to pull off the backing paper to inspect what was hidden behind it.

'As far as the art world is concerned you own the real version of Adeline Ravoux. Who else is there is to say, out of these two paintings, which one is yours?'

As if to make his point he put the real one back into Constance's case, closed it and put it on the floor behind his desk; metaphorically and physically out of sight. He picked up the version she'd brought with her from the States and laid it in the case they had taken from the safe in Lenisters Gallery, on top of his desk.

'Whoever took the original from the Ravouxs went to a lot of trouble to copy it and conceal its theft and then protect it from discovery for over a hundred years. At the time they couldn't have had any clue what an original Van Gogh would be worth in the 21st century. Now it seems they may also have hidden something in the back. I want to look at the backing paper and whatever might be behind it but we are not safe here at the moment.' He started gathering up the evidence from the various tests they'd just carried out in record time. Tests that would never hold up in court but were enough to convince him they were *now* in possession of the genuine Adeline. 'Tia is probably on her way with her father and I don't want you or the original painting here when he arrives. I have enough trouble to talk my way out of as it is and you don't need to be involved in that.'

'I'll go back to Claridge's with your mum and the original painting,' Ashley volunteered. 'I'll make sure she gets there safely. Eoin can stay with you when he gets here cos he's gonna need to talk to Tia's dad. They must know he was at the gallery before the murders by now! Where the hell is he? I thought he'd be here by now!'

Before anyone could answer, the door to the lab swung open clattering against the glass-topped room partition. A tall imposing figure with unkempt dark hair came into the room, pushing a thin, ginger boy in front of him and brandishing a handgun. The boy's arm was twisted up behind his shoulder blade, pulling him to one side, and he was clearly in pain.

'You'll be going nowhere!' Joseph Colthart said pointing the gun at the boy's head as he shuffled him in front of him.

'Matt!' Ashley yelled, instinctively wanting to rush towards her younger brother. Colthart pulled back slightly on the trigger, releasing the safety catch, as Henry caught Ashley's arm and dragged her back towards the workbench.

'Stay where you are girl, unless you want your brother's brains blending in with that monstrosity you are wearing,' Colthart said. 'You aren't getting the better of me so easily this time.' As soon as he'd seen the only photo in the living room of the Tottenham flat he'd recognised Ashley as the bogus junkie he'd shot at this morning. Even at 12 years old there was no mistaking the plump redhead who'd locked herself in the charity shop bathroom. 'I was hired to collect a painting for my client and I always deliver on my contracts.'

'How did you know where we were?' Henry didn't expect an answer but couldn't stop himself from asking. Apart from the people in the room, only Tia and Eoin knew where they were going with the painting and she was currently explaining the day's events to her dad. They should be here any minute if he could just keep this guy talking.

'You don't need to worry your pretty boy head about that, Mr Whittaker!' Joseph said, waving the gun to indicate that they should all

311

move away from the desk.

He kept Matt in front of him as he moved forward to check the contents of the aluminium case on top of the workbench. This was the right painting – exactly as his client had described.

'Get the case.' He pushed Matt towards the desk, and the teenager closed the lid on the aluminium case that was identical to the one Colthart had lost to the Chinese earlier. 'Now, little brother is going to come on a trip with me for a while. Thank you for deactivating the tracker, but I have a delivery to make now.' He moved backwards towards the door and pulled Matt with him. Normally he would never leave witnesses behind but he only had 3 bullets left in his gun. His extra ammunition was in the pocket of the coat he'd left in the charity shop.

Ashley stood at the end of the bench gripping its edge in fury and inching her way forward as slowly as she could. For the second time that day she was staring at this man's silenced gun, but this time it was pointing at her baby brother.

Matt picked up the metal case and turned towards Colthart, extending his arm outwards so the Zimbabwean could take the case, not wanting to get close to him again. Ashley watched carefully and waited until his fingers intertwined with the handle. His body was unbalanced now; his centre of mass was forward and unevenly weighted by the case itself. Her training allowed instinctive judgments of speed and timing to guide her attack. As his frame began to straighten she lunged forward onto her left foot and kicked out furiously with her right, launching the case forwards and upwards into Joseph's groin, at the same time pulling Matt backwards onto the floor behind her. The gun went off but the bullet shattered a glass flask on the next desk, spilling corrosive liquid onto the wooden surface. Yellow gas escaped into the room and Constance began to cough. Henry pulled his mother down behind the workbench and pulled open the outlet tap for his Bunsen burner. The colourless gas hissed as it escaped forward and he slammed the top of the tap with a metal canister from the chromatography unit. The spark ignited the gas, which sent a jet of flames forward towards the gunman.

'Ash! Henry shouted and Ashley spun sideways, rolling onto the floor out of the path of the flame.

Colthart clung tightly to the case. He stepped back and pulled his gun back up to fire at Ashley, who was now beneath his feet. She kicked the case up again towards his hand and the bullet ricocheted off the top of the titanium frame. Henry threw a heavy-based chemical jar of hydrochloric acid at Colthart and the room filled with more smoke as the acids and gases mixed.

Colthart backed up towards the door and pulled the gun upwards again, moving the case behind him, out of Ashley's range. He pulled back the trigger and the sound of the mechanical hammer aligning against the bullet casing ripped through the room. From behind the gunman a crunch of metal on bone added to the cacophony and Joseph spun round just as the air expanded and the cartridge left the chamber. The gunshot echoed through the room. From the open lab door Eoin had frantically struck the right of Colthart's head with a metal window pole, spinning him round and knocking both the gun and the gunman to the floor.

Visibility was almost non-existent in the room now. Ashley was shouting furiously for her brother to check he was okay and still in the lab. A door banged from somewhere outside in the corridor and Constance was coughing from the fumes. Henry turned off the gas outlet and opened the window behind his desk, allowing the smoke to clear.

Joseph was gone with the case. The gun was still on the ground. Ashley got up from the floor and turned immediately to Matt. Blood poured from a cut across his head where she'd hurled him against the desk but he was okay. Henry helped Constance up and moved her over to the window to get some air.

Heavy footsteps echoed along the corridor outside the lab and the group froze, fearing the gunman had returned. The door crashed backwards against the glass partition wall and the tallest black man Henry had ever seen burst into the room, closely followed by Tia who had ignored instructions to wait downstairs. He assumed this was her father.

'We heard a gunshot from the street as we got out of the car,' she cried, looking first at Henry, then at Ashley. She didn't know the boy on the floor but his red hair left her in no doubt that this must be Matt.

Stephen held out his hand to help Matt up from the floor. 'The police are at your mum's flat now. She's okay but she's going to have a few stitches in her head, as I suspect you may now need judging by that cut.'

Ashley wasn't listening to him. On the floor behind Tia, pressed against the wall and just visible in the haze, were black shoes and suit trousers that were too short. Motionless!

Ashley ran over and crouched down next to Eoin, turning him over without thinking. The ground was covered in blood and his right shoulder had a rip that tore through his jacket and his skin. The bullet had ricocheted off his shoulder blade and was buried in the wooden panelled wall behind him.

'Eoin!' she screamed at him.

Eoin's eyes opened slowly and he grinned.

'Looks like I'm not made of stone after all?' he smirked. 'Do I have any blood left in me?'

'Just about, you stupid bloody Irishman!' Ashley cried grabbing his hand and clenching it.

Stephen was on the radio calling for an ambulance when Sam arrived a minute later and took over the police work. Squad cars were despatched in all directions leading from the chemistry building. The gunman couldn't have got more than a few hundred yards' head start - but this was Central London on a busy Thursday evening in the heart of Theatre land. The streets were packed and it was dark. It would be difficult to spot anyone sensible enough to blend into the crowds.

The medics worked quickly to stem the flow of blood and regulate

Eoin's blood pressure. They fitted a saline drip and gave him a morphine shot as they lifted him onto a mobile stretcher. Ashley didn't let go of his hand the entire time.

'You saved me,' was all she could say.

His eyes flickered and rolled as the painkillers kicked in but he stayed conscious.

'Sorry I dragged you into this!' he said, and smiled weakly. 'It wasn't my intention to nearly get you killed! Even though you did threaten to kill me.' His fingers tightened around her hand.

Ashley left with Matt and Eoin in the Ambulance for the short trip to University College Hospital two streets away.

Stephen put a hand out towards Constance and thought how different this woman looked to the one he'd questioned this afternoon. Exhaustion and worry were now etched into the lines of her skin.

'Mrs Whittaker,' he said softly. 'Sorry to have to meet you again under these circumstances but I'm afraid I'm going to have to take statements from all of you. I need to know what is going on. I suspect only you really know what caused the two murders today and what happened here this evening.'

'Mr Hall I'm afraid I don't! I was hoping my trip would answer some very worrying questions I had about a precious artwork, but more just seem to keep cropping up. I fully understand you have your job to do but can we possibly do this back at Claridge's?' She picked up the case hidden behind the desk. 'I really need to get this back into the safe in my room.'

Chapter 41

Mayfair, London. Thursday 16th October 2014

It was almost 10pm when Derek Maltby, the concierge, spotted his most important guest and her son arriving back at Claridge's in a car topped by a blue light. He rushed from inside his booth to hold the door of the private lift open as they came into the building, and realised it was the first time he'd ever seen either of them without their bodyguards. Adams had arrived back just under an hour ago and he hadn't seen the FBI woman who usually accompanied Henry all day. Not that it looked like it mattered. Flanking them on either side were the two policemen he'd escorted up to the penthouse earlier in the day. He'd quickly established from his huge network of contacts around Central London that they were extremely high ranking officers, not usually seen actually investigating crimes these days.

Mrs Whittaker looked visibly shaken. Her head was dipped towards the floor and a film of some type of soot had settled onto her normally flawless make-up making her look grey and haggard. Maltby had seen her at least four or five times a year for the last twenty-eight years on her frequent trips to the Royal Academy and she'd always looked completely relaxed and self-assured. Something terrible had obviously happened and he suspected she'd been crying as mascara continued to streak down her cheeks. His inquisitive nature sparked his curiosity but his professional etiquette kept him steadfastly in his role of invisible, silent facilitator. Her son also stared resolutely at the floor, avoiding any eye contact. He was covered in the same dust like film and his eyes were bloodshot. Maltby didn't recognise the thin, beautiful, dark girl trailing behind them.

Henry was the first into the suite. He took the case from his mother, who'd been clinging to it all the way back to the hotel as if it tied her to a reality she understood but which was slipping away. He knew where the safe was, and the combination she would have used - the same secret date he'd used to pass his message to her via Ashley earlier this evening.

He thought about Ashley and Eoin, on their way to hospital. Twelve hours ago he hadn't even known Eoin, and now he was on his way to hospital to have his shoulder repaired after a day of drama that had indelibly bound the four of them together. If it hadn't been for his skill in opening the case, he would never have known that his family had unsuspectingly housed a fraudulent piece of art for over 70 years. He would find a way to repay him once he was out of hospital. Henry guessed he might need a helping hand after this!

Back in the living room Sam had resumed questioning Constance.

'Mrs Whittaker, when did Philip Charlesworth contact you about the painting?'

'It must have been some time in July initially,' she replied taking a cup of chamomile tea from the silently appearing butler who never seemed to sleep. 'The call came out of the blue and was completely speculative. He spoke to my assistant and wanted to know if I'd disposed of the Adeline portrait at any point since his father had seen it years earlier. She told him we hadn't and that it was still hanging on the dining room wall. I believe she was actually looking at it as he spoke so she didn't really understand his question or think very much of it. She knew there was no way I would ever sell it. When she told me about the conversation we both assumed he had a client who was interested in buying the painting, but it was the first acknowledged masterpiece my grandfather ever bought and one of the main reasons I became so passionate about art. I would never let that painting out of my family unless it was absolutely necessary; only if one of my family's life depended on it.'

'So what did he eventually say to convince you to meet him and bring such a valuable portrait halfway round the world?'

'He contacted me directly on a private phone number about six weeks later to say he'd come into possession of a painting that he had documentary evidence to suggest was the original Adeline painted by Van Gogh, and that what I had was actually a very well-executed forgery or a second copy. I reminded him that the provenance on my painting was almost unassailable. There have only ever been five people in possession of that painting: the artist, who gave it to the subject of the picture; the Ravouxs, who sold it to Harry Harronson for 20 francs; and finally my grandfather, who bought it directly from Harronson himself. Charlesworth's arrogance was unbelievable. He told me he had a very wealthy client who was prepared to pay for all the necessary testing to be carried out to prove that what he had was the genuine portrait. His client claimed to have documentary proof that Adeline herself had been party to the switch prior to her father selling the painting to Harronson. Of course those documents could have been forgeries themselves, but if that were true then we would have no claim to the original because that was not the painting Harronson bought, so I had no choice but to listen to what he had to say. He claimed that because I was a loyal customer of his father he would much rather do business with me than someone he described as "a shark with no finesse". He said if I were prepared to bring my painting to London so the two could be compared side-by-side we would surely be able to reach a satisfactory conclusion. I was under no illusion what that meant, inspector! Basically if his story turned out to be true he would allow me to take the original away for a fee and no one in the art world would be any the wiser. He was well aware of my ability to pay a significant sum to ensure I had the correct original. Any claims this other client might have had would then have been impossible to prove - documents or no documents. Whoever his other client was, it seems reasonable to assume they had to intercept the painting before Charlesworth brought it to me if they were to test their theory.'

'So what happened when you arrived at the Christopher Ingold building today?'

Henry walked back into the room and interrupted the story before his mother could reply.

'We took both paintings up to my lab and carried out a few rudimentary tests on them. They weren't sufficient to stand up in a court of law, but were enough to establish the chemical differences between the two. It was clear from the results that the one my mother bought from America was the original, and that is the one that's in it's case now in the safe in her bedroom. Whoever the gunman was, he's taken the case we found in Lenisters, which contained a portrait that was painted at least 10 years later, after Van Gogh died. My mother appears to have been the intended victim of some sort of elaborate scam that has gone seriously wrong for someone. I'm just glad Tia was able to help us stop it and at least we know what the murderer looks like now. That's much more important than a painting.' Henry prayed he was placating Tia's father in some way.

Sam was frustrated but maintained his composure. He'd wanted to get the whole story from Constance but he knew that if it weren't her son intervening it would be one of her army of lawyers. This was why they never interviewed witnesses together under normal circumstances. But these were not normal circumstances. He was already too far down the path of acquiescence to Stephen's request to help Tia to start playing by the rules. His priority now was to find out who had committed the two murders, not to establish the ownership of a painting, no matter its worth.

Constance looked at the floor, unable to acknowledge the policeman writing down the flawed statement. Only Ashley would ever be able to reveal the truth about their findings and she would never contradict Henry's story. Eoin might be a different matter, but the heiress was positive he hadn't been in the room when the provenance was being discussed.

'So you are saying that Philip Charlesworth and his secretary were murdered by this man you say sounds South African for a forgery? '

'Yes,' Henry replied again before his mother could speak. 'But he doesn't know it's the forgery. He thinks he's taken my mothers painting.' He calmly sat down in the leather armchair and leaned back as though the conversation were over.

'And you say he just turned up at your lab with your friend's brother as a hostage?' Sam knew he wasn't even close to the truth yet. 'How did he know you would be there?'

Henry froze.

He jumped up from his chair and waved his arms frantically in agreement with the policeman.

'That's it! That's what's been bothering me all evening.' He almost spat the words out as he paced the living room. 'The only other people who knew we were going to my lab were Tia and Eoin. How the hell did he get into the building? How did he even know where to go?' Even as his temples throbbed with frustration, he looked at her confused face and instantly calmed down. For some reason her presence today had kept him rational and under control; the very opposite of his normal reaction to stress, which was to lash out, blame others and fight whoever stood in front of him. He pushed aside the unwelcome thoughts and turned to Stephen, breathing deeply to compose himself. 'I doubt very much that Tia told anyone other than you where we were going to be. Eoin dropped me off but he couldn't have told anyone – we were all dragged into this because we were trying to save him!'

Sam sensed now was the time to increase the pressure to get to the truth.

'Mr Whittaker, someone knew of your whereabouts this evening. How well do you know Eoin Driscoll?'

'I only met him this morning but Ashley has known him for years. I think he's a friend of her eldest brother.'

'Did you know his uncle is a notorious thief?'

'No.' Henry didn't feel this was strictly a lie. Eoin hadn't mentioned his uncle when he'd picked the lock on the case at the hotel.

Sam reflected for a moment then changed tack.

'Both you and your mother are very high-risk kidnap targets. What precautions do you take with your personal safety?'

Henry thought for a few minutes.

'I have a bodyguard who lives in at the flat in the Barbican. They're highly trained and I've not had any problems or threats since they took over my security arrangements. I also a sub-dermal tracking chip implanted in my shoulder, but 5 years ago I got a court injunction to prevent anyone accessing the signal unless there was physical evidence that I was actually missing. Reactivation would have to be sanctioned by a judge in the US.'

'Who would have to submit the petition to have the information released?'

'Only a close family member can make the application and even then they need physical proof such as a ransom demand or blood evidence of a struggle. If I chose to go on holiday for a few days and didn't tell anyone then access would be denied under the terms I agreed.'

'Well I certainly didn't apply for the access,' Constance exclaimed. 'I'd completely forgotten about it to be honest. Once Ashley had told me Henry was okay I didn't even think about the chip.'

Henry recalled the bizarre conversation he'd had with his father this afternoon at the hotel in Ealing - had that been enough for his normally pragmatic dad to act?

'Did you say anything to Dad, or Richard?' he asked his mother.

The conversation was halted abruptly before she could answer by a loud commotion outside the door. A female voice could be heard arguing with the police guard and Adams, demanding access to the suite. The door burst open and Jennifer almost fell into the room.

'Oh my god Henry you're okay!' She ran over to him and threw her arms around him. 'I've been going frantic with worry all day! I came over because I couldn't get through to Constance on the phone and

Maltby told me you'd just got back. What's going on?' She stepped back and looked around the room at the two very official looking men she'd never seen before. She recognised Tia but regained her composure and ignored her. 'Who are these people?'

Sam didn't allow Henry to intervene this time.

'I'm Sam Ainslie, Head of Forensics with the Metropolitan Police and this is Assistant Commissioner Stephen Hall. We are in the middle of a very important interview and I'm afraid I'm going to have to ask you to step outside until we are finished.'

'But I'm his fiancée!' Jennifer held her left hand forward as if proof were needed.

'I'm sure you are, miss, but as you weren't a witness to any of today's events I must ask you to wait in the bedroom until we're finished.'

'Not until someone tells me what the hell has been going on all day! Witness to what events exactly?'

'It's okay Jen,' Constance said trying to reassure her. 'It seems someone tried to steal the Van Gogh but it's safe in the bedroom. We should only be a few more minutes with these gentleman.' Jennifer's arrival seemed to have woken Constance from her confused state. Her calm composure had returned and it was clear from her tone she would be saying very little else to the police tonight.

Chapter 42

Epping, Essex, Thursday 16th October 2014.

It was almost 11pm when Joseph Colthart stepped out into the car park at Epping. The suburban station was the final stop at the northeast end of the London Underground Central Line. The cold, cloudless sky was sprinkled with stars and the moon was almost full basting the night with a supernatural feel.

He'd been transport hopping for at least two hours, coming above ground on the other side of London just long enough to make a phone call before jumping onto a bus going back towards the centre of town. He'd switched coats and stolen a hat and glasses to change his appearance intermittently. He got back on the Underground at Liverpool Street station and headed north. The overtly placed CCTV cameras in the tunnels were relatively easy to spot and he kept his face hidden. Not that any police system anywhere had an image of him to compare for facial recognition. He was carrying the large conspicuous case but it was draped with a coat and had avoided drawing attention so far.

It was Thursday night and trickles of drunken City workers were still making their way home. He blended in effortlessly, appearing to be a weary traveller returning from a trip with his suitcase.

His final destination was almost deserted. A couple of commuters who had fallen asleep on the train and missed their stop were sluggishly changing platforms to make the return trip back towards London. There were no cars left to be collected and the taxi rank was out of sight on the other side of the station building. He was alone.

The lights from the car park barely seeped across the pavement as he crossed the road towards the black forest. The whole area was silent apart from the arrival of the occasional vehicle collecting a stranded passenger. The commuter traffic was long gone.

The Maybach was waiting a hundred yards up on the left-hand side as expected; impossible to miss, but not out of place in this prosperous suburb. He opened the back door and got in.

'You have the painting?' The Russian looked at the dishevelled Zimbabwean soldier whose shirt was ripped under his coat and who clearly had an injured arm. It was the first time they'd actually met face to face. Joseph had insisted on anonymity until the job was done, just in case anything went wrong, as it so nearly had. If he hadn't been alerted to a second opportunity to retrieve the correct painting he would have been on the first plane back home, photo or no photo. It would have meant spending the rest of his life looking over his shoulder but that risk was preferable to the certainty of what would have happened if he'd turned up at this rendezvous empty-handed.

Boris sat in the back of the leather-upholstered car in a handmade wool overcoat and black leather driving gloves. Both were unnecessary in the overheated limousine but Joseph suspected the gloves were rarely removed.

'It's in here.' Joseph indicated towards the aluminium case on the floor at his feet. 'The tracker hasn't been activated.' The case had been shut but unlocked and unconnected when he'd taken it from the labs.

The car began to pull away from the kerb unexpectedly, moving slowly and smoothly deeper into the forest. Vasily sat in the driver's seat, eyes intermittently glancing into the rear-view mirror. They turned left onto an unsurfaced track that led into the heart of the woods. It was dark under the slowly shedding canopy and leaves crunched under the wheels of the car. The moonlight barely broke through the densely spaced trees plunging them into a subtly mottled blackness. Without the headlights it would have been impossible to see more than a few yards ahead.

Joseph began to feel nervous. Where were they going? He'd expected to simply hand over the painting, confirm the transfer of the rest of his money and get back onto the last train into London, from where he would disappear for a very long time. He felt vulnerable, having dropped his gun at the university, and was now becoming acutely aware that he was unarmed and sitting between two dangerous strangers, whom he was sure would have come prepared to deal with a man like him if necessary.

'Do you believe your operation went well today Joseph?' Boris asked without looking at him, picking intently at the black stitching on his gloves.

Joseph could sense the threat in the comment even though the tone was calm and even. His training in the Zimbabwean army had prepared him for unarmed close combat. He knew he could take out one man, even if they were armed. Possibly two if they were both in front of him, but in his current position that would be virtually impossible given he was sandwiched between them. It didn't help that he was separated from one of the Russians by an internal glass partition that probably wasn't bulletproof, unlike the external windows. The driver could decapitate him before he even pulled back the door handle. He needed to get out of the car but it would be difficult to navigate through the trees in this darkness.

'There were a few hiccups but the end result was as promised. You got what you paid for.' Joseph turned towards the Russian, edging slowly backwards in the seat towards the door. 'Talking of which, have you transferred the rest of the money?'

As he spoke, trying to buffer some thinking time, his brain processed the options available to him. He could sit tight and negotiate or attempt to run. He'd taken all necessary precautions to protect himself – and his associate. Rubikov was not actually *his* client; he was essentially his partner's customer and Joseph was just a sub-contractor, designed and employed to keep them both safe from each other. He and his partner had gone to great lengths to protect themselves from any threat posed by the Russian, maintaining very discrete and separate roles. They set up the plans and dealt with communication and Joseph carried out the work. Neither of them had actually met with the Russian until now and Rubikov had not been aware of Joseph's identity until the very last minute. Boris would have had no time to prepare for who he was due to meet and no idea of his capabilities and potential weaknesses. They, on the other hand, had planned their defence rigorously. Between them they had gathered enough evidence, real and fabricated, to ensure that Rubikov would have to get out of England immediately if any of it should surface, which it would if anything should happen to Joseph. Law enforcement agencies would be the least of Boris's worries!

'I'm not sure killing two people could be classified as a minor hiccup, Mr Colthart. You have caused a lot of trouble today. This painting is tainted in a most unacceptable way. You have made displaying it, even in my own home very difficult now. Do you think the Rosenberg estate lawyers are just going to sit back and take the theft of such an asset lying down now that Henry Whittaker and his mother have been personally involved? Not to mention that the secretary's grandfather owns one of the biggest circulation newspapers in the country. We are not talking about an insignificant typist who will not be missed. What makes you think that I should pay you the rest of the money and not just shoot you and dump your body in the woods?'

Joseph was stunned. He'd had no idea who the victims of his work today had been, other than the gallery owner. He'd simply carried out his clients plan as instructed, without question, as he'd been trained to do. He didn't flinch. He'd taught himself to play poker many years ago to develop the skills he needed for scenarios such as this. It had been a profitable side line, and the expressionless visage he'd developed had kept him alive on more than one occasion. He remained calm knowing that as always he'd planned in precautions and safeguards at every step of the operation.

'I'm not an idiot Mr Rubikov. Do you think I would have gotten into your car without a gun if I had no back-up plan? I am well aware of your reputation in Russia. I know a number of your business partners have simply disappeared after serving their purpose in your assent from draft dodger. In Zimbabwe they teach us to be better prepared and to trust no one. You've been dealing with my partner and they're fully aware of our meeting tonight as you know. We have a significant dossier of evidence to prove your involvement in today's events, include the bank transfer details from your account, and photos of a number of other transactions you may not want shared with the world. If anything happens to me the police or the Russian Mafia, whoever gets there first, will be knocking on the door of your huge mansion in Egham I'm sure!'

'It would seem to you that I may have underestimated you, Mr Colthart.' Boris looked at the man sitting opposite him, who was almost as tall as he was. 'You do indeed appear to be more resourceful than I was led to believe.'

Boris picked up the handset for the car phone mounted on the partition behind the driver's seat and dialled a number from memory.

'Hello!' There was a short pause. Boris put his hand over the mouthpiece and stared at Colthart 'But then again, maybe not!'

Joseph looked at the phone pressed against Boris ear.

'Yes, he's here now. Would you like to speak to him?' Boris asked. Another short pause before he handed the phone over to Joseph. 'It's for you.'

Joseph looked at the phone as though it were radioactive - not wanting to touch it. How could anyone possibly know where he was? His client had only given him the location for the meeting less than an hour ago. He took it reluctantly.

'Hello. Who is this?'

He could feel the metal fillings in his teeth electrify as he listened to the voice on the end of the phone. An alien accent he'd known and worked with for the last two months. A voice he trusted and who was now betraying him.

'Joseph, I'm sorry, but business is business! I'm sure you understand.'

His brain tried momentarily to compute the possible permutations of outcomes but there were no good results for him that he could see.

'It would seem you didn't fully follow your own advice about trusting no one.' Boris took the receiver from Joseph and returned it to the cradle on the wood panelling. The car stopped in the middle of the dirt road. 'How far do you think you can run in this darkness?' Boris asked as Vasily switched off the headlights, plunging the deserted track into blackness.

Joseph reached behind him for the handle and threw open the leather-lined door. He stumbled out into the crackling undergrowth and headed straight towards the treeline. Vasily climbed out of the driver's seat and put on the night vision goggles that had been on the seat beside him. He could see the ex-soldier pushing deep between the second row of oaks. It was clear from the way Colthart moved that he was used to being out in the woods at night. Not that his survival skills could match the night vision technology of his goggles, or the speed of the silenced Heckler and Koch sniper rifle that Vasily was carrying as he followed his prey into the forest. Another 20 yards should leave him far enough off the track to delay detection for a few hours.

Boris didn't hear the hollow pop from the hunter's gun but he knew the job was complete when Vasily climbed back into his seat and restarted the engine.

As they pulled out of the service track back onto the deserted main road he picked up the phone and dialled the number he had just called.

'Its done. Your agreed fee is being transferred to your Cayman Island account as we speak. I must confess I am disappointed somewhat that I will not get to speak to you again. It has been my absolute pleasure.'

He hung up and turned his attention to the metal case on the floor. He hauled it up onto the seat beside him and opened the lid. A vibrant child in a blue dress with a woman's face stared back at him and he smiled to himself.

'Get the jet ready and let's get back to Fairoaks Airport as quickly as possible, Vasily,' he said as the driver turned the car onto Junction 26 of the M25, heading towards the west. 'I want to get this beautiful girl onto the plane as quickly as possible so I can examine the secret the banker described hidden within it.'

Chapter 43

Mayfair, London. Friday 17th October 2014

The meticulously maintained temperature of the Brook suite had dropped a couple of degrees in the last few minutes. Stephen knew they were unlikely to get any more details from the Whittakers this evening, or should he say this morning, as it was now 1am. Constance was already out of her seat and subtly ushering them towards the front door with promises to contact them if she had anything further to report. That was fine with him for now– his daughter was safe and he needed to focus on his job. His priority was to find the killer who had murdered Charlesworth and his secretary and put Eoin in hospital.

'Tia, come on, I'll take you back to Orpington tonight,' he pronounced to his daughter. He held out his arm to take her hand, as he'd done since she was a little girl. She didn't move and her gaze flicked involuntarily towards Henry.

'I think it would be safer for her to stay here,' Henry intervened, not doing anything to improve his standing with the imposing policeman. 'It's difficult to get access to this floor and we have a well-trained bodyguard outside the door. The man you're looking for is still out there and is obviously getting information from someone who knows our movements. We can protect her better from here and like you say, you'll be busy.'

'You haven't done the best job of looking after her so far!' Stephen retaliated. 'And who is we?' He looked at Constance, positive she would not be of use in a fight.

'Frank, our bodyguard, is outside, I can look after myself and so can Tia. Plus Jennifer is in the bedroom. She'll protect us.'

'Your fiancée?' Stephen couldn't keep the disbelief out of his voice. 'The girl that came in just a few minutes ago?'

'She isn't what she seems.' Henry looked at Tia apologetically and then at his mother, as if waiting for permission to continue. Constance nodded lightly in approval and he explained. 'Jennifer isn't my fiancée… she's my bodyguard. She trained with the FBI and graduated top in her year from Quantico but failed a sight test after an injury and came to work for us. We pretend to be engaged, as it looks more natural if I have a female constantly with me but don't underestimate her based on how she looks. I've never managed to beat her in sparring and I train with her every day.'

Tia could feel her face burning. Her day from hell just got better. He wasn't engaged, and he was asking her to stay here with him. Well, technically he was asking her father but that didn't matter.

'Dad I want to stay here. I'll feel much safer knowing you are just down the street and can get here in a couple of minutes.' Tia stared at her father, pleading and praying that he would trust her to stay safe.

Stephen thought for a moment. It was the middle of the night but he'd still be at the crime scene in Mount Street for another few hours and then he'd probably get a few hours' sleep back in his office on the daybed. Tia would be close enough here if she needed him. Closer than in Orpington where she'd have no protection.

'Okay, but I'm putting uniformed policemen on all the entrances to the suite.'

'That's fine,' Henry smiled. 'They can keep Frank company.' Frank was also ex-FBI and Henry had no doubt he would be able to keep a police constable under control.

Stephen and Sam left to get back to work as Jennifer emerged from the bedroom. She was fuming as she grabbed hold of Henry and began shaking him by the shoulder

'Will you please tell me what the hell has been going on? Where have you bloody been all day? This was the worst birthday ever.' She turned and glared at Tia. 'What the hell are you doing here? With my fiancé?'

'It's okay Jen you can drop the act.' Henry pulled away from her and went over to the drinks cabinet. 'Tia knows the truth about your security role.' He poured four brandies and handed them round.

'No thanks!' Tia said. 'Me drinking alcohol is what got you dragged into this mess in the first place.' It seemed so long ago since her first hangover had required him to collect her from her halls this morning.

'Well that turned out not to be the case. Seems my mum was wrapped up in this all the time.' He handed her the glass. 'Besides it will help you sleep.'

'Help her do what?' Jen was red with anger and embarrassment. Henry had often taken his frustrations and anger with his parents out on her over the past few years but he'd never made her feel like an employee. Not until just now! And it appeared that this teenager was about to be installed within the Whittaker circle right under her nose. Her life plans were all backfiring, but she'd suspected this for some time now.

From the day his parents offered her the lucrative contract to protect their son Jennifer believed she would eventually win him over - she always got her way with men in the end. She was beautiful, smart and feisty. Powerful men had tried and failed to tame her since she was in high school being pursued by the captain of the football team and the married headmaster simultaneously. But as the years in their service passed, his romantic ambivalence towards her remained solid. Her suspicions that she might fail in her ultimate mission had been growing for months, and then she saw the way he looked at Tia outside the Ivy, as they said goodnight on her birthday. Jennifer knew this was a battle she was never going to win. He'd barely talked about anyone else since meeting her; his feelings were out of her control and she hated it.

'I'm *paid* to protect you, not babysit schoolgirls. What the hell have you been doing all day? I thought we had plans?' Her anger and hurt spilled out in a stream of venom.

'Jen sorry about your birthday but I'll tell you tomorrow. Now we all need to get some sleep. You and Tia can take the second bedroom and I'll sleep on the sofa.'

Jen didn't respond as she turned and crashed out of the living room, torn between a contract that tied her to Henry's side and a burning desire to run back to the flat in the Barbican and hide. No one had ever made her feel like this and she had no idea how to deal with it. Unable to detach her logic from her emotions she descended into a sulk.

Jen was apparently asleep in the bed when Tia came into the room. The butler had somehow produced a nightdress and dressing gown and she climbed into the daybed that had efficiently been made up in the corner of the room. As she fought to calm her racing mind and claim some much needed sleep she reflected on how different her world would look tomorrow after what she'd been through today.

It was almost 4am when Tia felt a hand gently shake her before resting lightly over her mouth, prompting her to stay quiet. Henry was leaning over her, fully dressed and clearly in a hurry. He handed her a clean T-shirt and cashmere jumper stolen from his mother's drawer.

'Get dressed quickly,' he whispered. 'There's something we need to check and I don't want anyone else to know about it.'

Unquestioning, she signalled for him to wait outside while she pulled on her T-shirt, jumper and jeans. She managed to run a flannel over her face and brush her teeth before coming into the living room and retrieving her jacket and bag from the back of the dining chair. Henry really was getting to see her at her worst.

'We need to get back to the lab now,' Henry said, retrieving the metal case from behind the heavy drapes next to his mother's bedroom door.

'I thought you put that in the safe?' Tia asked.

'You were all meant to think that. There's no way my mum would let me do what I'm going to do.'

'How am I supposed to get out of the suite?' Tia asked, stalling him whilst her mind battled with the thrill of the excitement of going with him on his quest and the fear of failing her father again. 'My dad has a policeman standing outside both of the doors.'

'The same way food for 10 people comes up when guests are entertaining in this room,' Henry replied leading her into the kitchen. He pulled open a door in the wall, at chest height and the size of a small refrigerator. He removed the two shelves and put them on the floor next to him. 'You're agile and fit. You can go down in this. I've used it before to escape from my parents when I stayed here with them but I was a bit smaller then. The kitchen staff won't take any notice of you. I don't think I'm the only person who's used this method to escape their security teams. Send it back up once you're out and I'll send down the case. Then I'll tell the policeman I can't sleep and am going for a walk. He's not here to keep me inside the hotel. I'll meet you at the back of the main kitchen in 10 minutes.'

Tia felt as if she were climbing into an oven as she folded her almost six-foot frame into the space, pulling her knees up to her chin and placing her head between them. If she'd been a pound heavier she doubted she would have fit. As predicted, the mainly Eastern-European night staff didn't appear to even notice her as she climbed out and pressed the return button. The case came down with the two shelves propped up against it, which she replaced before leaving the kitchen by the back door.

Henry came out a few minutes later and took the case from her. It took a little while to find a taxi at that time in the morning, but by 4.30am they were back inside the taped-off lab. A police guard stood outside the front of the building, unaware of the concealed rear entrance through the bin store.

The damaged lab was just as they'd left it.

'Pull the blinds down,' Henry said as he started unpacking the

334

priceless Van Gogh from its monogramed case.

'What's going on?' Tia had been too scared to ask until now. Henry seemed to have forgotten that she hadn't been with them when he and his mother went through the painting's test results. He brought her up to speed.

'When we checked the two paintings earlier I ran a number of tests to compare them both. The killer got away with the case from Lenisters but what he didn't realise is that the painting inside wasn't the one that left the gallery yesterday morning. The tests showed that the painting that's been sitting in our house for all those years was the fake, albeit a bloody good one. The one that we've been carrying around all day, dumped in the boot of Eoin's car, was the genuine portrait of Adeline painted by Van Gogh! When we discovered the truth I simply switched the cases. Harry Harronson bought and sold what he believed were two genuine Van Gogh's and had all the paperwork to prove it. I don't believe for one second that the Ravoux's had the foresight, or even the money, to switch the original with a fake! What could they have possibly hoped to gain? They could never sell the original later without revealing the first dupe so it was worthless to them. I was trying to convince my mum that as far as the world was concerned she was the rightful owner of the original painting – whichever version that turned out to be. So I just put the real painting in her case and our fake into the case we took from Lenisters. Once the gunman turned up I didn't really have time to think about it until after he left with the fake.'

'How on earth did that happen? I thought your grandfather bought it directly from Harronson?'

'He did. Which means the painting must have been switched before it left the café in Meulan in 1905. The question is, why? My mom was right! Nobody would have forged a Van Gogh at that time for profit, so there has to be another reason for someone to go to so much trouble. I suspect hiring a master forger would have been more expensive than purchasing the real painting at that time. Whatever it is that the thief had planned it required the Ravoux's to believe they still had the original Adeline. I've just no clue what that reason is. Anyway, one of the tests was a spectroscopy analysis, which is a bit like an X-ray. Ashley saw something between the backing paper and the canvas that looked like a folded piece of paper. This is the genuine Adeline, not the one my mother brought over from the States. Someone has hidden something under the canvas. It might even have been Van Gogh himself.' Henry paused to let his working theory crystallize in his mind. 'What if it's the actual suicide note that was never discovered? That document would probably be as valuable as the painting itself.'

Tia was dumbstruck. He'd been so calm when he'd lied to her dad's face about not knowing anything else and about keeping her safe. She would never have been able to do that and get away with it.

'So the gunman left with the forgery?' Tia didn't care about a suicide note! Suddenly she felt the fear she'd been experiencing most of the day return with an unwelcome angry blast. 'Does that mean he will come back after us?' Her mind hazed as she thought of her friends all being held at gunpoint yesterday in this very room; of the two dead bodies in the gallery; of the bullet hole in the Windsor toilet door that missed Ashley by a centimetre. Her hands began to shake. What had he done?

Henry hadn't considered that possible outcome. He'd been so wrapped up in his excitement about the contents hidden behind the backing paper he'd not thought about the fake. He ran through the possibilities silently, calculating their likelihood of occurring. The main concern was if the killer discovered the painting in his case was the forgery. Based on the discussion of the results he'd had with his mother he was confident.

'I doubt anyone will ever be able to tell. It was only possible for my mum to make the call on which was which when the two were side-by-side and with a whole load of data, and she is an expert.' Henry cleared the shattered flask glass from the worktop and lifted the painting onto it, turning it carefully onto its front. 'I don't think there is anyone else in the world who would be prepared to do this to a $50m painting, but I sort of own it, and I have to know what is behind this backing paper. It may even help explain how two people have ended up dead because of it.'

Henry put the X-ray back into the light box and turned the painting so the top and bottom were correctly aligned with the film. He increased the magnification on the glass overlay and, using the photo as a guide, ran his fingers over the thin brown backing paper. Moving slowly and gently he traced out the slight ridges where something, most likely another piece of paper, sat behind the outer protector. He picked up a scalpel and scored the faintest line he could alongside the left hand edge of the inner page, applying virtually no pressure to ensure he didn't go any deeper than paper thickness. Using a long pair of tweezers he carefully lifted the backing paper up a few millimetres. It came away easily. Looking closer, Henry realised that the edges of this outermost sheet of paper had been painstakingly pushed under the wooden stretched frame, over the top of the original backing paper. Behind the additional sheet was a folded piece of heavy parchment writing paper. It was yellow with age and the ink was faded in places but the words were still visible. Henry slid the scalpel under the left edge of the parchment and gently prized the note out with the tweezers. He replaced the Van Gogh back into its case. He would need to remind his mother to repair the backing paper once she got it back to Washington.

Following a process he'd watched his mother use as a boy, Henry put on latex gloves and turned the unfolded parchment round to face them. He ran a black light over the top and the watermark in the paper became clearly visible. Henry's mood dropped slightly. It was clearly not Van Gogh's suicide note! The date at the top of the letter was 1957.

Tia typed the words on the watermark into Google on her phone and the image came up in a second. The paper bore the original crest of Swiss Re - the insurance company that owned the famous Gherkin building in the City. In a barely legible ornate flowing script was a simple message, written in French. Google translate gave them an English version which Tia wrote down.

1957

I have sought to make amends for the tragedy of this creator's life cut short. Avenues of the doctor's garden reveal, to someone of genuine passion, that which only God knows and which man must discover after I am gone.

RS.

Tia didn't understand the reference at all.

'What are we supposed to do now?'

'We talk to someone with genuine passion.' Henry took an A4 envelope from his desk and put the parchment carefully inside it. He knew his mother would be horrified to watch how he was handling this document, but they had to get back to the hotel before Tia's dad returned and found out she was missing.

Getting back into the hotel was a simpler process than getting out. It was 7.30am and a £50 note for Maltby confirmed the watch had changed. Henry explained to the new guard that he and Tia had been down to the restaurant for breakfast. The policeman saw no reason to question the large case he was carrying – no one had even briefed him as to why he was there, other than to keep an eye on Stephen Hall's daughter and she clearly looked fine. Frank simply smiled and said nothing. Tia wondered if he ever slept.

Jennifer had obviously dressed and left early as she was nowhere in the suite. Henry assumed she'd probably gone running as she did first thing every morning,. Constance was sitting at the table eating eggs benedict and drinking coffee.

'Where on earth have you been?' she asked.

Henry placed the envelop on the table in front of her.

'We went to check out what was hidden behind the backing paper. It's a note but I have no idea what it means.'

Constance removed the parchment from the envelope and laid it on the table. She took her glasses out of her bag and looked closely at the document.

'Did you identify the watermark?' she asked.

'Yes it's the Swiss Reinsurance group,' Henry said.

Constance looked up at him in surprise.

'Are you sure?' she asked pulling the paper closer to inspect it.

'Yes, Tia saw it too!'

Tia nodded in agreement that it was definitely their watermark. She pulled her laptop out of her bag and found the image again. She turned it to show Constance.

'This is extraordinary!' Constance put the paper gently on the table as if she were handling a sheet of spun sugar that might disintegrate in her hands. 'One of the most notorious stories in the art world surrounds rumours of the involvement of a young Parisian boy in Van Gogh's suicide. The only evidence that exists that Van Gogh actually shot himself is that he himself said he did. No corroborating evidence has ever been found and neither has the gun nor any of his materials. Then in 1956 the young boy, who was by then an old man, gave an interview that suggested the artist had not committed suicide at all. He never actually confessed to the shooting himself, but it began a long speculation that he may have been involved. Experts have been divided ever since as to the level of truth his words contain.' Constance paused, considering the implications of finding this note in the back of the original Adeline. 'The young boys name was Rene Secretan and when he died in 1957 he was a retired member of the board of Swiss Re.'

'So you think Rene Secretan is the RS who wrote this letter? But how did it get into the back of the portrait of Adeline Ravoux? How did he even get the portrait from them without them realising it. When Arthur Ravoux sold the paintings to Harronson in 1905 he believed they were genuine and so did Harronson.'

'Mrs Whitaker, was there ever any speculation that Rene Secretan knew the Ravoux's?' Tia asked.

'Yes! There were a number of reports at the time that Arthur Ravoux had loaned his gun to the teenager a few days before Vincent shot himself. Rene had a fixation with Buffalo Bill and was constantly trying to emulate him. He even represented France in shooting at several championships and was an expert marksman. The boy was the last one to be seen with the handgun. The police tried to interview him but there is no record of the conversation and the official report suggested he'd left the gun unsupervised in his bag whilst swimming in the river, allowing the artist to take it without his knowledge. You have to realise 125 years ago police enquiries were not the same as they are now. They had no forensic evidence. '

'But he knew them well enough to possibly know they had two of his works at their new cafe?' Tia was following her own trail of breadcrumbs.

'Yes, most art historians believe he knew them whilst he was in Auvers and he must have gone to the café to acquire the gun.' Constance studied Tia inquisitively. 'What are you thinking?'

'Just that Rene Secretan appears to have gone to great lengths to leave this message in a painting that he needed to be genuine if his note was to be taken seriously.' Tia pulled a sheet of paper from the desk and started to draw a mind map. 'So we have this Rene Secretan, who was linked to Van Gogh's suicide at the time, or at least linked to the gun, but never questioned in person. Then we have a note with his initials in the back an original portrait, switched under the noses of the Ravoux's some time before 1905, when it was sold to Harronson, and replaced with a remarkable forgery. Assuming it was Secretan who switched it, that must have cost him a lot of money, even then. Then we have an interview given by him in 1956, just before his death, claiming Van Gogh did not shoot himself. Finally, based on what Philip told you, we think he left the original painting in a safety deposit box to be discovered by an art dealer years later, for a reason as yet unknown.'

The three of them sat in silence considering Tia's summary, the unspoken question obvious to them all. Why?

Henry turned the parchment back to face him.

'It's obviously a message intended to remain hidden for a good number of years. Secretan clearly wants his identity known because he's used headed paper and his initials, but they would only make sense if you understood the significance of this painting. If the painting were not genuine, no credence would be given to the letter. If the letter had been separated from the painting, you would never know whose tragic life it refers to. But taking those things together it's clearly a reference to Van Gogh's tragic life - or at least the end to it.'

Tia wrote all of his words in a random pattern on her paper to reduce the associations and allow freethinking, as her father had shown her.

'So what about the doctor's garden? What could that mean? I've read that Van Gogh was in an asylum for a while. Do you think he's referring to that?'

Constance had a suspicion.

'The reason Vincent came to Auvers-sur-Oise was to be near his physician, Dr Gachet. He treated a large number of the Parisian art community at the end of the 19th century for psychiatric disorders and had one of the most extensive collections of Impressionist art in the world. He would definitely be considered to have a genuine passion for Van Gogh's work. In fact he was the subject of a couple of portraits himself, as was his daughter.'

Tia drew circles around some of the remaining words on the page as she thought.

'Did he have a garden?'

'Yes, it's still a tourist attraction today. You can visit the house and gardens, which have been preserved as a museum, although all the art is now in the Musee D'Orsay,' Constance had been to the small white house a number of times during her college years in Europe.

Tia tapped on the table for a few seconds considering the bits of the puzzle she now had. This letter itself was not what was important. It was merely a clue to the location of something that was. Something that had been worth hiding and protecting for decades. Something whose whereabouts was contained in this letter – almost like a modern day treasure map.

'I believe that whatever Rene wants discovered is in the garden of Dr Gachet,' she declared, tapping the final word with her pen. 'And based on what we've been through in the last 24 hours, I think someone else knows that at the very least that this painting was forged and stolen. Henry you said right from the start that whoever was trying to get this painting couldn't possibly hope to sell it after all this – especially not now it's linked to a double murder. But the killer came back for a second attempt to steal it. I don't think they want this painting itself. I think someone else knows that there is a hidden secret contained within it!'

Tia looked round expecting a wave of laughter to flood over her.

'Then we need to go to Auvers!' Henry said, deadly serious and already packing up his things. 'Now!'

Outside the suite door Frank Adams pulled out his phone.

'They are preparing to leave to go to a place called Auvers' he said in a hushed voice.

'Okay. You know what to do.'

The line went dead.

Chapter 44

Camden. London. Friday October 17th 2014.

Constance's chauffeur parked the limousine in Rochester Square opposite the entrance to Tia's halls of residence just after 9am. The decision to go with Henry to Auvers had taken her less than a minute, even though Constance had tried to talk them out of it. The heiress had pleaded with them to let the police follow the lead to the Parisian suburb but Henry was determined to go himself. He knew that the content of the letter was so vague no one would take it seriously until they discovered what exactly was hidden in the garden, if anything. The document was over 60 years old. Whatever it referred to could have been dug up and discarded years ago. Besides, if they were to maintain the story that the letter was in the back of the portrait that had hung on the Whittaker's wall for the last seventy years then how would they explain the date on the letter? More importantly, how could they explain it's connection with the murders of Phillip Charlesworth and Selena Holdsworth without revealing the truth about the switch? As far as the authorities were concerned, that was an attempted art theft of a painting that had turned out to be a fake, and which was now missing. Whatever story lay behind Rene Secretan's letter, they would have to literally unearth it for themselves. Constance had only conceded when Henry agreed to contact Stephen once they knew what the secret in Dr Gachet's garden was. In truth, she was amazed at the life that had been breathed into her son as he pursued this mystery. She'd not seen him this enthusiastic about anything since he was a little boy and she couldn't bring herself to rob him of this rare feeling of excitement. He would only be gone for a few hours at most. What harm could it do to let him follow this clue that no one other than her knew about?

Tia knew her father would be furious at her for leaving the hotel but she'd have plenty of time to repent once she was confined to her room in Orpington, which would be the inevitable outcome for disobeying him. She may be 19, but while she was financially dependent on her parents she may as well have been 12.

For now, all she could think about was helping Henry uncover the secret behind the art that someone had killed for. Someone who at any time could discover the paintings had been switched and come looking for them. This time her father wouldn't be so understanding of her decision to get involved in Henry's search for Rene's secret. She'd knowingly disobeyed his instruction to stay in the hotel and guilt was sparking against the surge of adrenalin she felt just being with Henry on this quest. She gave him her room keys and watched as he dodged cars crossing Camden Road before disappearing into the car park entrance.

Henry spotted the police patrol car sitting in the car park as he let himself into the Ifor Evans building and then into Tia's corridor. She'd suspected that her father would still have the premises under surveillance, and she'd been right, but the officers were less likely to recognise Henry with his hoodie pulled tight around his head. Her passport was in her bedside table. He didn't have time to pick up anything else. The Whittakers' private jet was on standby at RAF Northolt to take them to Paris and her name had been intentionally misspelt on the outbound manifest. The pilot understood the significance of the instruction when Constance herself assured him she would pay any resulting fines if they were caught.

Tia called Ashley from Henry's phone as they drove along the A40 towards RAF Northolt airport. She'd left hers in the hotel room, assuming her father would have put a trace on that just in case she decided to continue her first ever adventure.

'How's Eoin? And your mum and brother?' she asked. The events of the day before still seemed unreal and so long ago. Was it really less than 24 hours since Tia had walked into that murder scene in Mayfair?

'Eoin's out of surgery.' Ashley was glad to hear from her friend. She was finding it difficult to juggle her time between the three patients she was overseeing whilst constantly looking over her shoulder for the gunman. 'They operated on his bullet wound last night and stopped the blood loss. The doctors said it wasn't as bad as it looked and he'll make a full recovery. The main tendons were relatively undamaged fortunately. Mum and Matt are both fine and coming home today. Where are you now?'

'We are on our way to Auvers, in France,' Tia whispered, even though the chauffeur couldn't possibly hear her from his side of the soundproof glass partition. 'We went back to the lab this morning and Henry retrieved the paper you noticed in the back of the canvas. It appears to be a letter from a man named Rene Secretan, and has something to do with Van Gogh himself. We've no idea if it has anything to do with the murders but whatever it is, this Secretan person has gone to a lot of trouble to conceal something he obviously wanted discovered at some point after his death. If he didn't, he would have just got rid of his secret and be done.'

Despite the ordeals of the day before, being held at gunpoint twice, Ashley felt a pang of jealousy at not being with them but she said nothing. Tia continued her update.

'According to Henry's mum, Rene Secretan was a 16-year-old boy staying in Auvers for the summer when Van Gogh died. For years he was rumoured to have been the person Vincent stole the gun from, although it was never found. Apparently Rene borrowed it from Arthur Ravoux, who owned the inn where Van Gogh was staying. We've no idea what we are looking for. It may actually be the gun, although Henry thinks it could also be the suicide note, which was never found. Whatever it is, if it exists, it's hidden in the garden of Dr

Gachet, who was Van Gogh's doctor. This Secretan boy must have gone to great lengths to steal the original Adeline from the Ravoux's without their knowledge. Before he died he put something in the back of it for someone to eventually find and follow the clue. I'm sending you a photo of the letter now so you can see for yourself.'

Tia scanned the document and handed it back to Henry, then pressed 'send image' to deliver the evidence to her friend.

'Charlesworth told Constance that he'd been left the painting in his father's will three months ago and had recovered it from a bank vault in Zurich. Secretan died in 1957, so it must have been stored there for over 50 years, maybe longer, given he had to have stolen it before 1905. Whatever Rene was hiding, he didn't want it unearthed until long after he'd gone. The Whittaker's have the correct painting now, but the gunman hasn't been caught yet. There's a chance he, or whoever he's working for, may realise he has the fake so you need to take your family somewhere else until the police catch him. Henry's mum has said she'll cover the cost of a hotel or apartment until it's safe for you to return home. '

Ashley felt a wave of relief. She hadn't even begun to consider what she was going to do with her family now their front door had been broken off its hinges by a murderer.

'I thought the gunman wanted the painting?' Ashley was confused.

'So do the police, and so did we until we discovered that note but until we know what is hidden in the garden we've no idea if it's important,' Tia explained. 'I don't want to send my dad on a stupid wild goose chase if there's nothing there. If we find something then obviously I'll let him know.'

'Well be careful and I'll see you when you get back.'

Tia had one last request.

'Ashley, I'm sure my dad will be in to see you all before your leave the hospital. Swear you won't tell him where I am until I let you know what we've found!' Tia was hopeful that with the private jet at their disposal they could be back before evening, and before she was missed.

'Of course I won't. I've always been pretty good at bullshitting people! Especially policemen!' She laughed and hung up.

Tia knew her dad was going to be furious that she'd not only left the hotel, but the country - she'd repeated her trip in the dumbwaiter just after 8.30am, beyond caring about the trouble she was in. She didn't think it was possible for things to get much worse in her father's eyes. Besides, for now she was with Henry following the most exciting adventure she'd ever imagined. She felt alive and exhilarated. Her father would be focused on dealing with the murders now - not worrying about her. It wasn't her place, or her desire, to get any further involved in that.

Chapter 45

Auvers-sur-Oise, France Friday October 17th 2014.

The Gulfstream G550 jet owned by the Blue Star Corporation touched down in La Bourget airport just after 10am Paris time. A hire car was already waiting for them at the private hangar and the drive to Auvers took just over 40 minutes. Henry was breaking all the rules of his life insurance policy again today. He was travelling under his own name and without his bodyguard. There would be no pay-out if anything happened to him, the insurance company's lawyers would make sure of that, but they hadn't had time to make any other arrangements. He didn't care about the money or the risk! For the first time in years he felt exhilarated - as if he'd been set free from his prolonged exile from his own life. He couldn't explain his intuition but every sense believed this secret was something important - more important even than the art.

Whilst they'd been in the air, Constance had been on the phone to the curator of Dr Gachet's house and grounds. She'd agreed for her son and his friend to be given private access to the grounds. No explanation had been necessary. The promise of a sizeable donation to the maintenance fund from one of the richest people in the world opened almost any door!

As they drove the discrete Renault Clio along the bank of the River Oise, past the scenes of so many of Van Gogh's famous last works, Henry wondered how much had changed in the suburban town in the last century. Would the gardens really still be as they were so long ago? It was almost 125 years since the artist's death.

The place could be unrecognisable. Whatever they were looking for might have already been found and possibly destroyed.

They parked the car a few streets further up the hill from the house entrance, tucked away from the view of the main road.

The curator, Alain Petit was already waiting on the small, pebbled drive of the white house. The gate was propped open and Henry's concerns about the state of the grounds were immediately put to rest as they entered the property and stepped back in time.

'Welcome. Mr Whittaker, it's a pleasure to have you here at our little preservation of art history. I've just spoken with your mother and she explained you'd like a private tour and access to the gardens.' Petit's pride in his charge was obvious.

'Yes, my girlfriend loves Van Gogh and is desperate to find out about the real man and his struggle with his demons,' Henry replied as they walked into the cramped entrance hall of the doctor's house,

Tia could feel her skin flush as Henry called her his girlfriend. He really is an accomplished liar, she thought. I almost believed him.

'Might I ask you to sign our visitors book, Mr Whittaker?' Petit held out a pen, wondering how long after they left he could upload a photo of his signature to their website and Facebook page. Surely a visit by such an infamous American would reignite the interest in the great doctor's role in Van Gogh's life, and his house. It's popularity was waning now so many of the great works had been moved to the Musee d'Orsay, thanks to the doctor's son, Paul, and bills still needed to be paid.

'As I'm sure you know, Dr Gachet was a homeopathic physician and treated many famous artists during his time, as you can see from some of the portraits around the walls.' Alain pointed out the replicas that hung in the cluttered rooms as they moved through the interior. 'Obviously his association with Van Gogh is the most renowned, especially as he personally attended to the artist after he shot himself.' Alain was well versed in his material and desperate to impress. A benefactor such as the Whittaker's could solve all the museum's financial issues. He hated that none of the art on display were the real treasures once owned by the doctor, but even he had to acknowledge that the trust would never have been able to provide adequate protection as their value spiralled out of control.

'I've seen Van Gogh's paintings of his gardens.' Henry said. He'd been briefed as to what to say and what questions to ask by his mother. 'And the one of the house, by Cezanne. Has much changed outside since those works were completed?'

'Well the beds have been refreshed a number of times over the years, but most of the plants have been replaced by similar species to maintain the original appearance. The white roses and herbs have been replanted from cuttings taken from the original stock. That is, after all, what our guests want to see. The pathways, walls, stairs and structures are still the same as they were when the doctor lived here, although we frequently have to add more pebbles to the walkways to preserve them. A disabled access ramp, display stands and some benches have been added but they are the only external changes, I believe, so you should get a very strong sense of authenticity.'

Henry looked at Tia and smiled - that was good news. He moved across the hall toward the curator and put a conspiratorial arm around his shoulder before surreptitiously producing a small square box from his pocket, acquired courtesy of his mother again.

'Do you mind if we spend some time out there alone?' he confided quietly, opening the box to reveal an exquisite yellow-diamond ring.

Alain looked at the box and beamed, unaware that it was a copy of the genuine Harry Winston ring that had belonged to Henry's grandmother. This would almost certainly make the evening news once word of a proposal got out. Henry Whittaker was certainly on a par with European royalty in terms of American public interest and he'd been a recluse for years.

'Of course, young man, take all the time you need!'

Tia stifled a giggle at the thought!

The smell of herbs filled the air as they walked out into the steeply sloping grounds. As the pair surveyed the patchwork of stones and beds their enthusiasm rapidly waned. Where would they start? The pebbled and cobbled paths weaved an intricate pattern around the descending slopes and terraces. The flowerbeds were laced on all sides by a network of pathways and steps. Replicas of the doctor's own mediocre drawings were displayed amidst the beds but the view across the French countryside was breath taking.

'Well we know it's not in a bed or it would have been discovered by now,' Henry said.

'The letter referred to avenues, which I think means the paths. There are a few seats along the pathways, but whatever we are looking for has been hidden from sight, even from the gardeners, for decades, possibly longer, so I'm sure it must be buried.' Tia assessed the routes for possibilities. 'The paths and stairs have literally hundreds of flagstones and pebbled sections! It would take us hours to search under all of them. We don't even know what it is we're looking for. It could be another letter, which would be like trying to find a needle in a haystack in a garden of this size. It might have even rotted away after so long.'

'If you were hiding something in the garden of someone you barely knew, without their permission, where would you start?' Henry asked.

Tia though for a second, putting herself in the shoes of a scared 16-year-old boy who may have been a witness to one of the most notorious deaths in the art world.

'If I were him, and assuming I was acting alone and in secret, I would start either by the side gate or the section of the path furthest from the house and nearest the road so I could easily escape over the wall if I were disturbed.'

'The side gate is visible from the house - that would be a bit risky wouldn't it?' Henry said.

Tia agreed and they walked along the winding path to a shaded

351

spot where it almost skimmed the external wall. The bricks were coarse and uneven, and climbing over it would have been relatively easy for a boy or young man. They were working on the assumption that Rene had not come back here as an old man at the time he'd written the letter.

'I would start with this section!' Tia announced using her hands to indicate the extent of her assessment, which consisted of approximately 16 flagstones.

Henry rolled up the sleeves of his shirt, scraped away the crumbling mortar around the edges with a penknife and lifted the first stone in the section she'd chosen. The slab resisted momentarily but eventually it lifted. There was no mortar or concrete underneath fixing the stone in place, just the accumulation of over a hundred years of compacted pebbles, soil and humus.

Henry pulled out a metal meat skewer he'd bought from the plane to use as a probe and stuck it into the ground. The skewer was at least 12 inches long and it met no resistance as it pressed into the soil. There was nothing buried under this stone that he could feel. He moved the skewer around a few times, prodding in each corner of the exposed square, and at several points in the middle. Nothing!

'This is going to take longer than expected but I doubt anyone would have dug down more than a foot if they were in a hurry, don't you?' he said, without looking up at Tia.

There was no reply.

As he turned towards her, the midday sun blinded him momentarily. As his vision cleared he saw Tia being held with her arms forced behind her back by a balding man of over 6 feet. His right hand was cupped over her mouth, holding her neck in a position that Henry knew would snap it if he twisted hard enough.

'Maybe we can be of help?' came a voice from his right side, and he turned to see an even taller man, wearing a long black wool coat and gloves, with a distinctive Russian accent pointing a gun at him.

'How did you get in here?' was all Henry could think to ask, looking back towards the white house.

'The curator was most helpful' said the Russian. 'Although, sadly, it may be a while before he can walk around this garden again; assuming of course that he regains consciousness.'

'Who are you?' Henry already suspected he was now talking to whoever had initiated the deaths of Charlesworth and his secretary.

'That is not essential for you to know,' Boris said, taking Tia's arm and pulling her towards him, turning the gun towards her head. 'All you need to consider is that you are here because of my years of patient research. And now I intend to get what I set out to uncover when we deciphered the journals of Rene Secretan.'

'But you got what you wanted!' Henry took a chance that this man had not realised he'd received the painting that had been in Washington for nearly 80 years in plain sight. 'The person you sent to the gallery took the painting from my lab last night.'

'Mr Whittaker, do you think I am an idiot?' Boris ran the muzzle of the gun around Tia's temple.

'I don't know. Are you?' Henry instantly regretted the inflammatory comment as he watched Boris's hand grip Tia more tightly. He needed to control his temper, just as he'd been practising for years.

'Well Mr Whittaker you have been most troublesome for me over the last two days. I was almost back in Russia before I got word that the painting I had with me had previously hung on a wall in Washington.' Boris's leering smile disappeared and anger flared across his face. 'I'm not an idiot! I am also well aware of the switch you pulled and that the painting you gave my associate was the fake. But it is of no concern now. Thank you for deciphering the letter. Now you are going to help me get what I am really after.'

353

Chapter 46

Bloomsbury, London. Friday 17th October 2014

Stephen and Sam arrived at University College Hospital at midday, having lost most of the morning to bureaucracy. The list of people who required bringing up to speed was growing and included journalists, MPs and Police PR specialists once news of the murders got out. As anticipated, the various media publications were calling for blood at the killing of one of their own. So far any mention of Henry Whittaker and his own daughter had been avoided. That information had been contained to a group of just four. Stephen hoped it would stay that way.

The huge modern medical facility was spread over 18 floors, stretched across the northern end of Tottenham Court Road. His witnesses were scattered across various departments and would take some rounding up. The state-of-the-art glass building needed a map to navigate successfully and the policemen were already clocking up miles.

Stephen had spoken briefly to Constance about an hour ago, who confirmed Tia was still asleep, exhausted from the traumatic events of yesterday. She promised to get her to ring him as soon as she woke up. He was glad she was in a room on a secure floor of a top hotel less than five minutes away from him. Now he had to get down to the proper police work of investigating a double murder, attempted murder and art theft.

He'd been unable to question Eoin the night before as he'd been taken straight to theatre and stitched up. It hadn't taken long, but Eoin was asleep by the time the officers had finished interviewing the Whittakers at Claridge's. When they arrived this morning they had been informed by the policeman on duty outside Eoin's room that he was currently down in recovery having his dressing changed and was expected back shortly. For now, they would start with Patricia Rivers, Ashley and Matt, who had all seen the gunman and were currently working with the photo-fit artist to create a composite picture.

Patricia had been transferred by ambulance under police escort from Whipps Cross Hospital for her protection. She had seen the intruder but as a witness she was virtually useless. She'd been so drunk when her attacker kicked in the door of her flat that she couldn't remember a thing.

The boy was proving to be more helpful.

'Do you remember what time it was when he arrived?' Sam asked as Stephen sat back and observed.

'It must've been just after 6 o'clock because I could hear the news on mum's TV.' Matt was using all of his senses to recreate the scene in his head as Ashley had briefed him to do. In the absence of a lucid mother, she was sitting in on the interview with her younger brother in his private hospital bedroom, complete with police sentry on guard outside.

'And what did he say?'

Matt looked at Ashley seeking help on what to do or say. His hands were shaking and he clung to the bed sheets to steady his nerves. Despite growing up in Tottenham he'd never actually seen a real gun until last night. Years of playing combat games on his old console hadn't prepared him for actual confrontation. His voice was strained and croaking.

'He didn't speak at first. He pulled me out of my bedroom into the living room and hit my mum on the head with the butt of his gun and knocked her out. Then he picked up a photo on the windowsill and asked who the girl was. I told him it was my sister. That was when I realised he wasn't English.' He looked at Ashley for approval that his account was okay. She nodded and put her hand on his arm protectively.

Stephen already knew the man they were after had what sounded like a South African accent but the gun recovered from Henry's lab had failed to produce a fingerprint match against any of Interpol's databases. He had eluded the CCTV at Lenisters and an army of patrol cars last night despite having no more than a five-minute head start. Whoever he was, he was an exceptional professional.

'Okay and did he tell you why he wanted your sister?'

'No. He said he wanted Eoin, but I could tell by the way he looked at the photo that seeing her had pissed him off. She has that effect on people quite often so it didn't surprise me. I told him I hadn't seen Eoin since the previous evening and that maybe he'd gone back home to Edmonton.'

'And then what happened?'

'He threw the photo at the wall and then got a phone call. He didn't say anything and I couldn't hear who he was talking to but he ended the call and grabbed my arm and said we were going for a drive. He dragged me down the stairs and into a car that I assumed he'd stolen cos he started it with some wires under the steering column, not a key. It was a well old car. Not one with the fancy locks they have nowadays.'

'How did he know where to go? Did he have an address or write anything down?'

'He was using the map on his phone. I had no idea where we were going but we were driving for about half an hour. We pulled up in a side road and came into that building from behind some bins. He had a pass code to get in but he was looking in all the rooms on every floor so I guessed he didn't know exactly where he was going. Then we found Ash and the yanks in that chemistry lab.'

Stephen pulled out a sheet of paper from his folder. It was the finished sketch by the photo-fit artist, who had just left Patricia and produced a composite of their three descriptions. He pushed it across the table.

'And does this look like the man who took you?'

Ashley drew a deep breath but kept her composure.

'That's him,' she said. 'That's the man who came into the lab with Matt at gunpoint.' It's also the man who fired at me in Windsor, she thought, but you don't need those details!

Matt nodded in agreement. He was impressed by the accuracy of the likeness.

Stephen handed the photo to Sam.

'Get this circulated urgently. If we're not too late, we need to stop him getting out of the country.'

Sam left to scan the photo fit and brief his team. Stephen took advantage of the departure.

'We can't continue the interview until Sam comes back.' He directed his statement at Ashley. 'But I need to know! Has he done anything to my daughter?'

'Who? That South African bloke?'

'No!' Stephen almost didn't want to know but was compelled to ask. 'The American!'

'Henry?' Ashley felt her defences engage. 'Are you kidding! He's one of the nicest blokes I've ever met and I don't like many people! He wouldn't hurt Tia! He dotes on her! Doesn't stop talking about how good she is at Wing Chun or whatever it is she does! He's spent more time working with her than everyone else in the club put together. He thinks she can be a champion!'

Stephen slumped, relieved from her reaction that it wasn't the sordid news he'd expected but ashamed of his own preconceptions. He of all people should know better than to judge others at face value.

'Thank you,' was all he said.

Sam came back into the room and handed Stephen a slip of paper.

The Assistant Commissioners face screwed up in anger and he learned forward.

'Well it seems your 'decent' American friend just skipped town!'

Stephen scrutinised her for a reaction, his demeanour turning to steel again.

Ashley didn't flinch.

'We put an alert on his passport when this whole thing started and it registered earlier at Northolt airport, boarding his mother's plane. Funny that she didn't mention that to me when I spoke to her this morning. The flight manifest says he landed in Paris about an hour ago. Do you know anything about that?

'How would I know?' Ashley lied. 'I've been here all night.'

Stephen cursed his own instructions to not be disturbed while he interviewed the witnesses and dealt with the journalists. Henry could be anywhere in Northern France by now!

Sam's phone rang and the noise broke the tension. He answered.

'Guv, it's the officer we put on Eoin's door last night. He got worried when it was taking so long for the boy to come back from having his dressing changed so he went to look for the nurse who came in and took him. No one knew anything about him leaving the room to have his dressings changed. No nurse had been sent in to see him since they took his blood pressure at 8am this morning. He's checked everywhere he can think of but the lad's gone!'

Ashley looked bewildered as she listened to the officer. She had only spoken to Eoin less than an hour ago when he asked what had happened to Tia and Henry. Like her, he'd been gutted to miss the chance to go with them to France and continue their adventure but glad they'd recovered the real painting. That was just before 11.30am.

Stephen noticed her reaction.

'I take it you have no idea where he might have run off to?'

'Of course not!'

Sam wasn't paying attention. He was busy reading another text that had just come through.

'Guv, we have a more serious problem right now! I need to make a call.'

He didn't wait for Stephen to approve his exit. He was back in less than a minute looking haggard. The events of the last two days and virtually no sleep were taking their toll.

'We've had a response to the e-fit I issued already.' He rolled his eyes sideways to signal Stephen to leave the room so they could talk in private. Stephen ignored him. He wasn't letting Ashley out of his sight until he knew what had happened to Eoin. As far as he could make out, everyone, including his daughter, had been drawn into these events because of him and now he had disappeared. He didn't move and Sam carried on.

'Essex police discovered a body in Epping Forest earlier. They say it matches the man in our photo. He was discovered this morning by a jogger and his dog. Single gunshot to the back of the head. Looks like it was a rifle shot, probably from the road, but no confirmation yet.'

Sam paused to allow his boss to take in the news before offering a view.

'I think whoever hired him, took him out.'

Stephen was struggling to keep track of the barrage of developments coming at them. 'Who hires a hit man and then has him taken out by another hit man?''

'Someone who didn't want to get their hands dirty first time round?'

This time Ashley couldn't contain her reaction, anxiously shifting in her chair. Stephen didn't miss it!

'What's wrong? That should have been good news for you, now this guy is no longer a threat.'

Ashley battled her conscience. Her loyalty was being tempered by fear. Tia had sworn her to secrecy, but she didn't know about this development. Whoever the murderer was working for must have realised the painting they received was a fake. Surely having come so far they weren't going to give up now and she knew they wouldn't stop at another murder to get whatever it was they were after. They would almost certainly now be looking for Henry or his mum to recover the real Adeline. Ashley needed to warn them. She put her hands on the table and leaned forward, the urgency in her voice evident.

'I need to make a phone call!' she cried.

'You are staying right here until I know what's going on! Why are you suddenly so bloody worried? Whoever hired him is unlikely to have seen your face, or Eoin's.'

She knew he was going to explode if she told him, but what choice did she have? Tia and Henry could now be in trouble and not even know! She took a breath and composed her thoughts, staring at the table, running the possible consequences of this turn of events through her mind.

'The bloke who shot those two people in the gallery has now been executed by someone I assume is probably worse!' Her eyes lifted and Stephen could see the fear. 'And the person who dragged us all into this in the first place has disappeared! This isn't over yet. There is something you don't know. When Henry and his mum carried out the tests to make sure her version was the real painting, they found something behind the backing paper that had never been noticed before. They didn't know what it was, but it must have been there for years. Henry thought it was something to do with Van Gogh's suicide and wanted to check it out. He just thinks it could be a clue to what really happened to the artist and nothing to do with yesterday's murders. But what if that's actually why Charlesworth wanted his mum to bring the painting over from the States. If it's that letter that everyone is after and not the Adeline painting itself, them I'm guessing the person who wants it so badly has found out by now that he has the forgery. What if he's taken Eoin to find out where Henry has gone.'

She paused to let her edited version of the truth sink in.

'I assume Eoin knows that Henry has gone to Paris?' Stephen's accusation was clear. He wasn't happy they were still keeping things from him.

'Yes, I told him. But Henry hasn't gone to Paris alone.' Ashley looked directly at Stephen and pleaded for help. 'Tia is with him. They are on their way to Van Gogh's doctors house in Auvers.'

Stephen's professional veneer finally snapped! 24 hours of walking the line between loyalties ended. It was no longer a choice. Whoever wanted that painting - or letter or whatever this mess was actually about - was still out there, clearly prepared to kill - and so was Tia! He turned to Sam, who was just about keeping up with the rapidly changing events.

'Get me a direct line to the head of the Police de Nationale in Ile-De-France now. And then get a car to take us back to Claridge's!'

Chapter 47

Auvers-Sur-Oise, France. Friday October 17th 2014.

A cold breeze whipped the leaves of Gachet's garden into a wave of debris that circled the Russians. Henry assessed the two men in front of him and put down the metal skewer. He brushed the dirt from his hands and stood up slowly. He glanced apologetically towards Tia who raised her eyes to confirm that she was okay - for now.

Outside the main gate a group of loud American tourists could be heard complaining that the house and gardens were currently closed and their noise quickly faded as they retreated back down the hill towards the town hall. Their chance of being rescued receded.

'Let her go and I'll stay and help you with whatever it is you're searching for.' Henry said slowing his breath and preparing his body for whatever action became necessary. "I'm worth way more to you than she is'.

'True, but what is she worth to you? You've already caused the death of one girlfriend Mr Whittaker. I don't think you are going to allow another to sit on your conscience? You've already taken my painting, which was going to be a nice little bonus. A smart move as it will obviously now be impossible to retrieve without drastic measures. But I think you've seen first hand just what measures I'm prepared to take? Do you really think I'd let my main leverage over you just walk away?' Boris signalled to Vasily to search Henry.

He pulled the letter from Henry's inside pocket and passed it to Boris who read the cryptic note quickly but seemed unsurprised by its content.

'So, you found out about the banker? He has led me on what you call a 'merry dance' for over a decade. All I needed was this location. I doubt you even have any clue regarding the significance of what you are looking for, but you will not take away my chance of finally discovering his secret.'

'I don't know what you are talking about.' Henry said the first words that came into his head simply to maintain a dialogue while he tried to figure out a plan. They were unarmed and facing a gun – possibly two if the bald man were also armed. He needed to keep this Russian talking until he knew what they wanted. 'Yes we worked out that the initials RS in that letter were Rene Secretan and that he was referring to the garden of Van Gogh's doctor, but we have no idea what we are looking for. What do you want us to do?' As he spoke his eyes never left Tia. She was his only priority right now. Whatever secret laid buried under these flagstones it could stay there. Nothing else mattered other than getting her out of this garden safely. He glanced around quickly for something that could be used as a weapon. The garden was immaculate and nothing had been left lying around. It was unlikely he was going to be able to tackle these men alone. He knew Boris wouldn't hurt Tia until they'd found what they came for. He needed to get help.

Boris ignored Henry's question and signalled to Vasily to go in search of shovels. He was anxious to find what they'd come for after so many years of searching and there would probably be at least one more visit required if his suspicions were correct. He wanted to get away from this place before the American's security measures kicked in.

'Did your mother tell you about Secretan's interview with the journalist in 1956?' He asked as he waited for Vasily to return.

'Yes, that's why we came. She thinks that some clue to Van Gogh's suicide may be hidden here. She's dedicated her life to art, and a clue that reveals the truth about those events would be worth more to her than all the money in the world.'

'Your mother and I have much in common. I owe my life to a precious work of art. It saved me from the draft, funded my first company and signalled the deal that transformed my fortunes. Lost art is my lifeblood. My passion! Now you will start digging under each stone and pebble until we find whatever Secretan has hidden here.'

'You mean you don't know what you're looking for either?' Henry looked at Tia completely bemused.

'Lets just say I have a better idea than you'.

Tia stood silently, processing the situation and its possible alternative scenarios. None was playing out well for her and Henry so far. Once these men found what they were looking for, there was no way they were going to just let them both walk away.

'Just start digging!' was all Boris said. 'I'll know what it is when we find it.'

Vasily returned with a trowel and two spades that he'd found in the shed used by the gardeners. He gave Henry the small trowel and a spade to Boris, then moved to the other end of the wall and started digging up the pebbled pathway. Boris pulled Tia over towards one of the wooden benches and pulled a length of nylon rope from his pocket. He tied her hands behind her and lashed them to the back of the aged bench. He took off his coat and folded it on the seat next to her. Boris moved to the middle section of the pebbled path, knelt down and started to work his way towards Vasily, his gun still visible in his side pocket.

Each stone was taking Henry at least twenty minutes to check, as he had to be very careful not to damage whatever it was they hoped to find. Vasily was not being so gentle with the pebbled paths as his spade left a trail of destruction behind him. If what they were looking for was in any sort of fragile condition Henry doubted it would survive the thug's brutal digging. By 2pm they'd still only covered a quarter of the walkways between them.

'Go and check on the curator,' Boris instructed Vasily, 'and make sure the front gates are still locked. I don't want some coach party turning up unexpectedly.'

Vasily headed back towards the house as instructed.

Henry took his chance to try to negotiate with Boris. Everyone had a price eventually. He'd learnt that lesson at a very young age.

'If you don't know what it is we're looking for, how do you know it will be worth anything?'

'I suspect you and I do not measure value in the same way, American!' Boris twisted away from Henry to cut off the conversation. Henry persisted.

"I have a lot of money! And by a lot I mean third-world-debt amounts. How much will it take for you to let us go?'

Boris took the bait and got to his feet. He spat on the ground in contempt and moved towards Henry waving his spade like a club.

'You Americans are all the same! You always think it is about the money. Do I look like I need your money? If you knew who I was you wouldn't be using some pathetic attempts to bribe me. This means more to me than profit!'

He raised the spade and began to swing it towards Henry's head. As the blade crested the tension in the air was broken by a voice behind him.

'I know who you are!' Tia spoke for the first time since the Russians had arrived.

'Sorry?' Boris turned and looked at her in surprise. He lowered the spade and sneered. He'd almost forgotten she was there.

'I said, I know who you are!' Tia held his gaze, her heart pounding in her chest as she confronted her captor. She could feel her skin prickling as it so often did, but this time she was glad that he'd find it difficult to detect her nervous blush.

Boris just laughed at her. What could this stick-thin child possibly know about him?

'Tia don't!' Henry jumped up from behind the flagstone he was currently checking. He couldn't keep the panic out of his voice as he lurched forward, arms behind his back as though searching for something in his waistband. Boris dropped the spade and pulled his gun from his pocket, pointing towards Henry and forcing him to remain where he stood. He turned quickly back to Tia, scrutinising her face for signs of deceit and for any silent communication between them. Who was this girl anyway?

'What do you know?' His curiosity got the better of him. Few people surprised him but she just had and her boyfriend was clearly worried about what she might say.

'I know you bought Savil Court in Egham about three years ago! And that you have twins - a boy and a girl!' All Tia could think about was the absolute necessity to keep him talking.

Boris felt the anger searing his eyes as he stormed towards her and once again pressed his gun directly against Tia's head. How could she possibly know all this? She could feel the cold steel of the barrel tracing a circle on her temple as he pushed her backwards until he could see her face.

He turned back towards Henry, convinced they were somehow communicating. If they were then he couldn't tell how but there was no way she could know those things. Many people knew him by name and reputation - few people outside his immediate circle knew what he looked like; even fewer knew any details whatsoever about his family, especially his children.

'How could you possibly know that?' His usually cool exterior was fragmenting. It had been many years since he'd seriously lost his self-control.

Tia bit her lip and refused to let go of her advantage.

'Are you sure you trust your information source 100%?' She stared at him, right between the eyes, her nerves scintillating but her exterior frozen in resolve. Boris found himself locked in a compulsion to press her more. Any leak within his security team would need to be eradicated urgently.

'What are you talking about?'

'How would I know about your kids or where you live if I didn't have my own source of information? I assume they are not common knowledge for a man in your position? Being wanted by so many different groups as I suspect you are!' Tia couldn't see Henry, as Boris was now directly in front of her, blocking her view and leaning over her so closely she could smell his foul breath. Vasily was still not back and she prayed that Henry had taken the opportunity her distraction offered to climb over the wall. He was their only chance. She'd waited specifically until he reached that flagstone because it was the closest to the wall and behind a tree. He would now have a few precious seconds to escape and find help.

'What do you know about my source of information?'

'Only that you've known exactly where we were since yesterday afternoon. You knew where to send your hit man last night to recover the painting he'd lost. You must have given him the code for the back door of Henry's lab and you've followed us here today, despite having no clue until now that this location was important for whatever it is you are looking for. Your information must be coming from someone who knows us! Someone who knows where we are at any point in time and what we are doing. Are you sure they're not giving us information as well?' Tia could tell from his reaction that she'd touched a nerve with her speculative accusation. She'd suspected someone was divulging their whereabouts since yesterday – or specifically Henry's whereabouts - and now she was turning that assumption against this criminal. An untrustworthy man often trusts no one.

'Think about it! We've been one step ahead of you the whole time, despite being just a group of students. How do you think they cheated your hit man at the University? Information flow goes two ways. Henry was right - most people have a price. Why not extract it from two willing benefactors?'

Tia had run out of rhetoric but Boris was so close now, and he didn't have a chance to respond! As he processed the repercussions of her suggestion she launched a kick into his groin that knocked the gun into the nearest flowerbed. Whilst they were digging she'd broken through the rotten wooden bench slat with the nylon rope and had been easing off the shackles for almost 30 minutes. Boris collapsed to the floor in agony as her ropes finally unravelled and fell away, exposing her bloody, torn wrists. She was on her feet faster than he could lift his huge bulk and a right kick to his kneecap sent him down again. Boris was a brawler with no finesse. He was up onto his knees again quickly. He wouldn't need a gun to make light work of this twig!

Her punches to his head glanced off his slick receding temples and he barely seemed to feel them. He lunged and grabbed her ankle, knocking her backwards onto the bench, but she was up in an instant and her punches and kicks were furious and unrelenting. He was unable to regain his footing and fell backwards onto his haunches.

As her onslaught rained down on him, he reached forwards towards the flowerbed, trying to recover his gun, but her foot connected with his nose and sent him backwards again.

He still didn't seem to feel the blood running down his face and rolled away from her, jumping back onto his feet again. Tia glanced round for a fraction of a second wondering why Henry wasn't coming to her aid. He was nowhere to be seen. Maybe he'd taken the chance she'd given him after all, but the other Russian would be back any moment and she couldn't keep them both at bay.

Boris put his hand in his back trouser pocket and pulled out an ivory-handled flick knife. The deadly blade appeared from inside the illegal weapon's hilt and glistened. The little bitch may be able to fight but she wasn't made of steel. He'd carve her up like the Christmas turkey. Boris lunged but Tia was too quick, darting left off the bench, but catching the tip of the blade across her right arm, cutting through her jacket sleeve. She winced as she scrambled behind the crumbling seat, well aware it would provide no protection at all if he recovered his gun.

'Foolish move brave little girl!' Boris laughed as he threw the knife at her and dropped to the floor by the flowerbed, searching for his gun.

The knife knocked into the top of the bench and her jeans ran red as it hit Tia's front thigh. Thankfully the blow was partially absorbed by the deflection off the wood and the thick denim pockets, seams and rivets, embedding less than half an inch under the skin.

Tia pulled out the knife, and with a reaction speed only a professional fighter could manage, she hurled it back at the Russian, penetrating the back of his hand and causing him to drop his gun again.

Boris let out a yell just as Henry vaulted back over the top of the wall. He launched a kick at Boris's head that connected with his left eye socket and the giant fell to the floor. Henry picked up the gun that was inches from the Russian's hand and held it firm, looking around for the second man. As he turned he faced an approaching wall of blue uniforms waving submachine guns at him and yelling at him in French to get on the floor.

Chapter 48

Auvers-Sur-Oise, France. Friday October 17th 2014.

The tranquil, French suburban gardens were instantly ablaze with flashing blue lights and sirens as eight armed gendarmes circled the three of them.

The lead sniper waved a plainclothes inspector in. He was tall and thin and reminded Tia of her maths tutor at school. Unlike her teacher, his suit was immaculate and his shoes were polished to a gleam.

'Are you Tia Hall?' he asked in heavily accented English.

Tia looked at him as she clutched her injured thigh. Who on earth could have found her here?

'Yes!' she replied nervously has he held out a badge for her to check.

'Good, I am Inspector Robert of the Groupe d'intervention de la Gendarmerie. Your father said you might be here.' He looked down at the blood on her leg and hand and waved over an officer. 'Get her a medic! She's been injured.'

The paramedic who'd arrived by motorcycle ahead of the ambulance came over to inspect the wound. Inspector Robert turned to Henry and looked at the gun still in his hand.

'And therefore you must be Mr Henry Whittaker? You realise you are in breach of the terms of your visa, don't you Mr Whittaker?' He pulled out an antique silver cigarette case and removed a white consulate. He lit the end and the smell of menthol and tobacco wafted past them.

Henry didn't look up as he nodded, suppressing his instinct to react.

'I think in this instance we can overlook it given you've saved her life.' Inspector Robert took the gun from Henry and made it safe. 'I suspect this man is wanted for much more than trying to kidnap an heir. We have many questions for you two. Don't go away!'

He left the two of them to be treated in the back of the ambulance that had pulled up in the drive. The curator had already been taken to hospital and police tape was being wrapped round the entire premises. Henry held Tia's hand as the medic cleaned up her wounds. She was wrapped in a blanket with her jeans pulled down to her knees whilst they applied three neat stiches to her thigh. All she could think about was how unimaginable sitting in a French garden with Henry, with her underwear on display, would have been yesterday morning!

She started to laugh!

'Thank you for coming back!' she said, looking at Henry

Henry shot her a glance that signalled her to stay quiet. So far no one else was aware that he'd left the garden before the arrival of the police. She complied without question and let the medic bandage her wrists and apply two temporary sticky stitches to the top of her arm.

'C'est pas si mal,' the medic confirmed.

Tia pulled her clothes back on and got out of the ambulance. She felt fine and had no intention of spending the night in a French hospital.

They watched as Boris and Vasily were taken into custody, handcuffed and under heavily armed guards. Robert was on the phone proudly officiating over the political battle that had already started as to which country took priority for extradition, such was the list of their suspected crimes.

As the afternoon light began to fade Tia and Henry went back into the house to avoid attention as Inspector Robert gave a press briefing to the throng of journalists who'd already started to gather outside the historic grounds.

'Working with the British police, we have today apprehended an international criminal suspected to be behind at least three murders,

371

including that of art dealer, Philip Charlesworth and his secretary, Serena Holdsworth, whose bodies were found yesterday at his Mayfair gallery in London.'

No mention was made of the 'help' they'd received from Tia and Henry. That was the deal Tia's father had made. If someone *was* still after Tia and Henry and they were apprehended in Auvers then the French could take the credit! All Stephen wanted was for his daughter to be found safe and well.

Henry was glad. He had no desire to attract any more attention to himself ever! He was impatient to get out of the gardens and back on the road.

It was another two hours and a thousand questions before the French police allowed them to leave the museum.

'Your father is expecting you back at Northolt before 7 o'clock,' Inspector Robert warned 'I have arranged for a car to escort you back to the airport. He was most insistent that I made sure you got on that plane. An officer will be in to collect you shortly. I suspect your dad may have many more questions for you both when you get home. A patrol car will be waiting for you when you land. Au revoir.'

He left the two of them alone in the kitchen at the back of the house.

'We need to get out of here!' Henry whispered when the door had closed.

Tia could feel him move closer to her and her skin began to prickle. He put his hand round her waist and pulled her round towards him. Her face was almost touching his.

'I didn't just leave to find help, Tia. I would never have left you if it hadn't been essential. But I knew once they found what they were looking for they would have no reason to keep us alive any longer. You need to trust me, but we can't let them put us on that plane. If you want to go home then I completely understand. I should never have dragged you here in the first place but I couldn't help it. Now you're injured and in huge trouble with your dad. But I have to stay. I can't talk here, but if you don't want to come you can just tell them I ran off. You can use the plane to get home, that's no problem at all. I'll find another way home.'

Tia looked at the man in front of her whose eyes were staring unblinking into hers. Since the first moment she saw him in the cold gym she'd known he had a connection to her that she didn't understand. Before she could stop the impulse, her hand reached up and touched his face. His skin was cold from being outside all day but she didn't care.

'Of course I'm coming with you.' She said without hesitation.

Henry opened the back door that led into the potting shed and checked the garden. The police activity was almost entirely confined to the left hand side of the grounds next to the wall and the front of the house. Henry signalled for Tia to follow him to the right up the steep path in the opposite direction. The steel constructions displaying replicas of Dr Gachet's own artwork shielded them from view as they headed towards the back wall of the garden. Henry helped Tia climb over first and she felt the stiches in her thigh pull as she dropped down onto the path on the other side but they held firm. Henry was over a second later and they moved off the walkway into the cover of the hedgerow.

As they walked along the path, following the contour of the wall back down the slope, they could hear the voices of the various police departments working on different aspects of the evidence gathering process. They turned right through the trees and headed back towards the side road where they'd parked earlier today. Henry stopped suddenly as though he'd forgotten something and turned round on the spot. Once again his face was almost parallel to hers, with only a couple of inches difference in their heights. Without asking, he put his hands on Tia's face and gently kissed her. Her lips were soft and he waited for any signs of resistance or retreat. None came as Tia held her breath and sank into the moment. Her stomach flipped the way it had just before their first sparring session and she returned the pressure. He held her for what seemed like forever before kissing her neck and whispering.

'That's just in case we get into any more trouble before we get back to the car! I've been wanting to do that for over a month!' he teased. 'Do you know how many times in my life I've had to wait for something I wanted? Never! Not once! But it was worth every second.'

Tia knew she was turning her usual shade of invisible crimson but she didn't care. Inside she suspected this might be the last time Henry Whittaker ever made her blush! Her heart was pounding as she reached up and took his hands and kissed the tips of his fingers. Her wounds were forgotten and she wished they could stay her forever but any minute now someone would realise they'd left the grounds without their escort.

Assuming they were heading back to the car, Tia looked to the left as they neared the end of the lane, but Henry turned right at the next house, into the bushes, pulling her after him.

"Where are we going?' she asked, wondering what else he wanted to do to her.

'We're not done yet,' he smirked.

'What do you mean?'

'Come on - we'll have to double back this way I'm afraid.'

'Go back! Are you kidding me! We just ran away from the French police! What if they catch us?'

Henry didn't reply and just signalled for her to stay silent.

They emerged onto another steep, narrow lane that ran parallel with the one they'd just been on, behind the first line of buildings. Tall reeds and grasses brushed against their legs, as they proceeded slowly back towards the garden wall.

'You know I would never normally have left you don't you?'

'It's fine! It was the only way you could go and get help. Thank god they got there so quickly!'

Henry led her back under another row of bushes that were losing their leaves, creating piles of debris on the ground. They had to bend down to get under and Tia felt her wound sting again.

'I didn't call them. When I got over the wall, I came down here and saw one of their cars drive past the end of this lane.' He pointed to a spot about twenty feet from where they were now, and from where they had just come. 'I found a hiding spot and then crept back down to the road to see what was going on. The place was crawling with gendarmes and they already had Vasily in custody. Then I heard you scream so I jumped back over the wall.'

'Hiding place for what? And how did the police know exactly where we were?'

Henry stopped and dropped to his knees, clearing a mound of dead leaves.

'I've got an idea, but I'll explain that to you a bit later. Right now we need to get away from here with this.'

He pulled out a tin box about the size of a child's shoebox. It was rusted and dirty, but still intact!

'Just as you began your distraction I found this under the flagstone I was working on. You were absolutely right in your guess. It was the one nearest the wall and behind a tree. The perfect place to bury something without being seen by the occupants of the house.'

He stood up, pulled her towards him and kissed her again, the metal tin wedged between them.

'Now let's get out of Auvers, before they start looking for us again, and see what all this drama has really been about.'

They returned to the car and pulled out onto the road, following signs towards Paris to find somewhere to eat and check what they had found. Less than a hundred feet behind them another black Renault Clio pulled out unnoticed and followed them in the dimming light, back towards the city.

Chapter 49
Argenteuil, France. Friday 17th October 2014

It was almost dark by the time Tia and Henry pulled into the Carrefour Sannois, just outside Argenteuil, so Tia could buy a more comfortable skirt and basic toiletries. Her jeans were pressing against the stitches in her thigh and sitting was difficult.

As they left the shop and put their bags into the boot of the car Henry turned and kissed her again. Her hands move to his back as if they had a life of their own. They seemed to know instinctively what to do despite her complete lack of experience but her stomach gave a loud rumble and the mood was broken.

'Are you hungry by any chance?' Henry laughed and Tia cursed her body for ruining her perfect moment. 'Let's go and find somewhere to eat and see what's in this tin.'

Le Roy du Liban was a traditional restaurant in the centre of Argenteuil. They ordered brochettes d'agneau and the most expensive bottle of red wine on the menu.

As they waited for their food Henry recalled the moment Tia had thrown the Russian off guard.

'I meant to ask you, how did you know who that Russian was?'

Tia hadn't known for sure at the time but her stalling tactic had turned out to be a correct recollection.

'As soon as I saw him I knew I'd seen him somewhere amongst my dad's files. It took me a while to go through my memory and place the face but it eventually came to me. When I was little my dad used to tell me stories about criminals and how they had managed to escape justice because of loopholes and good lawyers. He would tell me how

376

frustrating it was to watch people walk away from their crimes because they had money, but that it was something I'd have to get used to if I ever decided to make a career in law or law enforcement.'

Henry flinched with guilt as she spoke but let her continue.

'We discussed dozens of cases over the years and every now and then he would show me an article or document about one of the people we'd discussed. About three years ago an alert was placed against the Russian when he bought a mansion in Egham and my dad was sent a copy of his Interpol profile as someone to watch. The list of his suspected involvements was huge but he'd never been charged with anything. I remember thinking at the time, how did someone under so much suspicion get to just go where they wanted buying houses and doing business and not get arrested? I remembered him because he was so tall, and because the photo had the other guy in it as well. To be honest his actual name only just came to me at the last minute. He'd never actually carried out any of the crimes he was suspected of committing personally and had been very clever to keep such a low profile for so long.'

'But not as clever as you, and now he's been caught in the act.' Henry knew first hand that even that wouldn't necessarily be enough to keep the Russian out of jail. Money was indeed often more powerful than the law. He knew that first hand.

He kissed her cheek as their dinner arrived and they didn't speak as they ate hungrily. The food was delicious and Tia even ventured a glass of red wine. The total bill was less than her main course at the Ivy but she couldn't have been happier. After they'd eaten Henry put the tin on the table and they both inspected it properly for the first time.

It was painted with red enamel that was chipped around the edges. A century of rust had eaten away at the spots of exposed metal but the condition wasn't as bad as it could have been. There were no complete breeches and the inside of the tin was still dry and waterproofed.

Henry lifted it onto his lap and pulled up the lid, shielding the contents from the waiting staff with the table top. He inched it forward slightly to allow in some light and for the first time they saw what was inside. Wrapped in a ragged oilcloth was a small pistol.

'Oh my god you don't think...' Tia couldn't bring herself to say the words.

'I do!' Henry lifted it out carefully and placed in on the empty seat beside him. 'Why else would you go to so much trouble to hide it?'

"Do you think they will ever be able to prove it?"

'Not without digging up Van Gogh's body and matching the bullet, which never exited his stomach according to the medical records and therefore should technically still be in his grave, but I very much doubt that will ever happen. What purpose would it serve? It still won't change the verdict of suicide. This matches the description of Ravoux's gun exactly and everyone believed it was this gun that was used anyway. The more interesting question is how and why it came to be buried in Dr Gachet's garden. Clearly Van Gogh didn't do that himself.'

Henry opened the chamber of the ancient pistol. Three bullets were still in the gun, clogged with dirt. The hammer was loose and the short barrel was filled with earth.

'This gun was buried without the tin at some point. Look, every crevice is filled with earth but there's no dirt in the tin. Someone must have dug it up and reburied it in a hurry, probably to keep it safe.

Henry looked back inside the tin. At the bottom were two metal tubes. The first was a tube of paint. Henry removed the lid but the contents had long since dried out leaving just a brownish filler in the neck. He passed it to Tia who studied the label.

'It's Indian Yellow. Does that mean anything to you?'

Henry tried to recall where he'd heard that name recently. He repeated it over and over in his head until a memory stirred.

'That's the colour my mum was going to test for on the original Van Gogh. She said it was banned around 1900 but it was the yellow Van Gogh often used. It contained high levels of lead, which is why it was discontinued. Given what we've discovered so far I suspect that this may have actually been Van Gogh's paint.'

He then took the second tube out of the tin. It was a cigar case. The brand on the outside was H Upmann - Habana, long since defunct. Henry pulled off the stopper. Rolled up inside the tube was a black and white photo. It showed an ornate marble fireplace on which stood two silver candlesticks and a photo frame. Above it hung a number of barely visible paintings. The photo was badly deteriorated and cracked from being rolled up for so long and Henry couldn't make out the subjects of any of the paintings. He passed it to Tia.

'What do you think this is?'

'It looks like someone's living room fireplace. It could be any house in the world.'

She turned it over but there was nothing on the back. Henry took it and reviewed it again.

"Well it's not the fireplace in Dr Gachet's house. That was made of wood and the living room was much smaller. You can't see the corner of the room in this photo, and I think that might be the edge of a grand piano. Wherever this was taken, it was a very large house.'

'So not the Ravouxs' Auberge where Van Gogh died?' Tia didn't believe it even as she said it.

'No. I've seen the Auberge and the whole building would have fitted inside this room. That was a very humble rural inn. This looks more like a city town house - like the ones they model dolls houses on.'

Tia thought about the evidence they had gathered so far

'Philip Charlesworth acquired the genuine Adeline at some point in the last three months. He said he inherited it in his father's will and that it had been kept in a bank vault for years. We don't know where the bank was, but we do know that a Russian gangster knew of its existence and planned to steal it.'

'Yes but do you remember what he said in the garden?' Henry was working through the facts with her. 'He said the painting was a bonus.

He was clearly looking for something else. Do you think he wanted the gun?'

Tia wasn't convinced.

'Unless he could get an exhumation order he would never be able to tie that gun to Van Gogh. I still think this is about the suicide note, or maybe even a secret letter explaining exactly what happened. Your mum told us Van Gogh wrote hundreds of letters during his lifetime that are on display in the Van Gogh Museum in Amsterdam. A letter from him saying who actually shot him would be much easier to verify and of much more significance. Finding the gun doesn't change any of the events from the past. Everyone knows Vincent was shot. Finding a letter that tells us what happened could change everything.'

'If Rene Secretan was hiding a letter for Van Gogh, why didn't he just put it in this tin?'

'I don't think he wanted any of the clues to mean anything unless they were found in order. Imagine if you just dug up this tin - what would you make of it?'

'Nothing! Without the letter from the back of the Adeline we would have no clue who put it there or who it was about.'

Tia jumped up, dropping the paint tube on the floor.

'Exactly! I know what we need to do!' she declared. 'Come on. We need to get some sleep. First thing tomorrow we need to go back to Auvers.'

'Why?'

'You'll see when we get there. Now it's your turn to trust me. It's a long shot but I think we might be able to identify where this photo was taken.'

Henry hated being one step behind her as usual but he trusted her judgement implicitly. They left the café and went in search of somewhere to stay. They checked into a tiny bed and breakfast just outside Argenteuil. As hoped, the family-run business did not ask for both passports when the generous handful of euros and Tia's passport were produced. Her name was unlikely to be recognised by anyone in

France. The owner gave Tia a disapproving glare as she showed them into their room, as it was clear they had no luggage other than a supermarket carrier bag.

Tia jumped in the shower while Henry phoned his mother to bring her up to speed with the day's developments. He got no answer and turned off the phone to conserve the battery. They had been expected back in London hours ago and neither parent would be happy. Tia had left her phone in England rather than risk her dad discovering she'd left the country but that had somehow happened anyway - and for that he was actually thankful.

Now they'd eaten, changed clothes and felt fresher than they had in the last 48 hours. It was only 9pm but they were both shattered.

'Why exactly did we need to share a room?' Tia teased as the bathroom door closed behind her and they were finally alone. Her heart was racing in anticipation of his answer. He had kissed her three times now and she had loved every second. She didn't want this evening together to end. Not even for the wild adventure they appeared to still be on.

'You need to protect me!' he joked. 'I'm still on the top ten list of kidnap risks remember, and I appear to have lost my bodyguard. I could still be at risk even if today's threat has been taken into custody.'

He took Tia's hands and held them, brushing her wet hair from her face.

Thoughts of intrigue flew from Tia's mind as she realised they now had to confront the sleeping arrangements.

'You take the bed, I'll sleep in the chair,' Henry said protectively. As he spoke he pulled her towards him. His lips pressed hard against her and he felt her return the pressure. His hand cupped her head and her hair felt soft entwining his fingers. She smelled of soap and red wine, and he realised she'd had a glass without protesting. It had calmed her nerves and removed her inhibitions. Her hand slid under his shirt and her fingers brushed against the skin of his back sending a bolt of energy through him. He couldn't remember the last time he wanted something so much.

They fell onto the bed without breaking their kiss and kicked their shoes off in unison. He felt her flinch as his thigh pressed against her stitches but she just rolled onto her back, pulling him up on top of her. He began to kiss her neck, slowly moving down her collarbone. It had been a long time since he'd touched a woman, but everything came flooding back to him as he slowly undressed her to reveal her perfect body, damaged slightly by the Russian's knife and rope.

Tia knew that the tingling sensation all over her skin was not the familiar flush of embarrassment. Nothing in her sheltered life had ever felt so right as kissing Henry and every progressive touch seemed like a perfectly natural next step. He made love to her gently, tenderly. Wanting to explore every inch of her and enjoy every second.

They fell asleep on top of the covers, ownership of the right to sleep in the bed no longer in dispute.

Outside the occupants of the black Renault Clio settled down for the night, confident nothing would happen before daybreak.

Chapter 50

Mayfair. London. Friday 17th October 2014.

Stephen Hall was alone when he arrived back at Claridge's just after 2pm. Sam had been dispatched to the gallery to oversee the continuing forensic investigations necessary for the triple murder enquiry that would now follow. Even though the murderer himself was dead, gathering evidence to tie him back to whoever had hired him would be their top priority.

As his patrol car pulled out of the hospital he'd called the French police asking for their help. The opportunity to lead an operation involving one of the richest families in the world had been seized upon by the ambitious Inspector Robert. Stephen was not interested in taking any credit and had agreed immediately to the officer's terms. As long as Tia was unharmed nothing else mattered.

Maltby hadn't needed ID this time to allow the Assistant Commissioner back up to the Brook Suite to confront the billionairess. He only needed to see a face once.

Constance was already waiting in the corridor when Stephan stepped out of the lift. Maltby was clear as to who was paying his wages, he thought.

'You need to start telling me the truth Mrs Whittaker.' He said brushing past her, back into the living room he'd left only 14 hours ago. 'The man who held you at gunpoint yesterday evening has been found dead in Epping Forest and the case he took from your son's lab is missing. Clearly whoever hired him wasn't happy with what he delivered.'

He turned and watched the colour drain from her immaculately made up face. Whoever was behind this was still looking for something. Her reaction confirmed she understood the danger that this posed for her and her son and Stephen needed to know what is was.

'I'm sorry I lied to you about Tia being asleep.' She couldn't keep the truth from him any longer – not if Henry was still in danger 'I think you better sit down Commissioner.'

The silent butler arrived as if on cue and placed a tea tray on the table. Constance poured two cups as she gathered her thoughts into a coherent story and then sat down beside the policeman to confess.

'Henry assured me they would be gone for less than 6 hours. He said he wanted to check out the gardens of Dr Gachet's house in Auvers Sur Oise, which is just outside Paris.'

"I know where it is Mrs Whittaker. The French police are on there way there now. What I don't understand is why they are there?

Constance drew a breath of comfort from the knowledge that police help was on its way to Henry. Please God let them not be too late! She calmed her nerves with a sip of tea and continued.

'When we examined the two paintings yesterday we found a shadow between the layers of the backing paper of the original version of Adeline. Henry wanted to know what it was. He thought it might have been Van Gogh's suicide note because the painting would have still been at the Auberge Ravoux when he died. He and Tia went back to his lab this morning and retrieved a letter. It took some deciphering, but Tia worked out that there was something hidden in the garden of Dr Gachet. Something that it seems a man called Rene Secretan had obviously gone to a lot of trouble to conceal. It may still be the suicide note, or even the gun, which has never been found. We don't know. That's what Henry and Tia have gone to find. This wasn't about the murders I assure you. Henry wasn't looking for more trouble or to hunt the murderer himself. He thought this might be evidence of what really happened in one of the most famous suicides in art history. Its discovery would be invaluable.'

'Mrs Whittaker did Henry or Tia speak to Eoin Driscoll before they left?'

'Henry didn't speak to anyone as far as I'm aware and the maid found Tia's phone in the guest bedroom a few hours ago. It's been switched off. Why?'

'Eoin has gone missing from the hospital. Someone is obviously passing information to whoever is behind all of this and background checks have shown that his uncle is a particularly dangerous criminal.'

Constance thought for a second. Eoin hadn't been in the building when the paintings had been switched. He'd only arrived just in time to save Ashley from being shot. He couldn't possibly know that the thief had taken the wrong one.

'He may have called him from the car.' She volunteered.

'Well I'm guessing whoever is behind all of this knew exactly what they were looking for and didn't get it. It would have taken a second to slice open the backing paper and see there was nothing there. We have to assume they are also after this letter. Have you spoken to Henry since they left?'

'No his phone has been switched off for hours. I've no idea where he is at the moment.'

The worried parents sat looking at each other, helplessly. Two powerful people whose only concern was the safety of their children. Despite their vast combined resources they sat in silence waiting for others to bring them news.

Jacques Robert called Stephen back just after 5pm London time.

'Stephen, events have taken an unexpected turn here, but Tia is safe.' His voice was proud and energised by the events of the afternoon. 'She has a minor knife wound but the medics have stitched her up and the boy is fine.'

Stephen felt the blood drain from his temples.

'Knife wound?' was all he heard. Beside him Constance began to tremble.

'Henry is fine.' He put a hand on her arm to calm her.

Roberts continued.

'You said they may be in danger from someone involved in your murders from yesterday. You didn't say it was Boris Rubikov. We have taken him and his head of security into custody and charged them with attempted murder whilst we sort through the question of jurisdiction.'

'Boris Rubikov?' Stephen frowned as he tried to recall where he'd heard that name before. 'The Russian billionaire?' Information stored in the annals of his mind began to surface. 'So he's been behind this the whole time? '

'It would appear so, therefore I thank you for handing me not just a possible high profile kidnap attempt but a notorious mobster who has evaded almost every law enforcement agency in Europe. I have already had calls from the Chief de Police and the Major of Paris to congratulate me. Tia and Henry will be leaving shortly and should be back in the UK in couple of hours. If I can be of any further assistance please let me know.'

'Jacques, thank you for saving my daughter,' Stephen said, and hung up.

Constance ordered room service for both of them as they sat and waited for their children to arrive back at the hotel.

By midnight the parents were worried yet again.

'Henry has been confiding in you the whole time,' Stephen said, 'surely he would have rung you by now to let you know what was happening?'

'Commissioner Hall, even if it crossed my son's mind to let me know where he was, unless he needed my help I would probably be the last person he would ring.' Constance was well aware that she had been paying the price for her overzealous protectiveness for the last eight years.

'What about the pilot? Has he had any word as to when they expect to take off?'

Constance knew that even if he had, her pilot, Mitch, would be loyal to Henry, who had graduated with him from college. Her son could be utterly captivating when he chose to be. She just shook her head.

'They must have discovered something in the garden that has made them stay in France,' was all she could think of.

'Inspector Roberts didn't mention anything. He said they must have left on their own via the back path to avoid the press. They had nothing with them at all. Has he not even contacted his fiancée?'

Constance looked up. She had completely forgotten about Jennifer. Where had she been all day?

'I have a confession Mr Hall.'

'Please call me Stephen.'

'Stephen, Jennifer is not actually Henry's fiancée. She had just graduated from Quantico and was set to become an FBI agent when she sustained an eye injury that terminated her federal career. We employed her as Henry's bodyguard and constructed the engagement to explain why she was constantly with him. She is stunning as you know, and the story was entirely plausible. She is actually responsible for every aspect of Henry's security. She plans his schedules, tracks his movements and is deemed lethal when it comes to close-up protection.'

'So where is she?'

'I guess I just assumed that she had gone with them! She wasn't here this morning.'

'Inspector Roberts made no mention of her presence and she wasn't on the plane manifest.'

'Trust me if she'd been there, she would not have allowed Boris Rubikov to get within ten feet of Henry.' Constance ran through the events of the day in her mind. 'Now I think about it, she was gone before Henry got back from his lab with the letter and I've not seen or heard from her since.'

'Would she have any way of being able to trace them?'

'Well she would if a judge gave the order for his tracker to be activated but…' She halted and then got up in a hurry, searching her bag for her secure cell phone. She called her husband.

'Harry, did you contact the authorities to activate Henry's tracker?'

The expression on Constance's face told Stephen the answer had been negative. She put down the phone and sat back down, thinking. A few moments later she picked it back up again and made another call.

'Mitch, it's Constance Whittaker. I'm afraid I need you to return immediately to London and be ready to meet me in two hours at RAF Northolt. I very much doubt Henry will need you tonight.' She put down the phone. Mitch might disobey her staff if Henry asked him to, but he wouldn't disobey her.

Stephen noticed that determination had replaced the worry etched into her features since they'd met.

'Where are you going?' he asked, knowing he was not letting another Whittaker out of his sight until he had his daughter back.

'Where we're going, Stephen. I've spent most of the day wondering how that South African man knew where we were last night when he turned up at Henry's lab. You had a police guard posted in front of the building yet he still managed to get in via a doorway that my company paid to have installed. Even Henry doesn't know that my security company built it, but others did. I'm sure your researchers have already told you that Henry had a sub-dermal tracker fitted in his shoulder after his second kidnap attempt. It actually saved his life the last time someone tried to take him. But when he was 21 he had a court injunction issued that prevented it from being activated unless there was proof of a threat to him, and even then only an immediate family member could make the application to have it turned on. I didn't ask for it to be activated and neither did his father. Only two other people can make that happen and I've a pretty good idea who did. I need to make some calls back to the US, and then we need to get to Paris as soon as possible.'

Chapter 51

Argenteuil, France. Saturday 18th October 2014.

For the second morning in a row Tia was awake at 4am, but this time she wasn't on the luxurious velvet sofa in one of the world's top hotels. She was lying in the battered bed of a run-down pension in Argenteuil, next to a man she had known for only a few months but who had quickly become the most important person in her life. She'd known this from the first moment she saw him in the gym, but she hadn't dared to hope he might feel the same way about her. Now she knew that he did.

The small bedside light was still on. They must have both fallen asleep without realising. Nicotine stained flock wallpaper was peeling away from the walls where the damp had risen up through the woodwork and the paint was flaking, but she was in heaven.

Tia moved Henry's arm that had been folded tenderly round her waist and turned towards him. She watched him as he lay in the umbra of the soft glow that permeated the suburban darkness, studying his naked body, which had been pressed against her for most of the night. He'd always been fully covered by his clothes or his fighting robes but as her fingers brushed lightly over his skin she could feel his arms were badly scarred. She looked closer at what appeared to be a mixture of cuts and burns, mostly faded with age but some still deep and red. On the right side of his stomach a three-inch wound had healed to a white translucent track of tell-tale metal staple holes. His left shoulder marked the start of a thin red scar that ran down towards his heart like a cartoon arrow. Tia softly traced the raised skin and wondered what horrors he had been through to have such a collection of wounds. Both scars had clearly been stitched and repaired by some of the best doctors in the world and could have been a lot worse. Tia wondered if his back had similar injuries. She hadn't noticed any of them last night. She had been too caught up in a whole new world that was opening up to her. As she tried to recall the sensation of what her hands had felt as she'd touched him, all she could think was that she never wanted to let him out of her sight again. Whatever he had been through in his life, its history was permanently etched into his skin and tissue. Her own small collection of injuries, which had mainly been invisible broken bones and fractures, seemed pathetic in comparison. For the first time in her life she understood how her father must constantly feel about her; what it must be like to be consumed with a desire to protect another human from being hurt.

Henry woke, as if he sensed she was waiting for him. He pulled her back under the bedclothes and kissed her.

'We have to get up and get back to Auvers!' she protested unconvincingly.

Henry didn't release her and she didn't fight him.

'It's Saturday - the museum won't be open for hours.'

'We're not waiting for it to open! I doubt even your mother's money will get us back into that building legitimately any time soon.'

He kissed her again and the urgency melted. Whatever they were looking for had been hidden for over a hundred years. Another half an hour wouldn't make much difference.

It was gone 5am before they were on the road back to Auvers. The black Renault Clio without headlights that held its position 100 yards behind them went completely unnoticed as they drove the twenty miles of dark road back to the doctor's house.

Henry parked in the same spot they had occupied the day before. They retraced their footsteps back along the overgrown path and climbed over the wall at the point hidden by the tree. The damaged pathways had been roped off with red-and-white tape and the bench that Tia had broken to escape her ropes was still in place in bits. They could barely see where they were going in the dark, pre-dawn cloak but they didn't dare risk using the torch on Henry's phone. It would be seen for miles if anyone was up at this ungodly hour. Tia led him carefully up the steep banks of the garden towards the house.

'Are you really suggesting that we break in to Dr Gachet's house?' Henry had a slight mocking tone in his voice as he teased her. 'What happened to the innocent young girl I fell in love with?'

Tia stopped in her tracks, suddenly drained of all her newly developed bravery. 'Do you think we shouldn't?'

'Hell no!' Henry laughed. 'I've done way worse than this in my life. I've forgotten how exciting it feels. Do they have any CCTV?'

'When we looked around the inside yesterday I remember thinking how little security they had on the property.' She guided him carefully around the periphery of an area she judged would be covered by the only intruder light on the outside. They reached the garden shed, and as she had hoped, no one had yet replaced the lock that Vasily had broken the day before to get the shovels. 'There are security cameras on the front gate, the front door and the side gate, but nothing inside the house. I bet it would be a very different story if the works inside were still originals.'

'The house would be more like Fort Knox if just one of the portraits that Van Gogh painted of Dr Gachet were still here. Last time one was sold it was for the second highest price ever paid for a painting!' Henry could imagine what the works of art given to the physician by his various artistic clients would be worth today if they ever came up for auction.

'There's an external door from the kitchen into this shed. I assume it's where they kept their coal or wood when the doctor and his family lived here.' Tia took Henry's phone from his pocket and turned on the torch, shielding the beam of light with her hand. She began searching for the tools she'd need to complete her plan. 'We need to get into the house without breaking any of the contact switches on the alarm system. That means we have to take out a pane of glass or wood, but the window and door frames are almost as rotten as the bench I broke yesterday. If we can find a claw hammer in here I think we can get that small wooden panel out of the bottom of the back door. Then I'll deactivate the alarm system from inside.'

'Do you know how to do that?' Henry was once again surprised at her resourcefulness.

'Well in theory, yes. I sat in on a seminar at Scotland Yard during my work experience week, but I've never actually done it. If the alarm goes off, run and I'll just make up some excuse about leaving my passport behind or something. How much more trouble can I possibly get in?'

'You still haven't told me what you're looking for.' Henry continued to search for a hammer. He found one stuck to the magnetic strip on the tool-shed wall.

'Do you remember the first thing we did when we arrived at the house yesterday?' Tia was enjoying toying with him.

'Yes we went round the house and listened to that curator guy, who I'm guessing is not our biggest fan right now.'

'Before that?'

'I don't know.'

'We had to sign a visitors register, which required our address.'

'I didn't put my whole address in there!' Henry still couldn't see how that was going to help. Most people had just written their country and state or county.

'Yes I noticed that! But most people don't have to spend their whole life worrying about kidnap threats like you do. I put mine down. Who ever reads the visitors books?'

'What's that got to do with anything?'

'Well that's were I'm running with a bit of a wild theory. If I'm wrong then I'm not sure what our next step would be.'

'Okay so what am I looking for?'

'We need to find the archived visitors registers.'

Henry clawed the rusting nails out of the wooden struts that held the thin wooden panel in the back door. He pushed gently on the bottom of the panel and the wood fell backwards into his outstretched arms. Tia then slid feet first through the narrow opening onto the kitchen floor. They wouldn't remove anything from the house and would replace the wood exactly as it had been before they left. She didn't want to add breaking and entering to her growing list of misdemeanours; especially not in a country where her dad had no influence.

The house seemed even smaller in the dark and she moved carefully, praying there were no motion sensors or infrared beams inside the house. She'd guessed when they first arrived that the property was struggling financially. Despite its historical significance to the life of Van Gogh, it was just too far and too steep for most of the elderly visitors who made the pilgrimage to cope with, and there was no parking in the tiny cramped streets. It was more than a half hour walk from the Auberge Ravoux and there was not that much to see.

She found the alarm panel and removed the front cover. The black power lead was in place just as she'd seen on the police training video, made for when they had to enter a building in an emergency. She cut the wire with the scissors, which shorted out the main fuse and removed the internal battery at precisely the same time. Then she held her breath. If her timing were precise enough she would have disabled both the mains power and backup supply simultaneous. Then the black wire fell onto the floor, completely severed from the whole unit. Tia laughed to herself. The alarm had already been disconnected! It was ancient and the house trust clearly didn't even have the money to spend on maintaining the existing system, never mind upgrading their security. She had been counting on that. No bells started ringing.

She went back into the kitchen and opened the door, letting Henry in.

'Right we need to find the books and get out of here as quickly as possible.' She walked back to the disabled alarm and screwed the front panel back on. 'When we get home can you ask your mum to arrange for a new alarm system to be fitted in here? Seems only right we do something to help them.'

They found the table in the small hallway where the current visitors register sat. Their names were about half way through the book. Each page had about 15 names and addresses on it and Tia estimated the book had about 200 pages. She opened the front cover and looked at the date of the first entry. September 2009 - 5 years ago. That equated to roughly 12 visitors signing in per day. Most people wouldn't bother. If she assumed a steady rate of growth and decline in tourists over the years then there should be approximately 25 more books somewhere.

'What are we looking for in these books?' Henry had done the calculation too and was envisaging going through thousands of names.

'Just find them and then I'll tell you.' She didn't want to reveal her plan until she'd checked her theory for herself. It was based on a whole lot of assumptions that could very easily be wrong.

The study was cramped and smelled of herbs and medicines. Clay bottles lined the walls to maintain the air of science and healing for the visitors who made the trek from Van Gogh's grave. Leather-bound medical books lined the shelves, alongside torturous-looking nineteenth-century pharmacological equipment. There were drawers and cupboards at the bottom of every dresser that lined the room, but most were empty. Under the window a small wooden desk, riddled with chemical spills and burns, sat facing into the steep gardens. The sun was just starting to come up in the east, casting a faint glow across the French countryside. It was a beautiful view, and Tia could see why the doctor would choose this as the place to sit while he was working. The top drawers contained all the paraphernalia of a small museum - visitor's guides, taxi cards and local attraction information leaflets filled the draws. In the bottom draw, neatly lined up in chronological order were a series of books identical to the one out in the hall.

Tia took the first one out and held her breath. If her theory was correct, Rene Secretan would be somewhere in this book.

Her first assumption was that Secretan must have taken the painting before the forgery was sold to Harronson in 1905. It would have been much easier to fool the Ravouxs than any potential art lover who might eventually make an offer for the two works.

Whilst Henry had been sleeping, she'd used his phone to check out some facts. Dr Gachet's house had been opened to the public for the first time earlier that same year. She suspected this was the trigger that forced Secretan to come back and rebury the gun, before an influx of visitors made access difficult.

She turned the book face upwards and opened it, turning each page slowly, scrutinising the names carefully.

Four pages in, she found it! Rene Secretan - and an address in Paris, written in full in tiny spidery writing. She could barely read it in the gloom.

'Pass me your phone,' she beckoned to Henry. She took a photo of the entry and expanded it so it was easier to read. Then she drew in a deep breath and gasped!

'Henry, look at this!' she cried, looking back at the original page to ensure there was no mistake.

'What have you found?' He leaned over her shoulder to see the torchlight-illuminated page. 'You've found his address?' Suddenly he realised what her plan had been. The girl was a genius!

'Yes but look underneath!'

He stared back at the book, to the line indicated by her finger, just under Rene's barely legible scrawl.

Adeline Ravoux, Rue Gambetta, Meulan, France.

Chapter 52

Paris, France. Saturday October 18th 2014.

'How did you know his address would be there?' Henry asked as he drove back towards Paris, ignoring the speed limits. The rising sun was climbing over the horizon, lighting the tree-lined highway beyond the town limit. It was a clear October morning and the sky was cloudless. The in-car sat nav told them they would reach their destination in just over an hour.

'I just guessed! Or rather I worked it out based on what I would have done.' Henry looked even more confused so Tia tried to explain her thoughts.

'Rene Secretan obviously went to a huge amount of trouble to leave a trail to that photo. He stole a genuine Van Gogh just so he could hide a note in the backing paper. He chose a portrait of a subject that was unlikely to have been painted by anyone else and that has two other versions for facial comparison. He replaced it with a copy that used paints not available in the 1890's but which looked identical to the naked eye. Then he left clues which if found in isolation or by chance would be meaningless. He knew that Adeline's stolen portrait would one day prove to be genuine and then hid the painting for over a hundred years waiting for science to be able to uncover the truth! Everything he did was to lead someone to that tin in the garden with the gun, the paint and the photo of a living room. It's not even of the outside of the house! What would've been the point if there were no way of knowing where the house was? He couldn't just write the address on the back of the photo if the clues needed to meaningless on their own. He needed them to be kept separately so that only someone following his trail would be able to understand the significance. I was thinking all night about where he might have written the address and then it came to me. He put in the best place to hide anything – in plain sight where it would not be out of context.'

'Not all night I hope?' he said with a wink. Tia smiled shyly and changed the subject.

'Do you think she knew what he'd done?'

'Who?' Henry asked.

'Adeline.'

'No idea. I guess we'll never know.'

They didn't stop for breakfast. It wouldn't be long before Tia's father came looking for them again, and the chip in his shoulder would tell them exactly where they were. Even if his mother refused to have the Verichip activated, he was pretty sure a judge would rule in favour of one of the most senior members of law enforcement in the UK.

It was 8am when they found the address that had been recorded in the visitor's book. The townhouse extended over four floors and a basement accessed by a separate entrance down a metal flight of stairs. The house was at least a hundred and fifty years old and typical of that period. The brass plaque on the wall read 'Ecole de St Vincent de Paul'

'It's a school!' Tia exclaimed with surprise.

Henry typed the name of the school into the web browser on his phone.

'It's been a school since 1960 when the building was left by a benefactor who made provision for its inception. I think we both know who that must have been. He obviously didn't want the building sold to anyone else. It's Saturday so I really hope there is someone here.'

Henry knocked on the door, ready to put his name to shameful use again. An austere-looking woman opened the door.

'Bonjour. Qu'est ce que tu veux?' Her expression remained stern.

She clearly had no idea who he was.

'My name is Henry Whittaker the Third.' He hated the numeral but it commanded attention. 'I was hoping to speak to the head or the bursar of the school regarding an item of art I was hoping to purchase. Blue Star Pharmacies have opened a new European office here in Paris and I am looking for works for our reception area. I understand the previous owner of the building was quite a collector.'

The mention of his mother's company triggered the association. Marie Saint-Pierre had read the newspaper reports several years ago about the teenage heir and the tragic death of his girlfriend following some kind of kidnap attempt in America. She looked closer and tried to recall the photo that had appeared in every newspaper around the globe for several weeks. Henry held out his passport to jog her memory - the photo was four years old and more like the one he hoped she would remember than his appearance now. It worked. As usually happened, once people charged with some form of financial responsibility met him and realised the extent of his wealth, the door opened wide and they were invited in.

They were shown into a drawing room that was now the school office. The woman introduced herself as Madam Saint-Pierre, the school bursar.

'I'm afraid no one else is here at the weekends. What exactly is it you are looking for Mr Whittaker? As you can see we are a school not a gallery.'

'I've been led to believe that you may have an art collection housed here, possibly left by a benefactor at some point in the past. I would very much like to appraise the works.'

'The house was left in trust to the school by the previous owner; all of the art in the building belonged to him, but I can assure you there is nothing of renown in his collection. I believe his brother, Gaston, had an eye for talent and quality but Mr Secretan showed no such interest. My predecessor spent a lot of time working with his personal secretary after Mr Secretan died and she never mentioned anything about the art in the collection. In fact she specifically said it was worthless and was not to be sold under the terms of the lease for the school. Apparently it had been very personal to the owner and he wanted it left exactly as it was.'

'Mrs Saint-Pierre, would you mind if we had a look in the main living room? I believe that is where the work I'm interested in may be located.' He held out the faded photo and watched carefully for a reaction. The bursar recognised the room immediately.

'Of course, Mr Whittaker, please follow me.'

Marie Saint-Pierre led the couple upstairs to the main ballroom. It covered the whole of the first floor and was used for school assembly and various functions. Tia looked round at the panelled walls and parquet flooring. They were in immaculate condition suggesting the fire was rarely lit. Modern radiators were placed at intervals around the room and the pipework had been carefully concealed behind the skirting boards.

The marble mantelpiece from the photo was the central focus of the room, surrounding the huge open grate. Up close it was magnificent. It was very ornate and decorative and it was easy to see why the bursar had recognised it so quickly. The room no longer contained the grand piano. Instead a small upright stood against the back wall, just under one of the windows.

Henry and Tia walked towards the fireplace together, their attention focused firmly on the artwork above. Six paintings hung in a random collage formation. All showed scenes in a rough Impressionist style but none had any significant quality that made them stand out from the rest. Henry took the crackled photo out of his pocket again and held it up for them both to see. Tia counted the paintings in the photo. There were five in total, arranged slightly differently to the ones currently on display. 4 were clearly in the same spot as they had been over a hundred years ago when the photo was taken, two new ones had been added at some point since, but one was missing!

Henry turned to the bursar.

'Madam Saint-Pierre, were there ever any other paintings on this wall?'

The old lady looked at him quizzically. How could he possibly know that? He had never been to this house before. She had worked here longer than he had been alive and would most certainly have remembered a visit from him!

'What is it you are looking for?' she asked, not giving anything away.

Henry held out the photo again and pointed to the central painting in the collection. The one that had commanded pride of place above the mantel but that was now missing.

'This is the one that I was actually looking for.' He had no idea what the subject of the painting was from the angle of the camera and the degradation of the surface of the photo, but it was obvious from its size that it had been removed and two different paintings had been hung in its place.

Madam Saint-Pierre put on her glasses and studied the ancient photo. This was most definitely the room in which they were currently standing but from an era long before her tenure. So much time had past, but so little had changed.

'This painting was moved over 40 years ago,' she declared. 'The headmaster at the time was something of an art lover and despite the work having no signature, he thought it was far better than the rest. He had it moved to his study and it's been there ever since.'

'May we look at it?' Henry could feel his pulse quickening.

'You may, but I think it is highly unlikely the head will part with it. The terms of Mr Secretan's will were very specific.'

Marie Saint-Pierre led them back out of the room and back downstairs to a doorway that adjoined her own. The room had clearly once functioned as a library, with almost every wall lined with bookcases. In the corner an old sliding ladder, which allowed access to the topmost books, sat neglected and unused. Above the small wooden fireplace, on the only space of bare wall in the room hung a painting of a scene that Tia recognised instantly.

'It's the bridge we drove over when we were leaving Auvers!' she said staring at it in awe.

Henry could tell just by looking that this work was indeed in a class of its own. The brush strokes, colours and energy were as good as any of the works painted by the Dutch master during his last few weeks in Auvers. He was no expert but he had seen enough of the real works to just know.

'It is almost certainly a Van Gogh!' he announced seemingly to himself. Marie Saint-Pierre's mouth fell open at the statement.

'But it's unsigned. How can you possibly know that?' was all she could say. The three of them starred up at the arched stone bridge.

The front doorbell ringing urgently down the hall broke their silence. The bursar excused herself and left them alone.

'Are you thinking what I'm thinking?' Henry asked.

'I suspect I might be, but I can hardly believe it – after all these years. How…? Who…?' She had so many questions forming she couldn't articulate any of them. They turned back to the painting and the door opened behind them. Their thoughts were instantly cut off by a familiar voice.

'I'm sorry guys, but I had no choice!'

They turned, and Eoin was standing in the doorway with his arm in a sling and cuts on his temple.

Chapter 53

Paris, France. Saturday October 18th 2014.

'You? You're behind this?' Henry couldn't think of anything else to say. Eoin looked at the ground, unable to face them.

'Not quite, lover boy!' said a voice that was even more familiar to him!

Jennifer kicked open the door and came into the room with Marie at gunpoint. The old bursar was shaking as the ex-agent pushed her into one of the visitor chairs and pulled the telephone cord from the wall to use as a rope. She bound her wrists without taking her eyes off Henry and used the gun to signal to Tia to move next to him.

'Make a sound and it will be the last thing you utter,' Jennifer whispered in Marie's ear. The terrified old woman nodded her understanding.

'What the hell are you doing here?' Henry was furious.

'Collecting what should have been mine.'

'You knew what was here?' Tia couldn't stop herself asking the question.

'Shut up, little girl! Grown ups are talking at the moment!'

Tia felt her face flush, but this time with rage, not embarrassment. Henry put a hand on her arm to calm her.

'What do you want, Jennifer? And why have you got Eoin with you? Has he been working with you all along?'

'No way man! She took...' Eoin never finished his sentence as the butt of Jen's gun connected with the back of his head. He dropped to the floor in a pile, unconscious for the second time in two days.

'I've been studying him for six weeks, but the idiot never had a clue. Henry you really are a sad little man having so few friends. Still, at least it cut down the background work I needed to do to find someone you would be prepared to help out if they were in trouble. Such a shame that she's not even here to realise it was all down to her. Jennifer walked over to Henry and rested the muzzle of the gun against his temple. 'Now, I'd like whatever it was you found in that garden, please!'

'How did you find us?' Henry held out the photo. He didn't look at her. His attention was on scouring the objects in the room looking for something that he could use as a weapon.

Jennifer lowered the gun and turned towards Tia, laughing.

'Now which particular time are you talking about? At the gallery? In your lab? Blocking your car and your phone was a clever move. You disappeared from my radar for a couple of hours in the morning and forced me to activate the Verichip. Luckily, officially being your fiancé counts as a family member as far as the ancient provincial judge I contacted was concerned. Once I had a court order my friends at the security company were only too happy to turn it back on. After that it was easy. Don't forget I set up all of your security protocols in the first place.'

'But why did you come looking for us in Paris? The South African took what he was after from my lab!'

Jennifer laughed again and moved behind Tia, pressing the gun against her side and causing her to flinch.

'Come on Henry, surely you realise I know you better than that. I've spent the last five years watching your every move; living through every tantrum and bad mood; witnessing you wallow in self-pity and self-loathing. I absorbed your rage as you punched and kicked your way through some sort of self-imposed sentence. I watched Joseph Colthart leave your lab with the case and did indeed think everything had ended up back on track. He's from Zimbabwe by the way, not that it matters now because he wont be going back there again. I came to

Claridge's to double check everything had gone to plan but as soon as I saw you at the hotel I knew you'd switched the paintings. You were just too calm. If Colthart had really gotten away with the genuine Adeline you'd have been smashing the living room to bits. Boris Rubikov is not the sort of man you disappoint so I warned him that he'd been fooled!'

'And he followed us to Auvers......' Henry finished her sentence, understanding now how Boris had tracked them to the garden yesterday. 'What could he have possibly offered you that my family couldn't match?' He was still searching for options to subdue her that wouldn't put Tia or the Bursar in danger. He needed to keep her talking.

'Oh yes I can just imagine what Constance would have said if I asked for $3m severance pay. Boris contacted me about four months ago when he discovered who owned the portrait of Adeline. He already knew that Rene Secretan had somehow been involved in the death of Van Gogh but he had no physical proof. I believe he even paid a visit to the old man's secretary right before she died. I'm sure you've guessed by now what this is... Van Gogh's last work!''

The Bursar looked up from her seat, her eyes wide with incredulity. How could that possibly be? Cecelia Roux's death was still an unsolved case. Had she really died to protect this secret?

'I may have mentioned you'd switched the portraits.' Jennifer looked coquettish in her admission. 'And I may have let slip that you'd already removed the letter from the back of the genuine painting. You didn't really think I was asleep when you crept out to your lab did you? Well as you can now imagine after your meeting yesterday, he was furious. He had a fake painting that he would never be able to sell or display given its inscrutable history, but that wasn't the work he wanted. His mission for the last ten years has been to find this final painting and to prove that Van Gogh did not kill himself. Sadly he did not have the patience to let you see through the investigatory work for him. I told him where you were and then drove through the port at

Calais less than three hours behind you. Do you know how easy it is to smuggle a gun into France through that port? He wasn't aware that her dad was a police officer and I may have forgotten to mention it.' Jennifer gestured towards Tia. 'I knew the idiot would get caught for something trivial after so many years of patience. Men just don't know the meaning of the word. He was never interested in the money. He wanted the glory of proving what so many had doubted for so long. I on the other hand am just interested in the money! I saw you jump over the wall, and I am not as stupid as that idiot Russian thug. I waited. I knew that between the two of you, you would lead me to exactly where I needed to go.'

Jennifer walked over to the wall opposite the desk and took the priceless painting off the wall so she could examine it.

She balanced it on top of the filing cabinet in the corner of the room so she could hold the gun currently trained on Tia.

'This is the painting Vincent was completing on the afternoon he died. That's why it's not signed. It wasn't quite finished. Boris knew it had to exist, since it was never found, and neither was the gun or any of his equipment. If someone had stolen the work whilst the artist was unconscious from his own bullet, they would have come forward over the next few years when the value of Van Gogh's work started to rise. The only person who could never produce the work, no matter what its value, would be the person involved in covering up the crime; maybe even committing the crime if the rumours are to be believed. The Russian wanted this painting but when his lawyers get him out of jail he may still be a bit pissed off about the real Adeline. He's already paid me and I know at least three potential buyers who would pay a fortune to own this, even if no one ever knew of it's existence. The trail of clues will be proof enough, which is why I want that tin!'

'So this is about money, Jen?' Henry barely recognised the women he'd shared his life with for the last five years. 'Was my mother's money not enough for you? What more could you possibly want that was worth killing two innocent people over?'

Jen looked at her left hand, at the diamond ring that adorned her third finger.

'I've known for a long time now that I was never going to be more to you than your bodyguard, and that one day someone would turn up and steal you away from me. Do you know for the first couple of years I actually believed I could make you fall in love with me.' She slid the ring off her finger and held it up in the air for Tia to see. 'I'd never failed to get a man to do what I wanted in the past and I was confident you'd be no different. But you spent years treating me as if I wasn't even there. Sure, you put on a good show in public and tried to kick the shit out of me every morning. Which he never managed, by the way.' The comment was firmly directed at Tia. As she circled Henry she ran the diamond down the side of his face. The sharp facets dug into his skin drawing a thin line of blood that ran down his cheek. Tia lurched forward ready to attack but Henry signalled for her to stay still.

Jen pressed her body up against him and ran the gun under his chin.

'I really did think you'd replace this inferior Harry Winston copy with the real thing and I'd be free from the financial chains that have bound me my entire life! But it never even came close to happening, and when you met her... I could tell as soon as I saw the way you looked at her that I would soon be relegated to the status of employee.'

'You've always been an employee!' Henry could barely look at her but he knew she was too dangerous for him to take his eyes off her for even a second.

'Well, the judge who allowed your 'fiancée' to activate your Verichip didn't seem to think I was just an employee! I used that right up until last night when your mother had my access revoked, but by then Eoin and I were curled up in a car in Argenteuil outside your crappy B&B.'

'Why did you involve Eoin in this?' Tia couldn't stay quiet. Her brain was racing to keep up with the implications this had for the last two days. 'Surely you could have just waited until Charlesworth brought the Adeline to Constance?'

'And who do you think the blame would have fallen on if a £50m painting disappeared from inside her suite? The whole place is covered by CCTV, and I would never have gotten the case out of the building. It would seem that your uncle Richard has had his suspicions of me for some time and Frank had been briefed to watch more than just your mother. I had to intercept it before Charlesworth left his building and Joseph knew exactly what he had to do. The stupid secretary turned off the CCTV system thinking it was you ringing the doorbell. I told her you wanted to buy something in secret and the silly bitch believed me. She literally just turned the whole security system off. '

'But that still doesn't explain Eoin! Why did you need to involve him if you could get in without being seen?'

Jennifer sneered at Tia.

'You appear to be so clever… You tell me!'

'You needed someone to take the blame!' Tia felt all the unsolved pieces of the puzzle fall into place into a horrific picture. 'Someone who could be tied back to Henry!'

'Eoin was almost too perfect a victim to take the blame for your demise. Did you know his uncle is a very bad criminal? I knew the stupid Irish thief would call that ginger freak and she would then have no choice but to call Henry. People with virtually no friends are entirely predictable in how they react in emergency situations and I simply made use of that knowledge. It's funny how you loners all seem to have found each other!'

'But Ashley didn't call Henry first – she called me!'

'Yes and that was my one piece of luck! She called you, on the one morning in your life when you were unable to get to her alone. She then called Henry to pick you up and the plan was right back on track. Besides, I didn't actually need Henry to be there. All I needed was for Eoin to phone Ashley and the link was secured. It wouldn't be hard to make a case for him wanting to steal from his over protective parents'

Jennifer signalled for the couple to move over to the desk. She pushed the painting back onto the filing cabinet and looked around for something to wrap it in.

Draped across the windows were two heavy velvet curtains. Jennifer pushed past the desk and started to pull one of them from its hangings. She momentarily turned her back to the room and Henry took his chance. He picked up the disconnected phone and slammed it over Jennifer's head and she dropped the gun behind the desk, out of sight. She turned with a start as a thin line of blood started to run down her forehead and sneered.

'Seriously? After all the times I've beaten you, you want to go again now?' Jen kicked Henry's knee and punched across her body at his chest, catching him in the solar plexus. Henry deflected the blow with his arm and countered with an upper cut which glanced off her cheekbone, but she anticipated his move perfectly and bobbed sideways causing his blow to land harmlessly.

'Let them go, Jen. This is just between me and you.'

'Henry, it will take me a couple of minutes to put you down and then I'll treat your little girlfriend and the thief to an experience from which they will never recover. You'll all be dead and I'll explain to Tia's dad that I couldn't stop Eoin in time. They won't know anything about the painting.'

Jen glanced over to where Tia had been standing. The skinny girl was untying the cord from the old lady's wrists. She couldn't let that happen. No one was getting out of this room today!

She jumped up onto the desk and launched a spinning wheel kick high into the air, her pivoting foot scattering papers and stationary across the room. She caught Henry square in the face, knocking him back onto the floor where his head crashed against the corner of the bay window wall. Blood ran onto the floor and his vision blurred as he passed out. She had been training Henry for too long to let anything he could do catch her out.

Jennifer jumped down to the front of the desk and Tia put herself between the ex-special agent and the Bursar, who continued to untie her bonds with her freed hand.

Jennifer launched a kick at Tia and caught her on the thigh. Tia felt a stabbing pain shoot through her stitches and she knew that her wound from yesterday had reopened. Blood seeped through her skirt and started to run down her leg, but she ignored it. She pulled her hands up into the cupped guard and pulled her right shoulder back. Adrenalin flooded through her body in a dose she had never experienced before and her energy soared. Fifteen years of dedicated training burst forth in a fury of relentless blocks and punches. The speed with which the punches flew caught Jennifer off guard in the same way it had shocked Henry not four weeks ago. Jennifer knew she had underestimated the teen as she continued to launch kicks furiously, but Tia's balance was gymnast-like in its precision as she blocked them and followed through with a high kick finish that sent the bodyguard backwards. Jennifer may have been taught by the FBI, but Tia had spent her whole life under her father's tutelage. He had never once allowed her to slack off or cut corners and every move was perfectly timed.

Jennifer changed her tact, picking up the wooden chair in front of the desk. It shattered as she smashed it into Tia's chest and face, causing blood to spurt from her nose. The impact slowed Tia's onslaught and Jennifer launched another kick, knocking Tia to the ground, but as she fell Tia swept her leg sideways and crashed into the leg on which Jennifer was balanced, sending her sprawling on top of her. Tia pulled her knee up to her chest and kicked into Jennifer's side, rolling her onto her back. Tia made a lunge under the desk and grabbed the gun, which still lay on the floor where the American had dropped it. Jennifer jumped to her feet and raised her booted foot to stamp on Tia's head. The teenager rolled onto her back and a gunshot reverberated off the wood panelled walls as Jennifer fell backwards, blood oozing from her shoulder. Tia pulled herself up on the desk, turned towards the fallen agent and pointed the gun again.

'Tia don't!'

Below her, Henry reached out and touched her ankle, stopping her from firing any more bullets into the injured woman.

As she stood there allowing her fury to subside the door swung open and her dad burst into the room flanked by Inspector Robert and armed French police.

Chapter 54

Paris, France. Saturday October 18th 2014.

'Tia give me the gun!' Her father spoke gently but firmly as his daughter stood staring at the woman she barely knew but who obviously hated her. She held her position; her hands steady but her heart thumping as adrenalin continued to surge through her. The two women glared at each other, each silently blaming the other for the events of the last two days.

Henry stood up and Tia felt a hand on her bandaged wrist; fingertips touched her fingers. He put his arm around her shoulder and took the gun, passing it to Stephen. Tia turned to face her father and he held her tightly as she burst into tears. Never in her whole life had she felt such uncontrollable rage. A rage she had no idea she was capable of. She had been trained to be able to kill another person with her martial arts and had kept her composure through years of fighting, but in a single moment of fear she had almost killed someone in an instant with a gun.

Constance came into the room and rushed over to Henry, wrapping her arms around her only child, who had pushed her away for so many years.

Medics attended to a still unconscious Eoin who had blood running down his right temple. Marie, who had been cowering behind the desk desperately trying to reconnect the phone, explained what she'd seen to the Inspector as more and more officers arrived to begin the process of investigation.

Constance pulled two chairs over from the corner of the room for

Tia and Henry, calling for medical assistance to stop the bleeding from their various wounds. Stephen refused to let go of Tia's hand, as if physical restraint were the only way he felt she would be safe now – or the only way to stop her running off again. Tia wasn't sure which.

Inspector Robert officially arrested Jennifer based on Marie's testimony and she was taken off in an ambulance under armed police escort. He came over to Tia and Henry and took out his notebook.

'I have just checked, and yes I definitely did tell you to go straight home yesterday.' He smiled. 'Do you want to tell me what has happened this time?'

Tia drew a breath and turned to Marie Saint-Pierre, who was now being checked by the medic.

'Madam, you mentioned your predecessor earlier. Would you mind telling me her name?'

Marie looked at the teenager who had just saved her life and smiled.

'Of course. It was Cecelia Roux.'

'And did she work for Rene Secretan by any chance?'

'She was his secretary for fifteen years and then looked after him when he retired. After he died she helped to set up this school in accordance with his will. She dedicated her life to preserving his wishes even after he was gone.'

'And was her death in any way suspicious?'

'Yes, how do you know this? She was the victim of a failed robbery in her home. The burglars broke her wrists and suffocated her but left with nothing as far as anyone could tell. She had nothing of any value to steal. '

Tia turned towards the French policeman.

'Inspector Robert, I don't think they did leave with nothing. I think that Boris Rubikov killed her and stole Rene Secretan's journals or diaries. If there is any DNA evidence at all from that crime I suspect you will find it matches one of the Russians you arrested yesterday.'

'But what did he want?' Robert asked.

412

Tia pointed at the painting still lying on top of the filing cabinet.

'That!' Tia turned towards the painting balanced on top of the filing cabinet.

Constance moved over to the painting and held it up, letting out a gasp. Her trained eye recognised the brushstrokes and paint hues immediately.

'Oh my god could it possibly be....?' was all she could say.

'What is it?' Stephen was completely lost. He was the most senior police officer in the room, and the only one who apparently had no idea what was happening.

'It's the painting that Van Gogh was working on when he shot himself,' Tia explained. 'Rene Secretan must have witnessed the incident and agreed to hide all the evidence which was why nothing was ever found.' She pulled the metal tin from her bag and handed it over to Inspector Robert. 'We uncovered this in the garden of Dr Gachet yesterday. It was what Rubikov was also after. We couldn't tell you then because we didn't know what it was, but if you have any detailed records left from 1890 I think you'll find that this is the gun used to by Vincent Van Gogh to shoot himself, and I'm pretty sure that tube of paint will be an exact chemical match for the oils used in his final works. I think Secretan put it in the tin so the gun could be verified'

Constance let her arms drop and the painting sank towards her waist as she listened to the story.

'But it's of the Bridge in Auvers? That's nowhere near the wheat fields where he claimed he'd been working. It would explain how he made it back to the Auberge with a bullet wound though. The riverbank is flat, unlike the farmlands.' Questions flew through her mind as she mentally mapped out the steps required for verification of this work. It's implications for the circumstances surrounding his suicide would keep art historians and technicians busy for months. Even she couldn't comprehend the potential value of what might truly be Van Gogh's last work.

413

A moment of silence was broken by chaos as everyone started to talk at once about what needed to happen next. Amidst the frenzy, from where he stood, Henry could just make out a series of letters and numbers written across the backing paper of the painting in barely visible charcoal. He quietly moved next to his mother and gestured for her to stay silent. He took the right side of the frame in his right hand so they were holding it between them and tugged gently to signal that she should follow his lead. Pivoting slightly, he turned towards the window as if trying to catch better light, his smartphone hidden in his left hand. He held the painting up in front of the unseen phone and photographed the back, then rubbed the back of his hand across the print, smudging the evidence so it was gone forever. No one was following them this time.

Given her training, Inspector Robert allowed Constance to package up the painting, which was now the subject of a huge murder investigation and ownership dispute. If Tia's theory was right, and without proof of purchase, Secretan had effectively stolen the painting from Van Gogh and if proved, ownership would revert to his original estate, which had been bequeathed by his sister-in-law to the Van Gogh Museum in Amsterdam. Once formal statements had been taken the foreigners were allowed to return to England. This time, under the watchful eye of her father, Tia did get on the plane.

'It seems we have one more clue to solve.' Henry whispered to Tia as they sat alone waiting for clearance to taxi down to the runway at Bourget Airport.

'What clue?' she wasn't sure she was ready just yet for more drama, although she was fairly sure there could be no more criminals involved.

Henry held up his phone and showed her the markings.

'These were written on the back of the painting. I've worked out the significance already. I spend hours of my life going through sequences exactly like that one' said Henry.

'What does it mean? asked Tia.

'Now it's my turn to make you wait!' He said smugly. 'We can't find out for sure until the building reopens on Monday.'

Chapter 55

Kings Cross, London. Monday October 20th 2014.

The rain was torrential as Henry and Tia sat in Starbucks on Euston Road at 9am on Monday morning. The constant throng of commuters from Kings Cross and St Pancras stations were fleeing for cover into the sea of black taxis, blaring their horns at rampant pedestrians. As the couple stared out across the gridlocked traffic towards the wedge-shaped red brick arch on the opposite side of the road Tia realised what the sequence of letters and numbers in the code Henry had shown her represented. The huge wrought iron gate, formed of the words 'British' and 'Library', welcomed them to the vast home of the biggest collection of books outside Washington.

Tia had managed to speak to Ashley briefly on the phone as they landed at RAF Northolt on Saturday evening. She was in Tottenham tending to Matt and instructed Henry to bring Eoin straight to her mothers repaired flat so she could stop him getting into any more trouble. Tia had promised to call her on Monday with an update and hung up without mentioning the code stored on Henry's phone.

She and Henry had spent most of Sunday in his mother's hotel room going over and over their statements with her father and his team. They hadn't been allowed one minute alone, and Stephen had insisted on driving Tia back to Camden himself once they were finished. It had taken all of Tia's determination and persuasion to convince her father to let her return to college, labouring the point that she'd already missed two crucial days of lectures and would struggle to catch up if she missed any more. In truth, she'd had no intention of making it to the 3-hour maths lecture once Henry told her there was still more to understand.

The only text she'd had from Henry since leaving Claridge's were instructions to meet him here at 9am and to bring two forms of ID.

'I've already registered you for a readers pass.' He told her, tapping unceasingly onto his laptop as he waited for it to connect to the free Wi-Fi. 'We need to pick it up once the library opens at 9.30am. I typed the code into the online catalogue but there is a bit of a problem. The digits are a library catalogue code specific to the British Library. Most libraries use the American Dewey system, but here that's only used as a cross-reference to their own bespoke Shelfmark. We need to find a single volume in a repository of over 150 million volumes and we don't know the name of the book, the author or the subject matter. All we do know is that it must be older than 1957, when Secretan died, and we have what I hope is a shelfmark - 7950.aa.76. Fortunately, most of the library's content is online now but here's the problem!' He turned the laptop to face her as a new screen loaded showing the search results in the digital catalogue.

'There are two books with the same Shelfmark?' Tia looked at the titles, which were both in French – at least, that made sense.

'Yes. I've never seen that before. It means we are going to have to check them both.' Henry clicked on the tab marked *I want it* and a digitised version of the second book filled the screen. 'As you can see, this book has been fully scanned so if something was hidden in here then it's either been found already or it's hidden inside the cover of the actual volume itself. I suspect it will be difficult to get it out without being captured on the CCTV cameras that are everywhere. I picked up a scalpel blade and tweezers from the lab on the way here and we are going to have to sneak them in. Do you have something for tampons in your bag?'

Tia looked at him in horror and felt her face flush! She had never discussed that with a male before – not even her dad!

'The security guards don't tend to look inside those,' He explained, smiling at the faint blush he could just about notice now. She took the implements and put them in her purse.

At 9.30am they walked past the bronze statue of Isaac Newton and crossed the red and white chequered square to the entrance hall.

The modern British Library, opened in 1997, was the largest public building to be constructed in the UK during the 20th century. The redbrick layers reminded Tia of a huge cruise liner, containing fourteen floors, of which 5 were below ground.

Tia collected her pass from the registration desk whilst Henry spoke to an official looking gentleman with a name badge who was asking about Constance. At 10am, when the 9 reading rooms opened, they headed to the second floor to the one dedicated to science where he sent so much of his time.

Tia looked across the vast expanse of wooden desks topped with reading lamps and scanned the modern purpose-built shelves that lined the room. The books on display represented only a fraction of what was available for reference.

Henry headed to the furthest information desk manned by a middle aged female, whose face lit up as he approached.

'Henry, where have you been? I haven't seen you for over a week,' the woman asked. The small plastic white doves that dangled from her ears fluttered as her head bobbed excitedly.

'Linda, did you miss me?' he asked with a cheeky smile.

Linda Clayton had worked here as a librarian for almost thirty years. She'd been present during the colossal move from the various old sites around London to the new building and often told her few friends that she had handled upwards of 1.5 million books during her tenure. Henry had befriended her early on, aware of the value of having an ally on the other side of the counter in a place like this.

'Of course Henry!' she blushed at the sound of her name. So few visitors treated her as little more than an anonymous form filler. She was a gatekeeper to be bypassed as quickly as possible. They were oblivious to the fact she had a degree in history, a masters in art history and a PhD in renaissance composition and could probably answer many of their questions without needing to find their requested books.

"I need your expert help again, Linda I'm afraid,' Henry said.

Linda bristled with pride. She loved any opportunity to flex her brain and Henry was her favourite student. Last year he'd bought her an exquisite antique paperweight for Christmas, that now took pride of place at her workstation.

'Of course, Henry,' she said again, stumbling over her words like a schoolgirl. 'What do you need to know?'

'I need to find a book, but all I've got is a shelfmark and the online catalogue says there are two books with that code. Can you help me?'

'Well I can see what I can do. What's the code?'

Henry handed her the piece of paper with the code copied from his phone.

'Henry you are silly,' Linda said, typing furiously into her computer. 'I take it you don't speak French?'

'Not since high school.' He admitted, looking at Tia, who also shook her head. 'Well the first reference is actually the forward of the second book. Look – its contained within the second Title.'

She read out the title of the book slowly and translated it for them. ' Le Science du Maître d'hôtel Cuisenaire; The science of the butler cook? That's not something I would have expected you to read, Henry. Normally you want to know about stem cells, DNA and chemical compounds.'

'My mother is in town and promised to check it out for a friend who thinks he may be related to the author.' Henry lied, forgetting he had no idea who the author was. 'When was the last time it was requested?'

'Its never been requested since its been housed here. According to the scanned records this book has only ever been withdrawn once and that was in 1954, when it was still housed in the British Museum. It will take 70 minutes to retrieve, as you know, and you'll need to wear

419

these.' She handed him a pair of white cotton gloves used to protect the fragile documents housed in the library.

The paternoster mechanical retrieval system kicked into action 65 minutes later and as the giant belt began to rotate, a thick, brown book made its way towards them. Henry lifted it carefully out of its tray and they took it back to their desks.

The book was bound with a plain mottled leather cover that had a large gash on the front. Inside the back and front heavy paper liners decorated with swirls were stuck to the covers, concealing the glued leather seams. The pages were almost stuck together through years of compression. The only time this book had been opened in 60 years was to scan its contents into the digitised system. A mundane job probably carried out by a temp listening to music while they worked.

Henry flicked through the pages but didn't expect to find anything. He scanned the seams of the front cover but they were all stuck fast. He turned the book over and opened the back cover. At first glance these seams looked well adhered also.

'Pass me the scalpel blade and lean across from my right.' He said to Tia nodding towards the camera that as trained on their area of the room. Tia handed him the blade under the adjoining desks and leaned forward as if reaching for something in his bag on the opposite side of his desk. Henry quickly ran the tip of the blade lightly around the seam of the paper inside cover. As he reached the top right hand corner the tip yielded suddenly and slid further under the paper.

'Its not stuck down properly at the top.' He told her as she sat back down in her seat. 'Hand me the tweezers and do the same again.'

Tia felt very conspicuous as she reach over again, this time grabbing the whole bag from the far side of the desk and lifting it over Henry's head. The move shielded his actions for a few seconds from the spy on the wall. Just enough time to pull out a small envelope, which had been forced into the top seam of the cover.

Inside was a letter, written on cheap rough paper that had yellowed with age. The handwriting was small and close and was written in

French. Henry laid it flat on the desk in front of them and read out words for Tia to look up on Google translate. It took almost an hour to piece together their crude version in English.

> *Rene.*
>
> *I implore you not to break our agreement. I send you this letter to remind you of your promise when I am gone. What happened was an accident and the gun had not been well maintained.*
>
> *You could not possibly have seen me in the rushes as I worked, until you heard me cry out.*
>
> *The world must believe I shot myself and must never know which weapon was used.*
>
> *I am filled with relief. Freedom from my life of torment will soon be over. Do not be so reckless with your own. Take this chance that God has given you and be a better man and fulfil his plan for you.*
>
> *Destroy all of the evidence and forget you ever met me and hopefully one day I will greet you again in Heaven.*
>
> *Vincent.*

The signature was underlined by the famous flourish Henry recognised instantly. He looked at Tia unable to take in what they'd found. He had no doubt this letter was from Van Gogh himself confirming he hadn't committed suicide but had been the victim of an accident.

'There's something written on the back,' Tia said.

Henry turned it over to reveal a very different handwriting. This one was almost illegible. A slanting scratchy scrawl suggested the shaking hand of a much older man. It was written in English.

The girl in blue tried to protect me, just as her father's guest had asked her to do, but she could not save me from myself.

For almost 70 years I have lived with the knowledge and the guilt of what I have done. I was a foolish boy and it was an accident. If you have been brought to this letter by the path I left then you will know the location of that fateful day - recorded in a beautiful scene, which I have had the privilege to look at every day for most of my life. A privilege I never deserved.

He was not angry with me; instead he was filled with relief. I believe he even laughed, claiming I had released him. He told me what to do and to tell the truth to no one. I was too scared to defy him.

I submit this document to history as the truth of those events. There was no suicide and I was to blame. I have never benefitted from my knowledge of the events or the items he asked me to get rid of. I have simply tried to protect my family's reputation and as I am the last, I can now go to my God in peace. I hope that he will judge me fairly, as will history one day.'   ***R***

Henry smiled as he thought about the 16 year old boy that Rene Secretan had been and compared him to the man he later became. The spoilt, reckless teenager, who had little regard for others and delighted in torment, had spent his entire life planning a way to make amends and reveal the truth without compromising his family or employers while he was alive. He had judged that time would make man less judgemental and his actions would be understood. He'd used the fortune that he'd amassed during the time Van Gogh had given him by keeping him from prison, to open a school dedicated to the education of underprivileged boys. Henry knew how it felt to be young and stupid. To think you are invincible until you watch helplessly as you realise no one is. To be spared the requirement to make amends for a tragedy you know was your fault. For over eight years Henry had enforced his own sentence, trying to atone for the death of a young girl who's only mistake had been to agree to go on a date with him. Now, at last, with Tia's help he'd been set free. She knew what had happened and loved him anyway.

Henry looked up at Tia, kissed her and folded the paper.

'What difference would it make for the world to think anything different now? Van Gogh's suicide made him famous. That legend keeps hundreds of people in Auvers in employment as tourists flock to see his last resting place and the room where he died. Does the world really need to know that he was shot by accident by a 16 year old boy?'

Henry put the letter back in the envelope and looked at Tia.

She understood. She took the letter from him and reached over again, sliding it back inside the cover where they'd found it.

'We have a beautiful new painting to share with the world. Let his legend live on.' She said.

Smiling, they took the antique French cookery book back to the returns' desk and left the library.

Epilogue.

Amsterdam, Netherlands Friday 2nd October 2015

The newly printed banners announcing 'The Final Work – The Exhibition' fluttered lightly on the flagpoles outside The Van Gogh Museum in Amsterdam. The image printed on the background was becoming one of the most recognised works of art in the world following the media attention surrounding its discovery. 125 years after his death, details surrounding his suicide still fascinated the art-loving public and were creating a new wave of interest.

Although the painting of the bridge had hung in the home of Rene Secretan for over a century, it had never actually belonged to him. The rapidly accepted version of events, that no one would ever be able to confirm, was that Rene had taken the painting, and the other items including the gun, after the artist left the riverbank to return to the Auberge. Experts assumed he had intended to sell or steal the items but must have hidden the gun and the paint in Dr Gachet's garden once he learned of the suicide, fearing he would be blamed if he were caught with them in his possession. The painting was unsigned so they agreed he'd just decided to keep it for himself. They concluded that his return to the house in 1905, as documented in the visitor's book, was probably a failed attempt to recover the evidence to dispose of it. Henry and Tia had no intention of correction these assumptions. What purpose would it serve now?

The untitled painting known simply as the Bridge had not been recorded as a gift to Rene or been paid for. He was not the subject of the painting and therefore officially Van Gogh's final work belonged to his family estate, which had been passed almost in its entirety to the Van Gogh Museum by Theo's wife, Jo.

In France, visitors to the small town of Auvers-sur-Oise soared following renewed interest in events surrounding the artist's death. The recovered curator at Dr Gachet's house was delighted that Constance had agreed to become the new benefactor for the estate. His personal account of the injuries sustained when Boris Rubikov arrived had become a central feature of his extended tour which now included the unfolding story of Rene Secretan's hidden evidence. The security system had been ungraded, the garden location of the tin had been taped off, and replica items added to a new display in the house. The documented police testimony of two eyewitnesses who claimed to have seen Vincent on the path by the river were recovered from the archives and added to the display in the town museum, which had been hastily rewritten for the summer tourist season. The only question no one was able to answer was *why had the artist lied about where he was that day?* A question powerful enough to ensure the controversy surrounding his death would continue to rage on for another hundred years.

Only two people would ever know the truth; that the artist had asked Rene to dispose of the work to prevent the world from blaming a foolish youth for a death he craved but could not bring about himself. The subject of the painting held the clue to the actual location of that fatal gunshot and Van Gogh had not wanted the area to be checked for blood or any other clues. With that hasty but well-intentioned decision, Vincent had given Rene a second chance to live a worthwhile life – and he'd taken it.

The museum had agreed a finder's fee of 5% to be shared between the four friends who'd found the painting and worked out its significance. The official valuation was set at £100m, giving a fee of £5m. - £1.25m per benefactor. The four agreed to each donate £100,000 of their reward to the school on whose wall the painting had hung for over a century as a tribute to Rene Secretan who had tried so hard to make amends for the accident he'd caused.

Tonight a gala dinner was being held to launch the exhibition and the friends had been invited as special guests.

Henry's mother had commuted between London and Amsterdam for the last nine months, working tirelessly with the museum to ensure the safe transportation and examination of the painting. Her company were sponsoring the dinner and she was giving the main address. In support of the evening, Constance had allowed the Adeline portrait to leave her family home for only the second time ever, to be displayed for six months next to the work whose discovery it had facilitated. Advanced ticket sales had already sold out and a major world tour was planned for the next four years.

Tia and Henry were staying in the Concerto suite at the Conservatorium Hotel opposite the Museum. They'd been inseparable since returning from Paris and even Stephen had got used to his daughter no longer being his little girl. They had so far managed to keep a low profile publicly and tonight would be their first official engagement as a couple.

'You know tomorrow will be my 20th birthday?' Tia said as she fastened his bow tie, a skill she'd learned practicing on her father many times for official police dinners. 'At least that will put us in the same decade for a while. Hopefully that will make things a bit easier for dad. He's still getting used to the idea of me having a boyfriend.'

'Of course I know it's your birthday' he said 'And as we appear to be celebrating early tonight I thought you might like your present now?' He handed her an exquisitely wrapped box roughly the size of a sheet of paper folded in half lengthways. She opened it carefully to reveal a bright red Cartier box. Inside was a necklace made of platinum set with a single 4-carat sapphire of the most amazing blue. It almost exactly matched the colour of the dress worn by Adeline Ravoux in her portrait, the original of which was now just a few hundred yards away.

Tia's eyes lit up. Even after a year together she still couldn't get used to this.

'Oh my God, Henry! It's gorgeous! I'm going to be too afraid to wear it.'

'After reading about what you did to Jennifer in Paris I doubt anyone is going to be foolish enough to try and take you on in the foreseeable future.' Henry smiled as he fastened the necklace around her slender cocoa neck. 'You look stunning!'

Tia caught a glimpse of herself in the full-length wardrobe mirror. She was wearing a brilliant blue Alexander McQueen gown that Henry had chosen for her. It matched the necklace perfectly and she suspected Constance had helped Henry with his choice; her taste was flawless.

'The others will be waiting for us downstairs,' Tia said looking at the clock by their bed.

'Nearly ready,' Henry said as he pulled her towards him and kissed her. 'You know I wanted to do that this time last year, don't you?'

'I had no idea! I thought you were with Jennifer, remember.'

Eoin and Ashley were already waiting in the Tunes bar when Henry and Tia eventually came down. Tia barely recognised Ashley. Her curly red hair had grown down to her shoulders in the last year, but now it had been put up into an elegant chignon, pinned with emerald studs to match the revealing emerald dress that Constance had selected for her. Tia had never seen her best friend in a dress of any description and her curvy figure filled this one to perfection.

Eoin was wearing a tuxedo, which clearly made him feel self-conscious but he relaxed a little when Henry arrived wearing the same thing. He would never get used to this lifestyle, he thought, but at least *this* suit fitted him.

Henry summoned a waiter and ordered a bottle of champagne, and a sparkling water for Tia, who at 20 was too young to drink in Holland.

'We need a toast,' he said as each of them was presented with a crystal glass of Dom Pérignon Œnothèque Rose.

'To Tia,' Ashley offered. 'Happy 20th birthday for tomorrow and congratulations on being let back into Uni for your second year.'

'To Henry,' Eoin countered. 'On getting his PhD despite nearly blowing up the chemistry building'.

'And to Ashley, on completing her psychology degree with a 2:1 despite her tutor asking who she was.' Henry laughed as he raised his glass again.

'No,' Tia replied. 'To us. We have come a long way in a year and faced a lot of trouble together. The French dropped charges against us in exchange for joint credit and even my father has almost calmed down and forgiven us all. But we got each other through it and came out on a much better side. To four people with few friends and plenty of insecurities who bought out the best in each other- we definitely all belong together.'

'To us!' they all repeated in unison.

As they toasted, Henry took a small folded piece of paper out of his pocket and opened it up to show them the artwork he'd commissioned.

'And here's to the unveiling of the official logo for our newly created fraud protection agency – H.E.A.T Ltd. The name is taken from each of our names and the capital is courtesy of our combined £4m finders fee from the Van Gogh Museum, and a 'donation' from my family for finally finding something I want to do with my life. The company will be run by the four of us; a rich man who spent his life in a gilded prison until being set free; a poor little wallflower who will give Sherlock Holmes a run for his money; the beggar girl with the courage of a lion and the thief with a conscience! Eoin and Ashley are off to Virginia next week to start specialist FBI training courses and we should have signed out first client by the end of the year. It will be my absolute pleasure to continue working with you all in the future.'

The four friends cheered as they raised their glasses again.

The End

Coming Soon

EUGENESIS

By JC Cole

The body of a man washed up in the Gulf of Mexico is identified as a member of staff at the Blue Star Pharmaceuticals plant in Houston. The autopsy reveals a biological mutation that could destroy the company's reputation.

On the same day Henry Whittaker's ex girlfriend, a leading geneticist, goes missing from her hotel after an MIT reunion.

The newly formed H.E.A.T investigative agency must span the US and Japan to save his mother's company and his friend.

For advanced notification of release dates and for bonus chapters sign up to the newsletter at www.jccole.co.uk

About the Author

JC Cole is a businesswoman who runs a coaching and career training company. She has two children and lives in Kent with her dog Milo.

She has degrees in Electronic Engineering (still not sure why) and Psychology and is fascinated by human behaviour and motivation.

Restoring Vincent is her first novel and she is currently working on her second, Eugenesis.

Janice@jccole.co.uk
www.jccole.co.uk